New York Times bestselling author **Christine Feehan** has had
over thirty novels published and has thrilled legions of fans

captivating and adrenaline-raising worlds is unsurpassed'
Romantic Times

By Christine Feehan

DARK GHOST

A CARPATHIAN NOVEL

CHRISTINE FEEHAN

piatkus

PIATKUS

First published in the US in 2015 by The Berkley Publishing Group,
A division of the Penguin Group USA (Inc.),
First published in Great Britain in 2015 by Piatkus
This paperback edition published in 2016 by Piatkus

1 3 5 7 9 10 8 6 4 2

A CIP catalogue record for this book
is available from the British Library.

ISBN 978-0-349-40568-1

Printed and bound in Great Britain by
Clays Ltd, St Ives plc

Papers used by Piatkus are from well-managed forests
and other responsible sources.

MIX
Paper from
responsible sources
FSC FSC® C104740
www.fsc.org

Piatkus
An imprint of
Little, Brown Book Group
Carmelite House
50 Victoria Embankment
London EC4Y 0DZ

An Hachette UK Company
www.hachette.co.uk

www.piatkus.co.uk

*For the members of my online community who are
always ready for a book discussion and share such a love
of reading with me. This one is for you, a tribute to your
sense of humor over all things Carpathian!*

For My Readers

Be sure to go to christinefeehan.com/members/ to sign up for my PRIVATE book announcement list and download the FREE ebook of *Dark Desserts*. Join my community and get firsthand news, enter the book discussions, ask your questions and chat with me. Please feel free to email me at Christine@christinefeehan.com. I would love to hear from you. Each year, the last weekend of February, I would love for you to join me at my annual FAN event, an exclusive weekend with an intimate number of readers for lots of fun, fabulous gifts and a wonderful time. Look for more information at fanconvention.net.

ACKNOWLEDGMENTS

With any book there are many people to thank. In this case, the usual suspects: Domini, for her research and help; my power hours group, who always make certain I'm up at the crack of dawn working; and of course Brian Feehan, who I can call anytime and brainstorm with so I don't lose a single hour. This time I want to thank my community members who have such passionate and fun discussions on the Carpathian walls. In particular Joan Colbert, who has made me laugh so often over the years with her declarations and funny, funny comments on the discussion walls and at FAN.

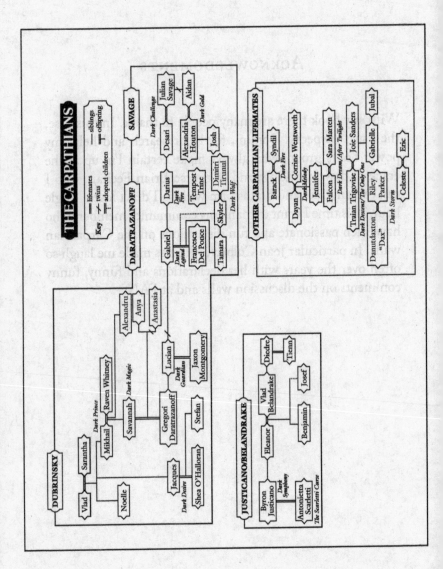

THE CARPATHIANS

Key: — lifemates — siblings ⌢ twins ⊤ offspring ⊤ adopted children

DUBRINSKY

Vlad — Sarantha
Mikhail — Raven Whitney *Dark Prince*
Noelle
Jacques — Shea O'Halloran *Dark Desire*
Stefan
Savannah *Dark Magic* — Gregori Daratrazanoff
Anya
Alexandru
Anastasia
Lucian *Dark Guardian* — Jaxon Montgomery

DARATRAZANOFF

Gabriel *Dark Legend* — Francesca Del Ponce
Tamara
Skyler *Dark Wolf* — Dimitri Tirunul
Darius *Dark Fire* — Tempest Trine
Josh

SAVAGE

Julian Savage *Dark Challenge* — Desari
Aidan *Dark Gold* — Alexandria Houton

OTHER CARPATHIAN LIFEMATES

Barack — Syndil
Dayan *Dark Fire* — Corrine Wentworth
Falcon *Dark Melody* — Jennifer
Sara Marten
Train Trigovise *Dark Dream/After Twilight* — Joie Sanders
Danutdaxton "Dax" *Dark Descent/The Only One* — Riley Parker *Dark Storm*
Gabrielle — Jubal
Celeste
Eric

JUSTICANO/BELANDRAKE

Byron Justicano *Dark Symphony* — Eleanor — Vlad Belandrake
Antonietta Scarletti *The Scarletti Curse*
Benjamin
Josef
Deidre
Tienn

THE CARPATHIANS

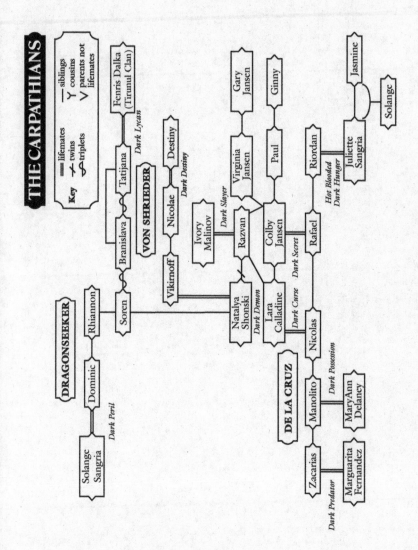

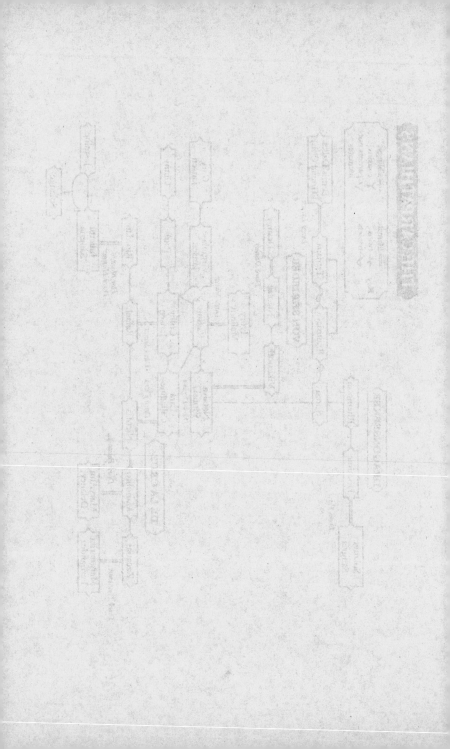

1

The mountain range was high. High enough that Andre could reach the lonely, craggy places others avoided. The higher up he went, the more fog swirled, enclosing him in a soft, wet, gray veil. He was the "Ghost," and he could easily disappear into the cool gray world he knew so well. He never used a last name if he could help it because the only name that mattered to him was not his own, and unless he found a lifemate, he would not chance ever dishonoring it.

Situated a couple more miles up, almost at the very top of the mountain, was the monastery, the one that had been there for centuries. Built on the precipices, the monastery was shrouded in mystery and the ever-swirling clouds. It was a sacred, protected place and few knew of its existence, although word had gotten out over the years that such a place existed. Only the bravest ever attempted to go there. Had he been inclined, he could have sought sanctuary there to recover from his latest battle.

The monastery, known as the Retreat in the Veil of Mists, held a virtual army of ancient Carpathian hunters—men who had not yet sought the dawn, but who, like Andre, could no longer trust themselves around others. They stayed strictly to themselves, avoiding all humans, all battles, and lived their lives simply until they were able to let go and seek the dawn.

For men who had lived centuries with honor, it wasn't easy to let go of life. Even without emotion and color, some felt it was cowardly, and without sustaining a mortal wound in combat, they couldn't just lie outdoors and allow the sun to take them. It felt ... wrong ... to too many warriors. Andre would have been welcomed among them, yet he had been too long away from others. He had thought to go there, but in the end realized he couldn't even accept the sanctuary and the camaraderie he might find there.

Andre didn't bother to stanch the flow of blood coming from various wounds. He knew he should. It was a trail leading straight to him. Still, it was also an invitation, pure and simple. Anyone who came near him was going to die. He would awaken—that was if he awakened at all—starved for blood, his body writhing with the craving, with the need, and that was the most he'd feel or ever could feel.

One didn't take blood from the ancients, not unless the need was dire, and certainly not without permission. Andre wasn't the type of Carpathian who ever asked for asylum or permission, not even from his own kind. He would find what he needed as he always had done on his own. His way.

Some things were a matter of honor. Andre had lived more centuries than he cared to count. He'd held out against the darkness with honor and served his people, hunting the vampire over several continents. He'd battled the undead so many times he honestly couldn't keep count of the numbers any longer, nor did he care to. There seemed so many more of them and so few hunters. They were losing the war.

He had searched centuries for his lifemate—the one woman who could restore his ability to feel real emotion. The one woman who could give him back color and life. He hadn't found her. He had long ago given up the idea that she could possibly be in this time realm. Had she been somewhere on this earth, he would have found her by this time.

The relentless whispers of temptation to kill and feel something, if only for a moment, no longer tempted him. For centuries he had carried that burden, but now it too was gone, and that was bad, because at least he'd felt something. Now there was only a dark gray void and endless weariness.

He wouldn't go to the monastery to rest because, among other reasons, he no longer trusted himself to be around anyone, humans or Carpathians. Once he realized how far gone he was, he knew, in order to preserve his honor, he would have to allow the sun to take him. That had been his intention until Costin Popescu had attacked him. Popescu, the name Costin had assumed was a joke. Son of a priest. Costin was anything but that.

Andre turned to survey the waning night. Light streaked through the gray, and already he could feel the first prickles of warning on his skin. That didn't matter to him, either. It only served to alert him to the rising sun. He didn't need the caution, he'd been alive too many centuries not to know the exact moment of sunrise and sunset anywhere he happened to be.

Had the master vampire Popescu attacked him man-to-man, vampire to Carpathian, as he would have in the old days, Andre would have been more than happy to go to his death with honor as long as he took the vampire with him. Battling a master vampire was very dangerous. They had immense power. Coupled with experience in battle, it made for a very fair fight.

The world had changed too much for Andre's liking. He no longer belonged and he was well aware of that fact. He'd never been a man to be around others. He preferred the high places or the wild places, anywhere he didn't run into masses of people. Or even a few. He wasn't civilized. He wasn't tame. He had his own code, and he lived by it.

Even vampires had changed. There was no longer honor in that battle. In the old days, vampires hunted and killed alone. Now, master vampires had begun recruiting lesser vampires, and they ran in packs. Costin Popescu had four following him, doing his bidding. Two were probably eager enough to follow Andre's blood trail. The rich ancient Carpathian blood would draw them straight to him. The other two had been around a while and Popescu had taught them a thing or two about battling an ancient hunter. Fortunately, he had managed to kill one of the more experienced followers, leaving Popescu with just three pawns in his little army.

Now, Andre couldn't go quietly to the dawn and rest as he should have been able to because he was honor bound to rid the world of Costin Popescu and his band of bloodthirsty underlings.

Andre found the narrow entrance to the cave he intended to use to rest and heal. He'd used this particular cave before. It wasn't easily accessible. One had to stumble upon the entrance to actually see it, and very few ever came up the jagged cliffs to this height. He had used this cave for a resting place since he was a boy.

He still remembered the glittering gems, crystals of every color sparkling across walls in the various chambers. Sometimes a gleam of light burst through the narrow chimney and lit the interior walls with veins of precious minerals.

He used to come back to the cave in the hopes of seeing that beautiful sight, the one that he thought he'd burned into his memory, the one he'd been so certain would never fade. He lost his emotions far earlier than the normal two hundred years, and the loss of his ability to see in colors followed quickly. The cave, like everything else, was gray.

He had made the underground chambers a home in his youth, long after he'd lost all family members. Everything that meant something to him from his earlier days was stored in an underground "vault" he'd fashioned out of rock, deep beneath the chamber where he often rested. A few centuries earlier, when he realized he would be the last of his family line, he had sealed the vault and only returned to the caves when necessary.

He sighed as he stepped inside the cool, narrow opening. He had to set safeguards. Popescu's minions wouldn't be able to be out in the sun, but it would be suicide not to ensure no one found him while he slept. He didn't have that luxury until he rid the world of the vampires preying on civilians. He lifted his hands and began the complicated but very necessary ritual of putting safeguards around his resting place.

He'd lost a tremendous amount of blood and unexpected weakness hit him as he began to open the earth. Perhaps he had waited too long. His injuries were severe and maybe, just maybe, fate would take a hand and he would not rise again.

Teagan Joanes sat on her sleeping bag in her small travel tent with her heart pounding. She'd made a huge mistake. *Huge*. She was an experienced traveler, and when she went hiking in other countries she always checked out the guide carefully. She knew better than to go off alone without a buddy in any foreign country. She had never, not one single time, considered it would be unsafe to travel into the mountains with a man she had known for over three years.

They were friends. Good friends. In the United States, at the university, she had tutored him, studied with him, ate lunch and dinner with him while they studied. He was from another country and very good-looking, with a deep accent, so therefore popular with the women on campus. He dated a lot. All the time. Rarely the same girl more than twice. Their relationship had been strictly friendship. He never made a move on her, not once. She'd always felt comfortable with him. What happened?

Teagan tried desperately to think what she could have done or said to make Armend Jashari think for even a minute that she suddenly wanted more from their friendship. They'd continued their relationship online, messaging back and forth every few days, just to keep in touch, but there hadn't been a hint of anything sexual. When she needed to visit the Carpathian Mountains it had been natural—she thought—to tell Armend she was coming.

He volunteered immediately to be her guide into the high country, and of course she'd accepted. She was comfortable with him. Correction. She *had* been comfortable with him. Now, the bad vibes had become really scary.

She slept dressed in her jeans and a tee, just to be safe. Now, she pulled on her boots quickly, hearing him prowling around her tent. He was working himself up, she could see that with his pacing. She hastily rolled her sleeping bag and fixed it to her pack, all the while wishing she could exit her tent without being seen.

She trusted her instincts, and right now they were screaming at her to run for her life. Without preamble, her tent door was ripped back and Armend launched himself into her space.

Teagan narrowed her eyes at the man who crawled into her

tent. Her guide. Her friend, so she thought. He wasn't acting the least bit like a guide or a friend, more like a spoiled rich kid who was entitled to take anything he wanted, including her.

"What do you think you're doing?" she demanded in her most haughty, how-dare-you, you're-going-to-die-if-you-come-one-step-closer-to-me voice. Most of the time, the voice didn't work. She wasn't tall and threatening in the least, but she could back the voice up whenever necessary, and right now she was afraid it was going to be very necessary.

"You want this. You've wanted me from the first day you ever saw me three years ago," Armend snarled at her. "Don't pretend. You've been panting after me all that time and then you decided to come over here and ask me to guide you into the mountains."

"You *offered*, Armend," she felt compelled to point out. "It was your idea."

"You wanted me to guide you."

"You were my friend and I thought . . ." She trailed off. She had never considered this would happen, but she should have.

"I know what you want. Stop playing hard to get."

"We went to college together, Armend," she said, keeping her voice low. She didn't want to agitate him or set him off. Sometimes logic worked. The tent was small and there wasn't a lot of room to maneuver. "We had classes together. We ate lunch and sat outside and talked. I thought you were my friend."

He rolled his eyes. "Women and men aren't friends. Did you think I wouldn't notice the looks you gave me?" His accent was thick and it thickened more with passion.

Armend Jashari had been sent to school in the United States. His parents were very wealthy in a land where few people had much. Clearly Armend had grown up believing

7

he could do anything he wanted, including keep coming at a woman when she unmistakably said no.

"I apologize for any misunderstanding that happened between us. I honestly did think we were friends. I have a very good reason for coming here, which I explained to you, and I thought you understood. It seemed a natural thing to do, contact a friend who was familiar with the mountains I needed to explore. I didn't mean to lead you on, or give you the idea that I was interested in being anything more than your friend," Teagan said.

She had never flirted with him. Not once. Armend hadn't given her any indication that he wanted more than friendship during the entire time he was at school with her. She was young to be in the master's program in geology. Armend was a good five years older than she was, and on top of that, she looked extremely young. Like a boy. Armend had treated her more like a younger sibling, He spent a great deal of time with her, but he dated a lot of women—women who looked like her sisters rather than looked like her.

She had three sisters. All were tall, with womanly curves and the faces of models. She had come along ten years after all of them. All three were athletic, beautiful, intelligent and now married with children. She was ... Teagan. She could see Armend being attracted to her sisters, but she wasn't five foot ten and she didn't have full breasts and curved hips. She didn't attract men like her sisters did. And she definitely didn't lead men on.

"You aren't really here looking for a certain type of crystal or stone," Armend objected. He inched forward.

Teagan picked up her one cooking pot. She used it to cook everything when she was hiking—which was often. The pot was black from spending so much time in flames. "Don't you dare come any closer."

"You're a tease. A bitch," Armend snarled. His face turned ugly, and he clenched his fingers into tight fists. "I came all the way up here for a pity fuck. That's what you are to me. My boys laughed when I showed them your letter. They're camping a couple of miles from here and waiting their turn."

She kept her expression blank. He had friends camped close by? She was in the Carpathian Mountains alone with him. She'd trusted him to guide her up the mountain in order to find the exact crystal or stone she needed. It was imperative she find it. She was on a quest—a mission—and she *needed* the crystal. She'd know when she found it. Her body was a tuning fork for such things. The moment she stumbled on the trail she'd track it to its location, but she had to feel a hint of it first. She'd come prepared to spend a month in the mountains, knowing sometimes it was very difficult to run across the faint sign that would allow her to find what she needed.

"I guess I should thank you for thinking of me, but really, Armend, a pity fuck is out. I don't want you to touch me, let alone get that personal. So pity or not, that's out of the question and off the table. Get out of my tent."

"You're just a stupid little virgin, aren't you? A cock tease."

She raised an eyebrow, gritting her teeth. She had a temper and he was pushing very close to it. He was definitely going to attack her, and she might as well prod him into it so she was ready for him. "There isn't anything stupid about me, Armend. I'm far more intelligent than you'll ever be. I had to tutor you, remember? You never would have gotten through any of your classes without me."

He flung himself on her, knocking the cooking pot out of her hand. She was small. Five foot two to her sisters' five foot ten and eleven, and that was when she wore shoes. She was extremely slight. She didn't exactly have lush breasts or

9

anything else that men found enticing. What in the hell was Armend thinking?

His body slammed into hers, carrying her over backward. Her head hit the frame of her backpack and her back hit the ground—hard. He landed on top of her, forcing the air out of her lungs. She punched him as hard as she could from the awkward angle she had, driving her fist into his left eye.

He swore and punched her back. Three times. In the face. She actually saw stars and the edges of her vision blackened. She refused to pass out. He tore at her clothes, ripping her favorite camping shirt. She had only brought a few changes of clothing, because when she hiked, it was all about the weight of the pack she carried. He'd just reduced that meager amount by one.

There was no bucking him off, no getting out from under him by rolling, so she used her very strong stomach muscles and sat up, into him, slamming her head under his chin and driving up with the top of her head. It hurt like hell, but she didn't care. It got him off of her. He rolled into the side of the tent, nearly bringing it down.

She scrambled on all fours to get out of the tent. He kicked her hard in the back of her thigh. Her leg went numb but the force sent her flying out of the opening. She landed on her stomach and rolled away from the tent as fast as she could, trying not to sob with the pain. He wasn't fooling around. He definitely meant business and he didn't care whether he hurt her or not.

She'd taken lessons in defending herself—a lot of them. She climbed, both bouldering and sport climbing. She hiked all the time, all over the world. She was in good shape and strong for being so small. She was *not* going to let someone like Armend Jashari beat and rape her, not without hurting him.

Her hand found the rock she was looking for. It was a good size and solid. As she pushed herself up, struggling to fight off the waves of nausea the punches to her face had caused, Armend hit her from behind, slamming her back to the ground. His hands found her hair and he yanked her head back savagely, turning her as he did so, still straddling her. He punched her hard in the ribs and then leaned down and bit her lip. Hard. The pain was excruciating. She tasted blood.

When he lifted his head, he had blood around his mouth. Her blood. He laughed. "I'm going to have fun with you, Teagan. And then my boys are going to have fun. You'll do whatever we tell you to do and you'll beg us to fuck you if you want to get off this mountain alive. You're not the first stupid bitch we've taken up here. A few are still wandering around trying to find their way off the mountain. Oh. Wait. They fell off a cliff. We didn't bother to bring their bitch bodies out, just left them for the scavengers."

Now she could put down "poor judge of character" beside all the other "cons" on her list about herself. As his head came down toward hers again, she slammed the rock against his temple, using his downward momentum and her strength. He grunted. His eyes rolled. He slumped over the top of her, a dead weight. Crushing her.

Teagan wasn't certain she could find the strength to move his body, but the thought of his friends being close by—and she was certain he was telling the truth about them—had her shoving him hard with every bit of strength she possessed. She managed to shift him enough to crawl out from under him.

Shock took over, adrenaline leaving her shaking and close to tears. Neither was a good thing when she needed to get out of there fast. She couldn't help herself, she had to reach over and feel for his pulse, just to assure herself she hadn't killed him. Touching him was abhorrent, but she did it. Unfortunately he was still alive. She scowled at him, staggered to her feet and hastily caught up her pack. She left her tent and started up the mountain rather than going down it as he would expect.

She had no idea how good he was at tracking someone, but she wasn't going to make it easy for him. She needed a plan, and she'd figure out what to do while she climbed. Her face ached and she knew it was swelling. Her ribs hurt. She wanted to go back and smash him again with the rock. At least there was some satisfaction in hitting him hard.

First, she had to calm her breathing so her ribs wouldn't hurt so darned bad. She wanted to climb into the high country so she could make a wide enough circle that she could head back down the mountain and not run into Armend and his friends if they really decided to come after her. Remembering the look on Armend's face and the way his eyes turned hot and eager at the thought of him and his friends having so much power over her, she was certain they would come after her.

Teagan pushed herself hard, using the trees and brush to hide as she moved steadily up the mountain. She kept herself in good shape and usually she could hike for hours uphill when needed, but she was at a higher elevation and the back of her thigh throbbed and protested with every step she took. Her face hurt so bad she wanted to cry, and one eye was swelling, along with her cheek. Her lip seemed the worst, which was silly. She poured water on a handkerchief and held it to her lower lip while she walked.

Eventually she came to a narrow deer path winding uphill through a much thinner grove of trees. Thin wisps of fog drifted through the trees—a few fingers only, but the air had cooled already considerably. She was grateful for the respite.

Up high, the sun and thinner air wreaked havoc and she had very fair skin and her ribs hurt like hell with every jarring step.

She cursed Armend Jashari with every breath she took. She'd gone a few more miles and was wondering if she dared to take a break. She needed one. She'd drank water and stopped a few times to find a place she could do her "girl" thing, and she hid any sign of that carefully, afraid it would help Armend find her trail much easier.

She spotted a depression in the low brush and thought it might be a good place to rest, even if it was only for a few minutes. Her leg needed it. She took several steps toward it and stopped dead in her tracks, her heart suddenly accelerating. There it was. Just like that. When she almost let everyone convince her she was crazy, she felt a strange fluttering along her veins, like a vibration.

Immediately she halted, allowing herself water while she absorbed the feeling. She needed to be able to tune her entire body to the vibration, until it was a song in her veins, rushing with her blood through her system. Her gift. The one she could never explain to anyone and not make it sound insane.

Elation swept through her. She hadn't thought she'd find the trail so quickly, but somewhere ahead of her, the wonderful stone or crystal or gem she needed so desperately was waiting for her. She had to make a decision right now. If she followed the trail of the stone she sought, she would be risking Armend and his friends finding her. If she didn't, she could lose this stone forever, and that meant losing her beloved grandmother.

Trixie Joanes had taken her and her three sisters into her home when Teagan was born. Her mother died in childbirth and not once had her grandmother ever blamed her for the death of her daughter. If anything, she had loved her all the

13

more. She owed everything to her grandmother and loved her beyond anyone else in the world. Lately, her grandmother's mind had begun slipping.

Her sisters were terrified she was drifting into a world of delusion and they kept taking her to psychiatrists. No one seemed able to help. Teagan had decided she had to do something herself, and that meant using her special gifts few wanted to know about. Talking about them put her in the same "insane" category as Trixie. Still, she knew what she could do with anything of the earth, minerals, gems, crystals, any type of rock. She knew the power each stone held and she was able to tune it to her, unlock that power and use it. Finding the right stone to help clear Trixie's mind was essential. Teagan was willing to risk everything for her grandmother.

She changed direction immediately and doubled her pace, determined to put as much distance between Armend and herself while she followed the trail of rock or crystal her body had tuned itself to. Armend had never believed her that her body could actually find the trail of types of rock and crystal.

She'd told him, of course, one time during an all-nighter at the university. He'd wasted a few days partying as usual and she'd agreed to help him study for an exam. She'd been a little tired and sometimes that made her talk too much. He'd laughed at her, just like everyone did, so she didn't bring it up again. Until now.

She felt like an idiot confiding in him, relaying her fears about her beloved grandmother, explaining why her quest was so important. She could understand him thinking she was crazy, but seriously, *he* was the crazy one. He was most likely a killer. A serial rapist. How was she going to explain that one to her grandmother and sisters?

She winced remembering his cold statement. "Pity fuck."

14

That was harsh. Mostly men ignored her. Well, okay. Not ignore; she had mostly male friends. But they always saw her as a friend. A little sister. Which was fine by her because she wasn't attracted to anyone. Not male or female. She had no idea why, but she wasn't.

Her sisters endlessly set her up, calling her and asking her over for dinner. Inevitably when she arrived, there would be a man—or a woman—one of her sisters had also just happened to invite, and of course she had to sit through dinner next to them and be hit on all evening.

But now, up in the mountains, all alone, without anyone around, she just had to get the attention of a man, and he turned out to be a killer. What was up with that? She sighed. She realized her legs were about to give out. The pain in her side now radiated up into her chest so her lungs burned for air. She had to rest, but fear drove her to keep going. She needed to find a place out of the way, somewhere she could lie down for a while.

She looked around, hoping to find a more hidden area to rest in, just in case she did fall asleep. She was exhausted, and the pain seemed to be worsening, although intellectually, she knew it hadn't, she just wasn't occupying her mind and keeping it at bay as well as she had been while she followed the trail. She had to pay attention to her body, to the strength of the song she heard in her veins. If she went too far in the wrong direction, the vibrations dulled. It took total concentration, which was a good thing to block out the pain, but she'd been traveling for a good part of the day and she had to stop.

Movement caught her eye. The trees were mostly gone up this high. Only a few straggly ones hung grimly on to life. While she'd been hiking, the mist had grown thicker and she hadn't really noticed. Around her, the world seemed gray, alien even. The wind blew, so that the fog swirled in

15

pinwheels, but it didn't seem to go anywhere. Still, even with the sounds muffled, she had *definitely* spotted movement a few yards to her left.

She bit at her lip and nearly swore aloud. Instead, as she crouched low to keep from being spotted, she heaped curses silently on Armend's head, wishing she was a witch and could consign him to a living hell. Maybe have fire ants crawling up his legs and biting the heck out of him everywhere, especially his manly parts. That might be nice.

It took a few minutes to realize it was no human being moving around in the brush, but an animal. No. More than one animal. Wolves? She knew there were all kinds of wildlife making homes in the mountain range. This was nearly the last refuge for larger predators.

She shrugged carefully out of her backpack, wanting to groan as the weight came off her back. Instead, she kept her eyes on the wide field of dense brush. She spotted movement in at least five different spots. Alarm grew. She hadn't cleaned up and the scent of blood probably clung to her. She brushed her hand across her face and it came back smeared with blood.

Her lip actually hurt more than her head, which was silly since her face was swollen up like a balloon, but the pain in her lip made her sick. It didn't help, either, that she had a habit of biting at her lower lip. The scrape of her teeth when she forgot was agony over the wound. She hadn't looked at it, not even once, afraid maybe she needed stitches. Or worse, the asinine idiot had rabies or something. *Sheesh.* She should have hit Armend harder.

Another strange thing was she felt inexplicable sorrow. Not just that, but despair. Hopelessness. An agony of loneliness. She knew it wasn't her own, but something carried in the mist. A song. A song of great sorrow, not just from one individual, but from many. The notes blended into the symphony of the mountain.

One of the animals moved out of the brush into the open. She stared at it, heart pounding. Mouth dry. She kept trying to make it into a wolf. Right size maybe. She could even think the shape was sort of right. But no way was that creature a wolf. It looked more like a sheep. Or a goat. Were there wild goats or wild sheep in the Carpathian Mountains?

The fog was very heavy and she hadn't even noticed it had become that dense. The air felt damp, but she was grateful for the cover. There wasn't as much foliage up this high and she didn't want Armend or any of his friends to spot her moving up the very faint trail she followed. The animal moved again, a slow steady few steps, and her body sagged with relief. Clearly the Carpathian Mountains were home to wild sheep.

She sank down onto a small, flat rock and let herself look around. Her tuning fork, as she called it, was leading her up higher into the mountains than she'd ever intended to go. Teagan drank more water. It was important to stay hydrated.

She glanced at her watch. She'd been hiking up the trail for several hours. She was hungry and tired and out of sorts. Worse, she was now totally enshrouded in the fog and wrapped in a blanket of intense emotions, none of them good. The notes playing through the song of the mountain were painful to listen to. She was a healer and she naturally wanted to do something to ease that pain. If it was pressing on her shoulders and crushing her chest, she couldn't imagine what it was doing to those who felt such despair.

She'd only taken a couple of small breaks because she was really afraid now that she'd decided to hunt for the gemstone or crystal that could aid in clearing her grandmother's mind. Of course, if Trixie knew she was hiking alone in the wilds of the Carpathian Mountains, with a pack of rabid men on her

17

heels, she'd get out the mythical wooden spoon she'd always threatened Teagan with.

She needed a place to rest. Her leg, where Armend had kicked her, cramped and throbbed alternately and she began to limp. She drank more water and searched above her for a place that might be hidden. There didn't seem to be any real cover other than the fog, but it was so thick, she couldn't really see anything above the elevation where she was.

With a sigh, she capped the bottle and stood. She couldn't stay there. She needed shelter of some kind, and that meant looking for it. While she did, she might as well follow the trail the strange vibrations in her body were leading her to. Both paths seemed connected. Both led up the mountain, instead of down toward civilization.

She shrugged into her pack and started up the trail, putting one step in front of the other, trying to feel her way. The blood sang in her veins. She was definitely close to her goal. She veered to her right. The song grew louder. She heard it in her ears, a pounding drum of satisfaction calling to her. Another few yards and the song burst through her body. She was that close—so close she actually could push aside those sad, weeping notes that counterpointed the song in her body.

Teagan stopped and examined the wall of rock directly in front of her. Her stone was somewhere inside the rising tower of rock. She slipped her palm over the small boulder. The fog was even thicker up here and she literally felt her way around the mountain. Her hand abruptly slipped off and she realized instantly she had found an opening.

She stared into the darkness for a long moment. She was small enough to fit inside if she took her pack off and carried it. Her heart pounded. Wild animals could live in the cave. Still, if nothing else lived in it, she could rest. The chances of Armend finding the cave were slim, and she desperately needed to go to sleep. More, she needed to try to calm the swelling in her face and take a look at her stinging lip.

"Courage, Teagan," she whispered to herself. "You've come this far for Grandma Trixie, are you going to fail because you're scared?"

She often asked herself that question. Was she going to fail because she was scared? She might be afraid of a lot of things, but she never once had allowed fear to stop her from doing anything she wanted to do. In fact, often times, that fear spurred her on, because she was so determined not to allow it to rule her.

She started to slip into the narrow opening and something stopped her. Something completely invisible. She put her hand out and felt the barrier. A shield. It seemed to be constructed of notes, like the music inside her body. She'd never encountered such a thing before, but her mind was all about puzzles and patterns. She loved to boulder because that was a world of puzzles and patterns. She could see a problem in front of her and her mind feasted on it, needing to solve it.

She didn't know if nature had spun that tight netting, or if something else had done it, but she knew she had to solve it. The compulsion was on her, and there was no going back from it.

She sank down in front of the opening and lifted her hands into the air, closing her eyes and tuning herself to the invisible threads of what she saw as a harp in her mind. The strings of the harp were all knotted, forming a tight net. She simply had to unravel them and set them straight again.

It was a complicated pattern, and she found herself completely absorbed, forgetting Armend and the sorrowful notes in the fog and everything else, even the pain in her body while she worked to sort out the strings of the harp. Everything had to be reversed and she had to do it by sound alone. There was no visible shield, just a song she felt in her body.

It took her two hours, she knew because she'd looked at her watch. She was shivering with cold, her clothes damp from the thick fog by the time she'd straightened out all the strings and knew she could walk through the entrance. Feeling triumphant, she got to her feet and, pushing her pack ahead of her, slipped inside. The moment she did, the despairing notes faded away, left behind in the thick mist.

Darkness swallowed her instantly and with it came the thud of her heart. Loud. Scary loud. She jerked out her flashlight and carefully examined the way ahead of her. The tunnel was narrow, but still, she could walk upright through it. She scrutinized the ground carefully for tracks of animals. She couldn't see that the dirt had been disturbed. She was fairly certain that if wolves occupied the cave, there would be evidence, like a pack surrounding and eating her.

She pushed forward. Her heart continued to pound, no matter how hard she tried to breathe away fear. She moved down the narrow passageway, realizing she wasn't only going deeper into the cave, but downward as well. The angle wasn't terribly steep, but she became aware of the heavy rock over her head. The cave had high ceilings and the farther she went into it, the higher the ceiling became. She stopped every few feet to shine her flashlight in all directions. She wanted to see the walls surrounding her and the ceiling above her.

There was no sign of wolves or any other animal, and she was becoming excited that she might have found the perfect base camp to hunt for her stones without Armend or his friends finding her.

The narrow passage abruptly widened and she had a choice to go left or right. She listened to the song in her veins and chose right. The tunnel was short and opened almost

20

immediately into a wide chamber. It was beautiful. The walls sparkled when she shone the light over it. Something drew her toward the very back, and she followed that need.

Teagan placed her backpack against the farthest wall beside another opening that, when she shone the light there, appeared to be an entrance into another chamber, just a bit smaller. She stepped inside to look around.

The dirt had been moved recently. She could see that, and when she flashed the light over the freshly disturbed earth, she spotted drops of dark red blood. Lots of it. And it was definitely recent. Her heart stopped pounding. Stopped beating. She was so certain her heart stopped that she put her hand over her chest and opened her mouth to drag in air. Blood. Right there in the cave with her. What now?

2

T eagan found herself following the trail of blood through the small chamber, down farther into the earth. The cave was far warmer as she went deeper. It should have been cooler, and that made her wonder if there was volcanic activity beneath her. The thought made her pause, but the compulsion to follow the blood trail was too strong to ignore.

She knelt down beside a particularly large splash of dark red blood and touched the substance with shaking fingers. It felt sticky, as if it had congealed there a few hours earlier. The moment she touched it, something inside of her answered. Opened. Needed. She should have wiped the blood off her hands in the dirt, but she couldn't make herself do it. Instead, she curled her fingers tight into her palm, as if holding him there. Instinctively she knew the victim was a man, and she had to get to him. She had to save him.

Teagan found him in the fourth chamber. It was a small

room, completely dark, and he looked to be in an open grave. Her flashlight caught the edge of his body, lying in the ground about two feet deep. The dirt had filled in around his body, but his face and chest weren't covered. Her mouth went dry and her throat closed. It was impossible to breathe for a brief moment. She couldn't run and she couldn't move forward. She could only stand still, praying, the flashlight shaking in her hand.

She stared at him, her heart continuing to pound as the song in her veins burst into a crescendo, as if somewhere on or beneath this man was the very stone she needed to cure her grandmother. She stepped closer, although she was reluctant, afraid he truly was dead, and she couldn't bear that, but if he was still alive, she needed to help him.

Teagan forced her feet to work, moving to his side, dropping down to her knees to feel for the pulse in his neck. The moment she touched him, the terrible dread in her increased. She needed him to be alive more than she needed anything else. He had to live. She waited for his heartbeat. Prayed for it. There was nothing at all. Not even the faintest thread of a pulse.

A small moan of fear escaped. Not of him. For him. For her. She knew, deep down, that she'd come to this place to save this man, but her injuries had slowed her down. Slowly she laid her head over his heart. Strangely, his body felt warm, although if he were dead, and had been for a few hours, he should have been cold. She pressed her ear to his chest and held her breath to keep from making the slightest noise. There was no discernable heartbeat, although she felt the heavy, defined muscles in his chest.

His shirt was bloody and torn. There were terrible gashes in his chest. Open wounds. Wounds that she knew should have killed him and probably had, but still, she needed him to be

23

alive and she had no idea why, but the need was so strong she shook with the force of it. More, there was evidence of old wounds. Four of them. One in each shoulder and one in each side. Circular scars that were a good two inches in diameter. This man had seen battle.

She closed her eyes, sorrow crushing her chest. The need to wail with grief rose in her like a tidal wave, coming out of nowhere, but so strong another sound escaped, an agonized cry that seemed terribly loud in the silence of the cave. She didn't know this man, but the blow was tremendous. She placed her hand in front of his mouth to try to feel air.

"Come on, sweetheart," she said softly. "Don't be dead. Unconscious is okay. I can deal with unconscious, but you need to come back to the land of the living." She dared to press her lips against his ear, needing him to hear her. He was so warm, it seemed impossible that she'd lost him before she'd had a chance to save him. "Stay here with me. Don't go. Come back to me." She didn't know why she structured her plea that way, but the compulsion inside her, the one that couldn't let him go, forced the wrenching words from—not her heart—but her aching soul.

His skin was pale, and hers was darker, a soft mocha latte, her grandmother had always described her. Her mother was African American but her father was Caucasian. He had been a businessman who had pursued her mother and then dumped her the moment he learned she was pregnant. Technically, her three sisters were half sisters, but never once had they ever acted like she wasn't part of them. They called her their heart because Grandma Trixie always called her that.

She could heal. She'd always had an extraordinary gift to do so, but not if someone was already dead. She couldn't raise the dead. Her throat closed in protest. This man couldn't already be gone, out of her reach.

She leaned down again, trailing her fingers gently over his chest as if the small sensation could penetrate deep to his heart. "Seriously, open your eyes right *now*." She tried to make it a command. Instead, it came out a plea. Tears burned her eyes as she stared down into his handsome face.

He was beautiful. Even in death, he was beautiful. If she'd been an artist, he would be the man she would want to sculpt. To draw. To put into any medium to preserve.

His lashes fluttered, and her heart fluttered right along with them. The breath rushed from her lungs. She stared at him. His eyelids remained closed. Had that been an illusion? She'd planted her flashlight in the ground, the light beaming toward the ceiling, casting a glow over him, but most of him was in the shadows. It had to have been an illusion. But still . . . Her heart began to pound all over again.

Whether he was dead or alive, she wasn't leaving him in this state. "Listen, handsome, I'm going to run back and get my pack. I can clean you up. That's the least I can do for you." Even as she spoke to him, whispered into his ear, her hand went to his chest, directly over his heart. Hoping. She was still praying. She needed him to be alive, but there was no indication whatsoever.

Pushing back a sob, she jumped to her feet, wincing when her leg protested—when her face told her the swelling hadn't gone down at all. She glanced at her watch as she hurried back through the various chambers to the one she'd left her backpack in. Sunset was approaching and hopefully, since Armend and his friends hadn't found her yet, they wouldn't as night fell. She'd be able to rest.

Andre only had one dream in his entire existence, a recurring one, and it was a nightmare—or more precisely, a memory he wished to forget. He slept the sleep of Carpathians. Heart stopped. Breath gone. Essentially, by human standards, dead. A paralysis settled over them and they couldn't move even if their minds were still active. But he had to be dreaming.

A soft voice—a woman's voice. His lifemate. The whisper of a touch against his skin. The little plea that touched his heart even though it wasn't beating. He dreamt in color. Bright, vivid color. It was so beautiful, so real, each color distinct, not bleeding gray into it, but there behind his eyes, in his brain. Blues and greens and vibrant reds.

He struggled to lift his lashes, to open his eyes to see. He hadn't buried himself completely in the soil as he should have. He'd lost far too much blood and he knew his safeguards were strong. The vampires would have gone to ground as well. All of them were wounded, including Costin Popescu, the master vampire. He knew he was safe enough and he was just too tired to do anything but lie down in the fresh, clean soil.

He lay there now, his heart beginning its slow revival. He took his first breath, drawing her scent into his lungs. She was real. He didn't know how to feel about that after centuries of hunting for her. Centuries of giving up on her. Centuries of being so alone he didn't know how to be with anyone else, or even how to be civil.

The brief moment when he'd managed to beat the paralysis and open his eyes just enough to glimpse her had to be real, not a figment of his imagination, because he saw her in all her glorious color. Still, how had she gotten into his sleeping chamber? Into his cave? He had put up safeguards. Intricate safeguards, not based on mage guards, but ones he had devised himself over the centuries. Guards that shouldn't have been penetrated.

He had to be dreaming. But in color? Nothing made sense. The moment his heart began to beat, blood began to stream from the various wounds on his body. Hunger struck. Clawed. Pain had to be shut off. Automatically he repaired the internal damage to his body, even as his mind went over every detail he remembered of the brief glimpse.

His lifemate had been very slight, very small, but he could see the steel in her. The determination. She was beautiful, more beautiful than any woman he'd ever seen—that in itself should tell him he was dreaming. Her skin was amazing, a dark soft expanse that any man would have a difficult time resisting touching. But she'd been covered in bruises. He could see blue and black in the mixture of color along her cheek, up by her eye and along her jaw. Her face was swollen, her lip torn.

She had a beautiful mouth, tilted at the corners, an inviting bow, her teeth small and white. Her eyes were a dark, dark chocolate. The lashes surrounding them were full and very black.

Her hair was long, a luxurious gleaming black, not dull gray, done in intricate cornrows and then swept back in a ponytail of small braids. The ponytail was easily as thick as his arm and fell to her waist. When she walked away from him, she was limping. He had to have been dreaming, because how could she be real after all the long centuries? And how could she have gotten past his safeguards?

He stayed very still, absorbing the feel of the cave. His senses told him he wasn't alone. He smelled her. There was a mixture of fresh air, fog, the mountains, sweat and something else, something that called to him, like a particular scent carried on a summer wind. Almost like the earth smelled after a fresh rain. He needed more of it. He wanted more.

He heard her then, the soft running as she returned to him, just as she'd promised. She thought him dead. He'd heard the sorrow in her voice. She had asked him to stay. To come back to her. Had she come to find him? Had he been close to dying? He doubted it. He had work to do. Several vampires to kill. He wouldn't have left them alive to harm others.

She dropped a backpack that was nearly as tall as she was onto the floor beside the entrance to the small chamber. She had a flashlight in her hand, the light dancing along the walls as she hurried toward him. He could see the colors of the wall. The rich veins of various minerals and the few gems that sparkled in the light. The edge of the light caught a crystalline rock jutting out of the wall. He remembered the formation from his youth, and was shocked that he hadn't noticed it again until her dancing light spotlighted it for him.

Her scent enveloped him. This time he recognized the interesting mixture of wildflowers and rain. He inhaled her. The moment he did, she cried out and dropped to the ground beside him.

"You're alive. Oh. My. God. You're totally alive."

Her hands ran over his chest. Her touch was featherlight, but everywhere the pads of her fingers touched he felt heat and something else, something that penetrated deep, right through his skin. He recognized the touch of a natural healer. She had immense power. He stayed very still, listening to the musical cadence of her voice. The sound of her struck an answering chord in him.

He realized she spoke English. Not just any English, but American English. She wasn't from the Carpathian Mountains. She didn't feel Carpathian. But she belonged to him. Absolutely belonged to him. He turned his head and locked his eyes on his prey. Seeing the swelling in her face hurt him. An actual pain. He couldn't leave her like that. He refused.

She was an amazing healer and should have seen to herself before recklessly running into a cave. What was wrong with her that she didn't see the danger to herself even now? Because she was in danger. Didn't she feel it? He was starving. He'd lost too much blood, and there she was, bending over him, her throat exposed, her pulse pounding, her heart calling to his. He could hear the ebb and flow of her blood. Smell it even, through the wound on her mouth. The tear.

Someone had hurt his lifemate very recently. A male. He could smell the testosterone on her. Her shirt was torn, exposing the curve of her breast. She was tiny, but he could see the small, beautiful curve and he ached. The ache wasn't enough to hold the beast at bay. Someone had attempted to harm her.

He lifted his hand to her face, his thumb sliding gently over the bruised swelling. "Who did this to you?" His English was good, but he had an English accent. He was unfamiliar with the American accent. His first words to his lifemate. He spoke softly, his voice pitched low, but there was a distinct growl, a note that made her entire body go still.

She pressed her lips together and then winced. "Let's concentrate on you. Your wounds are horrific. I'm Teagan. Teagan Joanes."

"I do not want to invade your privacy by taking this information from you, but I refuse to argue. Give me his name."

Her long lashes swept down and then back up. She sank back on her heels, wincing as she did so, as if that movement hurt as well. He saw trepidation in her dark eyes, the beginnings of fear. He knew what she saw. He'd been alarming humans for centuries—and she was definitely human. He'd alarmed his own species. He wasn't a man to trifle with. But his first obligation was to the safety and health of his lifemate, not the other way around. Fear or not, he *would* get his answer.

"Armend Jashari," she replied, her voice a whisper. "He's

somewhere behind me. He told me he had friends camping nearby and they were going . . . " She trailed off.

He scowled at her and decided to take the information from her. He wasn't the coaxing kind. This was too important. He needed to know what this man had done and what he intended to do. He needed to heal his woman and decide a course of action. Her dithering wasn't helping the situation at all.

"Look at me," he commanded, keeping his voice low. He deliberately didn't move from his resting place, allowing her to keep a false sense of security.

Her gaze jumped to his. He didn't allow her to look away. The moment her dark eyes met his, he ensnared her, whispering his command to her, so that she would accept his dark embrace. He sat up, pulling her into his arms, his mind reaching for hers, pushing past barriers, seeking information.

He found himself snarling. Lethal. Furious. His lifemate had been in jeopardy, nearly raped. She'd been beaten. Some man she trusted, the man he could see in her memories who she believed had been her friend, had assaulted her and then threatened her. Armend Jashari would be receiving a visit from him, and then Armend Jashari would know what real terror was.

He laid his hands on her face gently, the pad of one finger over the jagged tear on her lip. Before all else, before he allowed himself to taste her, to stop the terrible clawing need in his body for sustenance, he was compelled to heal her. He couldn't look one more second on her bruised face, or feel her discomfort and pain beating at him.

Andre sent himself out of his body. Letting go of one's self to become pure healing light had always been a little difficult for him, but this time, for the first time, he did so easily. For her. For his lifemate. He tasted the word even as he entered her body and began to heal her from the inside.

He didn't forget to examine her leg—the one she'd been limping on when she hurried away to get her backpack. He found dark bruising almost to the bone. She'd been kicked hard, hard enough to do major damage. Jashari was going to pay for that as well.

Andre made certain every damaged place on her body was healed before he returned to his own body. The pain of his wounds jolted through him. He'd stopped the bleeding, but he had suffered a severe loss. He needed. The need was becoming desperate. More. Much more. His lifemate's scent called to him. He could already taste her. A perfect addiction he would crave for all time, would never be able to get enough of.

He pulled her into his arms, wrapped her close to him to warm her. Her body shivered against his, and she blinked, looking up at his face. She looked a little frightened and he knew she was coming out from under his thrall. Part of him wanted that, but he knew she wasn't nearly ready to understand she would be coming into his world and what that would mean for her.

"You are safe with me, Teagan," he said. "Safer than you have ever been in your life. When you are frightened, look to me."

He pushed at her mind again to send her deeper under even as his lips found the pulse beating so strongly in her throat. His tongue stroked the rhythmic throb that told him she was alive and healthy. He kissed her heartbeat. Listened to it. Absorbed it. Savored it. His lifemate. A gift beyond any price. A treasure. *His.*

His teeth sank deep and the taste of her burst through his mouth. He had thought the colors she'd returned to him were blinding and vibrant, but he had no idea what the real gift was, not until that moment. Hunger took his body, sharp

31

and terrible. Not the addiction to her blood, but physical. His cock swelled. His nerve endings came alive. Life came to his body. The beauty of it was painful and yet a miracle he had never considered or expected. His body craved hers. Just as his need for the taste of her, spicy and addicting, settled deep into his veins, his need of her body settled deep into his bones.

He didn't hesitate. He had waited centuries for his woman. Beyond centuries. She was his reward. She was his miracle. She was ... his. *Te avio päläfertiilam*—You are my lifemate. The ritual binding words resonated deep. His ancient language rose like the tides from his very soul.

Teagan Joanes held the other half of his soul. He didn't question why or how. It simply was. And he was driven, bound, to seal their souls together. *Éntölam kuulua, avio päläfertiilam*. I claim you as my lifemate. *Ted kuuluak, kacad, kojed*. I belong to you. That in itself was a miracle. To belong to anyone. To belong anywhere. He hadn't had a home in centuries. Even childhood memories had faded. Now there was this one small woman—this tiny vessel who carried his life in her.

He forced himself to close the small pinpricks on her throat. *Élidamet andam*. I offer my life for you. *Pesämet andam*. I give you my protection. *Uskolfertiilamet andam*. I give you my allegiance.

Her body was very warm and fit perfectly into his. She moved restlessly in his arms. He waved his hand to remove all bloodstains and the tatters of his shirt from his chest so that she was tight against him. Instinctively she turned her face against his heart, her lips rubbing gently over his pulse beating so strongly there.

The simple movement inflamed his body and he reveled in his ability to feel. To come alive. To know that the woman in his arms was truly his. He whispered the command to feed, to take his blood. He needed the first exchange with her to be complete while he completed the ritual binding.

She would be forever bound to him, unable to be away from him for long, just as he would be the same with her. They would be able to speak mind to mind. He would always know what she needed or wanted and he could see to that every need or desire.

More than anything else, at this moment, he had to feel her mouth on him, drawing his blood into her to connect them in the deepest possible way so that the binding of their souls would last for all time, in this world and any that came after.

He drew a thin line over his pulse with a sharpened fingernail. His blood seeped out and he pressed her mouth over the spot, his heart beating hard as her lips moved. It was erotic, so much so that he couldn't move or breathe for a moment. It was also beautiful to him. He could feel the connection growing quickly between them.

"*Sívamet andam.* I give you my heart." He spoke aloud in both languages because later—much later—when he allowed her to remember—he wanted her to know just what she meant to him. Just what he gave to her and demanded from her. It was complete surrender by both parties. Since he'd been a boy, he had never had a heart to give to anyone until she came into his world.

"*Sielamet andam.* I give you my soul." His soul had always been hers. He had walked for centuries, half alive, always the darkness in him growing because his other half had the light he needed to exist. To live.

She made a sound and her palm slid up his chest, over his shoulder to curl in the length of his hair. He was an ancient and he wore his hair in the way of his people in ancient times. It was thick and long and pulled back with a leather cord. His hair had always had far too much wave in it and sometimes, like now, there were long, unmanly spirals, but he'd never bothered to change it even in his mind. Now he liked it when her fingers sought one spiral and slipped through it.

"*Ainamet andam.* I give you my body. *Sívamet kuuluak kaik että a ted.* I take into my keeping the same that is yours."

He had never given much consideration to sex. He'd learned everything he could about it, because down the long centuries, a Carpathian acquired as much knowledge as possible on every subject they could. It was a trick they used, a way to keep their minds occupied, and it served them well. Now he was grateful for those long centuries of study.

He had been so removed from those studies, absorbing all the erotic positions, every way a man could take a woman to please and pleasure her. Every way a woman could please and pleasure a man. With Teagan's mouth moving against him and his cock full and hard and throbbing, all those images were uppermost in his mind.

"*Ainaak olenszal sívambin.* Your life will be cherished by me for all my time." More than cherished. She would be worshiped. Adored. She would be his everything.

She moved restlessly, her buttocks rubbing along the length of his cock, sending an electrical current radiating outward from his groin. The blood in his veins thickened with desire. He had to stop her feeding. She'd taken enough for an exchange, and he didn't dare lose too much more blood. He'd only taken enough from her to get by until he went hunting the man who had tried to rape her.

"*Te élidet ainaak pide minan.* Your life will be placed above my own for all time." And that meant any enemy of hers was his enemy. Any enemy of his could never touch her. His enemies did not last very long.

He gently inserted his fingers between her mouth and the wound in his chest. Her tongue instinctively followed the little trickle of ruby beads away from the slash. The movement was naturally sensual, and his breath hissed out of his lungs as he closed the wound and tipped her face up to his, using two fingers, forcing her eyes to meet his.

"*Te avio päläfertiilam.* You are my lifemate. *Ainaak sívamet jutta oleny.* You are bound to me for all eternity. *Ainaak terád vigyázak.* You are always in my care."

He took her mouth. Gentle. Reverent even. Tasting the mixture of their blood now flowing together to form a mutual path. He closed his eyes, savoring her. Savoring the moment. She wouldn't remember other than in a dream. He wanted that for her. He wanted her to get used to his world slowly, taking it in a little at a time so she wouldn't be too frightened and she would be able to accept her fate over time.

He used his tongue rather than his mind to remove all evidence of his blood from her lips and mouth. He loved touching her. Loved having her next to his skin. He especially loved the silk of her hair against him. Sensations were sensual. He craved them now that he could feel. Every sensation she could give him. How could he possibly let her go, even for a moment, after waiting so long for her?

Still, he set her to one side, his hands reluctantly leaving the warmth of her body. He took a breath and gave the command for her to awaken fully. Her lashes fluttered. Lifted. He found himself looking straight into her dark melted chocolate eyes. So dark a man might get lost there.

She brought up a trembling hand and touched her lips, her gaze moving over his chest—a chest that had no shirt but revealed heavy muscles, four circular older scars and wounds that were healed. Completely. Absolutely healed. Gone.

She swallowed and glanced down at her watch. "I feel like I missed something important." The moment she spoke, she touched her lip where it had stung, especially when she talked. Her hand moved from her lip to her face where it had been swollen.

He smiled to reassure her. "I, too, am a healer. The sight of you bruised and battered was abhorrent to me. No man should put his hands on a woman like that. Especially you. I felt compelled to heal you," he added honestly. "Are you in any pain at all?" Because he would start all over if she was.

She shook her head. "I was supposed to heal you."

She sounded a little disappointed and he hid a smile. He had forgotten smiles. He doubted if he'd ever smiled much. The sensation was wonderful and a little shocking. "Next time. I seriously couldn't allow you to be in pain."

"Are you an empath?" Her eyes were on his chest.

She had a difficult time pulling her gaze away, and he was suddenly grateful he hadn't donned a clean shirt. That meant he would have to manufacture a stash of clothes for the time being, enough that she would be eased into his world as gently as possible. She liked his chest and the muscles there. He had plenty from so many centuries of battling the undead.

He also had a few scars, including the four circular ones that would never leave his body. Carpathians rarely scarred. The wound had to be mortal—one that was deadly. He'd taken a few very nasty jabs to his heart when a master vampire had nearly managed to rip the organ from his body. He'd been lucky that time. Skill had little to do with saving his life, although his vast experience had definitely aided him. The worst scar was there, and he saw her gaze fall to it several times, no doubt wondering why the scar was the size of a fist and looked as if an animal had tried to rip him open.

"I'm Andre. Andre Boroi." His heart leapt when he gave himself that precious last name—the surname that actually meant something to him. The one he had vowed he would never use unless he used it with his lifemate out of honor. Out of respect. "It is my pleasure to meet you, Teagan Joanes." Which didn't tell her anything. Her eyes told him she was afraid and he didn't blame her.

He was a Carpathian and that meant he was a predator. There was no doubt that showed in his features, in his eyes, probably even in his carriage. He didn't want his lifemate frightened, but there was no softening of what or who he was.

"What happened to you?"

Her voice was very soft, trembling even. Her hands dropped to her lap, fingers twisting together. She'd been attacked by a friend. He was a total stranger and they were alone in a cave. Her fear beat at him, making his belly knot up. He found having a violent and unexpected physical reaction to her fear interesting and yet disturbing.

"Be still, Teagan." He dropped his voice low, using a hypnotic tone. A soothing one. "You are safe with me. I would never harm you."

Her lashes fluttered. He couldn't help staring at them. She had long, thick lashes that curled just a little on the ends. They were midnight black, just like her hair. Black—not gray. He liked that.

She moistened her lips with the tip of her tongue and instantly his attention was on her lips, that soft perfect little bow of a mouth. He found himself fascinated with her mouth. Her skin was beautiful, flawless, and as soft as it looked. He knew because the feel of her was already imprinted in his mind.

"You're staring at me," she said in a small voice.

"You are quite beautiful. I have never seen a woman as remarkable as you are."

She frowned at him. "I'm not, you know. Beautiful. I'm just me. I like being me, and I don't need compliments and lies to make myself feel good."

He touched her mind at the suddenly fierce flash of pride in

37

her eyes. He saw her sisters, the women she viewed as beautiful. They were all tall with lots of curves. Her half sisters. She loved them and thought they were the most beautiful women on the face of the earth. He pulled her recent encounter with Armend Jashari out of her brain, hearing the ugly things he'd said to her.

He frowned. *"Ainaak enyém*, to me, there is no one more beautiful for a variety of reasons. I love the look of you. Your eyes and skin, the shape of you, but more, the way you make me feel. We are sitting in a cave, both injured, both healers, and I can feel your fear, yet you have not abandoned me. You did not abandon me when you found me and that took courage. I find that—and you—quite beautiful."

The hint of defiant pride faded to be replaced by a small smile. "I'm not all that brave, Andre. I'm afraid of everything, I just refuse to give into it."

"Do not be afraid of me, *csitri*. I can tell you this. There are few men walking this earth more dangerous than the one in this cave with you. I will not allow any harm to come to you. Not now. Not ever. That simply is."

His voice rang with sincerity. He looked her in the eye, hoping she would believe him. He wasn't a man who talked much. In fact, probably, this was the most he'd spoken at any one time to any human being. But he didn't want her to fear him. He didn't like the way her fingers twisted in her lap and the slight tremor he could see in her hands, although she tried to hide it from him.

She sent him a faint smile. It didn't light her eyes, but it was real. Her lips curved into more of a bow and a shallow dimple appeared on either side of her mouth. "Is that supposed to reassure me? That you're more dangerous than most men walking the earth? Do you have any idea how that sounds? Not to mention, it might just be a little arrogant."

38

He wasn't about to argue. He didn't really know what to say. He wasn't being arrogant. He wasn't bragging. He was stating a fact.

"I am not used to talking so much with others," he admitted. "Perhaps my wording is not correct. Nor do I normally converse in this language."

She looked a little relieved. "Of course. That makes sense. Thank you for healing my face. My lip was really hurting, which seemed a little silly since the injury was so much smaller than the others. How did you know my leg hurt?"

"When you walked away from me you were limping. I heard you."

Her eyes moved over his face. Watched him. She was very still, other than her fingers twisting in her lap. He couldn't help himself. He laid his hand very gently over both of hers, his touch calming. At the same time, his mind sought hers. He was very careful about that as well.

Her eyes widened. She took a deep breath.

"Do you feel me? In your mind?" he asked gently. "I established a connection when I healed you. That sometimes happens." He was being honest, although he knew he was misleading her just a little.

"You're psychic? You can read minds?" Teagan asked.

He nodded slowly. He couldn't deny that and he wanted her to become comfortable sharing their thoughts and speaking telepathically to each another.

"Wow. That's not good. You're sort of gorgeous, and I'm not certain I want you able to read anything I'm thinking about you," she blurted out.

That was the last thing he expected, and somewhere deep inside, he felt the beginnings of a smile again. It didn't quite reach his face, but his mouth twitched. He had never liked the company of others. He always felt too caged in. Too exposed.

And he disliked the inane small talk that always seemed necessary in the company of others. He wasn't good at it and he never would be.

Frankly, he chose his own path and he followed it. The feelings and opinions of others didn't enter into the equation. He had relied on his own judgment for centuries and had learned from hard experience. The less civilized entrapments he had to deal with the better, as far as he was concerned. The only company he ever kept was with his semi-adopted brothers, triplets he'd shared his youth with, but they would never call him civilized.

"I do not mind if you think I am gorgeous. That is a good thing, is it not?"

Her answering smile was slow in coming, but some of the tension drained out of her. He was fully connected to her now and gently pushing soothing calm into her mind.

"It's a good thing."

She was exhausted. She'd hiked uphill all day and covered miles. She needed rest, water and food. His blood had helped to revive her, but even that shot of energy wasn't going to last her long.

"You can set up your camp in one of the chambers," he said. "There is a chimney in the one just through there." He indicated a narrow opening she hadn't noticed. "You can cook in there and you'll be safe. Although I would like to know how you got through the safeguards I placed at the entrance to the cave." He could have taken the information from her, but he was practicing being polite. If she didn't answer him satisfactorily, he would take it then.

Her face lit up. "That was you? That was so incredibly cool. It took me a long time, but I really enjoyed it. You set some intense patterns. Of course you're psychic, you'd have to be to do that. I never thought of trying something like that to

40

guard a place I was sleeping. With you wounded so severely, I could see you blocking the entrance."

She still hadn't told him *how* she'd done it. He liked that she wasn't bothered by it, instead excited that he could do it and eager to try it on her own.

"Teagan." Her name rolled off his tongue, sounding strange. Beautiful. His crazy, daring woman who had no business being out on her own. The sound was also his only warning to her. He wanted an explanation.

"I see patterns and hear musical notes. Your safeguards were a combination of both. I could see a harp in my head, the strings all tangled and messy. I had to just sort them out carefully to open the lock."

She was not just beautiful, intrepid and daring, she was brilliant. And she was his. For one moment, Andre could barely breathe with the knowledge that this woman was the woman he had searched centuries for, had given up on, and then she just simply unraveled his safeguards and walked into his life.

3

Andre stepped out of the cave into the gathering darkness. He stretched, feeling his muscles respond with eager anticipation. He was starving. The clawing need had started the night before and was far worse now. Ordinarily, that was a dangerous thing with an ancient as old as he was, but he had a lifemate to anchor him now. He could exact his revenge and put the fear of demons into Armend Jashari without worrying he would lose his own soul in the process.

The fog was thick, but he fed it, adding in the frightening whispers of dark shadows, the ghost and phantoms he was legendary for. No one could quite face the terror of the demon packs living within the fog, not when he created them. The sound effects were particularly good, he decided. He'd never had the ability to feel the effects before or the satisfaction of knowing if anyone came near his woman, the faceless ghosts would protect her.

He'd left Teagan after she built her fire and had put on

a pot to boil water for tea. She planned on making a small meal for herself and offered to share. He'd politely declined, stating he had business to take care of. She'd looked at him sharply, clearly leery of what business could possibly be in the mountains, but she didn't ask any questions.

He thought he'd be relieved to be away from her company. He didn't share space with anyone other than the triplets, Matais, Lojos and Tomas, and even then, he traveled loosely with them. He battled, killed and burned the bodies of his enemies. He didn't converse with them or worry about their feelings. He was a Carpathian hunter, close to the end of his time, no, *past* the end of his time.

Now his world was different because of one small miracle. He could look into her eyes forever. He'd restrained himself. She'd had a man assault her already, and he didn't need her more frightened than she already was. He was already beginning to bring her gently into his world and he wanted to do so one small step at a time.

He turned back to the entrance of the cave and used a much more difficult pattern for his safeguards. He had no intention of holding her prisoner. He was certain she could get out should she choose to, but it would take time. Time she wouldn't have. He intended to return as soon as he'd taken care of Jashari. Still, anyone else, such as the undead or Jashari's friends, would never be able to unravel the safeguards and any vampire would think he was inside the cave rather than outside of it. That would give him an advantage.

He shifted with ease, the change sweeping through him as he took on the shape of the night owl. He was comfortable in the form, second nature to him, as was the wolf and a variety of other shapes. He'd been shifting for centuries and had never considered how extraordinary it was until the moment he took to the sky.

The world was breathtaking from above. Even within the dense fog and the nightmare faces and voices he'd created, the night was different. Exhilarating. He couldn't wait to show it to Teagan. He felt the wind in his feathers, and through the bird, on his face. He smelled the wild mountain and the creatures living on it. The wet mist felt like soft touches on the bird and through it, on his skin. She had done that for him. Teagan. She'd brought this to him. His own personal miracle.

How many times had he slid through the sky on silent wings, the owl's sharp eyes scanning the ground for prey? Millions. It had to be millions. Yet he'd never felt it. At least he didn't remember feeling anything. He circled high because he could, now out of the fog bank, just to watch the way the sliver of a moon played through the canopy of the trees, turning all the leaves and needles to silver.

The owl covered ground fast, familiar with the country-side and the best places human men would choose to camp. He also looked for signs of vampires. They'd been severely wounded, every single one of them, and he was fairly certain they had gone to ground to heal, perhaps even for a couple of days, but the master vampire wouldn't be happy without fresh blood.

Popescu wouldn't go looking for blood himself. Not with his heart nearly ripped from his body—and Andre had come close to disposing of the undead. The four lesser vampires had returned in the nick of time, saving their master, inflicting damage, but receiving terrible wounds themselves. The price of battle had been high for both sides.

Popescu would definitely send his least valuable minion. The newest recruit. He would expect the vampire to return with human fodder for the master to consume first. If he left any blood, the others could use the victim as well. Sometimes they kept their prey alive for several nights in order to remain beneath the ground and hidden from a hunter. Many, many times, Andre had found the remains of the vampires' human food source. In each case, the human had died hard and brutally.

The owl suddenly banked sharply, its sharp eyes finding their target. There was a small tent pitched away from the wind, down in a slight depression where it was protected on three sides by rock. A small fire burned. The owl flew to the nearest tree above the tent and settled on the branches, slowly and carefully folding its wings, never taking its gaze from its prey.

A single man emerged from the tent carrying a pouch, which he tore open and emptied into the boiling water. Instantly Andre recognized him from Teagan's memories. This was Armend Jashari. He was alone, and he clearly was comfortable being alone.

Jashari dropped down onto a rock beside the fire and pulled a small object from his belt. A handheld radio. Andre knew cell phones didn't work along this particular stretch of wild mountain range. So there were others—Jashari's friends— probably out searching for Teagan's trail.

"Armend here, all of you report in, over."

"Giles." The radio crackled with static as Giles gave his dismal news. "Didn't find crap. She's disappeared. Vanished. If she gets down the mountain and tells anyone, Armend, you could be in trouble."

Armend scowled. "Who's going to believe the bitch? She's a stupid tourist, although I don't need the hassle. My dad's been a bastard lately. Insists I get a job, make something of myself. He's pissed because he had to have our lawyer settle with a couple of women who claimed I was overexuberant with them." He laughed. "Anyone else out there find her trail? Gerard?"

"I found a faint trail leading up the mountain, but it disappeared. The fog is so thick I couldn't see anything at all, but it's the only thing I found so maybe I should continue to try to scout around and see if I can pick it up again in the morning. If it's her, she's good in the mountains. She knows what she's doing." Gerard's voice came over the radio.

So that made three men who were enemies of Teagan. Andre remained very, very still, the owl partially hidden by sweeping branches.

"I got nothing either," another voice said. "I'm just a little south of you, Armend. She hasn't come this way."

Armend cursed under his breath. "Keep looking, Keith. She has to be somewhere. I would have picked up her trail if she'd gone down the mountain. Kirt, what about you?"

"Nothing here either, Armend," Kirt reported.

So Armend had four friends who had gone out in different directions to try to pick up Teagan's trail while Armend stayed close to the first camp area to see if she would go back to it. That told Andre a lot about the man. He used his friends while he did the least amount of work. He definitely thought himself entitled to take anything he wanted. So Andre needed to give him that opportunity.

"We'll meet here tomorrow morning," Armend snapped, and clicked off his radio abruptly without the slightest courtesy. He shoved it back on his belt and turned to stir the meal in his cooking pot. Clearly he was out of sorts.

The owl spread its wings and sailed down to the ground. The moment the talons touched earth, Andre shifted back to human form. He chose a spot in the deeper tree line just below where Armend had made his camp. Lifting his hands, he made the motion of a circle. At once fingers of fog began to drift from the trees toward the campsite.

At first the droplets were no more than the finest mist,

curling along the ground, sliding out between branches, forming its own layers, both high and low. He made certain the vapor stayed thin enough that one could see through it. Next, he called to the wolves. The pack was a long way out, but they answered him, first one cry and then another. They would obey him. They always obeyed him. Andre watched Armend carefully the entire time the pack was taking up the hunting cry. Armend hadn't failed to notice that the first wolf had sounded close by.

Armend stood and paced nervously, his hand dropping twice to his radio as if to assure himself he had friends close enough to call should there be trouble. The hunting cry of the last wolf died away and silence reigned once more. At first the abrupt quiet increased the tension in Armend.

The man checked his weapons. He didn't have a gun, but he had three knives, and he positioned them close to where he sat, even going so far as to practice reaching for them. Next, he built up his fire and went to the trees to get more wood. He stacked it close to him.

Andre moved with the fog. He sent his phantoms ahead of him, directing the mist so that it wound through the trees and crept upward from the ground toward the rocks and boulders several feet above the tree line where Armend had made his camp. The fingers of fog had already reached the stones above the trees where foliage tended to grow in clumps along the mountainside. The fog drifted over the field of boulders, layering in almost gently, nonthreateningly—unless one noticed that there was little wind and when there was, the mist paid it no mind.

Armend sank down on his rock seat and stirred the concoction in his cooking pot. He glanced around him, still a little wary after the wolves' hunting calls, but Andre could see he'd already begun to dismiss the animals from his mind.

Hunger beat at Andre, so that every cell cried out for sustenance. He needed blood. He could smell Armend's blood. He could hear the blood pumping through his veins and the strong beat of his heart. Andre's lips drew back in a snarl as he felt the sharp points of his teeth. Still, Armend needed a lesson. A serious lesson before he met Andre. He needed to experience fear. Terror even. That was something Andre was very good at showing his prey.

The thicker fog inched along the ground, rising as a wall, cutting off Armend's vision. One moment he glanced down at the food he was heating and the next he looked up and couldn't see anything at all but the swirling, very dense vapor clouds. Alarmed, he stood up again, one hand nervously dropping to his radio.

Armend didn't pull the radio from his belt. He was the leader in his group of friends. He always had been. He was that little bit richer and much more dominant. He was the one who had realized early on that women—particularly young college-age girls who were backpacking across Europe—were especially vulnerable. He'd been the one to slowly get the others to accept more and more violence.

He had been the one to think of their guide service. Armend made certain the few couples or older people they took into the mountains had the best of times. He won them over with spectacular service, taking them to the most beautiful places so they would rave about their guides.

His victims he chose very carefully. He made certain there was no paper or Internet trail to follow. The girls came alone or in pairs. Those were the ones he chose for his sport.

He beat and raped the first girl alone, but in front of his friends. He'd known his accomplices since they were little kids together, and he'd chosen all four as carefully as he chose his victims. All of them had tendencies toward violence, but he knew without him, they probably would have taken a lot longer to act out their fantasies.

He made certain he bought plenty of porn vids, all with themes centering around rape and hurting women. He took them down that path first with stories of sharing women, treating them like the toys they were, then the videos and finally actual snuff porn. All of them got off on it.

He kept the girl with him, soothing her, promising her money, saying he was sorry that things got out of hand, all the while winking at his friends and letting them know he was working up to a second round. The second round had Kirt and Giles joining in. By the third time, Keith and Gerard had leapt at the opportunity. From there, it had been easy enough to convince them that she couldn't live because she'd endanger them, and they all beat her, taking turns, laughing and jacking off on her as she begged and promised them anything they wanted.

Armend was fairly certain his father suspected what was going on, and maybe even wanted to join in, the hypocrite. Still, his old man paid to keep silent the few girls he'd dated throughout his school years, the ones he'd shared a little bondage with and then his sadistic tendencies. He'd made certain they agreed to be tied up before he ever did it, and that kept the police out of it.

He was charming and persuasive. The girls all thought he loved them. He always taped them agreeing to the fun of being tied or handcuffed. Sometimes even whipped. Of course once he had them at his mercy, the compulsion to hurt and humiliate them took over and he couldn't stop the things he'd done. Hell—he didn't want to stop. He reveled in it.

Then he'd met Teagan Joanes. She wasn't anything like the women he generally chose for his victims. If anything, she was the exact opposite. She should have looked like a boy—she

49

didn't really have much in the way of breasts, just a handful. She shouldn't have caught his eye at all. For one thing, she was half black and half white. Not his thing *at all*.

He couldn't stop thinking about her. He obsessed over her. Her skin was the softest, smoothest skin he'd ever seen and the color of a mocha latte, absolutely beautiful. Her laugh was just plain sexy and could cut right through a man. Her waist was so small he was certain he could span it with his hands if he tried. She had nice hips and a really fine ass. She just grew on him until he couldn't think with wanting her.

She never gave him a single opening. For a while, those three years of college together, he thought maybe she was a lesbian, but there weren't any women that she dated. Had there been women, he knew he would have killed them. Same if a man had come between them, but she didn't date. She had a lot of male friends. Climbing friends. Hiking friends. Biking. She seemed to be busy all the time in her off-hours.

Teagan was brilliant, and he hit on the idea of hiring her as his tutor. He'd struck gold with that. He had plenty of money—he didn't give a damn about geology—but if he wanted his inheritance he needed a degree from a university in the United States. She spent a great deal of time with him. He'd poured on the charm. Spent money on her, although she didn't seem to like it much. He'd brought picnic lunches on the pretext they could spend more time studying.

He woke some nights with the sound of her laughter in his head. He began to dream about her constantly. No other woman seemed to satisfy him and eventually, every fantasy he had was about her. He wanted her under him. He wanted to hear her screams, although he honestly didn't know if he wanted to hurt her or pleasure her.

He kept in touch with her because he had to. He couldn't

50

let the relationship go, although he knew he was obsessing over her. When she'd emailed him and told him she was coming to his part of the Carpathian Mountains, looking for a particular stone or gem, he was certain she'd been just as obsessed with him. He'd been elated. Wild with joy. The dreams had turned so erotic he could barely eat, and he couldn't stop thinking about her.

She couldn't even tell him what kind of rock she was looking for, only that she knew vaguely where it was and she'd be able to find it. What kind of crap was that? Of course she was coming to see him. She had to be. She'd thought of him the way he thought of her. But then, all the way up the mountain, she'd played her stupid little game, teasing him, acting like they were just friends and nothing else.

She was nothing more than a damn cock tease and he was going to give her a lesson. He was a little sorry the others had followed him up. He still wasn't certain he wanted to share Teagan with anyone, let alone kill her. But if he did, maybe the obsessive thoughts would stop and he could get on with his life.

A low moan came out of the night. Very low, a woman's soft cry as if she was in pain. He shivered. He'd always liked that particular note and he worked hard to get it when he had a woman at his mercy. He paced around the fire, his eyes narrowed, looking into the thick fog.

Was Teagan out there? Hurt? The moan rose again, this time closer. The note played through his body like a violin might, soft and stroking. He stopped and stared directly toward the sound. His heart accelerated. "Teagan? Are you there?"

Silence met his call. He waited. He wasn't going to step away from the fire, not with such heavy fog. He could barely see his hand in front of his face. The gray wrap of vapor seemed much thicker than normal, dense, a live wall of mist surrounding him.

Armend shook his head as fingers of fear crept down his spine. He'd hiked the mountains his entire life. They were his personal playground. He wasn't ever afraid. Still, his hand dropped to the radio. Once again he didn't pull it off his belt, but he needed the reassurance of it.

The moan came again, muffled, but definitely closer. It had to be Teagan. She was afraid of him.

"Teagan, just come toward the fire. We'll talk it all out. Are you injured?"

He could almost taste her. *Finally*. He had her. Elation swept through him. His body hardened with anticipation. He'd have a long night alone with her and decide in the morning whether he'd share her with his friends and then kill her or just keep her for himself. There were a lot of places he could stash her and make her dependent on him. That might be fun. Hold her prisoner, give her food and water when he felt like it, force her to need him. His fantasy took off in his mind, and he really liked that idea.

Something moved in the fog, and his gaze immediately riveted there. The fog swirled, seemed to come alive. He saw a woman's face pressing toward him through the gray vapor. No, the mist actually formed the face. He recognized his first kill. She swayed and moaned, staring at him with accusing eyes.

He gasped and stumbled back, nearly falling into the fire. All around him, in the tight ring of fog, faces began to appear. Women. Moaning. Calling to him softly, arms outstretched first in pleading and then to take him into the bank of fog with them.

Everywhere Armend looked, the women were there, surrounding him. Eyes on him. Arms out. Faces accusing. The sound of their moans continued to rise until he couldn't hear anything else. Until the sound penetrated his bones, pierced his organs and frayed every nerve he had. He'd forgotten a couple of them, but each had been his victim over the years, his and his friends'.

"You're not real," he muttered. Then he raised his voice and shouted at them. "You're not real." He found his rock beside the fire and sat down because his legs trembled so much he couldn't stand any longer. It wasn't real. His mind was playing tricks on him.

Jerking the radio from his belt, he pressed one hand to his ears in an effort to drown out the terrible moan. He would never be able to hear that particular note again as long as he lived. "Giles, come in, over."

Static answered him, and then faintly, very faintly, he heard a woman's voice calling to him—*over the radio*.

Join us, Armend. Come to us. Forever is a such a short time to spend with us.

He dropped the radio into the dirt and kicked it away from him. "Shut up!" he yelled. "All of you, shut up! You're dead."

The moment he uttered the words *you're dead*, those faces in the fog turned to skeletons, horrible bones with teeth and sunken holes for eyes. All of them. Surrounding him, bony fingers reaching for him.

The wind picked up and the women moaned louder, the sound making him feel sick. He couldn't escape the terrible penetrating moaning note of pain, and now it was consuming his body, bit by bit, as if it were eating him alive. He could feel the reverberation biting into his flesh, taking him, wanting him to join the women in the fog.

He pressed both hands to his ears, trying to drown out the sound. The moan was physical, ripping and tearing at his body like teeth. The sound of their bones only added to his mounting terror. He circled the fire, trying to find a way to escape, but the ghosts had him completely surrounded.

Ghosts. He took a deep breath. The women were dead. He was alive. They weren't real. They couldn't come out of the fog and drag him into it. Very carefully he backed away from the few wisps that strayed from the main wall of dense gray matter. He found his rock again and slowly sank back down. He didn't take his eyes from the thick fog bank as his hand reached toward the ground to feel along it for his radio.

The ground felt damp. Wet even. He dared to take his gaze from the macabre sight of the skulls with their empty eye sockets, opening their empty mouths and calling to him. He glanced down and froze. There on the ground, he could see tendrils of fog, much like the root system of trees, creeping along the dirt. Alive. Searching. He had a terrible feeling the creepers were searching for him.

What did roots do? They *fed* the tree. They were searching for him. For his body. His blood. He was nearly hysterical, and he tried to force himself to think beyond the fear. This couldn't really be happening, no matter how real it seemed.

The moans continued, but one woman—his first kill— changed her note, her voice rising on the wind to a howl. A call to the hunt. He knew that sound. He'd heard it earlier. An alpha calling his pack to the hunt. Another chill went down his spine and his heart thundered.

He fed the fire quickly, building it up. All around him, along the ground, the veins of fog, tubes of gray stretched like the bony arms of the women in the fog bank. His body stilled. He felt them. The wolves. When he dared to peer into the dense wall of mist, he saw the red eyes staring back at him.

There was nothing worse in his imagination than to be killed and eaten by wolves. He counted at least seven in the pack. They surrounded him just as the women in the fog did.

Strangely, the bony hands looked as if they were petting the wolves, although he couldn't see the creatures through the dense fog.

He heard them. The growls and snarls. He felt them. The hair on his body stood up. His heart pounded so hard he feared he would have a heart attack. Occasionally he glimpsed a large beast pacing back and forth, waiting for some kind of signal.

The fog swirled, forming another shape. At first it looked like a wolf. A huge wolf. The animal turned its glowing eyes on him and then, to Armend's horror, stepped right out of the fog as if it was really alive and not a part of the mass of dead creatures. The wolf took several steps toward him, and then he wasn't a wolf, but a man.

The man was tall, broad-shouldered, solid. Real. He wore a long, hooded cape that fell to his ankles. It was difficult to see his face as it was in the shadow of the hood. There was no denying he was real. Not a wolf. A man. The sight of him had Armend's shoulders sagging. He nearly sobbed with relief. His imagination had gone wild. He'd been experiencing a hallucination, but now, with this man, things could get back to normal. He forced a smile.

The man didn't smile back. He looked at Armend with ice-blue eyes that seemed to look straight through to his soul. Eyes that could see his dark perversions and his need to see women in pain. Women suffering for his amusement. Suffering because he enjoyed the pain of others—particularly women. This man knew he had killed and that he craved killing and would continue to kill because he needed it just as much as he needed air to breathe.

Armend's mouth went dry. He dared to take his eyes from the man sitting in judgment of him to glance at the moaning skeletons with the beckoning arms. The women were still

55

there, watching. The wolves were still there, waiting. Armend backed up again, reaching for the knife he'd positioned right on his pile of wood.

His hand closed around the hilt. Fire burned through his body. The hilt glowed red just like the eyes of the wolves. His palm and fingers melted into the knife, the burning so bad he went to one knee. He tried to fling the blade away from him, but it stuck to his hand, burning and burning. He screamed and plunged his hand into the ribbons of fog that crawled along the ground.

He heard the sizzle as the fire spluttered against the cool, wet mist. The knife fell free, and he turned his hand over. His palm was covered in blisters, but he could see beneath the raw wounds that something else burned into his skin. His hand looked as if the flesh was falling from it to leave bones behind. White bones. Scored deep in blackened charcoal was a single word. *Murderer.*

He screamed again. He didn't know how long he screamed, but his throat was sore by the time he got control of himself. He shook his head. "This isn't real. None of this is real. I'm having a nightmare. That's all. Just a nightmare."

He steadfastly refused to look at the moaning women or the glowing red eyes of the wolves pacing just a few feet from him. He wouldn't look at the man who had to be the grim reaper, coming for him. "I'm going to go into my tent and get into my sleeping bag. When I wake up, all this will be gone."

"Unfortunately, Armend," the grim reaper said—and his tone was chilling—"your tent cannot aid you this night."

Armend moistened his dry lips and forced himself to meet the reaper's gaze. The impact of those eyes was terrifying. "What do you want?"

"You attacked my woman. What do you think I want?"

The voice was low. Soft even. Gentle. There was no threat

in the tone, but the way the reaper stared at him, unblinking, the eyes of the predatory wolf, the face always in the shadow, kept Armend terrified.

"I don't know your woman."

"Of course you do. She thought you were a friend. She trusted you, and you beat her savagely. You tore her mouth with your teeth. You attempted to rape her. You would have allowed your friends to use her body and then you would have tortured and killed her just as you did the others."

The voice never changed pitch. That was more chilling than if the reaper had shown some kind of anger.

Armend held up his hand. "No. No. That isn't true. I wasn't going to let the others have her. You're talking about Teagan."

"Do not say her name. Do not ever call her by name. You are not worthy of speaking her name. I know where every single body is. The women you tortured, raped and killed. They will all be found and returned to their parents."

He shook his head. "No. You can't do that. My mother. My father. It would kill them. My family's name would be dragged through the mud, and for what? Who were they? Stupid women. They wanted me. They liked what they got. They begged for it." He pointed his finger, the one that burned and hurt but he refused to acknowledge because none of this was real.

"I woke hungry. Starved. I need to feed. We'll talk after," the reaper said.

Armend blinked. He looked down at his cooking pot. He'd forgotten he was making food when the fog bank had rolled in. Suddenly, without any warning whatsoever, the reaper was directly in front of him. One moment he'd been several feet away and the next he was close, in Armend's personal space.

He was big up close. Solid. All muscle. Intimidating. He threw off the hood and looked down into Armend's face.

57

And then he smiled. Armend shrieked like a woman, a high-pitched, terrified cry that echoed around the boulders. Armend was looking directly into the mouth of a vampire.

The moan of the women rose to a fever pitch. The wolves snarled and growled, their impatience rising with their dinner but a few feet away. Armend tried to move, but his feet were frozen into the ground. Stuck. Leaden. He could only stare at the man who appeared almost beautiful, his face wholly masculine, his eyes cold as he lowered his head toward Armend.

"Get away," Armend yelled, trying to punch at the vampire's face as it came closer to him.

The unholy smile widened. "Are you feeling what those women felt, Armend? The fear? The terror of being helpless? Are you afraid of what I will do to you? Tear through your skin with my teeth? Bite you savagely the way you bit my woman? I'll drink your blood. I can make you my puppet. I can take your mind. What will I do? Isn't that the game you played with those helpless women?"

"Please. My family has money. I'll do anything." The teeth kept coming closer and closer. The pulse throbbed in Armend's neck. He couldn't stop it. Even holding his breath didn't stop it. His heart hammered away, calling to the vampire.

"Did begging and pleading and bargaining work for any of those women you murdered? Even one of them?"

"Oh, God. This can't be happening," Armend wailed.

The hand on his shoulder, turning him, was gentle, but there was no way to break the implacable grip. The other hand went to his head, pushing it to one side to expose the throbbing vein. He felt hot breath. Teeth tore into him savagely. Mercilessly. The pain was excruciating.

He screamed again until his throat felt shredded. Still the mouth drew the blood from his body. He began to moan. In pain. A single note. The sound he'd always craved to hear from the women he tortured and killed. The women in the fog picked up the note and harmonized with him. He was surrounded by their moans. He felt the moans in his body. In the fiery never-ending pain in his throat.

He was cold. Shivering with cold. With fear. Where were his friends? He couldn't die this way. He couldn't die by the hand of a vampire, surrounded by the stupid bitches who had drooled over him and then screamed and cried when he gave them what they wanted—what they deserved.

Why are you doing this to me? He wanted to scream the words aloud, but he couldn't talk, not with the vampire ripping out his throat. *Those women were nothing. Nothing at all. They were put here to be used.*

That's how you viewed my woman? As nothing?

Armend knew he'd made a terrible mistake. It was there in the soft voice moving through his mind. He couldn't take back anything. There was no way to undo it all. The vampire could read his thoughts, and that meant he could see into Armend's mind. He could see the truth there. He could see the ever-present need to feed off the pain he inflicted on the women. He liked the power. He craved it. He would always need it. This vampire knew it.

Make me like you, Armend whispered in his mind. *I'll serve you. We can have such fun together. Make me like you.*

The vampire jerked his teeth from Armend's throat and stepped back, eyes blazing fire. "You could never be like me. You have no honor."

Armend stumbled back and found himself on the ground. He was weak. Very weak. The vampire stared at him as if he were no more than an insect crawling on the ground. And he had to crawl. He could barely find the strength to drag himself toward his tent.

The vampire simply watched him. The women fell silent. The wolves followed suit. The sudden hush chilled him even more than the growls from the wolves or the moans from the women. He turned to look. The skeleton faces were still there, staring from the sunken sockets where their eyes had been.

Armend's breath caught in his throat and he paused, his fingers digging into the wet ground. Blood dripped steadily from the wound in his throat. He looked back and saw red staining the dirt and turning the tubes of fog that stretched along the ground pink.

The wolves emerged from the fog bank, glowing eyes fixed hungrily on him. They didn't rush, they moved with precise steps, infinitely slow, almost inching their way. First their heads came through, then the necks and bodies. He looked around him. The wolves had formed a ring around him, just as the fog bank had.

He saw his mistake. He'd left the safety of the fire. He switched direction, clawing at the ground with fingernails. The sight of those nail marks in the dirt gave him pause. So many times, he'd seen those marks in the dirt where he'd dragged the woman along, her bloody body naked to feel every rock and twig, every sticker as he pulled her toward a cliff.

He clamped his hand over the wound in his throat, knowing the scent of blood called to the wolves. He could feel their eyes on him. The alpha stepped closer, head down, nose scenting the blood. The wolf drew back his lips in a snarl.

Armend looked around him, trying to get his bearings. He had knives stashed around the campsite, but he couldn't remember where. When he looked back, the alpha was standing over him. They stared at each other for what seemed a lifetime. He felt hot breath on the back of his neck and then excruciating pain as another wolf clamped down on his shoulder and began to drag him farther away from the fire.

Armend screamed, looked toward the vampire, begging for mercy, but the vampire was gone, nothing but vapor, a fog streaking away from his campsite. He screamed for a very long time. His last thought was that he'd lasted as long as the strongest of the women he'd tortured. He wished he hadn't.

4

Andre scouted around the mountain for signs of Costin Popescu and his followers. They had to have stayed in the ground to recover from their wounds, and that gave him a little time with his lifemate to cement their relationship. He unraveled his safeguards, entered the cave and replaced the guards. He added a warning for humans as well, just in case any of Armend's friends happened upon Teagan's trail.

He moved through the network of caves quickly, finding himself eager to get back to his woman. She wasn't where he left her, nor was the fire burning. He followed her scent through a series of narrowing corridors leading deeper underground. He could see the trail of shoe prints; it looked as if she was searching for something.

Teagan sat on the floor of a small chamber, right over the spot where he'd buried his family's treasure. She had her eyes closed. Each foot was drawn up and rested on the opposite thigh and she formed an *O* with her thumb and index finger. She hummed softly under her breath in a chanting rhythm.

Andre watched her for a few minutes. She didn't seem to be aware of his presence at all, and that disturbed him. In her deep state of meditation, an enemy could easily sneak up on her. That was unacceptable to him.

"Teagan," he said softly. "Teagan, open your eyes."

She didn't comply. She continued her ridiculous humming.

"Teagan, obey me." This time he "pushed" at her, insistent on obedience.

Her long lashes lifted and she scowled at him. "You didn't just use the word *obey*, did you? As if you were giving me some kind of an order?"

Andre studied her face. She was so beautiful it hurt to look at her. Right now, her eyes sparkled with what could only be a hint of temper. He'd forgotten the modern world had moved on without him. Women didn't obey their men, even when it was for safety reasons. That didn't bode well for either of them. He wasn't about to allow her to put herself in jeopardy for some modern nonsense of equality.

Of course she was his equal. Well, perhaps above him. Which was the very reason he needed to guard and protect her. She was a treasure beyond any price. Clearly she didn't get that.

He thought it best—and much safer—to ignore her question. "What are you doing in here? I was worried about you."

She studied his face for a few moments before she slowly took her feet from her thighs and stretched a little. "You were gone for a while. I'm looking for something very important to me and I think it's somewhere in this chamber. I can't quite get a lock on it though."

He reached out a hand to her. Teagan hesitated, only a half second, before placing her hand in his, but he caught it. She'd

63

had a nasty experience with a man she considered her friend. She wasn't going to be so trusting of a man she didn't know, no matter how drawn to him she was. And he'd ensured she would be drawn to him. The lifemate ritual had sealed them together as had their first exchange of blood. She might not remember it, but she wouldn't be able to be far from him for very long.

Andre drew her gently to her feet and let go of her, making certain she was a little distance from him so she would feel safe. She wasn't, but she didn't need to know that.

"Perhaps I can help in your search."

She glanced at him from under her long lashes, a small frown on her face. She gave a little shrug accompanied by a sigh. "Actually, if I tell you, you'll think I'm totally crazy. Everyone does."

He waited in silence for her to continue, but she didn't, forcing him to have to pry the information out of her. "Tell me." He did his best not to make it sound like an order, but even his softest voice appeared to be a command.

Her frown deepened. "I came here looking for a certain item. A stone. Or a gem. I'll know it when I 'feel' it. I know that sounds crazy, but it's what led me up here. My body tunes itself to the precise stone, gem or crystal I need for my work in healing. I knew it was here in the Carpathian Mountains and I had to come. I knew the general location and what part of the range to search because I was drawn to it on the map." She waited for him to laugh. To make fun of her.

He studied her face. She didn't know it of course, but he was already in her mind. She could do exactly what she said she could.

"Why would I not believe you? You are a gifted healer."

"I didn't get the chance to heal you. How would you know that?" she countered.

He hadn't talked so much in ages. It was rather wearing. "I feel your power. Why do you need this particular stone?"

Her face crumpled. She looked almost as if she might cry. Her look did strange things to his insides. His belly formed hard, protesting knots and his chest ached in the region of his heart.

"My grandmother. Grandma Trixie. She raised me, and she's the kindest, most thoughtful, wonderful person you can imagine. She raised my three older sisters as well. It wasn't easy. She had to work all the time but she never complained. She even helped us out with school when she didn't have to. She's incredible."

"Is she ill?"

Teagan looked down, studying the toe of her boot as she scuffed it in the dirt. "She's gone a little crazy. Her mind isn't right. A while back she began to mutter under her breath about this mythical man named Gary. She despised him. I asked her about him numerous times, but she just said he was a man who had betrayed everyone. He was a spy and he needed to die. That's totally not like my grandmother."

He held out his hand to her. "Keep talking. We should go back to your campsite and start a fire. You are beginning to shiver a little. That is the only chamber with a decent chimney."

She took his hand without hesitation, more because she wasn't paying as close attention than because she was no longer leery of him.

"About two months ago, she began talking about Gary to my sisters. She's become totally obsessed with him. She said he runs with vampires and he has to be stopped. My sisters took her to a psychiatrist. He said she was slowly losing her mind. She wouldn't back down. She swore vampires exist and that this Gary is a traitor to the human race and needs to die."

Andre knew a man named Gary Jansen. He was highly respected among the Carpathian people. He had fought beside them in battle, led the way in research to find the cause of why their women couldn't produce babies and worked to find a way to save the children who were born. He was also instrumental in finding the flower needed for their fertility. Gary was fully Carpathian now and a brother to Gregori Daratrazanoff. He was a little alarmed that his lifemate's grandmother might actually know something about Gary.

He remained silent. Teagan sent him a hesitant look. He nodded at her, making certain he looked interested.

"I found a vampire-hunting kit she bought off the Internet stashed in her closet. I wasn't snooping. She'd asked me to get her yarn and knitting needles. I didn't even know she knitted. I think she plans on using her needles to stab someone through the heart if she can't use her vampire-hunting kit."

"What's in a vampire-hunting kit?" he asked, genuinely intrigued.

"She has some gun that shoots wooden stakes. A rosary. A bible. A silver cross and holy water. There are all kinds of bottles filled with stuff, but I don't know what's in them." She sighed. "My grandmother wouldn't hurt a fly. Seriously, we had to put spiders outside rather than kill them, and now she's going to hunt vampires, specifically a man who I can't find out about anywhere, and shoot them with a wooden stake. It's scary that her mind is going so fast."

"What else does she talk about? Why has she fixated on this Gary person? Surely you must have asked her."

"We all did. She just told us that he had once hunted vampires but now he's in collusion with them. When I asked her if she'd really kill him, she said she didn't want to kill anyone, but he deserved to die for what he'd done. She'd heard of a monastery in these parts and hoped he was there already asking for forgiveness and then she wouldn't have to lead justice to him, he'd spend the rest of his life doing penance for his sins. Seriously. That's how she talks. Penance for his sins."

Andre's alarm rose. He'd heard of a few individuals who had a specific psychic gift. If her grandmother were one of those gifted who could follow the path of a Carpathian or vampire, it would answer the question as to how her granddaughter had unraveled his safeguards. She had the same gift. The difference was, Teagan had never been told about vampires. Her grandmother obviously had.

If he had to guess, he would say that Trixie Joanes belonged to the human vampire-hunting society. The same society killed Carpathians and vampires alike, without distinguishing between the two. They also occasionally targeted humans they didn't like, or had grudges against, such as Gary Jansen.

Andre had run across them a time or two, but they'd never had anyone who could actually follow the trail of a Carpathian or vampire. It was difficult to do. And he was more difficult than most. He had never understood how it was done, but after seeing how Teagan had unraveled his safeguards, he realized it had something to do with the way their bodies "felt" or "sang" when near their quarry.

"Where is your grandmother now, Teagan?"

"She's at home. In the United States. We live in California. My sisters are watching over her while I try to find the specific stone or crystal that will help me heal her mind."

"Will they be able to stop her if she tries to get on a plane and follow you here?"

They were back in the chamber where her sleeping bag and backpack were stashed. He waited until she had her back turned and was rummaging through her pack before he waved at the fire. Instantly flames leapt. When she turned, shocked, he was dumping a load of wood next to the ring of rocks.

"Where did you get the wood?" she asked, her eyes wide.

He gestured toward the darker shadows where the cave curved deeply and a small amount of water trickled to the floor and seeped under the dirt. There was a large pile of wood neatly stacked.

"I have used this cave many times," he said. Again, it was strictly the truth. His statement was misleading, but it wasn't a lie. He had just acquired the wood for her fire, but he had, in the past, often used the cave for his retreat when he was wounded.

"I didn't even see it. I guess I was so obsessed with finding the stone I need, I didn't really look around."

"Teagan." He used his most gentle voice, to counteract the tightening of the knots in his belly. "This mountain is not safe. You should not be unaware at any time. There are wild animals as well as poisonous insects and snakes that could harm you. And that is not even mentioning the men who hunt you."

She shuddered and threw a blanket down over the dirt beside the fire. "When you went out, did you come across Armend's trail? Did you see him? I was worried he might attack you if he thought you'd spoken to me, or helped me. He told me things he wouldn't want the world to know." She frowned. "He's a dangerous man. I don't know how I couldn't have seen that."

"You were afraid for me?" Andre wasn't certain how to take that. He'd never had anyone, let alone a beautiful woman, be concerned for his safety. On the other hand, did she think that puny Armend could possibly best him? That might be a bit of an insult.

"Of course I was afraid for you. He admitted killing several women. If it was true, he wouldn't think twice about killing you as well."

He was silent. Had it occurred to her, even once, that he

68

could be one of Armend's unknown friends? She was too friendly by far. Too trusting and open with strangers. He couldn't tell her that either because he didn't want her fearing him. She was nervous enough as it was.

"You're really a nice man, Andre. Very thoughtful and kind. Men like Armend are very dangerous. I wouldn't want to think of you meeting up with him," Teagan continued, in a worried tone.

Andre's heart fluttered. It was a physical reaction to her concern for him. Clearly, Teagan perceived him as nonthreatening for the most part—at least until she remembered she was alone with a stranger, which didn't seem nearly often enough to him—but she thought Jashari was dangerous. She made him want to laugh out loud. She also conveniently forgot that Andre had warned her that he was a dangerous man.

"I do not think you will have to be afraid that Armend Jashari will ever harm another living soul."

She went still, her hands freezing around the sweater she was pulling on over her arms. She tilted her head to look up at him. He felt her fear, the sudden jump of her heart. "What do you mean?"

"I came across his trail a few miles down the mountain. He pitched his tent right in the middle of a territory belonging to a wolf pack. There was not much left."

Her breath hitched. Her long eyelashes fluttered. She sank slowly back on her heels, all the while looking up at him, straight into his eyes. "Are you certain it was him?"

He couldn't help but admire her. She was definitely afraid, but still, she was fearless in her questions and in her attempt to hide it from him. He nodded. "There is no doubt at all. I did not, however, see any evidence of anyone else around his tent, or even within a few miles of it."

69

"I didn't want him to die." She chewed on her bottom lip. "Well, unless you count the fact that I did want to bash him over the head with my cooking pot with every step I took. Hard. Really hard. Do you think I put that out into the universe and I'm responsible for his death? Because I believe in karma. I don't want wolves to come hunting me." She blinked rapidly, and he thought he caught the sheen of tears, but if he had, they were gone when she looked at him again. "Are you really certain it was him? I did hit him pretty hard. Maybe I killed him and the wolves came later."

"I have hunted in these mountains for many years, Teagan," he reassured her. He sent a small push to soothe her. "He had moved his camp from where he attacked you to this place."

"How do you know?"

"I backtracked him looking for his friends and found the original campsite. He was very much alive when you left him."

"Thank God I didn't kill him. I wanted to bash him one but, you know, without the consequences of him dying."

He hid a smile. She was different from the other humans he'd met. Intriguing. But then she was his lifemate, and everything about her, down to the smallest detail, was captivating and fascinating to him.

"Do you often bash men over the head with your cooking pot?" he asked, amusement in his voice. He barely recognized the emotion. He didn't know what humor was until that moment. She made him want to smile. She made him happy just by being in the same space with him.

She grinned at him a little mischievously. "Only if they deserve it. Well, once I hit Jimmy Baker over the head with my book bag and nearly knocked him out. I was in kindergarten and he was in first grade, and he was picking on me. I was always really small so I was an easy target. I learned to pick up equalizers." She bit her lip. "Um. I put a couple of really heavy books in my bag. I took them off the teacher's desk. It's important to be totally prepared, but the school didn't see it that way and I got in trouble."

He didn't like that she'd been picked on, but he liked that she defended herself. Where the hell was her family when some boy was being mean to her? He pushed down the need to go find Jimmy Baker and have a little talk with him.

"That was very intelligent of you. What would you like for your dinner?"

She pressed a hand to her stomach. "Actually, I'm not really that hungry. I'm thirsty, but I think I'm too tired to eat. It's the middle of the night already, and I spent too much time being a tuning fork."

He raised an eyebrow and walked over to the darkened corner of the room, keeping his body solidly in the way, even going so far as to blur the chamber enough that she couldn't see him as he created a small cupboard with human supplies such as herb tea and a kettle. She needed to eat and drink something. She was feeling the effects of the first blood exchange between them.

To bring his human lifemate fully into his world, he needed three blood exchanges with her and she had to have psychic abilities, which clearly she did. It seemed a little ironic to him that her grandmother—a vampire hunter who clearly didn't have the good sense to discriminate between her victims—could have been a lifemate to a Carpathian male in need. She probably was. He had the urge to find the woman and shake her.

"I will make some herbal tea," he announced, returning with the kettle and the tea.

She shook her head. "Thank you, Andre, but really, my stomach is a little upset. Maybe it was the news about

71

Armend. He deserved to be arrested and should have gone to jail, but being eaten by wolves ..." She trailed off.

"That is probably justice if he really killed other women as he boasted to you," Andre pointed out as gently as possible.

She nodded before she could stop herself and then looked guilty. "Well, I hope he didn't suffer."

"Like he would have made you suffer?" he asked as he filled the kettle with water from the small trickle of water coming out of the side of the mountain. "As he made those other women suffer?" Again, he kept his body blocking her sight of what he was doing so he could just wave his hand and fill it.

Keeping the fact that he was a different species from her was going to be difficult. Other Carpathians lived among humans and had perfected the art of blending in. Andre had perfected the art of avoiding contact with them. This woman was his lifemate, and she would have to know, sooner or later, that she was his and belonged in his world, but she'd already suffered a trauma and he didn't want to compound that, especially after she'd confided in him about her grandmother.

"Well, I didn't suffer so much as I was scared," Teagan admitted reluctantly. She watched him set the kettle in the flames. She winced. "Andre, you're going to get burned doing it like that. It's hard to believe you camped out before."

He hadn't felt the heat of the flames. He could call down lightning and not get burned, fire wasn't going to do anything to him, not unless he was in the paralyzed sleeping state of his people. "I will be more careful."

She studied his face. "You don't like to be around people, do you?"

Andre turned his gaze to her face. She was definitely a natural empath. He had been intrigued with her gentle nature and the unexpected strengths that suddenly rushed to the forefront. Her very nature had to always be at war. She was a fierce little warrior who definitely had a clear line of justice she didn't want crossed and would fight if necessary. She was also a healer and protector, one who would face her greatest fears in order to help others.

"I find I like being around you," he admitted. He wasn't certain if that was something he should say, but she was his lifemate and he didn't want to lie to her. "Ordinarily, I find people trying, but you are very soothing. You also make me want to smile. I had forgotten what that is like." That also was the truth. He had forgotten emotion.

Like every Carpathian, he had clung to his memories of emotion after feelings had faded, leaving him in a bleak world of gray. Unfortunately, as the centuries went by, he had even forgotten the memories—at least any good ones, if there had been any. He found he couldn't relive them through the minds of others. Emotions had receded too far for him to recapture them. Now, feelings were so vivid and alive, pouring through him, he was nearly overwhelmed, and most centered around this woman.

She sent him one look from under her lashes. Her features were so beautiful to him, he had to keep himself from staring, so he busied himself making certain the water in the kettle boiled fast. He couldn't resist touching her mind to see what that look meant. He found wariness. She wasn't used to compliments and it made her a little nervous that he gave her one. But she was pleased. Secretly she hugged his words to her. That made him want to smile as well.

She didn't see herself at all the way he saw her. In her mind, she had an image of what beauty in a woman was. Her sisters. Taller. Curvy bodies. Long legs. Lots of curly hair and makeup. He supposed they were beautiful in their own way, probably by human standards as well.

Teagan was so much more to him. He would never be able

73

to explain it to her. He liked that she was petite and slight. He liked that she had the spirit of a warrior. It didn't mean she didn't have fears, but she faced them head-on. He especially liked that she loved her grandmother with the same fierce protection she would have for their children.

Teagan shifted back and he could see immediately she was uncomfortable.

"Is your leg hurting again?"

She shook her head. "No. I climb." At his raised eyebrow, she gave him a faint smile. "You know. Boulders. Cliffs. Rock. I love climbing, especially bouldering, but I took a pretty bad fall right before I came here. I was working on this problem and I was literally on the last move before I topped out and I knew I should have pushed off from the boulder and let it go when my foot slipped, but I was so close to victory that I could taste it, so I hung on like an idiot."

He had scanned her body for injuries, but he had concentrated on injuries she'd suffered from the attack on her by Jashari, not older ones. He cursed silently. He would have to be much more thorough in the future with her.

She shot him a small grin. "Grandma Trixie says I have a stubborn streak with a dash of crazy."

"What happened?"

"I fell, of course. First I tore the skin off my fingers and when I fell, it wasn't the graceful falls I'm so known for. I hurt my shoulder." She rubbed her hand along her right shoulder. "It was my fault, but it still hurts. Funny that I can heal everyone's injuries but not my own."

"Let me." It wasn't a question. Or a plea. He had to heal the injury. He had no choice. The need was more than a compulsion, it was as necessary as breathing.

Teagan gave him a faint smile and shook her head.

Andre ignored the head shake as if he hadn't noticed. He didn't wait for her consent. She was his woman. She was injured. There was nothing to talk about. He moved with his blurring speed, one moment on the opposite side of the fire so she felt safe, the next he was beside her, his hands gentle on her shoulder.

Her bones were small. She was very slender, but her muscles were surprisingly firm. She was in very good shape. He could feel her strength beneath her soft skin, the gentle ripple of muscle. Still, his fingers could close around her upper arm.

"Um ... " Teagan trailed off, biting her lip. She didn't trust him enough to touch her so intimately, and up close, he was just plain scary. But his hands felt warm and gentle on her and already she could feel the heat going into her muscle.

"It would be impossible for a man such as me to allow you to continue in pain," he said softly, distractedly.

She bit her lower lip a little harder, reminding herself he had taken that pain away and with it, the memory of how Armend attacked her had diminished just a little. His body was close to hers, almost surrounding her. The way he sat, his knees apart, her back to his front, her body wedged between his thighs, his heat warming her more than the fire, was terrifying. Not because she feared him or felt threatened, but because her body reacted to his.

The reaction was shocking, exhilarating, astonishing and proved there was absolutely nothing wrong with her when it came to men and sex. She'd never felt the rush before, the heat moving through her veins or the way her breasts could ache with sudden need. She loved the sensation, mostly because she'd never managed to feel it for anyone else.

Still, it was a little unsettling having him so close and she was afraid he would notice the change in her breathing, the slight trembling in her body at his touch. His hands were large and very soothing on her aching shoulder, but the effects of his touch didn't stop there.

"Um . . ." she started again. "Andre, maybe this isn't such a good idea."

"Csitri. Ainaak terád vigyázak."

She frowned. When he spoke in his language—and she couldn't understand a word of it and she was pretty good with languages—he sounded sexier than ever. His tone was pitched low and seemed to move over her skin in a caress. She really didn't understand how a voice or tone could do that to her, but it did.

"I don't understand what that means."

"Csitri is"—he frowned—"little one. But affectionate."

Teagan didn't ever want to think of herself as "little," but she liked the affectionate part and she couldn't deny that beside him, she was on the smaller side. Okay, maybe beside most people, but still. "And the other part?"

"Ainaak terád vigyázak." He mulled that over for a minute. "I have difficulty translating that properly, but it means you are in my care. Always in my care. I do not have the proper English words to convey the full meaning."

He sounded distracted. She was totally okay with him being distracted. The healing warmth penetrated deeper, right into the muscles and tendons she'd strained. She could feel the difference already. She also preferred that he wasn't paying close attention to her reaction to his touch.

The longer he was close to her, the more her breath stayed captured in her lungs. Even her thighs seemed to dance with fingers of desire moving up and down them from his voice alone. The heat between her legs increased and she felt her womb pulse and her feminine channel go damp with need.

It was beautiful. Perfect. Scary strong. Very intense. She'd gone from not being able to react physically to a man to wanting to turn her head and see if his mouth tasted as good as it looked. She also wanted to dance a little jig or something to celebrate that she wasn't totally frigid.

His breath hitched. She felt the warmth on the nape of her neck as he swept her hair out of his way. The pulse in her throat jumped. Throbbed. She reached up and covered it because, just for a moment, she felt his mouth there, against her skin, his tongue sliding across her pulse. She knew it wasn't real, because his mouth was close to the nape of her neck—she could feel his breath. Still, she captured the sensual feeling of his tongue over her pulse with the palm of her hand and just held it there, pressing it into her skin.

She hoped the memory burned deep so when she went to bed, she could take that with her and keep scary dreams of Armend at bay with Andre's presence.

"I need your hand, *sivamet*."

Even as he told her, he already had taken possession of it, so very gently. His touch was a caress, and it sent a shiver of awareness down her spine. He examined the raw fingers, smoothing them out in his palm. Her hand looked very small inside of his. The pads of his fingers stroked over the raw wounds. Her toes actually curled, and she felt her very core spasm and spill damp heat between her legs.

Teagan nearly jerked her hand free, but his fingers closed around hers and he brought them to his mouth before she could do a thing. She was so mesmerized, she stared at him over her shoulder as her fingers disappeared into the warm haven of his mouth. The reaction of her body was shocking. She could have sworn she had a mini-orgasm just from the sensation of his tongue stroking caresses over her fingers.

She couldn't move. She should have—but she couldn't. Her entire body was on fire and that was just ... remarkable. She didn't want the feeling to go away, yet at the same time, she didn't want this strange bear of a man, so gentle and kind, to know what she was feeling.

Her hand tingled, and then grew warm. She felt his tongue slide over each individual finger a second and then third time. Each slow, sensual movement sent desire knifing through her body. It took a moment for her thought processes to kick in.

Her brain felt slow and sluggish, dazed and mesmerized by the lines carved so deep in his handsome face. His hooded eyes filled with concentration, the blue so deep and true, she'd never seen such a pure color on anyone. He had to be the most sensual man in the world, and she was alone in a cave with him.

There might be something to vacation flings after all. She'd never understood the concept. It seemed so wrong, sharing your body with a stranger and walking away. She wanted intimacy and emotion. A connection beyond physical. She wanted everything—or nothing—with a man. She'd accepted, a long time ago, when her body didn't respond to anyone, she was going to have nothing.

She took a breath and let it out to calm her wildly beating heart and maybe get air to her brain so she could actually think. He removed her fingers from his mouth, although he did so reluctantly, slowly, as if he didn't want to. He held her hand up for his inspection, turning her fingers first one way and then the other.

Teagan stared at her hand. There no sign of injury; the skin had completely healed over the raw wounds where she had torn them. She held her other hand up for comparison. Both hands had suffered the same fate when she'd slipped off the rock with her foot and tried to hold on.

She loved climbing, but she seemed to have thin skin. She didn't develop the necessary callouses the way others did.

"How did you do that?"

Looking at him over her shoulder as she was doing, she saw him in profile, and his eyelashes were outrageously long. His mouth was perfection. His nose straight and his jaw strong. She liked the scruff on his jaw and the blue of his eyes. She could stare at him for eternity and that wouldn't be long enough.

"I have a healing agent in my saliva," he said.

"Wow. That's awesome. Amazing. I can't do that, but it would come in handy when I climb. Maybe I should take you along so you can heal my hands after I tear them up again." The words tumbled over one another. She couldn't help herself. He had possession of her other hand and once again he was inspecting the damage.

Her stomach performed a slow somersault. A million butterflies took wing. Her feminine channel throbbed and pulsed. She stared at his face. God, he was just beautiful. The concentration gathered in his eyes as he focused completely on her injury was just plain sexy.

Once again he brought her hand toward his mouth. She held her breath. Waiting. Needing the touch of his mouth. The velvet rasp of his tongue. Without warning his lashes lifted and he looked straight into her eyes. Instantly, she had the sensation of drowning. She lost her breath and allowed herself to fall.

"Teagan."

Just her name. That was all he whispered. The tone of his voice was a caress. Fingers moved over her bare skin, down her back, tracing her spinal cord. She swore she felt a light touch, but he hadn't moved. He hadn't relinquished possession of her hand.

She couldn't look away from his eyes. The world was there. The entire world. Her mouth was suddenly dry, and she wanted desperately to touch him. Her palm itched with the need to run her hand over his heavy chest muscles.

79

Even as he stared into her eyes, he brought her fingers to his mouth and sucked on them. His tongue curled around each finger separately. It did something to her insides. She melted until she was soft and boneless—until there was nothing but Andre and his eyes and mouth and the scent of him surrounding her.

Teagan couldn't have spoken if she wanted to. She was totally incapable of extracting her fingers from the heat of his mouth. It was so completely unlike her. She stared into his eyes and let herself just be with him. Connect to him. It was sexual—but so much more. She could live there with him. In that cave. A primitive world. Just as long as he was with her. It was crazy, but true.

She knew she was in danger. She knew the danger was not just to her heart. This man could take her soul if she let him—and she would let him if she stayed much longer. She had no idea why, but she felt the truth of it with every cell in her body.

80

5

Teagan both feared him and was totally enraptured by him. Andre had a very strong compulsion to pull her into his arms and hold her close. Her heart beat too fast and her breathing was nearly nonexistent. When he was certain he had healed her fingers, he released her hand, and pushed the heavy fall of her braided hair from her neck.

"Breathe, *sivamet*," he counseled softly. "Just take a breath."

He moved in her mind with the lightest of touches. She was physically attracted to him and wondering why. She was shocked by it and that made him want to smile all over again. She'd never been with another man, she hadn't kissed one, or even felt attracted to one. She was all his. *All his*.

Andre hadn't ever had anything in his life. Anyone. His childhood had been unhappy, with very few good memories, and those memories had faded beyond his ability to recapture them. He remembered a tall bear of a man who had eyes for his mother and little else—certainly not for him. His mother always looked right through the "ghost" in the house and never saw or acknowledged him. Truthfully, he couldn't remember what she looked like. Teagan had eyes for him. Only for him. He liked that. More, he needed it.

She took a breath and smiled at him. "I don't think I've ever seen or heard of anyone who could heal such injuries with saliva. My skin was completely gone. It doesn't seem possible that you could actually regenerate skin that quickly."

"When you heal wounds, you are sealing off the injury," he pointed out. He reached around her for the kettle.

She caught both his wrists firmly and jerked his hands away from the fire. "Andre, can't you feel that heat? You'll get burned."

The concern in her voice caught at him. She was so incredible. How had it been possible to live for centuries without her? He'd never seen hair like hers before. So much of it. Long and thick and shining like a raven's wing. Glossy hair. Braids everywhere. He loved her hair.

"I want to make you a cup of tea," he said, his face close to her neck, inhaling her scent. He had never felt such soft skin or seen that particular shade of mocha, so beautiful it made his eyes ache just looking at her. He wanted to rub against her like a cat, but he was afraid the shadow on his jaw would scrape her soft skin.

"That's so sweet of you, Andre, but let me get my hot pads from my backpack." She looked around the cave. "I should get a couple of lanterns as well if we're going to set up camp for the night."

The last thing he wanted her to do was go to sleep. He needed her exhausted so she'd sleep most of the day away. She could get through safeguards. The vampires wouldn't be a threat to her because they would need to go to ground when the sun rose, but Armend's four friends would certainly be a threat, although it was possible they'd leave the mountain once they found Armend's body.

"I sometimes come here," he said, again, strictly true. He didn't need to reveal yet that he'd been using the cave for centuries when he was in the area and it was the closest thing he'd had to a home at one time.

She turned her head to look at him over her shoulder. Their faces were close. He could see the dark chocolate melting in her eyes. Liquid chocolate. Beautiful. For a moment he just stared at her, wondering how he'd gotten so lucky. How he'd managed to find her just when he'd made the decision to let go of life and go out with honor battling a vampire.

There she was. Saving him. This little slip of a woman. He needed to make certain he brought her into his world as gently as possible. She looked fragile, but he knew from touching her mind so often that she had a will of steel. If she got her back up and tried to fight him, it wouldn't be good for either of them.

"I have another chamber set up more comfortably. It is difficult to get to, but a little safer than this cave."

Deliberately, Andre had not gone fully to ground, luring the vampire with his trail of blood. Carpathians buried themselves deep in the earth when they went to ground, not shallow where a master vampire's newly acquired apprentice would unravel safeguards meant to delay, not keep out. His plan hadn't worked; instead, his lifemate had somehow wandered into his cave and found him.

"You do? What's *more comfortable* mean?"

He reluctantly moved away from her. He didn't have any more excuses to wrap his body around hers, so in order not to look like a pervert taking advantage, he had to move to the other side of the fire.

"A few chairs, torches up above to the light the room. A bed. Nothing great."

Teagan smiled at Andre as he settled across from her, grateful for the respite of not having him so close. She didn't understand how he could look so clean and fresh and smell so great when they were in a cave and he'd been horribly injured. His clothes were no longer bloody or tattered.

She was the one who looked disheveled, and she was quite certain she needed a bath after hiking for so long. She'd been hiking up the mountain with Armend for a few days before he'd gone psycho rapist/serial killer on her. Now, she had to sit with the sexiest, most *gorgeous*, probably hottest man she'd ever meet in her life, and she looked like something the cat might drag in.

Worse, she was totally crushing on him. His black hair was long. Wavy. Pulled back with a leather cord. He looked like he'd just stepped out of the shower, and he smelled yummy, too. He was sweet, too, making her tea, or trying to without getting burned. If she had any imagination at all, she would pretend he'd nearly stuck his hand in the fire because he was so absolutely enamored with her. Unfortunately, she didn't have that much pretend in her.

"It was thoughtful of you to want to make tea for me. I appreciate it, thank you." She dragged a cup from her pack, poured the water from the kettle into the cup and added the herb teabag he'd given her from his stash of supplies. It gave her something to do besides stare at him.

Strangely, her stomach rebelled a little at the thought of food. Even the herbal tea looked like it might not go down well. She hoped she wasn't getting sick, not when she was just deciding a vacation fling might be the right way to go.

She allowed herself a quick glance at him from under her lashes, just sneaking another peek. He was watching her. When Andre looked at her, he focused wholly on her. That gave her the sensation of being the only woman in his world.

She cleared her throat. "Would you like some tea as well? I don't have another cup in my pack, but you must have one somewhere."

He shook his head and held out his hands to the fire, warming them. "Tell me about your life, Teagan. Where you live. Your family."

She let her breath out. She was good at chattering. She'd learned if she could make small talk, she could feel a part of the activities around her. Most of the time, she pursued solitary things, such as her beloved bouldering, but she could appear social with the best of them. Staring into Andre's eyes had already proved dangerous to her so she decided she wasn't doing that again soon.

She liked looking at him. She was drawn to looking at him. Worse, it was becoming a compulsion. Up close he was even better, and with the firelight casting shadows across his face, he was spectacular.

"Teagan."

There it was. The way he said her name. Just her name. That low, sexy voice, with his super sexy accent. Totally impossible to ignore. She forced the cup of tea to her lips in order to keep from staring at him.

"Teagan."

He said her name again. Low. Gentle. Mesmerizing. She had no choice. She lifted her gaze to his. Found herself drowning again. Who had blue eyes like his? Blue eyes and black, glossy, glorious hair. She blinked several times and found the tea in the cup gone, her stomach warm but a little upset. She was so hypnotized by him she didn't even remember gulping the tea. She *had* to get ahold of herself.

She swallowed. Licked at her lower lip with the tip of her tongue. His eyes followed the movement. He was just plain sexy, and she didn't know how to handle sexy.

85

"*Sivamet*, you are not breathing again." He placed his palm over his heart. "Your heart beats too fast. Listen. Hear the rhythm of mine. Allow your heart to follow mine."

Andre was right. She wasn't breathing. She had forgotten how. Even his words, whispered to her in a velvet tone, sinful as midnight in a cave with a stranger, tangled in her brain until she thought he was asking something else of her. She didn't know what, but whatever it was, she knew if she did as he said, she was committing to more than just slowing her heart rate.

Still, she took a breath, observing his hand over his heart. It was a big hand, strong, with long fingers. She couldn't imagine what it would feel like to have his hands stroking her skin. She fought down that particular vision—want, need, whatever—and placed her own hand over her heart.

"Listen."

She noticed that just about anything he had to say, he said as briefly as possible—with the least amount of words he could use. He spoke English, but then maybe he was unsure of the language, like when he was trying to interpret his own language.

She did as he said. She talked a lot, but meditation and stillness were important to her. She quieted her mind and reached for sound. To her surprise, her hearing was acute enough to pick up the steady beat of his heart when she actually listened for it. Strong and rhythmic, his heart pumped blood through his veins and arteries. She listened just as he instructed, her hand over her heart, and to her surprise, her own heart rate slowed to match the strength and beat of his.

Her body was a tuning fork, so she shouldn't have been so shocked, but still, she usually heard notes to music. Or for a musical instrument. Songs. Gems and crystals tended to be actual songs, where rock was more notes. Each variety, or composition, emitted a different note to her. Now she even heard the steady trickle of water, the splash as it hit the dirt. She heard the scurry of insects through the dry wood stacked against the wall of the cave.

What she found really wonderful and terrifying was the unexpected fact that when she tuned her body to Andre's, she could hear not only his heart beat, the flow of blood through his veins, but also an echo of his thoughts.

She is so beautiful. I must protect her, even from herself. From the men searching the mountain for her.

She nearly scrambled back from the fire, feeling as if she'd invaded his private thoughts. *But.* Seriously? *Beautiful.* She was cute in her dresses and boots. In her darling jacket with the bustle of ruffles falling down the back. But beautiful? In her camping clothes and her hair in braids to keep it from going wild?

She examined the tone of his thoughts. They seemed sincere.

"Is something wrong, Teagan?"

He had to quit saying her name. He drawled it out and curled his accent around it until the sound of her name became a caress. Literally, the sound penetrated her skin and sent darts of fire straight to her most feminine channel where a lot of activity began to take place that shouldn't. Not there. Not with him this close to her and the firelight playing on her face so he could read her every expression. She couldn't even play poker, how was she going to hide her attraction to him?

"No. No, I just thought I should be doing something besides sitting here. The authorities need to know about Armend." She blurted the first excuse she could think of.

"You are exhausted."

"I know. I ... That's true." What an idiot. She was

stammering. Her face was growing redder by the moment. She shouldn't be able to blush, with her skin, but she did. She wanted to kick her birth father for that trait.

"Tell me about your family, please. Your life."

She realized she still held her hand over her heart. Her beat matched his exactly. She dared to look into his eyes again. He was watching her with the same focus, his entire being centered on her. The way he looked at her sent tiny electrical currents zinging through her cells to join the darts wreaking havoc in certain places of her anatomy.

"I have a noisy family. Nosy, too. They're great, and we get into each other's business all the time. I have three sisters. I adore them. You'd adore them. Everyone does, but me especially, although Tarita's husband argued with me that wasn't true, but it is. I know he loves her, but Tarita is *my* sister and very special. I've known her my entire life and he's only known her a few years."

"She must be very special."

"I was so lucky growing up. I had Grandma Trixie, who is really the best of the best. She laughs all the time, and no matter how difficult things got, she would just shrug her shoulders and tell us to make some lemonade. Then she'd laugh. We always had lemonade in the house and that's how we'd solve problems. We'd sit together as a family, all with a glass of lemonade, and talk it through. We'd come up with ideas to raise money if one of us needed it for anything. I loved our family meetings."

"I can hear that you do." Andre stood, reaching out a hand to her. "Come with me. I find your life intriguing and would very much like to hear more, but you need to be comfortable. You are still sore. I know where there is a hot spring."

Teagan blinked at him. That sounded like heaven. She'd even brought a bathing suit. A nice modest one-piece, and she had a wrap to go with it. Maybe she'd actually feel like a human being again.

"Lead the way."

The moment she put her hand in his, her heart turned over. Melted around the edges. Her stomach did a series of backflips and there was a definite spasm, hot and a little out of control. It was the way he watched her. His totally focused stare that made her aware of everything about herself. The way she moved. The way she breathed, as if he was interested in the very breath coming in and out of her lungs. She was even acutely aware of the way her hair swayed and dropped down her back in a fall of braids.

His hand enveloped hers, and yet he was so gentle that when he wrapped his fingers around hers she only felt warmth and a prickle of awareness that always ended up south of where it should be.

He snagged her backpack with one hand, lifting it as if it didn't weigh anything at all. He pulled her close to him, so she was virtually walking beneath the protection of his shoulder. With every step she took, she felt his heat. She could feel the way his muscles rippled and glided so fluidly beneath his skin. And that was through his clothes. She couldn't imagine what he would feel like skin to skin.

She bit hard on her lip to try to steady her mind. "Um. Andre. We can't just leave the fire burning."

"I dealt with it." He kept walking right through to the next chamber.

She glanced behind them, and as she did, the firelight was gone and the chamber went totally dark.

"I don't have my flashlight."

"I do not need one. Your eyes will adjust in a moment."

"How did you ..." She trailed off. She hadn't seen him pour water on the fire. She had been so absolutely enamored by him she might not have noticed him dumping the water from the kettle on the fire. It hadn't been that big, but even so, could a kettle full of water actually put out the flames?

"Tell me more about your family. Your other sisters," he prompted.

It was strange, she actually could see where they were walking. Her eyes really did adjust to the darkness. More, she liked walking so close to him. She didn't need safe. She didn't want to live her life safe. She wanted adventure.

She had grown up with four strong women. She had never felt strong. She was the smart one. They all said it. Not the beautiful one. Not the one with the confidence to get up and sing in church, although she had the voice to do so. Or the one who could model. Worse, she was totally afraid of everything. It wasn't just a small panic attack, sometimes she was actually paralyzed with fear.

Teagan refused to live her life with fear ruling her. She took martial arts. She worked out. She climbed, facing her greatest fear, of heights. She loved the wilderness and was determined to see as many places as possible, even if she had to go alone, which was often—and that was terrifying. Still. She did it.

Over the last couple of years, she had gained some confidence. No matter how she really felt on the inside, she could project confidence, but walking with Andre so close to her made her safe in a way she'd never felt.

She felt the brush of his gaze like a physical touch. She knew if she looked up, he would be looking down at her. The knowledge sent a little shiver of delight down her spine. She wasn't flirty, but she suddenly wished she were. She wasn't daring, but she *thought* about putting a hand on his rib cage as if to steady herself. Of course she wasn't going to actually do it, but the fantasy was there. She suspected she wouldn't have the courage to have a vacation fling with him, either, but she'd come away from this with one nightmare and a million fantasies.

She sighed. Instantly, Andre let go of her hand and swept his arm around her. He had a big arm. Lots of muscle. The moment his body was against hers, she considered fainting. It was the only viable option other than sliding her hands under his shirt to run them up his perfect chest. All that muscle and those intriguing scars. Yeah. Perfection.

"This is not an appropriate question I asked you?"

She blinked. What was he talking about? She had no choice but to look up at him. The moment their eyes met, her stomach went on a roller-coaster ride all by itself. Her knees went weak, which was stupid but true. Her toes even thought about curling, but she sent them a fierce command not to react. Still, she couldn't stop the tremor that ran through her body at the impact. Who knew that ice blue could go dark navy?

"What question?"

"About your family. Is that not what strangers do when they try to get to know each another? Ask about family?"

He didn't blink. She knew because she watched and blinked for him. Like a million times. Staring into his eyes was just plain dangerous, but she couldn't look away. Her body was tight against his. In a lover's embrace. Except it wasn't actually a lover's embrace, it was more like a—Teagan was making a fool of herself and was going to fall at his feet and he was keeping her up embrace.

His body was cool at first. His skin cool. It heated quickly in all the places she touched him until he burned right through her clothes. Her *dirty* clothes. She nearly groaned. Why did these things happen to her? Why couldn't she be totally glamorous and assured like her sisters? By now, there was no doubt about it, her deodorant had failed. He smelled—yummy. He'd been lying in dirt, covered in blood when she found him, but somehow, he looked and smelled like heaven.

"Teagan."

There it was again. Her name. That caressing voice. His accent. Her toes totally ignored her earlier command and had a field day curling right along with her stomach doing flips.

"Um." *That* was certainly showing him her intelligent nature. Her witty conversation. Her mind was blank. Well. Okay. Not exactly blank—it was filled with all sorts of things that shouldn't be there. Like Andre with his shirt off. It was as far as she dared to imagine. Seriously. Anything else would have made her head explode.

A slow, amused smile lit his eyes for one small moment and faded, but the dark navy receded a little and all that beautiful glacier blue began to return.

She narrowed her eyes. "You'd better not be reading my mind."

"I am doing my best to be courteous."

Color swept her face. She dared to put a hand on his rib cage to push him away from her. His body didn't so much as rock back an inch, *and*, touching him was a huge mistake. Like *huge*. Her hand seemed to mold to his body. She was fairly certain it had melted into his skin and there was no way to ever remove it again.

"You're lethal, Andre. Really. I don't even know what to do with you. You'll have to just step back and give me some breathing room so I can act like a normal human being again." She made the confession in a little rush.

"You are not acting normal?"

She gave him her darkest scowl. "Do you think I plaster myself all over every strange man I meet?"

"I am strange?"

92

There was no trace of amusement on his face. She wanted it back. The steady, focused stare was getting to her. Now she'd insulted him. Damn the language barrier.

"I meant as in *stranger*. A stranger. I don't plaster myself against men."

"I would hope not."

She didn't see amusement on his face, but she heard a hint of it in his voice and for some reason, her body wanted to melt at his feet right then and there.

"Well, you're just … um … gorgeous." Confession was supposed to be good for the soul, right? And what else could she do? She'd insulted him by calling him strange. She hadn't meant to, but she'd done it. And anyway, telling the truth seemed the only thing she could do, because she'd blurted it out without thinking. It was already out there, and she couldn't take it back.

"Gorgeous?"

Great. He didn't know what the word meant. She sighed again and wished she could unmelt her hand from his skin. There was a thin piece of material between her palm and his skin, but she was fairly certain she'd melted that away as well. Even if it was still there, she could no longer feel it.

"Hot. Seriously hot."

He blinked. Why had she wanted him to blink? He had long lashes. Black like his hair. Not dark brown. His hair and lashes were the real thing. Black. Glossy black. Beautifully black. She was so perving on him. It was wrong, but impossible to get her mind to work properly enough to stop.

"Good-looking and sweet. That's a lethal combination," she added, her mouth running away from her. The ground needed to open up and swallow her. She needed to add a disclaimer. "But you're safe. Really. I'm just going to stare at you a lot, but I won't be all grabby and touchy. Well. Except for my hand.

93

That's kind of melted into you and there's nothing either of us can do about that."

How was that for recovering? Now she was just plain crazy in his eyes. Like her grandmother. It obviously ran in the family. At least she didn't think he was a vampire; but really, weren't vampires supposed to be sexy? Dracula had been really sexy at times. And he did make her tea. Men didn't do that, did they? She'd never seen one of her brothers-in-law make tea for her sisters. Her sisters always made dinner and put it on the table in front of their already seated husbands. Did vampires make tea?

Andre actually smiled. A flash of white teeth only, but for a moment he'd smiled. Even in the dark she could see his teeth were very white and not sharp and pointy like a vampire's teeth should be. No bloodstains. Her neck was safe. Her pulse gave a disappointed little throb. The idea of him nibbling at her neck was sexy, too.

"You think I am this . . . gorgeous?"

"Um. Yeah. You're drop-dead gorgeous. The kind of gorgeous women like me just view from afar."

His smile was completely gone now. But his eyes had gone soft. Liquid almost. So beautiful she wanted to cry.

"Women like you?" he repeated.

She gave a small shrug, still leaning into his body. Still with weak knees and a stomach doing flips. Worse. Serious, serious chemical reactions, little mini-explosions taking place in secret places she didn't want to think about—not with him so close. She couldn't pull her gaze from his any more than she could unmelt her hand that was now permanently glued to his side.

"Ordinary. Normal. You know. Not goddesslike status. We don't associate with men like you. We just worship from afar." Yeah. She was making a total fool of herself. Now she

94

knew why it was a total blessing she'd never been attracted to a man before. She was an idiot. She had to stop talking. She just couldn't. She was too nervous and when she was nervous, she chattered.

"Teagan."

A million bird wings fluttering in her stomach joined the roller coaster. He could *not* continue to say her name like that or she was going to have a mini-orgasm just from the sound of his voice. That was gospel. Absolute.

"Um. Andre. You have to stop saying my name."

His face changed. Subtly. All those carved lines, like a sculpture of the god of masculine beauty, softened. More masculine beauty. She blinked and his face was closer. His hand slipped around to the nape of her neck, his thumb sliding along her cheek. Her stomach bottomed out, did a series of flips and began churning. The air actually whooshed from her lungs so that they burned. Her throat closed.

She didn't close her eyes. She couldn't. He didn't close his eyes. He watched her reaction, and she couldn't stop it. The disaster of his mouth finding hers. She didn't know how to kiss. He was gorgeous. He had to have kissed a gazillion times. Still, even now when she was going to make more of a fool of herself than ever, she held very still. Waiting. Holding her breath. Needing. Craving. Her perfect disaster.

His mouth touched hers. Featherlight. An exquisite brush that left behind tingles. The tingles radiated right down her body to her breasts so that she ached more than she'd already been aching. The sensation kept traveling, using her veins as a highway straight to her sex. She felt heat. Fire. A spasm of need.

She blinked. His other arm moved to her back, pulling her even tighter to him. The hand at her nape crept into her hair, fingers bunching her tight braids, pulling her head back. His mouth returned and she couldn't stop herself. She closed her eyes and just let him take her over.

She had never kissed a man before. No one actually, other than her grandmother and sisters and that was more an affectionate kiss on the cheek. This was something altogether different. His lips moved over hers, sending little darts of fire shooting in every direction, all over her body. His tongue slid along the seam of her lips and a spear of fire shot to her feminine channel. Burning her there.

She had a mad desire to press herself against his thigh, but she lost even that thought when he deepened the kiss. Gently. Almost tenderly. Still, his mouth was pure fire and she was drowning in him. With him. She hadn't known a woman could feel this way. She just gave herself up to him. Let him take her over, needing his mouth and the taste of him and the burn that just kept threatening to spin out of control.

He lifted his head and stared down into her eyes. She knew she looked dazed and confused because she *was* dazed and confused. She wasn't even certain she knew her own name. She blinked rapidly to try to bring herself out from under his spell. She shook her head and touched her lips.

"Are you all right?" His voice was gentle. Sweet. Sexy.

No, she wasn't all right. *Hell*, no, she wasn't all right. Was he crazy? She heaved a sigh. "Clearly I'm not in my right mind. I don't kiss strangers."

"It was a good kiss."

She rolled her eyes at him. "It was more than a good kiss. It's official. You're the best kisser in the world and therefore we can never—and, Andre, I mean *never*—do that again."

His eyebrow shot up. "If it was a good kiss, why would you not want to repeat the experience?"

"My hand is already melted to your side. Do you want my entire body melted into yours? Because, let me explain this so you understand. It could happen." She stared up into his incredibly blue, so sexy eyes, willing him to comprehend the graveness of the situation. "Seriously. You could walk around to the end of your days with me just stuck to you."

Faint amusement crept back into his eyes. She didn't like how much she loved seeing it there.

"Normally, I'm really intelligent. I am. But you've short-circuited my brain and fried a few necessary cells. I can't think clearly around you. So no more kissing." She tried to sound decisive. Really firm. She didn't sound that way at all, not even to her own ears. "On top of being gorgeous, did you have to be a world-class kisser?"

Yep. She blurted that one right out there, too. Of course. Because no matter how much she tried, she couldn't stop her mouth from talking. She even pressed her lips together and seriously—really—she had to remove her hand from his side. Unfortunately, she was afraid if she did, she might just put her lips there.

She groaned. Out. Loud.

He smiled and smoothed back her hair, his thumb sliding lower, over her pulse. His gaze dropped to her mouth. "I think there will be many kisses in our future."

"Really?" She sounded more hopeful than shocked like she wanted to sound.

"Yes. Really. I think kissing you is a must. I like the taste of you. It would be impossible for me to kiss you just once. One taste and already you are an addiction."

She shook her head. "I get that you could be an addiction for me, but I don't know how to kiss. I've never done it before. You're the first. And the only. So see, I just don't have enough experience for the kind of world-class kissing that you do. You're so far out of my league it isn't funny."

Oh, lord. Her runaway mouth struck again. She just had

to get the "world-class" in there *twice* so he couldn't possibly miss it. *And* admit she had never kissed anyone. That was just great. Now she looked pathetic and desperate. What had Armend called her? A pity . . .

"Stop." Andre growled the command in a low, almost snarling voice.

His eyes glittered and began to fill all that ice with a dark midnight blue color. Turbulent storms swirled through the blue. It was fascinating and scary at the same time.

His fist tightened in her hair. "Do not even think about that man and the disgusting things he said to you. He wanted you. You refused, and he said things to hurt you. To make you think less of yourself. I will not have *avio päläfertiilam* thinking anything but that you are beautiful."

Teagan had no idea what *avio päläfertiilam* meant, but he definitely was referring to her and she could tell he meant every word. She had no idea why she knew he was so sincere, but for some reason, this gorgeous man really thought she was beautiful. It didn't make sense. Maybe his eyes shone in the dark because he was blind.

"Did I make myself clear?"

She swallowed. He could be scary even when he seemed to be defending her. "Very clear. Thank you. But you have to stop reading my mind." Oh. Lord. He was reading her mind again. She really had to control all her thoughts. That was not going to be easy. "Please do me a favor and remove my hand from where it's all melted into your side. I need to get a handle on this and touching you isn't helping."

"I can do that for you, but first, I really have to kiss you again." He made it a statement.

"You do?" Who was she to stop him if he really had to kiss her? There was a difference between want and having to do something, right?

She watched as his head bent slowly to hers. Her tummy did the roller coaster and a million bird wings all at once. Her heart forgot all about following the steady beat of his and began racing overtime. His lips brushed caresses over hers, and she was fairly certain the only thing holding her up was the hand in her hair and the arm locked around her back.

If she wanted to survive she needed to stop him. But really? Was survival all that important? His tongue touched her lips and the bottom dropped out of her stomach. No. Survival was one of those things people talked about that really wasn't all it was cracked up to be. Not when a world-class kisser was taking his time with you.

His mouth slanted over hers. *Open for me, sivamet. Give yourself to me.*

His sexy voice played along every one of her nerve endings, leaving her burning in need. She should have paid attention to her inner voice for survival, but there was no listening to her brain. She opened her mouth to his. An invitation. Giving herself to him. Surrendering.

The fingers in her hair moved to her hand, the one melted to his ribs, and he very gently brought it up around his neck. He did the same with the other one. She had to go up on her toes and he simply lifted her as if she weighed no more than a feather, his mouth never moving from hers.

She did the unthinkable and wrapped her legs around him. Still kissing him. Still burning for him. Kissing. Burning. Floating. It was absolutely wonderful. Perfect. Unbelievable and so unlike Teagan Joanes.

6

Andre dazzled her. Cast a spell. He had to be a sorcerer. There was no other explanation. One moment Teagan was standing with him in a chamber with narrow passages leading in a couple of directions and the next, when he took his mouth away from hers—and it had to be said, she mewed her disappointment like a kitten in distress—she was in a completely different chamber.

This one still had a dirt floor, but it was warm and there was a pool of very inviting water. Steam rose, indicating the water was hot. There was a bed that actually looked clean, not filled with insects, and the chamber was lit up with fantastic stars on the high ceiling. Torches on the wall gave off a dancing light that flickered across the room much like flames from a fireplace.

Andre lowered her feet to the floor, one arm holding her steady so that she didn't just collapse into a melting pile of boneless flesh—which was exactly how she felt. Her mouth wanted his mouth back. She could taste him. He tasted as good as he looked and then some.

"Um . . ." She trailed off, looking around her. *Um* seemed to be her favorite word. She sighed. "Honestly, I do have a college education. As a matter of fact, I have my master's and I'm quite young for that. You fried my brain." She couldn't help sounding slightly accusatory because he really had fried her brain. None of this was her fault.

His eyebrow shot up and the amused look she was growing so fond of crept back into his eyes. She found Andre was doubly dangerous when he gave her that particular look. She'd already melted. Then she lost her mind and kissed him all the way into another chamber and never even noticed they were moving. Well . . . she did feel as if she were floating.

"Your brain is just fine," he assured. "I checked."

She scowled. She was good at scowling. She'd practiced all through school when she was trying to study and some of her rowdier friends—all guys—bugged her to wrestle, do martial arts, climb or just plain diverted her attention when she needed to stay focused. She'd even used the scowl most effectively on her brothers-in-law when they called her "shrimp" and "mini-hotcake." Seriously. They really called her that.

"Mini-hotcake? They really called you that?" Andre proved he was immune to her scowl by reading her thoughts.

"Will you stop? Andre, I'm telling you, you don't want to know what's floating around in my head. Especially in regard to you. And right now, I don't want to argue with you, I want to sit in the hot spring."

"Actually, you want to kiss me again. I have no objections."

"Actually, I'm thinking about kicking you in the shins. You're a total stranger. I don't know the first thing about you, and I'm not kissing you again. I don't know what happened, but I'm telling you I don't do that sort of thing with everyone."

"I heard you the first time, *sivamet*. I believe I pointed out that was a very good thing. I would frown on *avio päläfertiilam* kissing other men."

He had to stop talking in his native language. Not because she didn't know what he was calling her—and she didn't—but because it sounded ultra sexy. *Bonehead* was most likely.

She waved her hand airily and stepped around him. Well, she *started* to step around him. He was a big man and stepping around him took a little time. It didn't work, because he wrapped his hand around the nape of her neck and tugged. He was strong and she found herself hitting him full on, her front to his. Up close. Very, very close.

She tilted her head up to look at him, always a mistake, but then she couldn't stop herself. She pressed her palm to the side of his face. Gently. A caress really. It was the way he looked at her. The look in his eyes. Like she was everything to him. The air he took into his lungs. His very breath. His world. No, his entire universe. She didn't understand how that could be so, but she felt the way he was so alone and then not. Then filled—by her.

"*Susu*." Andre whispered the word aloud.

She knew instantly whatever he'd said was important, and she filed the word away to ask him later. He still had that look in his eyes and she couldn't pull her gaze from his.

Andre covered her hand with his, pressing her palm even closer so she could feel the prickle of the shadow on his jaw. His eyes went bluer than ice blue. Beyond blue. The color was incredible. She stared into his eyes for a long moment and then she made another mistake. Again, she couldn't stop herself. She went up on her toes, pulled his head down to hers and brushed a kiss across his lips.

She didn't understand what was happening between them, but no one had ever looked at her like that. Not ever. Not even

Grandma Trixie, and her grandmother loved her like crazy. No one could look at her like she was the only one in their world. No one other than Andre, who had to be even crazier than Grandma Trixie.

Still, she couldn't stop herself. She touched her mouth to his. She needed to give him something back. To acknowledge his look. His lips were warm and firm and soft and a blatant invitation to more.

Andre's hand cupped the back of her head and his mouth moved against hers. For the first time she recognized hunger in the gentle coaxing of his tongue. She should have pulled back. She didn't know him. She was alone with him. She'd already given one man the wrong impression, with disastrous results . . .

Andre folded her closer, his mouth dominating, commanding even, short-circuiting her brain so that every thought disappeared and she leaned into all that heat and simply caught fire. The rush in her veins was like a fireball spreading through every part of her body. It was the most beautiful, amazing moment in her life. She didn't want it ever to end.

His mouth was hot and perfect, and she knew she was giving herself to him even as he was taking over. Taking charge of her in a way she would never have allowed if she thought about it. The fire spread fast, out of control, and she wanted it, wanted that burn to consume her. Mostly, she wanted him. She wanted to be his. She felt as if she was his, pure and simple.

You are mine.

She absorbed the soft statement, the one more in her head than whispered in her ear. His mouth kept moving on hers, his tongue stroking and caressing until she couldn't breathe. She couldn't catch her breath. For a moment, she thought she might die of kissing if that was even possible, but her lungs refused to work, burning her raw. And then, somehow, weirdly, he filled her lungs with air, exchanging breath with her, air with her, so that she felt him inside her. Close. Twisting through every organ and cell she had, lodging there. Branding himself in her very bones so that if she died and they did an autopsy, his name would be there, on every bone she had.

He lifted his head reluctantly. She clutched at his hair, his neck, hating to give him up. She felt dazed and a little shaky. He held her steady so that if her legs gave out, he wouldn't allow her to fall.

She stared up into his blue eyes. "What's happening here, Andre? Because it's scaring me just a little bit. I'm not like this. Not at all. I'm acting totally out of character, and you're a total stranger and I'm scared."

"I know you are, *csitri*," he murmured gently, his hand at the nape of her neck, his thumb sliding along her cheek and then finding her pulse in the sexy way that he had. "You do not ever have to be afraid with me. I would give my life before I would ever harm you."

It was impossible not to hear the utter sincerity in his voice or see it in his eyes. That was just as scary. She was always afraid, but she'd made it a priority to face every fear. This was different. This endangered her heart. She could fall for him, hard. She realized that, looking at his handsome face. If it was just his looks, that would be one thing, but she knew it was much more. They were connected in a way she didn't understand.

"See?" It had to be said. "Even that is bizarre. You don't know me at all and yet we're so wrapped up in this craziness you'd be willing to give your life for me. Does that makes sense to you?"

She forced herself to step back. Away from him. Away from the threat and potency of him. He was too mesmerizing.

Casting his spell over her and holding her prisoner. It wasn't all him. She was honest enough to evaluate her own behavior. She would have fought to save him. She might even go so far as to give her life before allowing something or someone to harm him as well, and that was *really* scary.

Teagan backed farther away from his heat. From the fire. From the gentle promise in his eyes. She could barely breathe again. The only sane thing to do was put distance between herself and this man. A lot of distance. A country or two. She picked up her backpack with one trembling hand. Grandma Trixie might have to stay crazy just a little longer, living in her world of vampires and monasteries.

She actually turned to go, but somehow, he got there first. She hadn't seen him move. She hadn't heard him move. Not a single rustle of clothes. Not a footfall. Not even a breath. She just blinked and he was there. Solid. An immovable rock. His hand, so very gently, took the backpack out of hers.

"Teagan."

Her name. That accent. His low reprimand. She shivered and bit at her lower lip. She was not going to make the mistake of looking into his eyes. That way led to complete and utter disaster and she wasn't going there again.

"Now you are just scaring yourself. You are tired and your body aches. I can feel the way your muscles are screaming. Please get into the water. It will make you feel so much better."

His voice was velvet soft, smoothing over her skin like the caress of fingers. She had the feeling if she tried to leave, he would find a way to stop her, and that would really freak her out. Maybe he was a psycho just making her feel safe with him, only she didn't anymore. Why? Because her entire body melted at his touch. No, it was even worse than that. Her entire body melted when he looked at her.

"*Sivamet.* I do not like to feel your fear. I am not this psycho you are afraid of. *Te avio päläfertiilam. Ainaak terád vigyázak.*"

Steadfastly refusing to look at him, she took a breath. "Andre, I don't know what that means."

"If you get into the hot spring, I will tell you."

She glanced up at him. His blue eyes were the colors of the purest glaciers she'd ever seen. The hot spring was tempting. She was tired. Exhausted. She needed rest if she was going to hike back down the mountain and tell the authorities what had happened to Armend.

"All right. But I'm putting on my swimsuit, so you need to go into the other chamber." That was definite and she put command into her voice. She could be really firm when she needed to be. Her nieces and nephews always obeyed her when she used that tone.

He just looked down at her, and slow amusement crept into his eyes. Her stomach took off again and her toes threatened to curl. He reached out and ran his knuckles gently down the side of her face. "I had no idea what the English word *cute* meant until I met you. When you get all fired up, that is what you are."

Cute was not what she was going for. He might be a foot taller than she was, and outweigh her by more than a hundred pounds, but he needed to take her seriously. She scowled and pointed to the narrow opening, the only one she saw, although there were two shadowy spots that might be entrances as well.

"Go." She hissed the command. She'd practiced that one and then used it on her naughtiest nephew. He always obeyed the hiss instantly.

Andre continued to look down at her and the amusement in his eyes moved slowly to his mouth. For one moment, she held her breath, waiting. His smile was brief, but it was there, showing his strong white teeth—no vampire teeth—and just as quickly it was gone, but still, she felt triumphant. She could tell he didn't smile often and it was nice that she could make him. Even if he wasn't reacting to her scowl or her hiss or her best scary tone.

"Andre. I want to change."

He bent and kissed the top of her head before he turned and walked out of the chamber. She stared after him, her heart beating a little too fast to suit her. He moved so beautifully. Like a great jungle cat, fluid with muscles rippling subtly beneath the surface. He was truly gorgeous. Maybe it was just his body she was after and she was safe after all.

"Get moving, Teagan, or I will have to come help you."

She was staring right at the entrance to the other chamber and he wasn't there. He was out of sight, so how did he know she was totally lost in a daydream about him and his fantastic body? She sent a fierce scowl his way and hoped he felt it right through all the dirt and rock.

She found a corner out of sight of the entrance and pulled on her swimsuit, thankful it was a one-piece. She traveled a lot to foreign countries—not to the cities or tourist areas, but to the wilderness and mountains and rivers. Many of the places she went, the cultures frowned on women showing too much skin. Often she went alone and it was just safer.

"I'm dressed," she called out, the moment she was close to the pool of steaming water. She dipped her hand in cautiously. It was hot, but not too hot. Hot enough to take the ache out of her muscles and bones.

She felt him before she heard or saw him. He was directly behind her, close, but not touching. She knew because she felt safe and warm. He had a way of making her feel as if she was in a cocoon of safety. Which was silly when she actually was scared of him.

"You are not afraid of me."

107

Andre's arms went around her waist from behind and he pulled her close to him. Her back to his front. He was barechested. Her heart stuttered. Was it possible to have a heart attack just because a man showed off his chest? She wasn't even looking at his bare chest, and already her heart was racing. Faltering. Stopping and starting. *Misbehaving.*

"Actually I am, Andre."

"No, *csitri*, you are afraid of change. Of what this means to your life. I do not blame you for that. You love your family, and they live in the United States and I live here."

"Um. No. That's not what I'm afraid of."

She tried to pull his hands away from her waist so she could swing around and face him, but his hands didn't budge. Strangely, his grip didn't even feel tight. More as if she were encased in a cocoon of safety.

Andre lifted her off her feet and, stepping into the pool of steaming water, set her slowly down. The hot water was a shock, but it felt good. She was short and the water came easily to her shoulders so she was mostly submerged when she was standing.

Andre took her hand. "There is a smooth rock you can sit on over here. Do not go too far into the middle because the pool becomes deeper."

He settled her onto the rock and then sat close to her. Close enough she could see him breathe, far enough away that she couldn't easily reach out and touch all that muscle in his bare chest.

"If you are unafraid of change, and I disagree that you are, what is it, *sivamet*, about me that frightens you?"

She closed her eyes against the velvet mesmerizing tone that just sank into her body and made her boneless. And spineless. And captivated. The hot water lapped at her breasts. She had very small breasts, but they were sensitive, and the water, coupled with his voice, wreaked havoc on her senses. Her nipples were hard and her breasts ached for his touch. The water actually felt like tongues licking over the slight curves.

Why did Andre have to be so gentle and sweet? Armend would have eaten him alive. Armend's friends would probably kill him when he tried to defend her. She would have to be fast. She knew martial arts and she could defend him. Andre. The gentle bear of a man.

Teagan knew he was watching her closely because she felt his eyes on her. He had that kind of intensity. He remained silent, expecting an answer to his questions. She'd already made a huge fool of herself, what did it matter if she continued?

"I'm way over my head with you," she blurted out. "You're this gorgeous stranger, sexy and sweet, and I don't have a clue why I'm so drawn to you, but I am. If we were talking about a little fling, I might consider it, although honestly, I don't know if I would. I'm private. Really private. I don't want some mindless night with a man, no matter how good it is. And that tells me I'm in real trouble with you."

"Why?"

Could he really be that clueless? She risked a glance at him. Yeah. He was watching her all right, with darker blue eyes, the midnight color that told her he wasn't happy with what she was telling him. He was totally focused on her, making her feel as if she was the only woman in his world. Not just there in the cave, but in the entire world.

She let her breath out slowly. "Andre, you get to me. Inside, I mean. That means when we walk away from each another it's going to hurt like hell. For me at least. I don't think it's a good idea to chance it."

"Why would we walk away if we both want the same thing?"

109

She waved her hand at the cave. "Do you have any idea how bizarre this truly is? We're in a cave in the mountains. I'm on a visa. You live here. We've known each other for a few hours."

He nodded his head slowly. Thoughtfully. She let out her breath again, reminding herself to breathe once in a while. At least he was listening.

"I have been in your mind. It is not a few hours for me, Teagan. When I healed you, I connected us together. You can touch my mind, see inside of me any time that you wish. Once you do that, it will not be a few hours for you either. You will see me, the person that I am, just as I see you."

She hadn't expected his answer. He'd been in her head a couple of times reading her thoughts, so maybe he did know more about her than she was comfortable with anyone knowing—especially a gorgeous man who looked kind of godlike.

"I can't read your thoughts, Andre. I'm a healer, but I'm not psychic. I don't have that kind of gift—or curse, depending upon how you see it."

"You can, Teagan. You feel the connection between us. It is too strong for you not to."

She shrugged and shifted a little. The water swirled around behind her, lapping at her back. She slid a little on the rock until the water covered her to her neck. The heat felt good, easing the tension out of her shoulders and neck. The backpack was heavy after miles of hiking and a bit of a strain on her small frame. She packed as light as possible, but when packing for a month in the mountains, and maybe a day or two in a town to wind down, the weight began to add up.

"I've never read anyone's mind in my life. If I could, Andre, do you think I would have put myself in Armend's hands? Clearly he's a psychopath. He's a killer. A serial rapist and a killer. If he was telling the truth about his friends, he isn't alone in that kind of behavior. If I could read minds, I would have known when we were at the university. I tutored him. I was with him five days a week, sometimes a few hours a day. He never once acted anything but friendly toward me. He never crossed a single line with me. In fact, not one of the women he dated looked a thing like me."

Andre studied Teagan's face closely. She was upset now. He couldn't blame her. She knew Jashari had killed several women, and he didn't want her taking on that responsibility, but she was. He could see it on her face.

"You can read my thoughts because we are connected, Teagan. At this time, you will not be able to read others."

Her gaze jumped to his face. He could get used to the way she looked at him. He hoped she would always look at him like that—until the end of their days and well into their next life together.

"How? How do I do that?"

"Be still. Let your mind be still. You have not wanted to look into my mind. You fear what we can become together, not me. You fear what you will feel for me, not me. You already know I would never harm you nor would I leave you brokenhearted. It is impossible."

"What does *csitri* mean?" Teagan asked again, wanting to hear his explanation a second time. She loved the way the word sounded in his language.

"Little one." He ran his fingers through his hair. "But more. Little slip of a girl, little slip of a thing. Little one. It is a term of affection. Simply that. An exact translation is difficult."

She made a little round *O* with her lips for just a brief moment. He'd seen her do it a couple of other times and once he looked at her mouth, it was difficult to pull his gaze away. She was finally relaxing, the hot water easing the tension

111

from her. He couldn't allow her to sleep, not until dawn, not until she was so tired that when he pushed sleep on her, she wouldn't realize the difference.

"Quite a bit earlier you used the word *susu*; what does that mean?"

He was silent for a moment, turning over in his mind what he would say to her. He couldn't lie. She was his lifemate, and lifemates didn't lie to each another. He shrugged, tried to be casual when the meaning was anything but. "It means, 'I am home.'"

Teagan frowned, trying to comprehend what for now was impossible for her to understand and it would only frighten her if he tried to explain.

She bit her lip, something she clearly did when she was nervous. "What else did you say in your language? *Sivamet?* Was that it? Something like that. It sounded beautiful."

"That one is a little more complicated," he admitted. "There is no precise translation I can give you. More like, of my heart. To my heart. In your language a man might say, 'my love.' But again, it is more. A little different." Her eyes went dark. A deep chocolate that seemed to melt into a liquid. So dark the color was almost black, but not quite. "What else?"

He shook his head. "I am only making things worse between us, and that is not my intention, Teagan. I want you to feel comfortable. I have not been in the company of humans ... people ... for a long while and I have forgotten more skills than I remember."

"You haven't been around people much?"

She was sharp. He was giving her too much information. She needed time to process. More time to be with him and grow closer. He didn't want to bring her into his world too fast. In fact, he wanted her to choose his world. To choose him. If she didn't, he would find other ways to persuade her,

112

but in the meantime, he wanted to court her. To give her the things his woman deserved.

He shook his head. "I've talked more to you than I have to anyone else in a year." Centuries. But he couldn't say that and not have her ask questions.

Teagan made little patterns on the surface of the water. He found the swirling images fascinating. "Andre? I know there's a monastery around here. At least I've done a lot of research of this area, and there are enough references to it that I believe it's there. Up higher, shrouded in all that mist. Were you there? Is that why you haven't talked to anyone in a year and now you're living here in this cave?"

She lifted her gaze once more to his and the impact hit him low. Like a punch. Hard. Desire burned through him. Her dark eyes had gone even softer. She thought she understood where he had come from and why he was there.

"No one goes up there, Teagan. Those inside are not like one would expect monks to be. They are warriors. They believe in the ancient ways. It would not be safe to go into their home."

He knew that wasn't an answer. He also knew how she would take it. She had a soft heart. Her compassion was going to be her greatest downfall if someone didn't look after her. He was even a little disappointed in her beloved grandmother for not stopping her from traveling alone.

Teagan began to draw a picture in the water, right through the swirling patterns. His breath caught in his throat. She drew curls of fog and inside of it, there were faces. He recognized the faces. Women Armend had killed. He had called to their spirits and joined them together in the whirling mist so they could see justice brought to the man who had betrayed their trust, raped, tortured and murdered them.

Teagan was in his head whether she knew it or not. There

was nothing good for her to find in his memories. His life had been endless battles against the undead. If she dug too deep, she would find things that would scare her to death. She'd try to run and he couldn't allow that—it would be far too risky for both of them—and then she'd be more afraid than ever. How had she managed to get inside his head without him knowing? Was that a part of the gift her grandmother had passed on? If so, it was an extremely dangerous one.

Andre was fairly certain Teagan's grandmother had been approached and recruited by the human society that hunted vampires. They were a secret order that left their legacies of murder to their children. They were ruthless and used pawns to draw out anyone they wanted to accuse of being the undead. He had heard rumors that vampires had actually penetrated the society and were using it to find women psychics. Women like Teagan and her grandmother.

If both women were proverbial tuning forks for those who needed blood to survive, and they were capable of slipping undetected past shields into the heads of both Carpathians and vampires alike, they were extraordinarily dangerous to his people.

He went very still, looking inward, reaching for the small intruder. He wanted her in his mind, but only looking at the memories he gave her, not finding everything at once. Eventually she would know everything—she would have to. As his lifemate, there would be no secrets between them, but not now. Not this early. She was still finding her way with him.

It took a moment to find her presence. Her spirit was barely there—and it had nothing whatsoever to do with being a tuning fork or even his lifemate. This had everything to do with her being a genuine and powerful healer. She was such a strong empath that she had reached out to him without either being aware of it. Or was she?

"Teagan?" He said her name softly. Whispered it. Put the emotion into it that he couldn't say aloud without her bolting.

Her head came up. Her eyes met his. She was having a difficult time looking at him. She didn't trust or understand the physical attraction she had with him. It was new to her and too extreme and intense for her to be comfortable with. Still, right there, in the shy, dark chocolate of her eyes, he saw the truth. She knew she had touched him. She wasn't looking for memories. She wasn't trying to see who he was. She wasn't there for herself and so to her, denying she was in his mind was the truth. She was there to heal him.

"You have already healed me," he said softly. "Teagan. Just you. Just your existence has healed me. There is no need to take on the burden of what I was before you came into my life."

"You didn't go to that monastery because of your faith in God," she said. "I know you didn't. You hunted . . . men. Like a bounty hunter. Or a sheriff. I can't tell which and it doesn't matter. You've had to kill and it took its toll on you."

Andre was amazed at her insight. She got it right, and yet she got it wrong. He hadn't lost his emotions or the color in his life because he'd killed. He could kill, even men he had grown up with and considered his friends, *because* he lost his emotions. He was Carpathian and that was the life of the male. Their world became bleak and stark and gray after a couple of hundred years. He needed Teagan. Only she could give him back the light. And she had.

His heart hurt. He put his hand over his chest, feeling the steady beat. She could do that. She had that much power. Just because it mattered to her that he felt sorrow for his lost friends, for those who would never know the sheer beauty of what he had sitting next to him in a pool of hot water. He wanted to curl his fingers around the nape of her neck and pull her to him. He knew she would come, but neither had many clothes on and he wasn't certain of his own discipline, not after waiting for so many centuries for her. Not after giving up hope. Not after finally finding her and tasting her.

"I cannot remember ever having anything in my life that was mine. Anything or anyone that I wanted for myself. I hunted, yes. I did my duty to my people and the cost was great, but I knew the cost before I ever accepted the job." That much was true. Every ancient had a choice. Every Carpathian male. They didn't have to hunt the undead. They didn't have to keep humanity safe. For Andre, it had been a calling, and he was good at it.

"Andre, you don't have to tell me this," she whispered softly.

The sound of her voice, so silky and threaded with concern, moved through his blood like a stream of molten gold. He could almost see musical notes in the air between them when she spoke in that tone.

"I want to tell you. I need you to understand what you are. Who you are. All those years I hunted, I knew there was only one woman and I looked for her—for you. I have found you. I knew the moment I heard your voice and felt your touch. The moment I looked at you. You cannot give a man like me the taste of paradise and then take it away. I do not work like that."

She frowned. "I don't understand what that means."

"It means I want you to at least consider the possibility of getting to know me. Of letting us explore this situation with the idea we can have a future together."

She bit her bottom lip, instantly drawing his attention to the full, tempting bow of her mouth. She didn't think she was attractive or sexy and he found her both. Intensely so. Beneath the water, his body stirred. Grew hard. Thick. Full and painful. These were not things he was used to, but he didn't attempt to block out the sensations. He was grateful for them. Grateful he could feel them. Grateful his woman had been given to him.

"I wouldn't know what to do," she admitted.

It wasn't a firm no. If anything, she wanted to do just as he asked. He liked her personality. He liked the way she was compassionate and intrepid and willing to face her fears. And she was afraid. He could feel it. He had to resist the urge to tone it down for her. That wouldn't be fair to her, but he knew if her fear grew much more, he would have no choice. He found there were some things a man like him couldn't take. His woman being uncomfortable was one of them.

"I know what to do, Teagan. Give me a chance, that is all I am asking." For now. He couldn't say those words, but they hung in the air between them.

Her teeth bit down harder on her lower lip, and he suppressed a groan. He leaned toward her. "I am making an effort to go slow here, *sivamet*, but if you keep doing that, I will no doubt kiss you again and then things will heat up. You will be even more frightened. That will not be good."

"What? What am I doing?"

"Biting your lower lip. Giving me ideas, and I have enough of my own."

She blinked. Quit biting. Sent him a shy smile. "I like the idea of getting to know you better, Andre. I'm here for a month. I really do need to find a particular stone in order to facilitate healing my grandmother's insanity. I also need to tell the authorities about Armend and where his body is so his family can have some closure. Hopefully the authorities can find some of the bodies of the women he killed and give their families closure as well. If you're going to be up here . . . "

"I will be wherever it is you are," he said firmly.

"Do you know these mountains?"

He nodded.

"Well, clearly I need a guide. We can spend time together while I'm hunting for the right stone."

He leaned back, automatically adjusting the rock behind him to the contours of his body. For the first time since he'd found his lifemate, he fully relaxed. She'd agreed to stay with him. To get to know him. He planned on making very good use of that time.

"You haven't told me anything about *your* family, Andre," Teagan said.

"My immediate family is long gone," he said. "But I have extended family. Quite a bit, actually. The three closest, those I would consider brothers, have left for the States. I grew up with them. Triplets. Matais, Lojos and Tomas. I was to join them, but I had one last hunt."

"I thought you'd quit."

"I had. It did not work out that way. I ran across the trail of a very dangerous killer. He is still up here somewhere."

Her breath caught in her throat. He heard the soft gasp. "That's why you were wounded. You caught up with him. Andre. Were you planning on ... " She hesitated.

He opened his eyes. He felt her then, in his mind. He couldn't throw her out after inviting her in, but he could lessen the impact of what she saw.

"You were hoping he took you with him when you killed him," she said, in a soft voice that left his heart stuttering.

He shrugged. "Hunting and killing men is not an easy task, *avio päläfertiilam*. I have grown tired. And out of the blue, I find you. My greatest reward. The one thing I never expected to ever find. My savior."

Her eyes searched his. He let her see it was true, both in his mind and his eyes. She lowered her long lashes, but he knew she was grateful he was alive.

"It is a strange thing to give up on life. To think one welcomes death only to find that had they allowed their life to slip away, their greatest happiness would never have been experienced. I want to have the opportunity to go to the States, find my brothers and tell them this. It is important they know. It is important they realize we cannot give up. Not ever. Our lives can change in an instant at the least expected moment."

"I'm really that for you?" Teagan asked.

"You are really that for me. My miracle. My savior. And I want you to stay with me. Please stay with me and get to know me before you make a decision."

She nodded her head. "I want this to work out, Andre, as strange as it all seems, I really do."

7

Teagan groaned and tried to roll over. She couldn't move because something heavy draped over her waist and something even heavier hooked over her thigh prevented movement. She gave up the fight and snuggled deeper into the warmth.

She was comfortable. Definitely not in her sleeping bag. She was very warm, and she knew for a fact she wasn't in her jeans. Still, she didn't—or couldn't—open her eyes. She felt hungover, but she hadn't been drinking at all. For a long time, she lay there, drifting somewhere in the twilight between waking and sleeping.

Andre. Gorgeous Andre. He was so lost and alone. His life didn't seem to be a happy one. She didn't understand that. She'd grown up in the happiest of homes. They might not have had all the money in the world, but they were certainly the richest of families when it came to love.

She could call any one of her three sisters, tell them she

needed them, and they would be on a plane trying to get to her. She had that. She'd always had that. And Grandma Trixie had shown her what unconditional love was. Teagan had always been a little different from her sisters. She was driven to learn. She sought knowledge all the time. She even snuck out of the house as a child and they'd find her in the library reading everything she could get her hands on. She was never punished. Not really. Not for anything she did. But truthfully, she loved her grandmother so much she didn't want to disappoint or hurt her, so she'd toed the line as best she could.

But Andre. Her heart broke for Andre. He looked at her as if she were his world. He'd just met her, but she was his lifeline. The healer in her had been inside his mind, trying to figure out how best to aid him. She'd found overwhelming sadness. His emotions were strong, almost as if they were so new to him he had trouble toning them down. He didn't go out during the day. An allergy to the sun, perhaps? He hadn't told her, and she didn't know if she could heal that.

She *had* to get up. Strangely, she knew, without looking at her watch, that there wasn't much left of the day. If she wanted to scout around and try to find the trail of what she was looking for, she would have to get moving. Andre had explained to her that he slept during the day and wouldn't wake up until evening. He was a heavy sleeper, he said. If she woke first, not to worry, he'd be up soon after.

Andre also made her grit her teeth when he'd said, in his commanding, *sexy* voice, that she shouldn't leave the cave under any circumstances, to wait for him. She didn't like bossy. Or commanding. Still, it was sexy on him, but then everything was.

Teagan took a deep breath and forced her eyes open. Andre's chest was pressed against her face. One of his arms wrapped around her waist. She could tell by the way it felt that he was not only asleep, but *sound* asleep. His leg was over her thighs, pinning her to him. She didn't move because it felt nice up against him.

He'd carried her to the raised mattress. It was not too soft and not too firm, exactly how she liked her mattresses. More, it was far better than her sleeping bag and the ground. She couldn't believe the sheets were clean. So was the blanket. That made no sense at all. Even more strange, the faint scent was lavender, one she particularly loved. How sheets and blankets in the wild of the Carpathian Mountains managed to smell like her favorite scent, she had no idea. Still, it was wonderful, and she wasn't going to complain.

She didn't remember Andre getting into bed with her. Surely she would remember an event *that* big. Yikes. She was actually in bed with Mr. Gorgeous and his very hot accent. Just lying next to him sent all kinds of very erotic and inappropriate thoughts through her head. And visions. All sexy. Some of the things made her blush. Okay. All of the images made her blush, but some were impossible to do, weren't they? And why was she lying next to Mr. Gorgeous thinking of things he could do to her that she'd never even heard of?

She'd never woken up in a bed with a man, and even though he was asleep, she wasn't certain what to do. She didn't want to wake up. The weird thing was, she couldn't hear or feel his heartbeat—just like before when he'd been injured. He'd been a monk. Maybe they taught that in the monastery. He had very long hair. She loved his hair, although she would never have thought she'd be a fan of long hair, but if that was a monk kind of thing—and all this time she thought monks were bald—maybe she could be a little grateful that he had wanted to be a monk.

"You don't look monkish," she murmured. "You're too

122

gorgeous." What if *all* the monks in the monastery were hot? "I can just see the monk at the gate. 'Sorry, buddy, you're not hot enough to be one of us. We're the hot monks. We only allow gorgeous men like Andre inside these gates. That's the reason we're up here in the clouds—to hide away from all the women of the world so we don't wreak havoc among them.'"

She pressed her face against his chest. "Did you escape, Andre? Are they looking for you because you're the one they use to measure the hotness of any applicants?"

Sivamet, go back to sleep. You make me smile when I should be resting.

She went very still. She heard him in her mind. He wasn't just reading her thoughts, he was communicating with her, and his heart was still not beating where she could hear or feel it. He heard her. While he was sleeping. He heard her.

"Now I'm totally embarrassed. You weren't supposed to hear that. And why isn't your heart beating properly?"

She ran her hand over his heart. She lifted her palm and replaced it with her lips. A compulsion. She couldn't stop herself. Strangely, she felt as if she'd done that before. She dared to use the tip of her tongue, to slide it over the very place his pulse should be.

Do not play with fire, csitri. I am a man, after all, not a saint.

There was lazy amusement in his voice. He didn't move. Not a ripple of a muscle. Still, he knew she was playing with fire.

"I have to get up."

No.

One word. Authoritative. Very Andre when he wasn't being the sweetest man on earth. Bossy almost. No, super bossy. She wasn't the kind of woman who did bossy very well. Ask her grandmother. Ask her three older sisters. Ask anyone.

123

She lifted his heavy arm and slipped out from under it. His leg was an altogether different proposition.

Teagan.

There it was, the voice that made her go weak. She didn't move for a moment, because the way he poured emotion into his voice curled her toes and stole the air from her lungs. She almost wanted to obey his commanding "no." Almost. But she didn't want to stay in bed. She had work to do and she doubted if she could climb around a mountain in the dark.

She shifted his leg, withdrawing her own in one surprising burst of strength and determination. She was free, but something kept her right there, glued to his side. She was reluctant to leave him unprotected while he was sleeping the sleep of the dead.

Her body felt strange and sluggish, like she was trying to move through quicksand. Even her mind felt fogged and a little hazy. If they hadn't been up for hours talking, she might have thought something had been in the tea, but she knew better. Determined, she forced her body into a sitting position.

Stay here, Teagan.

She actually felt a compulsion to obey. It was strong, and that scared her more than the command in his voice. She had never wanted to obey anyone, not from the time she was a baby. Grandmother Trixie often regaled anyone who would listen with tales of how even before she could walk, she didn't like anyone telling her what to do.

Feeling as if she wanted to oblige him when he used that tone with her shocked her. More, it told her she was getting in over her head, and it was way too soon for that. If she felt that way now, what would it be like if she fell in love with him? She could never disobey Grandmother Trixie because she loved her so much. Loving Andre was out.

She turned her head to glare at him, but she couldn't see his face. Or his eyes. His hair covered both. She took a breath. It wasn't his fault that everything in her wanted to surrender to him. She realized she didn't want to leave him. Not just because he was unprotected, but because she needed to be with him. That was even more terrifying.

Did he feel the same way? Was that why Andre's sweetness had turned bossy? Maybe he was as frightened of what was happening between them as she was. She didn't want him to feel afraid or sad or so alone, like she'd felt when she was in his mind. Her throat burned. Her eyes stung. For him. For his life. For the fact that her life had been so wonderful in spite of losing her mother before she ever had a chance to know her. Andre's life had clearly been so different.

Once she felt the onset of tears, it was imperative to get away from him. She didn't cry in front of anyone. Not ever. She was the tough girl in martial arts, the one that could hang no matter how banged up she got. She was the same when she climbed. She refused to give in to the panic attacks when she was up over thirty feet on a rock that was mostly slab. Well, okay, she cried her eyes out, but then she got ahold of herself and climbed even when her heart beat so hard she thought she'd have a heart attack.

For the first time she tried to answer him back, mind to mind. *Stay asleep. I just need a little alone time.*

She gasped and pulled back, touching her fingers to her lips. Sorrow was in his mind. Terrible images of battles. Of blood. Of death. Of friends. He hadn't just been in law enforcement in some capacity, he had been a soldier of some kind as well. He'd seen terrible things. It was no wonder he had sought the peace of a monastery.

She felt such sorrow in him. Just touching his mind had shaken her. She leaned close to him, swept back his hair and

125

daringly brushed a kiss over his mouth. For one moment, in her mind, she felt him try to shake off his sleep, but he subsided. He wasn't feeling sorrow, it was more like a dark determination that didn't bode well for her. He definitely didn't want her to leave him.

"I'll be back," she promised, and forced her body to move off the bed.

The moment her bare feet touched the floor of the cave, she drew them back up. She didn't mind dirt or rocks. She was okay with insects. In fact she liked and respected most insects for their extraordinary part in the world's ecosystem. But she detested slime. She looked down at the floor. It looked like regular dirt without a hint of water on it, but it hadn't felt that way. Water and dirt would have equaled mud, and she hadn't felt mud, she felt *slime*.

Teagan pulled her foot to her and inspected the bottom. The sole of her foot was perfectly clean. There wasn't even dirt clinging to it. She frowned and looked around her. That was another thing. How could she see? She wasn't using her flashlight and the torches had long since gone out, yet she could see. She'd been in caves quite often and she'd always used a headlamp or her flashlight. Mostly the headlamp.

She pushed her hands back through her hair, smoothing the braids at the side of her head and then running her fist down the long, thick ponytail of braids that fell down her back. Was this all real? Maybe her grandmother's illness was genetic and she was having hallucinations.

"Great. I'll be seeing vampires next. She was right about the monastery. I just have to meet a man named Gary and then I'll know I'm as nuts as she is," Teagan muttered to herself.

She had to be alone and figure out what was going on. She couldn't stay in Andre's company like this. He was everything that drew a woman like her. A fantasy man. He probably wasn't any more real than the slime she thought she'd put her feet into.

She put her feet down quickly and forced herself to stand up. Her stomach lurched. Definitely slime. She didn't look down at her feet, but walked quickly to her backpack and found her clothes. With every step she took, she felt as if the slimy substance covered more and more of her feet, crept up her ankles and even onto her legs.

She had to breathe deep to keep from gagging because the sensation was so real. Still, when she went to pull on her jeans, there wasn't a single bit of dirt on her feet or legs. The moment she had her jeans on, she put on socks and her hiking boots. Thankfully, with her boots on, the sensation of slime disappeared.

She dragged on a shirt and slung her climbing shoes around her neck just in case, and then with one last glance back at Andre's still form, she took off through the labyrinth of chambers to make her way back to the entrance she'd used to enter the caves—only it wasn't that easy.

First, the ground seemed unstable when she tried to move quickly. The floor of the cave rolled and pitched as if there was an earthquake. She lived in California and she'd experienced a few minor quakes, and although this was like an earthquake, it wasn't the same. She stood very still and waited to see if she was dizzy, but it wasn't an inner ear problem either. When she looked at the ground, it seemed stable enough. She even used her headlamp to make certain, but nothing was out of the ordinary.

She forced air through her lungs in an effort to clear her head. Every step she took away from Andre seemed harder than the last. Her body felt leaden, her feet heavy. She had to contend with that as well as the pitching floor. That served

127

to disorient her, and she took a wrong turn somewhere along the line.

The moment she realized she didn't recognize the chamber she was in, she backtracked. The rolling of the floor made her feel sick. She hadn't eaten, nor did food sound good to her. Even the thought of her beloved tea ritual made her feel slightly nauseous.

Grandma Trixie drank tea, and they had their own ritual. She always used cold water in the kettle and brought it to a rolling boil. Loose leaf tea was the only *real* tea, according to her grandmother. All three of her sisters believed their grandmother was totally right about that. The few times Teagan had snuck a teabag for convenience when she was backpacking, the tea wasn't quite as good, but then she was certain she'd been brainwashed from the time she was an infant.

The memories rose of her grandmother and sisters sitting around the table laughing together, drinking tea with her. She loved those times. She was ten years younger than her next sister, and she knew her older siblings treated her more like their child than their sister, but it was straight-up love. She'd been doted on and loved from the moment she was born.

Her sisters had a different father, a man who had, sadly, died of cancer. From everything Teagan had heard of him, he had been a wonderful man and he loved and took care of his family. Her mother had been devastated when he died and she'd moved in with Grandma Trixie. Ten years her mother had been alone with her girls and Trixie, and then she met Charles Drake.

He'd been a charming, sweet-talking man who, by all accounts, chased after her mother for months. The moment he heard she was pregnant, he was gone and things turned ugly. Her mother had died in childbirth, and Grandma Trixie and her sisters welcomed the baby with open arms in spite of her father. Teagan never wanted to see or meet him. She was given her mother's maiden name and she loved it.

Teagan allowed the memories to absorb her mind so that her body went into automatic and instinctively found the way through the chambers to the entrance. There was that shield again. The harp strings in a terrible jumble, but through them, she could see the light of day.

She sank down onto the floor of the cave, right beside the tangled strings and began to tune to each note, just as she had when she first encountered them. She was faster than before because now she knew what to do. She had them all in place and began to rise when one string broke, flipped over the others, knotted and ripped the other strings free, tangling them all over again.

Teagan scowled at the mess. In another couple of hours she would lose the light for certain. If there were wolves hanging around the area, she didn't want to be out at night, but she needed to go breathe the air, climb a little, take some time to think about what was happening.

Mostly, she hated the fact that even while she made plans to go out on her own, every single cell in her body demanded she turn around and run back to Andre. That was—unacceptable. Totally unacceptable. She had the sudden fear that when she left him, he needed her. That he wasn't breathing. That his heart had stopped.

She sank down in front of the narrow opening, staring out into the light. Her skin prickled as if the sun might burn her. She'd never really had that problem, a legacy from her mother, but still, the feeling was there. She wanted to weep and run back to Andre, to hold him close and assure herself that he was breathing. She didn't. Like everything else, the slime, the earthquakes, the labyrinth, even this shield, it had to be an illusion.

Andre was just fine. She was the one who needed to control her thoughts. She took another deep, calming breath and lifted her hands. She sang the notes softly this time, putting more power behind them, more resolve. As each string slid back into place, she tied a knot by adding a note on. Still, she was ready, standing this time at the end of the song. Just as she sang the last note and the string untangled, she pushed through the barrier into the light of day.

The sun hit her hard, nearly blinding her. Her eyes burned. She had to close them and rummage blindly for her sunglasses. It had to be the altitude. Her eyes were never particularly sensitive to the sun, but not only did her skin feel like it was burning, her eyes hurt—so badly tears leaked down her face.

She pulled on her windbreaker to shield her bare arms from the rays of the sun as she took a careful look around. The mountains were truly beautiful and wild. This range was one of the last preserves for wildlife in Europe. If her eyes hadn't been swimming with tears, she would have enjoyed the view. She squeezed her eyes closed and took off her glasses so she could wipe the tears away.

Unfortunately, her mind kept returning to Andre. Asleep—or dead. Unprotected—or dead. Alone—and dead. She definitely wasn't enjoying the view. Andre Boroi had been living just fine without her.

Existing. Not living.

She blinked. Her breath caught in her throat. She was a distance from him. He was definitely sleeping. Now was she hearing things as well as hallucinating?

Come back to me, Teagan.

Yep. There it was. The sexy, but bossy tone that grated on her nerves. She was not going to give into her strange compulsions or obey a stranger just because he was the sexiest man alive with his looks and his accent and his sweetness. Who knew sweet could be bossy? And most likely, along with all her other hallucinations, his voice in her mind was just that.

"I really am going crazy. At least my illusion is a very hot man with a sexy accent, and not some vampire who wants to suck my blood and make me into a crazed, bloodsucking monster, and have me sleep in dirt or a coffin filled with dirt," she whispered aloud.

She needed to get back on track and find the stone that would not only cure her grandmother, but cure her as well. She had crossed the path once, thought it was in the cave, but she knew she'd taken a wrong turn.

It was entirely possible that there was something in the cave that caused hallucinations. That seemed a likely explanation, although she was out of the cave, but with every step she took away from it, she felt a terrible weight pressing down on her. Sorrow built. Andre was dead. She knew it. She had to go back. She couldn't go on. Not without him.

Teagan found her face wet, and this time it had nothing to do with the sun. She touched her face and looked at the smear of tears on her finger. Definitely time for another illusion, like his voice. Of course it didn't come. Illusions didn't work that way.

She pushed herself to keep walking back to the point where she'd first felt the tuning in her body toward the stone or gem she needed. She was cautious. She did her best to stay low to keep some cover around her. She continuously scanned the mountain below her for any movement. She didn't want a surprise visit from Armend's friends or the wolves that had killed him.

That brought her up short. If Andre was an illusion born of something in the cave, did that mean Armend was still alive and hunting her? The thought made her shiver and she nearly turned back, but if she went back, she'd be inside the cave where the origins of the trickeries began. Was it possible that the shield had been designed to keep people out of the cave so they wouldn't get caught in the delusions?

Worse, what if Andre *wasn't* an illusion, but real, and he'd been caught in the cave and couldn't get out? She bit hard on her lip. She just couldn't stop thinking about him, no matter how hard she tried. The harder she pushed him away, the stronger the compulsion became to see him.

"I have to think of something else entirely or I really will lose my mind," she muttered. She was nearly to the spot where she'd found the trail of the stone. Now, she wasn't certain she should try to find it. The sun was beginning to dip in the sky, and she had to occupy her mind to keep it away from thoughts of Andre. Clearly, thinking about Andre was insanity.

She looked up rather than down the narrow path. The mountain range wasn't particularly suited to bouldering and she was far from any well-known climbing crags. There was no mention of this area in the climbing circles, but the sides of the cliff jutted out in places and a few larger boulders butted up to the mountain, or were a part of it.

Once she focused on a climbing problem, the rest of the world dropped away and that was the only thing in her mind. Climbing was a form of escape to her, a place she could go and no one else could follow. Of course, she did climb with friends and they shared beta—information—with one another and encouraged one another, but for her, once she focused on a new problem, that pushed everything else out of her brain and her mind became still.

She *needed* her mind to be still. Right now, even with spotting a potential climb, her mind kept reaching out to Andre—trying to tune itself to his—but she found only emptiness. A void. Silence.

She tried calling to him mind to mind. *Andre. I'm going a little crazy here. I'd appreciate an answer. Something. Anything from you.*

It was crazy to reach out, to expect an answer, but she needed him. She needed to know he was real. The connection was so strong. That didn't make any more sense than her grief, especially when she no longer was certain whether or not Andre was real. If he wasn't, and she'd been hallucinating, then that meant Armend was still alive and was looking for her. If Armend was looking for her, she was nuts to be out in the open, bouldering. If he was dead, she had to tell the authorities.

Andre *felt* real to her, more real than Armend. She was certainly more concerned about him. She couldn't understand the need to rush back to the cave and see if he was there or not. Check on his heartbeat. She should have checked to make certain he was breathing. Grief filled her again, pressed down on her chest until she could barely breathe herself. Once sorrow got ahold of her, she couldn't make it go away.

She had to stop. There was only one way to keep from rushing back to the cave, or worse, throwing herself over the cliff. Her gaze went up, searching. She knew exactly what she was looking for and she spotted a boulder about seventeen feet high. It butted up against the mountainside just to the left of her position and looked interesting.

This part of the Carpathian Mountains wasn't known for limestone, it was too high up, although the gorges were cut deep throughout the entire area, and she was just a little shocked to see that part of the rock behind the boulder, showing through the dirt and small grasses growing out of cracks, looked from a distance like limestone.

She took a deep breath and forced her mind into that place that was hers alone, where nothing else could touch her.

Climbing. She needed full concentration in order to work through the problems. There was no room for error. No room for any other thought. She let the face of the cliff consume her mind.

Teagan took another careful look around for safety and then made her way slowly toward the boulder. It was taller than she first thought, beautiful, with an almost vertical face. Midway up the vertical face, the boulder jutted out fairly far into a striking roof. Limestone ... a mix of grays, blues and pearly white. She took a moment to take in the sight of it. So perfect just sitting there waiting to be climbed. The desire to climb it was strong. Her eyes devoured the rock looking for the easiest way up.

She then inspected the ground. She didn't have a crash pad with her and if she fell, which was possible—even probable—when bouldering, she didn't want to break something. Of course there was no avoiding it, she would have to go over the roof and then falling wouldn't be an option anymore. The ground felt soft and had a lot of give to it. There were a few small rocks beneath the boulder, but she tossed them out of the way, all the while looking up at the shining surface of the rock.

She stepped back, frowning, trying to make out a sequence up the face and assessing risk. The start looked somewhat challenging, with only a couple of small crimps and tiny footholds. The next hold was pretty high up, but with a little dynamic power she was certain she could stick the big pinch and then maybe throw a heel hook to gain the sloper. Definitely the crux would be sticking that next sloper, but the heel should make it solid. A little committing with no pad, but at least all the hard moves seemed to be at the base. It looked significantly easier after that. In fact, the roof appeared to have plenty of large hand and footholds. She just hoped it was solid and not hollow up there.

Limestone had a rough, almost sandy feel to it. Often, when climbing, she took the skin off her fingers, but there was something about the texture that called to her. She liked limestone. The stone itself could be used for enhancing other healing stones. The properties in limestone were centering and positive. Climbing limestone always made her feel better.

Teagan decided to go up the down climb and investigate further. She couldn't have asked for a better down climb. The boulder nested next to the mountainside, almost as if it was part of the cliff edge creating an easy and safe walk off. Upon looking down from on top of the boulder she saw that there was indeed a series of juggy holds going up from the roof. Definitely the hard part was over at that point. Relief and excitement flooded her. It was the best she could have hoped for. Falling from there would be rather unlikely and to her it was an acceptable risk. She made sure to clear off the little bit of debris she found and brushed off some of the top out holds she could reach from above with her climbing brush.

After making her way back to solid ground, Teagan sat down to put on her climbing shoes. Not much to look at, the once vibrant yellow leather was now quite faded, but the sticky rubber soles were new from a recent resole and the webbing for the Velcro straps had also been replaced with some bright orange webbing that stood out in sharp contrast. The talon shape of the toe box and thick reinforced heel spoke of her love of overhang climbing, and while they weren't the best shoes for vertical or slab climbing, they were her comfort shoes and ones she reached for the most often with disregard to the climbing terrain. They were dirty, smelly, and to the average person looked two sizes too small for her feet, but she loved them like a best friend and once warmed up they fit her perfectly.

Teagan shook her head. Her mind was beginning to

wander to Andre in spite of her best efforts to keep herself focused. The moment she allowed him into her head, he consumed her just as much—if not more—than the climbing did. Sorrow pressed down until she was crushed under the weight of it. Grief was all too real. She choked on it, and before she could stop herself, she actually had a foot on the trail, as if she could run back to the cave and either make him real, or save him.

She forced her body under control and then her mind. She was strong. Whatever hallucination had taken hold of her in that cave had to end before she lost her mind completely. She was going to make herself crazy by allowing herself to think about Andre. She had to shut him out. She just needed a few quiet moments to relax with something that totally consumed her, totally occupied her brain. She needed to clear her mind, focus, and let go of everything else. Resolutely, she turned her attention back to the rock and immediately felt the tension dissipate as the problem solving took hold of her mind. A puzzle to solve. A challenge.

Her shoes felt stiff and tight as she pulled them on. She warmed up her body by doing some shoulder pushups, a few leg swings and stretches. She tried wiggling her toes in her shoes and slowly she felt the leather start to warm and mold to her feet. After a little while she took her shoes halfway off, leaving her toes inside to keep them warm.

She concentrated on the boulder one more time, mentally climbing the problem first from start to finish, visualizing herself doing the moves successfully. After she had successfully topped out the climb in her mind she pulled the shoes back on completely, and sure enough they felt perfect.

The first contact with the crimps felt a little cold but the solid rock felt amazing to her hands. Teagan felt the rock lightly at first and then once she found the perfect place to crimp she pulled onto the rock, her feet resting on tiny footholds. She moved into a small under-cling with her right hand and then set herself up for the dynamic throw with a scrunched drop knee. She focused on the pinch, quickly calculating the amount of power she would have to give as she visualized herself sticking it.

She launched herself, letting out her breath and tightening her core, the wave of extension starting from her left toe and flowing through her body in one clean motion. The moment of contact with the hold was empowering. She absolutely loved the feeling that big moves gave her. She felt strong and in control of her body. Being in control was important to her.

The pinch was wide in her hand and the texture was rough. Her right foot cut as she hit the pinch—it would have been impossible to keep it on with her small size—but her left foot stayed on as she stretched to full extension and kept her core from collapsing from the strain. The hold to the right wasn't the best for a hand, but it made a nice heel hook and she quickly took advantage, giving her right foot a home.

Teagan locked off on the pinch, drawing her body up and close to the rock face as she pulled down on the heel to gain the large sloper. She cupped the top of it with first her right hand and then matched with her left. She kept her body under the hold as she pulled straight up, trying to maintain the best friction with the smooth hold. As she moved up she transitioned her heel to a toe as she stood up to gain the next smooth ledge above her. It was worse than she had hoped for, but good enough to keep going.

The sun fell further and shades of gray sliced through the light. With the gray came wisps of fog sliding like fingers toward her. She glanced up the mountain toward the highest peak where the mountain was always encased in mist. Now, the mist had crept down so that up above, where the cave

137

was located, the fog appeared so dense it looked impenetrable. She didn't want to be on the boulder when mist came in that thick.

The next few moves she executed swiftly, and she was happy to find her assessment correct in that the holds got better toward the roof. It was a little daunting coming up underneath the roof thinking about going over it and committing to the slab above it, but seeing those large holds gave her the confidence she needed. As she made her way up she tapped on the larger holds to make sure they were safe.

The last thing she wanted was to go flying to the ground because she pulled on a hold that was too fragile. The moves might be easier now, but the risk was far greater. Caution was now her main priority and each move was executed with more care and more precision than the last. She took her time, feeling around for the most solid holds, using as little force as needed, and planning her strategy over the roof. Her caution paid off and soon she stood above the roof, feeling satisfied. Only a few more moves to go to reach the summit.

She glanced up and saw nothing but gray mist. Her heart stuttered. The fog couldn't have come in that thick, or that fast. There wasn't even a wind. She became aware of the utter stillness. There was no drone of insects. No cries of birds. No slight movement anywhere around her.

This wasn't good. She was clinging to the side of a boulder, a good sixteen feet in the air. She felt cautiously for her next hold. She had practically memorized the climb in her mind before she'd started and she knew where it was, her body just had to pull the information from her head.

The first fingers of mist reached her, touching her hand when she reached for the small pocket she knew was there. She jerked her hand back and nearly lost her footing. Gasping, she caught at the rock again and flattened herself against it.

The moment the fog had touched her skin, she knew it wasn't normal fog.

The vapor was sticky, clinging to her, sending prickles of fear through her and a chill down her spine. Worse, something moved in the fog. She knew it. Whatever the entity was, it was using the spreading mist as concealment.

She bit her lip and tried to calm her breathing. She had to think. Was it better to take a chance and bail, or climb the last foot into the fog? Her skin crawled, and the dread grew to full-fledged fear. *Something* was coming toward her and it felt wholly evil. She had to make a decision and she had to do it fast.

8

Teagan made a quick decision to down-climb while she had the chance. Getting back over the roof was going to be difficult, but once under it, it would help shelter her from the fog. Her skin hurt as if burned from the small exposure to the unnatural droplets of mist. She knew it didn't make any sense, and maybe it was another hallucination, but if so, it was one that was all too real.

She swore out loud, words her grandmother would have washed out her mouth for, as she looked at the skin of her hand. There were blisters. Actual blisters. She sucked in her breath. Real or not, she was getting the hell out of there before the fog enveloped her entire body.

Reversing her moves back over the roof, especially with her body trembling and her heart going crazy, was unthinkable, but sometimes life required the unthinkable. Going up into the blistering fog would be a far worse fate. She turned her focus on her breathing and tried to steady her mind to the task at hand. She moved cautiously but swiftly down to the roof. As she made her way to the roof's edge she tried hard not to look up at the fog or down at the ground. Relax. She had to relax.

The easy moves coming up over the lip proved much more difficult in reverse. Not being able to see the footholds under the roof was a challenge. Plus the holds that felt so nice on the ascent felt much worse when lowering her body over the edge. Her left leg dangled under the roof feeling around for the good foothold she used coming up. She knew it was there somewhere, but it was as if it disappeared completely. As she struggled to find something to stand on she made the mistake of looking up. Fog was coming toward her fast. She needed to get under the roof immediately.

Teagan lowered herself even further, dangling both feet under the roof and feeling around. There. A large pocket was her salvation. She felt immediate relief as she shifted her weight onto it. She moved quickly, underclinging to the roof with both hands. Able to see under the roof now, she made a few more moves until she was safe. Sweet relief flooded her as she huddled under the cover of the roof just in time to escape the fog.

She still was in danger though. The fog could still reach her, and now she was trapped half way up the rock face. The roof provided some coverage but the fog was still moving. As crazy as it sounded, it almost seemed as if the fog was hunting her. She needed a plan and she needed to move quickly.

Risk assessment was a common part of climbing and she let that part of her brain take command. Staying put seemed like suicide. She could probably down-climb the next two moves, but after that it would be extremely challenging and she would probably be too slow if the fog kept coming. Two moves and then she would need to drop if the

141

fog was still coming. A ground fall, but a risk she would
have to take.

~~~~~~~~~~~~~~~~

Teagan was gone. Andre's eyelids snapped open and he rolled
to his feet, waving his hand automatically as he'd done for
centuries to conceal his identity. Fresh clothes, fresh body,
completely clean as if he'd just stepped from the shower and
dressed. He was already running and on the third step he
shifted, becoming nothing more than tiny molecules streaking through the caves toward the entrance.

He reached for her, the connection strong, and found he
was already too late. She had inadvertently strayed almost
straight into the hands of one of Costin Popescu's lesser
vampires.

Teagan. Hear me.

He burst into the open. The sun had just set and darkness
had not taken over, but he could see the thick, dense fog. It
was oily and sticky to the touch. It carried the taint of evil.
His heart thudded in his chest and he tasted terror in his
mouth.

Teagan, answer me now. He pushed command into his
voice.

He felt her then, a small stirring, tentative, following the
thread of the path he created between them. She was afraid.
She felt the danger surrounding her.

Andre? There was a tremor in her voice.

I am coming to you. He tamped down his fear for her—fear
that he would be too late. Just as he'd been so many years ago.
He had many memories, but over the centuries they had faded
until he had nearly forgotten them. But not the one he wanted
to forget. The one that haunted him every rising.

I don't know if you're real.

Her breathy little voice tugged at his heartstrings. She was frightened, and he detested that she was. Even more, he detested that she had reason to be.

Look around you, sivamet.

The fog is close. Teagan's voice wavered as if she was going to lose it but then she continued. *Something's in it. It touched my skin and felt wrong. It felt evil. Where it touched my hand burns. I down-climbed and I'm just under the roof which gives me a little shelter but I can feel the fog reaching for me.*

He cursed silently in his ancient language. She was definitely in the path of a vampire's trap. If the fog had touched her skin, the vampire sitting in the middle of that web had just felt the tug on one of his lures and he would be creeping out to find out what kind of prey he had snagged.

I'm sorry, I know I sound a little hysterical, but I don't want whatever is in the fog to get me.

She thought he didn't believe her. He wanted to wrap his arms around her and hold her close. Protect her. But right at this moment, he needed to push those thoughts away and make certain he *could* protect her.

I need to see around you. Keep your eyes open. I am in your mind and I can see through your eyes. You have to do this, Teagan. You have to be brave and allow me to guide you through this.

He felt her take a breath. Felt her release it.

Okay, but if I'm crazy like my grandmother and you're just a figment of my imagination, I'm going to be really angry with you.

That nearly broke him. He wouldn't lose her. He couldn't. Not to a vampire. Not to anything. She was full of life. Strong. And she had a sense of humor that got to him every time.

Andre knew he was close to her, but close wasn't good enough, not now that he knew the vampire was also targeting her position. He slipped further into Teagan, using their strong connection, gaining her vision. He felt her first

143

reaction, a revulsion of feeling his presence so strong in her mind.

Her terror mounted. Whatever was coming for her was close and she didn't know what to do, whether to push off the rock and chance landing wrong, stay where she was and let the fog reach her, or try to down-climb to get a little closer to the ground before letting go. Having made it over the roof, she at least had a shot at not hurting herself when she jumped.

No. Do not do anything yet. Do not move.

She clung to the side of a boulder feeling vulnerable and exposed. Her body trembled. She wasn't certain if he was real or part of a hallucination, yet she remained as calm as possible, even though sharing her mind with him totally freaked her out. He wasn't altogether certain what the term *freaked out* meant, but he assumed it wasn't good.

The fog is almost on me.

Now there was panic creeping in. He felt it in her and realized the emotion was coming from him as well. He forced himself to shed all emotion. He couldn't afford to think of her alone and vulnerable.

Look around you. I need to use your vision. Let me see exactly where you are in relationship to the fog.

He pushed into her mind, connecting to the pathways of her vision. At once he could see her predicament. The dense, unnatural fog was creeping toward her. She either had to allow it to envelop her or she had to let herself fall from the boulder.

Keep looking at the fog.

His tone left no room for argument. His tone, his power, every bit of ancient warrior and primitive predator was in his voice. He stared into the fog, using Teagan's eyes. Even as he streaked through the darkening sky toward her, he narrowed in on the vampire making his way toward Teagan.

A fierce wind hit the fog, rushing through the dense, sticky trap to disperse it. At the same time, clouds burst open to dump rain on the vampire's web in order to neutralize the acid hidden within the mist. A bolt of light shot into the mass of fog, lighting up the sky, illuminating the interior of the fog.

Like a deadly spider, the vampire was exposed, crawling cautiously toward the boulder and his prey. The bolt nearly pierced him, forcing him to spring sideways, screaming at the intense light hitting him. For a moment he was completely visible.

Teagan screamed and closed her eyes to block out the sight of the monster. His mouth was wide open in a hideous shriek, revealing his sharpened, stained teeth. His eyes glowed red and burned with a fierce need to rend and kill. He had hair, but it was dirty and hung in mats.

"This isn't real. This isn't real," she chanted.

Open your eyes, Andre commanded. Relentless. Implacable. Forcing his will on her when it was the last thing he ever wanted.

The vampire shrieked again, and this time Andre heard the piercing cry of triumph. The lightning hadn't struck him, hadn't even slowed him down. He wanted his prize, the rich, fear-based adrenaline-spiked blood in the human. It would give him a rush, give him more power for the battle he knew was coming.

Open your eyes, Andre hissed a second time.

She obeyed. *I have to let go. The boulder is slick now, making it harder to hold on to. The fog is coming. I have to jump.*

Not yet, he cautioned. He saw the fall in her mind. She'd fallen many times bouldering and she knew what she was doing. He could help, floating her to the earth. *Wait until I tell you. I am close by. He is dropping out of the sky toward you. Wait.*

He felt her need to close her eyes, but he refused to allow it.

145

He needed to see what was happening. He smelled the vampire now and felt the taint of evil in the air. He detested that smell and he knew, no matter how long he lived, he would never forget it. Just like the memory of his youth, that smell was locked into his mind for all time.

Do not take your eyes off of him.

More than anything else she wanted to look away, to jump and try to run, but Andre held her locked there, refusing to allow her to give in to her fears. He refused to allow himself to feel her terror, but he couldn't drown out the hammering of her heart, and he knew that sound drew the vampire like a beacon.

Breathe, slow your heart, sivamet. Do not give him the satisfaction of hearing or feeling your fear.

He didn't want her to shut down on him. He should have known she wouldn't. She stared up at the rapidly descending monster.

Now.

Andre didn't need to tell her twice. Looking down, Teagan made a visual with her landing zone then lowered her body as far as she could off the holds she was on. She let go with a small push off the slab and lifted her arms above her head to keep from hitting the rock as she fell straight down. She'd come off boulders before and she knew to keep her feet flat so there was less chance of twisting or breaking an ankle. She focused on relaxing, on keeping her body straight, and on softening her knees for impact. She fell like a cat, experienced, as if falling from this height toward the hard earth without a crash pad was the most natural thing in the world.

She expected to hit fairly hard. The fall was a good distance and she knew without the crash pad, most likely it would jar like a son of a bitch and she'd fall back on her butt. Two feet from the ground, she actually seemed to decelerate, as if time had slowed down and with it her. When her feet touched the ground, it was truly the softest landing she'd ever had.

"What the hell?" Teagan whispered, earning her another mouth washing from Grandma Trixie. "What the *hell* is going on." If she was getting her mouth washed out with soap, it might as well be for a good reason.

Already she was on the ground, pulling off her climbing shoes and wiggling her toes to make certain she could run again. Grabbing her hiking boots and socks, she dragged them on as fast as she could.

The monster in the fog dove at her from above, his eyes burning right through her, streaking like a comet from outer space. She sat there, frozen for a moment while the thing just got bigger and scarier. Long, bony arms reached for her. Each hand had long, talonlike fingernails. They looked more like blades than fingernails and she was certain each was razor-sharp.

"This isn't real. This is an illusion. This isn't real. This is an illusion." She chanted the mantra over and over.

"You will give yourself willingly to me," the thing snarled, exposing his fangs as he pushed his will at her.

Her body jerked, notes in her head jarring and crashing, so far out of tune the sound hurt her ears. She didn't take her eyes from the face. He was muttering something and he looked triumphant. She realized he believed she wasn't moving because he'd forced a compulsion on her. She did hear a buzzing along with the jarring notes, but her mind refused to tune itself to the jangled tone. The sound made her stomach heave and bile rose in her throat.

"Uh. *No.* Not in your wildest dreams, you freak," she snapped. "Illusion or not, I'm outta here."

Her heart pounded louder, hammering in her chest, and she forced air through her lungs, remembering at the last

147

moment what Andre had said about not giving the creature the satisfaction of hearing her fear. Andre wasn't real either, damn it. She was just losing her mind. The tea had mushrooms in it. Something. Right? There was no stilling her pounding heart.

The hell with that, Andre. You aren't here. I'm scared and there's no way to control it. Still, she didn't move.

I am with you.

How could he sound so arrogant? So confident? How could his voice resonate with her body so that every single cell reached for him? And where exactly was he? Invisible? Because she sure as hell didn't see him. Real or not, if this thing wasn't a vampire, she didn't know what it was. She was in desperate need of her grandmother's vampire-hunting kit.

The undead's burning eyes widened and his mouth stretched in glee as he reached with his bony hands. She rolled fast, away from the rock, toward the narrow trail. One fingernail sliced open her shoulder, ripping right through the material of her shirt. It burned like nothing she'd ever experienced before. She had presence of mind to snag her climbing shoes as she rolled and then she was up on her feet and running.

"This isn't happening. There's no such thing as vampires. There's *really* no such thing. I'm freaking out, having delusions!" she shouted as she kept running. "They aren't real. My grandmother's nuts and I'm nuts, too. None of this is real."

Something streaked above her head. She felt a terrible wind nearly blowing her off her feet as it passed, and then she heard the vampire shriek. She halted abruptly, spinning around, her heart in her throat. Andre was in front of the vampire, his solid body between her and the terrible creature. His fist appeared to be *inside* the undead. Black blood ran in streams down the monster's chest. He spit venomous acid at Andre. Teagan knew it was acid because it burned Andre's skin.

"Oh my God. Oh my God." She wanted to cover her eyes and ears and drown out the horrible creature's screams.

The vampire raked viciously at Andre's face, tearing long, deep furrows in the skin, opening the wounds so that his blood flowed freely. She gasped as the creature drove his teeth into Andre's throat—or rather tried to do so. Andre, with his fist and now part of his arm buried in the vampire's chest, turned his body slightly so the teeth sank into his shoulder.

The vampire tore out a chunk and, to Teagan's horror, began gulping at the blood. She couldn't run. Real or not, she couldn't leave Andre to face such a terrible thing. She had no garlic, she didn't have a stake or holy water, none of the things in her grandmother's kit. She looked around and found a rock, one that would fit her hand, her only weapon. Maybe if she bashed the vampire over the head, it would give Andre time to sharpen a stick so he could drive it through the heart of the beast. If her grandmother actually wanted to hunt and kill one of these things, she really *was* nuts.

Teagan caught up the rock and took two steps toward the two men. Andre was covered in his own bright red blood as well as black blood from the vampire. Everywhere the vampire's blood touched him, it burned his skin. Worse, it burned *through* his skin. Teagan didn't see how he could stand the pain.

Andre didn't move. Didn't defend himself from the raking nails or the savage teeth. He began to pull his arm back. There was a sickening sucking sound. The vampire screamed horribly, the sound nearly bursting her eardrums. She saw his hand rear back, his terrible, bony fingers curl into a fist, and he drove it straight into Andre, right beneath his heart. She cried out and ran toward them.

Stay back.

Andre's voice was absolutely devoid of all feeling. There was no pain, no fear, only a cold order.

Teagan skidded to a halt. There was no question of leaving. Andre's body was shredded by teeth and talons. Up close she could see the vampire had buried his hand in Andre's chest, and Andre was withdrawing his own arm from *inside* the monster's chest.

This was a scene straight from a horror movie—and she hated horror movies. Seriously, under any other circumstances she would have thrown up. There was no time for that sort of thing, even if the bile was right there in her throat. She had the rock, and Andre was being ripped to pieces.

He's killing you. I'll just bash him with this rock. I don't have good aim and if I throw it, it might hit you. That was strictly the truth and she tried to convey it to him with her voice, but even mind-to-mind—especially mind-to-mind—her voice was all wobbly and she sounded like a girlie-girl ready to cry. She wasn't ready to cry. She was ready to run. If that thing tore at her face and neck and gulped her blood like it was doing to Andre, she'd just keel over and faint or something.

Teagan took a firmer grip on the rock and stepped closer. The moment she did, Andre yanked his arm. The sucking sound was horrendous. Disgusting. Bile rose into her mouth, and the vampire shrieked loud enough to wake the dead. Rocks began rolling down the cliff face above them.

She couldn't move, her gaze on Andre's hand as he withdrew it from the vampire's chest. His fist was closed tight, his arm and hand covered in black blood. Everywhere the blood touched him—which was pretty much everywhere—his skin was burned. In some places, particularly his hand and upper arm, the burn was all the way to the bone. She gagged and pressed her hand to her mouth, unable to pull her horrified gaze from Andre's closed fist.

The vampire withdrew his hand from Andre's chest and rich, red blood poured down Andre's clothes. The creature seemed captivated by the flow of blood, unable to look away from it even as he reached, with a torn cry, for Andre's closed fist.

Andre opened his hand and tossed the prize away from him. Teagan saw it was a heart, blackened and shriveled. It rolled away from the vampire and Andre.

Stay back. Well back.

It was her only warning and the tone of voice Andre used had her scurrying back several feet. The movement immediately garnered her the monster's attention. He leapt past Andre and straight at her.

"I'll kill her if you don't give it back to me," the vampire snarled.

Teagan stepped into him as he reached for her, sweeping with one foot to take his legs. As the monster went down, she slammed the rock against his temple and leapt back, running toward Andre, with a vague thought of protecting him.

Teagan.

Andre simply said her name softly. In that voice. The voice that could move mountains or just plain send shivers over her body. His tone sounded just a little exasperated this time, but she couldn't imagine why when she'd just knocked the crazy monster to the ground. She heard a sound and glanced behind her.

Her heart went into double time, thudding now. The vampire was already on its feet. So much for rocks and martial arts.

Andre held out his hand to her. The good one. The one not covered in black acidy goo.

151

She hurried to his side. "We need a stake. Do you have a knife?" She tore off her shirt and ripped the hem while he ignored her, doing something else with his hands.

The vampire roared and ran toward the heart on the ground. The heart actually rolled toward the creature. The entire thing was just plain wrong. She kept tearing at her shirt, telling herself none of it was real.

A bolt of lightning slammed down, hitting the blackened heart, incinerating it completely. The spear of white-hot energy leapt from the heart to the vampire. He disappeared in the bright glow, completely disintegrating to become a fine ash.

Andre had shoved her body behind his to protect her, but he hadn't moved a muscle. The lightning strike didn't seem to affect either Andre or her. Andre did the craziest thing and actually stuck his arms and upper body in the white, glowing light. The moment he stood straight, she shoved the torn shirt into the hole on his chest.

"We've got to get you to a hospital. I can heal things, but this is really bad and you're losing way too much blood."

His hand slid up her back to the nape of her neck and then into her hair. His fist closed around the thick ponytail of braids. "Would you like to tell me what you were doing?"

His tone gave her pause. He spoke slowly. Distinctly. Enunciating each word as if he was biting them out between his teeth.

She looked up at his face streaked with blood because she had no choice. He tilted her head back, forcing her gaze upward. She had presence of mind to keep pressure on the wound in his chest. He looked terrible. He had four long, very deep grooves in his face, and his shoulder was a hideous mess. Part of his chest was streaked with deep furrows and then there was the hole the size of the vampire's fist.

He should have been on the ground. She expected him to topple over any moment. Her legs were shaking and she was ready to fall to the ground in a girlie faint, but she had to take care of him. He didn't seem to understand that he was wounded. In shock maybe. That had to be it.

Teagan made certain her voice was soft, yet very firm. "Andre. You're injured. You need to sit down and let me take care of this as best I can. You're losing way too much blood. It's already dark and the wolves are going to smell this and come running."

He ignored her as if she hadn't spoken, his gaze moving broodingly over her face. His glacier blue eyes were hooded and in spite of everything, all the gore and shock and horror of what she'd seen, his amazing eyes were just plain sensual.

"Tell me what you were doing, Teagan," Andre repeated. "Do not make me ask again."

He reached for her hand, his fingers shackling her wrist, and he tugged it to him, even though she tried to resist. She needed both hands for pressure. He ignored the fact that she was saving his life when he used that scary tone, the one that said she'd better come up with an answer.

She opened her mouth to respond, but he was looking at the blisters on the back of her hand and arm from the acid in the fog. He dipped his head, and she felt the stroke of his tongue. Her breath stopped right in her lungs. Her throat closed. Her eyes burned and she blinked rapidly to stop the tears.

Teagan knew exactly what he was doing. He stood there, torn and wounded beyond anything she'd ever seen, and he was healing her minor little burn. "Andre." She whispered his name.

His tongue was a caress. A velvet rasp that sent shivers through her entire body. Everywhere he touched, the pain vanished. She wished she had a healing agent in her saliva in order to heal him, but her gift didn't work that way.

His gaze jumped to her face, and she took a breath. He was angry with her. Not just angry, but *really* angry. She had thought the vampire scary, but Andre's anger turned the air around them into an electrical heat wave. Worse than the lightning bolt. He waited in silence, one hand in her hair, the other holding her healed wrist. She knew he wasn't going to allow her to help him until she answered.

"Andre, this is all crazy to me. I mean, I came here to find something to heal my grandmother's mental illness, and suddenly everything around me is making me think I'm mentally ill as well. I thought you were a figment of my imagination. A really, really gorgeous one. I should have known I couldn't conjure up someone like you. I don't have that much of an imagination ... " She trailed off.

Her mouth was running away from her. When she got nervous, she talked and anything in her head came out of her mouth. She pressed her lips closed, willing him to understand.

His eyes softened at her ranting, but she could tell he wasn't finished with the topic. "We are too exposed here. We have to get back to the cave. That one has friends."

"We need to get you to a doctor, Andre. You need a transfusion. Seriously. This wound can kill you."

He wrapped his arm around her waist and pinned her to his side. "Close your eyes, Teagan."

"What?" She pressed her hands tighter to his chest now that she had both of them. "Andre, you're in shock."

"Close your eyes."

She huffed out her breath in total exasperation. He was really annoying when he went all he-man macho on her. She wasn't certain all that gorgeous was worth the attitude. Still, she closed her eyes to humor him. She had the feeling healing him was going to be up to her anyway. How could they climb down the mountain at night? Especially when there were wild animals everywhere and he was bleeding so much. Her shirt was soaked with blood. It had been useless tearing it. Now she was in her bra, and he could see she had no curves whatsoever.

She had that floating sensation again, the one she got when he kissed her. She lifted her lashes just a little and saw the ground was gone. *Gone.* Completely gone. As in she really was floating. Well, flying. Technically she wasn't flying. Andre was flying and just carrying her along for the ride.

She closed her eyes again because if she didn't, she was going to scream very, very loud. "This isn't happening. This isn't happening. This isn't real. This isn't real." She chanted the denial, hoping she was caught in the throes of a terrible nightmare.

Just in case it was real, she continued to press both hands tight against the hole in his chest. The wind on her body told her it was true, that she was flying through the air, with his arm locked around her waist. If he was flying, what did that make him?

Um. Andre. What exactly are you?

Teagan peeked at the earth below her. Yep. Still flying. Maybe it wasn't the best time to ask him. What if he realized she peeked and he just dropped and smashed her body against the rocks below? She knew how to fall, but not from this kind of height. It made her a little dizzy to look down so she closed her eyes again and pressed her bloody shirt tighter into the wound on his chest.

I hunt the vampire.

A monk *and* a vampire hunter. A monk, a law enforcement bounty hunter type and a vampire hunter. She hadn't really expected that from him.

She bit her lip. He really wasn't very good at vampire

155

hunting. Maybe he hadn't been at it long, with his career change and all. He didn't even carry holy water with him. Or stakes. Or a bible. She had seen her grandmother's vampire-hunting kit, straight off the Internet, and in spite of the fact that, at the time, she thought her grandmother was absolutely bonkers, the old case with all the hunting tools inside was very cool. Surely if he really hunted vampires he'd have all kinds of weapons.

May I make a teensy observation? She didn't want to upset him, but he needed a little help.

I cannot wait.

That sounded a little sarcastic but she forged on. *If you had the proper gear, such as the stuff Grandma Trixie has, you wouldn't have to get so close to that horrible creature and you wouldn't get so torn up.*

The only way to destroy a vampire is to remove his heart and incinerate it. Even if you chop off his head, he can repair himself. He is the undead.

She kept her eyes closed tight. She would have put her hands over her ears and sang *la la la* at the top of her lungs to keep from hearing him. Unfortunately, he was talking in her head, so that luxury was impossible and she had to keep her hands pressed to his chest to keep more blood from spilling out at such a high altitude.

Is that really true?

Yes.

Well. That was bad news for her grandmother. She'd been swindled on the Internet. So many people preyed on the elderly. She'd have to check into that and maybe find a way to put those people right out of business.

Andre landed lightly and ducked inside the cave, still holding her to his side. She didn't open her eyes to see how the two of them managed to fit through the narrow entrance, because if she had any more surprises she was going to just scream. Hysterically. Scream at the top of her lungs. She needed to focus on healing him so he wouldn't die.

"Andre." She kept her eyes closed as he carried her through the various chambers. She was fairly certain they were headed back to the room where he had a bed. "You're going to need a transfusion. Do you know your blood type? I might be able to donate my blood if we're compatible."

He paused at every entrance, just for a few moments, and she risked peeking. He seemed to be the one setting up shields, because right before he turned away, she saw notes and strings shimmering for one moment before they disappeared.

"We are compatible."

He was still angry. She opened her eyes and glared at him. "Are you still angry with me? I'm saving your life. I sacrificed my shirt and I only have a couple, which necessitates going into town to buy more. And I need to find the stone to heal my grandmother."

"Your grandmother is not in need of healing, although I am beginning to suspect you are."

She narrowed her eyes at him, giving him her most fierce scowl. "That wasn't nice. You can put me down anytime, Andre."

He paused to weave another shield over the last entrance before his hidden chamber. Ignoring her squinty eyes and really mean scowl—the one that always made her nephews behave—he carried her right on through to his living quarters. Only then did he set her on her feet.

She kept her hands pressed tight to his chest. Deciding the best thing to do was ignore his bad mood—she was fairly certain she'd be grumpy if she had a hole the size of Texas in her chest—and take charge.

"Get over to the bed, Andre, and lie down. I can take a look at this and see what I need to do to fix you up."

He looked down at her for a long time. He sighed. "I will heal my wounds as best I can and if you are willing, I gladly accept your offer of blood."

"Of course I'm willing. We have to do this now, Andre."

"I have sustained far worse wounds than these. His fist didn't penetrate that far."

He sounded as if he was running out of patience. And she was being as nice as possible under very horrendous and scary circumstances. She thought it best to point that out to him.

"Just so you know, I'm not my grandmother. I do *not* hunt vampires. In fact, I prefer to believe they are figments of the imagination. Or at least very bad nightmares. So if I'm not handling this situation to your satisfaction, I apologize." She gave him another glare just to make certain he realized *she* was losing patience with him.

"I told you not to leave," he said, and his voice went scary quiet. Soft. Scary soft.

If she didn't have to press so hard into his bleeding chest with both hands she would have given an airy wave to dismiss his orders. As it was, she decided to be the bigger person. After all, he was bleeding to death right in front of her.

"Just because you've sustained worse wounds, doesn't mean this one won't kill you. Get on the bed, Andre. And I mean it." She used her firmest I-mean-business voice.

158

hunters and the strange things he could do, she wanted to heal him. The compulsion grew in her the longer she looked at the rake marks on his face and the blood flowing from his chest.

"I *was* afraid," she conceded. "I was afraid I was losing my mind. Please, Andre, let me help you. I'm not as good a healer as you, but if you don't let me help, you're not going to make it. You can't sustain this kind of blood loss."

He turned and went to the bed, taking her with him. He sank down on the edge, his thighs apart, and he pulled her down in front of him, seating her with her back to his front. "Sit still."

He made it an order, and she winced, but at least he was sitting on the bed instead of standing like some crazy macho man, bleeding out right in front of her.

"I will heal my wounds and then I will need your blood. I will be weak and I need you to sit still and not fight me."

She turned her head to scowl at him over her shoulder. "I *volunteered* to give you blood, Andre. And just an FYI, I bashed that vampire over his head in order to save you. I may have wanted to run away, but I didn't." She knew she sounded snippy, but *as if.* She was the one who pointed out he needed a transfusion, and she'd told him she would donate if they were compatible.

Andre wrapped both of his arms around her waist and drew her close. She was instantly aware of her bare skin. She'd almost forgotten she was in her bra and nothing else. She'd just have to pretend she was wearing a bathing suit. It wasn't like she could jump him when he was so seriously wounded.

She huffed out her breath and turned back around. It was far too daunting to look into his eyes. She couldn't see pain there, but she *felt* it beating at her. Both the healer and the empath in her needed to help him—needed to heal him. She couldn't bear for him to be wounded one more moment.

Still, she had the feeling that he wanted her to experience this with him. He was still angry. She felt that as well, a kind of repressed fury smoldering just below the surface, and she wasn't altogether certain why, but she wasn't going to ask. She just wanted him to get on with however he was going to heal himself.

Teagan felt him push into her mind. It wasn't subtle, the move was a powerful force, a thrust, taking him past every natural barrier and merging them together in one swift take-over. He felt predatory. Invasive at first. Scary. He poured into her, filling her. Finding her. *Seeing* her.

The swift invasion was both uncomfortable and yet sensual at the same time. He would know her every secret. Every thought. Everything. She couldn't hide from him. Still, she'd been lonely all of her life. She'd been different and never fit anywhere. He filled those empty spaces with—him. With his strength and courage. He gave himself to her, opening his mind to her.

She found herself moving into him. Not as decisively as he had her; she was delicate about it, not wanting to give him the feeling of a takeover. She discovered that where she'd *felt* alone in the midst of her family and friends, Andre had *been* alone. There was a huge difference.

He had no one. Not a single person of his own. She really was that person to him. She poured herself into those lonely places, just as he had done for her. She felt him still. His hands tightened, nearly cutting off her breath, but she didn't move. He needed this. He needed her, and she gave herself to him.

Heal yourself now, Andre. I want to be with you when you do.

She might never be able to do what he could, but she could share it with him, just like this. Mind-to-mind. It was far more intimate than she could ever imagine. She couldn't lie to him. Or hide from him. She saw him just as he saw her.

161

He had killed to protect others. She saw that. She accepted it. Andre's integrity shone through every other thing about him.

She actually felt him shed his body. It was almost a glorious thing to feel him lose his ego, his more human and predatory senses, all sense of self, to become nothing but a pure white healing light. She felt his heat like a laser, moving through his body to find the hole in his chest. He repaired veins and arteries, removing the venom from the places where the vampire had clawed through his flesh. She hadn't even known vampires had venom in the nasty, razor-sharp talons they called fingernails.

He was meticulous, taking his time, and she realized it took a great deal of energy to stay out of one's body and do the kind of work that he was doing. She was so deeply connected to his mind, moving with him through his body that she could actually feel the repairs and "see" them, although it was much more of an internal visualization.

She could feel hunger clawing and raking at him, a brutal assault that tore through him worse than the pain of his wounds. Weakness. Weariness from too many battles. Too much death. She saw the gray, bleak world he'd occupied before she'd come to him and the one of color and passion after she'd arrived.

Her breath caught in her throat as she realized his skin was becoming smooth. Perfect. The black vampire blood that seemed to contain acid had been bathed away right there in the battlefield, when he'd incinerated the vampire and somehow controlled a lightning bolt. *He'd controlled a lightning bolt.* How freakin' awesome was that? She'd tried not to think about it, in fact, she'd just buried it deep so she wouldn't have to figure out how he did it, but even that wasn't as awesome to her as the miracle taking place in his body right before her eyes.

162

The tattered remains of his shirt were gone, leaving his chest bare. She was up close, and she could see every torn muscle. The rake marks. The bites at his neck and shoulder, great gouges of flesh and muscle torn away. The worst was the fist-sized hole that had gone about an inch deep in his chest and looked to be positioned over his heart. Of course, he had those old circular scars she always wanted to touch—or kiss. Those felt so much a part of him, she couldn't imagine his body without them.

There were four long furrows, extremely deep on his face, long rake marks torn with the horrendous talons the vampire had on his hands. One of the lacerations was very close to Andre's left eye. Even as she stared at the wounds, they were closing. *Closing.* Right in front of her from the inside out. His healing abilities were insane, off the charts, his gift a true miracle.

As a healer, she'd seen things that shocked and amazed her. As an empath being merged so close with him, feeling his pain and hunger, seeing his life so empty, tears burned behind her eyes for him. Everything that she was, the very essence of her reached out to him. She poured herself into his mind in an effort to soothe him, to make his life better in some way.

Mostly she looked at his skin, now nearly perfect. There were no scars other than the older, circular ones. Not on his face. She could see faint lines there, where the wounds had been, but she knew those would fade with time. She couldn't stop herself from turning completely around to face him so she could run her hand over the smooth muscles, feeling with the pads of her fingertips as if touching him would help her process how he had managed such a phenomenon.

It was the most powerful and beautiful thing she'd ever witnessed. She had no idea how much time passed, but she

163

knew he was swaying with weariness. The blood loss was too great and he desperately needed a transfusion.

Teagan wanted to call him back to her, but she didn't know if that could possibly damage him further so she remained silent, but stayed close in his mind. Almost abruptly he returned to his body, and for the first time she felt him shudder with both pain and exhaustion.

She smoothed her fingers gently over his face. He touched hers and his fingertips came away wet with tears.

"Andre." His name came out breathy. She hadn't wanted it to, it just did. "I've never been able to heal anyone in my life like that. You're a gift, a precious gift to the world."

Andre's eyes went from pure glacial ice to electric blue. Intense. Beautiful. She could see the long lashes, lashes that should have made him look feminine, but there wasn't one single feminine thing about him.

"Do not cry for me, *sivamet*. I have you now and all of it was worth the wait." He murmured the words softly as he brought his finger to his mouth and tasted her tears.

"You need blood, Andre. I can feel how weak you are. We have to give you a transfusion." One of them had to be practical. His sitting there looking gorgeous and hot with nearly perfect skin didn't negate the fact that she could still feel his weakness and exhaustion. Blood loss would do that.

"I have dreamt of the taste of you," he whispered softly.

She found herself shivering in anticipation. Of what, she wasn't certain. He swept back her hair, pulling it from around one side of her neck to the other, so that the long ponytail of braids hung over her right shoulder. His touch, as his thumb slid over her skin was sensual. So was the way he moved her hair. Her heart jerked in anticipation. Of what, she had no idea, only that her body came alive at his touch.

He dipped his head. She felt his breath, warm against her

skin. His tongue stroked once, twice, over the pulse beating so strongly in her neck. She had time for one swift inhale, the comprehension. She was in his mind. The terrible hunger. The craving for her unique taste. For the rich substance she could provide to help heal him. She made a single sound, started to lurch forward, knowing she couldn't escape. His arms were two steel bands wrapped around her middle.

His teeth sank deep and she cried out at the bite of pain. Instantly it gave way to pure, erotic pleasure. She shared his mind and she felt his body heat. Harden. Need. For her—only for her. There was no other. There could be no other.

She felt her blood go into his body, spread through his starving cells to answer the terrible need. She tasted—exquisite. Perfect. His fingers splayed wide over the bare skin of her abdomen, rubbing gently as he fed. She relaxed into him, gave him more of herself, willingly allowed him to feed from her.

She knew he hadn't put a compulsion on her, and she saw the memory of the first night with him, that first taking of her blood. She hadn't remembered and yet she did, right then, that thrill, the same erotic feeling she had right now.

Teagan couldn't help herself, she reached up to stroke the perfection of his face right where the vampire had torn the long lacerations, so deep they should have scarred. She'd wanted to smooth those faint lines away. She'd wanted to heal him. To be the one who could take away his pain.

You have done so already, avio päläfertiilam. Everything I have done these long centuries has been wiped out by the gift that is you.

He swept his tongue over the two small holes, closing them, and she murmured a protest, not wanting the sensation to end. His mouth continued to move on her neck, tiny kisses and stinging bites followed by his soothing tongue. He turned her easily, using his strength to set her on his lap.

She was deep in an erotic-filled daze, lulled by Andre's

sheer sensuality. She could barely think, feeling so connected to him. Having him in her mind. Being in his. Even the way he took her blood, she could accept that—accept him because he didn't feel evil at all, not to mention it was the most sensual thing she'd ever experienced.

It was entirely possible that the erotic-filled daze was just Andre and the chemistry between them that seemed to be off the charts. She had nothing to compare him to, because he was the only one she felt anything for.

"It is your turn, Teagan," he whispered. "You will take my blood."

That managed to penetrate her sensual fog. She frowned, her eyes searching his for the meaning of that. Because no. He was hot. Gorgeous. Her body was singing and hot and needy, but ... *you will take my blood*. Okay. *No*. No way. No *f-ing* way. That was not happening no matter how hot he was. No matter how sensual. Even if he was dying.

She took a leap right off his lap and got exactly nowhere. She didn't move one inch. She planted both hands on his chest, right above where the terrible wound from the vampire had been and tried to shove him back on the bed, so he'd at least lose balance and she could escape.

"You will take my blood for our second exchange."

Not only was there command in his voice, but she felt the subtle "push." Her heart went wild. Her mouth went dry and she exploded into action, uncaring that he was injured or that he was hot and gorgeous. *Second time?* She'd taken his blood once already? And didn't remember it? He'd kind of left that part out.

She tried for his eyes, and then his throat, but she found she couldn't move. Not a single muscle. His eyes drifted over her face. There it was again. His anger. It was tangible. She felt his anger like a black cloud surrounding her with heat and if she hadn't been completely locked down where she couldn't even lift an arm, she would have gone still anyway.

"You have capabilities that few have, *sivamet*, and it has become clear to me that you are very headstrong. I cannot protect you during the daylight hours and you insist on leaving my side. There is no other path."

What path? That didn't sound good. There was always more than one path. Her mouth went dry when she saw him bend his head toward hers. He turned slightly, presenting the side of his neck the vampire had shredded. His skin she couldn't help marveling over because there was nothing but perfection there. In spite of everything, she had a strange compulsion to bury her face in his neck, fling her arms around him and seek comfort.

You're scaring me. She couldn't speak, but she was still in his mind and it felt intimate and right. *You said you would never harm me.*

You are the safest person on this planet from me. I would never harm you. I am incapable of harming you. However, csitri, you have taken all choices from me.

There it was again. All choices. She hadn't taken *all* of them. There had to be other ways than this, right? She swallowed, but she still wanted to bury her face against his neck, right over the vein where she could feel his heart.

Her gaze was captivated by the pulse beating so strongly in his neck. He had a great neck. Great shoulders. Awesome muscles. She leaned into him. It wouldn't hurt anything to touch his bare skin, with her lips, right there. To taste him. She wanted his kisses, but he wasn't giving them out, so she could just get a little whisper of a taste.

Abruptly she pulled herself together. What the hell was wrong with her mind? She had to stay focused if she was going to get out of this.

You will not be getting out of anything, Teagan. Running is not the answer.

Maybe running isn't the answer for you. She tried to glare to let him know he was being a total jerk. *You can fly.* She made that an accusation, because really, who could fly? Superman maybe, but Andre wasn't wearing a big geeky *S* on his chest so he had no real explanation.

Running sounds really good to me about now. I am so not drinking blood. I don't judge. I'm not in the least judgmental. Well—she hedged because he was in her mind and he'd see that was a teensy lie anyway—*I totally am opposed to vampires. I might have judged him a little harshly when I bashed that one over his head, but I'm not judging you. I'm just saying, blood is not exactly my cup of tea.*

She watched in a kind of fascinated horror as he lifted his hand, fingers up, and one nail slid across that beckoning pulse point in his neck. Small ruby red beads welled up and dotted his skin. Anticipation beat at her. Her mouth watered. She could taste him in her mouth. It was both horrifying and wonderful. Wonderfully horrifying.

His palm shaped the back of her head and pressed her face toward him. She closed her eyes and immediately was enveloped with his warmth. She felt secure. Loved even. Comforted. Her racing heart slowed to match the steady beat of his. She heard them, two hearts, beating in exact synchronization.

With his one hand at the back of her head and the other wrapped around her, holding her close to the incredible heat of his body, she was completely surrounded by him. She kept her eyes closed and let herself sink into his warmth. He was there in her mind, comforting her, gently pushing her mouth to taste his skin. To just kiss his shoulder blade and move up his collarbone to his throat.

She had to breathe him in. He'd been in a battle and yet he smelled fresh and clean. All male. As wonderful as the forest after a rainfall. She inhaled, taking him into her lungs. He was there in her mind, filling every lonely place, caressing her, whispering encouragement.

Teagan felt his swift intake of breath when she dared to press her lips to his skin. She felt the impact on his body, the incredible moment when she realized the chemistry between them was just as great for him as it was for her. She tasted his throat, a slide of her tongue, and his body was instantly hard.

His heavy erection pressed shamelessly against her bottom, so hot she thought he might burn through their clothing to touch her skin. She kissed her way to the fascinating place where his shoulder and neck met. His arm tightened, and he groaned.

She heard him. He groaned. She'd made gorgeous Andre actually groan just by burying her face in that warm, perfect spot on his body. Just by skimming his pulse with her lips. The tip of her tongue teased and caressed his skin, needed his taste, wondering if he tasted the same or different on various body parts.

You are killing me, sivamet.

His voice was husky, sensual, brushing along the walls of her mind. She felt the stroke of his whisper over her skin. Her nipples peaked, pushed against the lace of her bra, seeking contact with his heat. Needing his touch.

Avio päläfertiilam, I have given you my heart. I need you to give your heart to me. I need your body. Give yourself to me. All of you.

She felt him moving again, in his mind, and she was skin to skin with him. She was hazily aware that suddenly neither of them had a stitch on. She should have been embarrassed, but she was elated. She wanted to touch him. To run her

169

hands over his chest and down to his lap. She needed to feel every bit of him against her, so she simply turned her body and pressed her front to his front as she lapped at the hot spice spilling from him.

She'd already given herself to him. She didn't sit in a man's lap without her clothes on and not want more. Want everything from him. And she did.

As if hearing her unspoken answer, Andre's hands slid over her bare skin, a delicious feeling that sent little flames dancing through her. Delicious. Her tongue tasted him again. A rich spice. The flavor of him burst on her tongue, addictive. Wild. Exotic. Nothing like she'd ever tasted before, but she craved it. Needed it. Or had she tasted that exact richness before, setting up her addiction? Her obsession. Once maybe. She had a vague recollection, and hadn't he said something to that effect? She found herself licking at the tiny beads, no longer caring, only needing.

Andre groaned again, his body shifting restlessly against hers. His palms stroked caresses along her rib cage. His fingers traced each rib, every indentation, the soft mound of her belly and then up the sides of her breasts. Perfect. She melted into him, against all his hard muscle, feeling the incredible softness of her own body. Her mind was so firmly entrenched in his that she could feel everything he was feeling, not just the sensations his sensual hands gave to her, but his actual responses.

She felt his heart, the love he already had for her growing deeper and stronger. She felt part of his soul, tiny threads binding them so that instead of two lost souls, they were one very strong soul. She felt his hunger and need of her body. She drove him wild with her soft skin and the feel of her mouth and tongue against his skin.

A delicious burn between her legs spread flames through

her. The fire started right there, as she spread kisses over the droplets of hot spice. She needed more. She *had* to have more. He was in her mind. She needed him inside her, flowing through her veins. She wanted him inside of her, in her body, so they were one, not two.

She tried not to be greedy, but the taste was exquisite and there seemed to be an endless supply. Better yet, as she drew out the spicy liquid, Andre's body got hotter and tighter, and she felt his hunger for her growing. It was there in her mind, a need that seemed to grow, matching her own almost desperate desire for him.

His hands cupped her breasts, and her breath left her body. His thumbs slid over her hard nipples and she gasped, arching into him. His fingers and thumbs tugged and rolled, until fire spread straight to her sex and sent hot flames licking over her skin.

She tried to gain some control, but once she closed her eyes, she couldn't open them again, which was strange, because her body was her own again. Her hands moved up the strong column of his broad back, spreading across his skin to take in as much of him as she possibly could. She had to touch him. There was no stopping herself. She wanted all of him. She was desperate to have all of him.

His back was every bit as muscled as his chest. Beautiful, deliciously defined, very masculine muscles. She had a thing for muscles and he had them everywhere. His skin was hot and hard and smooth. She couldn't get enough of touching him, of kissing him. Of tasting him. An addictive taste she would crave forever.

Enough, sivamet. This is our second exchange. You are close now. Next rising it will be done. Come to me now. I need you.

He gently pulled her head back, using her long, thick pony-tail of braids, depriving her of the exquisite addictive flavor that was uniquely him. She licked her lips. He watched her, his eyes darkening. Turning more intense than ever.

"Andre." She murmured her protest and tried to lean into him.

"Teagan."

There it was again. Her name. His accent curled around it. Soft. Low. Husky with need. She recognized that note in his voice for what it was. So sensual. So hungry. She slid her arms around his neck.

"I have no idea what I'm doing, Andre," she whispered the admission. "But I want to do it all with you. Everything."

He fell back against the mattress, taking her with him so that her body sprawled over his. His skin was so hot she just melted into him. He dragged her up along his thick chest, until she straddled him, her legs over either side of his body so that his very heavy erection was pressed deep into her belly. She loved the feel of him. And the look of him.

His eyes were hooded, more sensual than ever. The look of love and lust mixed together was hot, and she wanted that fire. She found herself so drawn to it that she couldn't think of anything else but Andre and his hands and mouth. His body. She wanted to put her own hands and mouth all over him. The compulsion was a hunger, a need that grew into a coiling ball of tension and settled wicked, sinful and low in her body.

Teagan ran her palms up his chest, and followed the trail with her tongue. She couldn't stop touching him, especially in the places that had been wounded. She would have given anything to have a healing agent in her saliva and to be able to turn herself into pure spirit to heal him when he was wounded.

You heal my heart, sivamet. You heal my soul. You are the only woman who can make me whole.

Well. There it was. When you were the only woman in the

172

entire world who could make a man whole, who could heal his heart and heal his soul, you did it. Right? His words were an incandescent shimmer in her mind. Warm. True. She felt his honesty, and she also felt the way his body responded to her touch.

What woman had the kind of power to make a man like Andre come alive? He was beautiful and powerful and so sensual she couldn't resist him. She couldn't look away from his blue eyes. He had so many colors of blue there, depending on his mood. This was a new color, a deep, beautiful sea blue.

His hand moved gently over her hair, sweeping over the top of her head in a gentle caress, as if he was memorizing the intricate braid work. He followed the length right down to the end of her ponytail.

There was something about the way he touched her with just a hint of possession that sent tingles down her spine and had butterflies taking flight in her stomach. His head dipped and he kissed her again. A long, slow, heart-stopping kiss that went on forever, and yet it wasn't enough.

His hands slid down her back, a slow sweep to match the kiss that sent streaks of fire dancing through her body. His hands were big and his fingers were splayed wide. She was very slight and his palms took in her entire back as they slid downward. Then his hands cupped her bottom and it felt incredible.

His mouth moved from hers to her chin. His teeth nipped and his tongue slid over the tiny sting. He placed a series of kisses along her jaw and then trailed more down her neck and over her throat. Her body caught fire. She closed her eyes and let herself drown in the flames.

He took her hand very gently, slid it down his body. Her heart nearly stopped and then began pounding when her palm encountered the heavy length of him. He was hot and hard and his erection jerked against her hand when he wrapped her fingers tight around him. It was scary and wonderful at the same time.

"Um. Andre. I really have never done this before." She didn't know if that would make him want to stop. She didn't want to stop, but she knew it was unusual for a woman of her age to be a virgin. And quite frankly, she was just a little intimidated by his size. He was a big man, and she wasn't certain he was going to fit. That could be a real problem because she really wanted him to.

"You were made for me, *sivamet*, my other half. I will be gentle with you."

His voice turned her heart over, sounding tender and filled with love. Still connected in his mind, she *felt* his love for her. It made no sense that he could already be so intensely attached to her, but it was there and it was real. She felt his love envelop her, surround and enfold her.

Every lonely place in her mind was already filled with him. She knew she was already gone, drowning in him, in the spell he'd woven around her. His mouth was driving her crazy, moving over her skin almost leisurely, as if he had to take his time to get to know every square inch of her body. As if he were worshiping her, imprinting everything he touched or tasted in his mind to last forever.

She couldn't stay still, and her hand moved over his erection. His hand guided hers, so that she memorized the shape and feel of him, sliding over the thick pulsing shaft to the large, velvet helmet, slick with pearl beads. Her breath caught in her throat and she had a mad desire to bend down and lick the beads off of him just to see if his taste was as addictive as she thought it would be.

"Give yourself into my keeping, Teagan. Your body. Your heart and soul. You are safe with me. I have entrusted you with my heart and soul. I give you my body and trust I am safe with you."

Her heart contracted. Her sex spasmed. He had such an old-fashioned way of talking, but it was beautiful. She leaned forward to lick at his neck, right over the pounding pulse. She smiled and kissed her way over his stubborn jaw and up to his ear where she licked and kissed until the breath left him in a long hiss. His cock jumped in her hand and she actually felt him grow scorching hot right there in her fist. She loved that. She loved that she could make a man like Andre fight for his control.

His hands cupped her breasts. She was very small, so slight as to be nonexistent and she'd always been self-conscious of that fact. His hands were large and she felt him cover her completely, his thumbs sliding over her nipples with absolute expertise. She felt each stroke roll through her like a tidal wave, sending streaks of lightning straight to her sex.

She lost her ability to breathe when he abruptly rolled, sliding her beneath him. With him on top, she couldn't move. It felt a little like being captured, but all the more thrilling because of it. He should have felt heavy. Instead, everything feminine reached for him. Wanted him. Needed him. She loved how hard his body was. When his mouth covered her breast and suckled she cried out. When his teeth and tongue laved and nipped she couldn't even find her voice.

"Easy, *csitri*," he whispered. "We have all the time in the world."

She realized her hips bucked under his. Her body writhed and she was pleading in little gasps for him to do something. She hadn't even realized, but she couldn't stop. One hand slipped lower, trailing down her belly until he was there. Virgin territory. He pressed one finger to her and her hips jerked hard. Her sheath contracted. His mouth pulled stronger at her breast and she felt hot liquid welcome his invasion.

It felt ... unbelievable. She wasn't certain she could stand much more. The tension in her body coiled tight. He nuzzled her breast with his shadowed jaw and then kissed her, a long, lingering kiss. His finger slid deeper and she gasped against his mouth. She couldn't help herself, she hooked her leg around his hip, opening herself more to him, needing more. Needing him inside of her.

"I waited lifetimes for you," he whispered against her mouth. He slid another finger inside her and flames spread like a wildfire. "So beautiful. You are worth all those years of endless nothing. Centuries, *sivamet*. So much ugliness. So much brutality. Wiped away with the sound of your laughter. Your nonsense. With your smile and your kisses. You taste so sweet, Teagan. I am holding you in my arms, looking into your eyes and I still cannot believe you are real."

She was real? More like *he* couldn't be real, not and be so sweet. So loving. Teagan wanted to cry at the things he said to her. He really meant them. She was that special to him. How could he have lived such a lonely existence for so many years—years filled with hunting and destroying friends and even family? He didn't have anyone left alive. No brothers. No sisters. No parents or grandparents. She'd lost her mother, but she'd never really known her. Her father had abandoned her before she was born. Still, she was raised in a loving environment and her family always, always had her back.

She couldn't imagine what his life was like, so bleak and gray and barren. His memories were mainly those of battle, blood, wounds, pain and death. She didn't want to see those things in his mind. It was difficult not to burst into tears. At the same time, she wanted to give him everything he wanted or needed.

She stretched up, bringing his head down to hers again, needing his mouth, needing to show him how much he mattered to her. It wasn't just about what his clever fingers did to her body, or the fire raging in her, she wanted him to know she felt so much more. She kissed him, sliding her lips over his in a caress. Teasing with the tip of her tongue along the seam of his mouth.

Kissing him was a miracle of sensation, especially combined with the delicious feelings his fingers stirred as they pressed inside of her. There was a tiny bite of pain from the stretch, but that was a little wicked and delicious.

Look at me, sivamet.

She reluctantly lifted her head so her eyes met his. There was something there, deep, important. Something that took her breath away.

You are giving yourself to me.

It was more of a statement than a question, but she knew better. She knew he needed to hear her say it to him.

She lifted her head, found his earlobe and tugged gently with her teeth. "I'm giving myself to you," she affirmed.

His eyes darkened. The glacier melted. Went pure liquid. He took her mouth and it was no leisurely kiss, no gentle kiss. It was hard and hot and spectacular. She hadn't known anyone could kiss like that and she lost herself completely, there in his mouth.

10

Andre took a breath to gain control. Teagan had only a glimmer of an idea of what and who he was. He knew that. He knew the pull between lifemates was so strong that they couldn't be apart for long. He also knew she wouldn't be happy when she realized the full of extent of the commitment she was making.

It should have mattered. It had mattered before she walked away from his protection and the safety of the cave. Now it didn't. Not after seeing a vampire dropping out of the fog straight at her. The vampire was newly made so it had the advantage of being able to hunt right at sunset, but thankfully it didn't have the skills to overcome the terrible need for fresh, fear-based blood.

Andre wanted Teagan with every breath in his body. He knew from kissing her, no one had kissed her before. No one. Not a single man. There was no childish fumbling in her school years. She had kept herself away from other men. No one had ever been inside of her, or put their hands and mouth on her. She belonged only to him. Only him.

The thought of her loyalty to him before they'd ever met and her gift of herself to him now, left him wild for her. He wanted to give her everything. Be everything for her. He wanted to see her first orgasm take her, looking into her eyes, his name on her lips, knowing *he* gave her that pleasure. He wanted to feel what she felt. He had bound their souls. He would bind their bodies, and then he would work for the rest of their eternity together to bind her heart to his.

He tried to gentle the kiss, but possession had taken over. Teagan belonged to him. She was worth every sacrifice he'd ever made. He kissed his way to her chin. To her breasts. She was so small and perfect. He'd never seen a woman more perfectly formed and so sensitive. The expression on her face, the hitch in her breath and the glaze in her eyes when he tugged and rolled her nipples, when he sucked them into the heat of his mouth, wiped out every horrific place he'd ever been, even if it was just for the moment.

Her skin was softer than anything he'd ever felt. He craved her, and he allowed himself to feel that craving. To embrace it. He kissed her throat, laved the pulse in her neck, but resisted taking more of her very essence. He kissed his way along her collar bone, holding her easily beneath him.

Her hands smoothed his back, shaped his shoulders and then tangled in his hair, pulling out the cord so his long hair fell free and she could grasp the thick length of it with her fist. He loved that. He loved her ragged breath and writhing body, the way her hips bucked against him. She held nothing back from him. From his touch. When she gave herself to him, she meant it and she gave him her complete surrender. Her trust.

It had never occurred to him that trust would be such a gift. She put herself in his hands when she'd never made love before.

She trusted him to make it good for her. She trusted that whatever he chose to do to her body would ultimately bring her pleasure. He was not about to abuse her trust—not ever.

He lavished attention on her breasts, and then when she was moaning softly, he kissed his way down to her belly button. She wrapped both legs around his hips, pressing herself close to him. She was naturally sensual and with him, uninhibited. Her soft skin had gone hot. Her breath came in sexy little pants. He spent some time on her belly. She had muscle but there was woman under that soft skin, sleek and beautiful, and her belly had a faint soft curve to it that he reveled in.

He knelt between her legs, pulling them over his shoulders. She gasped, and for the first time he felt a hint of fear creeping in, but it wasn't strong enough for her to retreat. He kissed the inside of her thigh.

You will like this, csitri, I promise.

Her gaze clung to his. Watching her face, he kissed his way up her thigh until he was at the junction of her legs. Her soft belly contracted in anticipation. She held her breath as he leaned close and the shadow along his jaw rubbed along her thighs. She gasped. He did a slow tongue swipe. Her body jerked and she let out a small cry.

He didn't wait. She needed to be prepared to take him and just with one small taste, he was already so hungry for her he couldn't have stopped himself. He plunged his tongue deep, all the while watching her face—her beautiful face. She came apart for him. Just that fast. That hot. On fire. He knew he would need to see that particular expression millions of times and he'd still crave it as much as he craved the taste of her sex and the taste of her blood.

Teagan cried out, nearly overcome with sensation. Tears burned behind her eyes. She hadn't known she was capable of feeling like that, or that an orgasm could be so strong. Like a tidal wave, washing over and through her.

He moved over her fast, pushing into her slick heat, stretching her beyond anything she'd imagined. It burned, and yet at the same time, she wanted more. He was thick and long and he moved one slow inch at a time, careful to allow her body to become accustomed to his invasion with every inch he gained.

You are so tight, sivamet. Relax for me. As much as you can.

He wasn't hurting her, not really. She knew he was aware that he wasn't hurting her because they were so deeply entrenched in each other's mind. It only added to the intimacy between them. She did her best to do as he said, especially when every single cell in her body was on fire. She was desperate to have him inside her.

He was going at an excruciatingly slow pace. She pushed up, trying to impale herself on him, needing to be filled.

Let me, csitri. I do not want your first experience to be painful.

She didn't want it to be painful either and she'd heard it could be, but still, she couldn't think clearly with wanting him. Each time he moved in her, he took her breath. She felt stretched and full and so much a part of him. He slipped inside deeper and she couldn't stand it anymore. She tried to buck, to push onto him, but both his hands pinned her hips beneath him and he stopped.

Take a breath, sivamet. We are almost there.

She felt his breath. She heard his heart and she automatically tuned her body to his. He surged into her. The pain was more than a bite, but he was lodged deep. So deep she could feel him bumping her cervix.

Andre paused again to allow her to adjust to his size, to being filled by him. It had been a fight, even as slick as she was, to move through her tight channel. His cock was being

181

strangled by hot silk and it felt like paradise. She was so tight he could barely breathe with the way her muscles constricted him. The pleasure bordered on pain, but then her body slowly accommodated his size.

Are you all right? He was in her mind, he knew she was, but he needed to hear her acknowledge it. He needed her soft little moans telling him she wanted more—she wanted all of him. He hadn't given her a lot of choices and if she wasn't ready for this last commitment, he had no problem starting over and making certain she was.

Please do something. Anything. I need this. I need you.

Her breathy voice took the last of his control. He withdrew slowly, feeling the fiery friction, the tight muscles trying to hold him. Burning with pleasure. Scalding him. Taking him to a place he hadn't known existed. He never wanted to leave her body. Never. If there was a heaven, he was fairly certain he was in it.

She gasped and her nails scraped down his back. Her hips moved to follow his and his hands tightened on the sweet curves to keep her still. He waited a heartbeat, savoring the moment. Imprinting a new memory. Her face. Soft. Beautiful. Her eyes. A little dazed. Filled with something he dared not name—for him. All his. All for him. For the first time in his life, he had something—some*one* who cared about him. She might not know it yet, but it was there in her eyes, the beginnings of love.

He surged forward and she cried out, her hands moving up his back to anchor in his hair. He loved that, too. He loved the fire. The intensity. The way her body moved and the breath left her lungs. In his life there had only been violence and blood. She was the reason. His purpose. Not duty and honor. That was more who he was. She was the reason the males of his species wanted to keep the world a safe place.

He began to move in her, a tight paradise, slowly at first to allow her to get used to the movement. His cock stretched her, filled her so tightly every small movement was exquisite. Her foot slid along his thigh, and he lifted her leg and wrapped it around him. She immediately followed suit with her other leg, wrapping him tight. Her arms came next and she seemed to melt into him.

He moved faster, hard, deep, jolting thrusts, until she was chanting his name, and the fire was consuming them both. They shared the sensations, the mounting tension coiling so tight inside her, building, always building. The same tension coiled in him, that powerful gathering even as pleasure washed over them both.

Look at me, Teagan.

He had to watch. To see it in her eyes. On her face. What he gave her. What only he would ever give her. He wanted his name on her breath when she dropped off the precipice with him.

Her lashes fluttered and she lifted them. His heart stuttered in his chest. She was so beautiful and the way she looked at him . . . her eyes . . .

Let go, sivamet. Give yourself to me. I want this. Keep your eyes on mine and say my name. I need you to know who you are with. Where you belong. Where I belong.

Her eyes went soft. Tender. Loving, even. Her heart beat close to his, the same wild, pounding rhythm. The blood rushed hot through her veins. Her legs and arms tightened around him. The delicate muscles in her sheath clamped hard, holding him to her. He felt the wonder of it sink into his bones. Her brand.

You belong to me, she whispered in his mind. *Definitely.*

Give yourself to me, he said again.

He surged into her, holding her to him, thrusting deep and

183

hard, feeling her scalding sheath tighten, clamp down to grip and milk. She shuddered, and then the tsunami hit, taking her, and he breathed through it, holding on to his control by a thread because he had to see. He watched the sheer beauty of it. The miracle.

Andre.

There was wonder in her voice. Shock. Pleasure. He had given that to her, but she'd given him so much more. The breathy sound of his name was a miracle in itself.

He waited for the aftershocks and began to move, building the pleasure for her again. She was more than he had ever imagined a woman could be. No one could possibly feel for her what he did. He knew that. He wanted her to know it as well.

Andre bent and nuzzled her throat. Everything about her was perfection. Her scent. Her laugh. Her eyes. The way she looked at him. Her indomitable spirit. He liked her sass and her nonsense and the way she chattered on when she was nervous. He liked her sense of humor and how she used it in difficult situations.

Tet vigyázam. It was too soon for her, and she wouldn't understand in his language. Only the feeling in his mind when he told her he loved her.

He shifted his body more fully over hers, gathered her to him, once more sliding her legs around his hips because he liked the way it felt with her surrounding his body while her feminine sheath surrounded his cock. He allowed himself the freedom to lose himself completely in her body.

They caught fire together, an out of control wildfire, burning hot and long, his thrusts fast and deep, each one jolting her body. Her keening cries for more with each hard stroke drove him higher and higher. He felt her moving over the edge again and he forced himself to wait, just one more time, watching, letting the beauty on her face sweep him with her. They fell together, locked together. He listened to their hearts beat the same rhythm and he'd never felt so content and at peace as he did in that moment.

Bodies still connected, he rolled with her, so that she was on top of him and his arms were safely around her. He held her, listening to her breathe. Stroking caresses down her back, reveling in the feel of her soft skin. He wanted her hair down, wanted the long sweep of silken strands across his body.

He caught her face in his hands, thumbs sliding along her cheeks, fingers delving into the mass of braids. He stared into her eyes for a long moment. She didn't look away. Instead, her hands stroked his chest, one right over his heart where the vampire had tried to rip it from his body.

"You are the reason I hunted all those centuries, Teagan. Why I held on to my honor. You are the reason the monastery up at the top of the mountain exists. Others, like me, at the end of their ability to hold on, those who have given up ever finding their other half, yet still cannot walk into the sun. Because of you."

She didn't understand the enormity of what she was to him, he could see that and feel it in her mind. She had no way of knowing what she would be to others who needed their own lifemate—a beacon of hope. He was older than most, but younger than others. He had given up, and yet here she was.

He ground his hips deeper into her, held himself inside of her, feeling every aftershock through her tight muscles.

"Are you all right?"

She nodded slowly.

"You are not hurt in any way?"

She shook her head. Bit at her lower lip. He leaned into her and swiped her lower lip with his tongue.

"You have to know I will cherish you for all time, Teagan.

In this one moment, you managed to wipe out every horrific battle, all those centuries of loneliness. You made all of it worthwhile."

Teagan felt her heart still in her chest. The things he said to her made no sense and yet it was everything. She knew she would have to ask him questions, but not right that moment. Right then she wanted to be the woman who wiped out centuries of loneliness for him. Wiped out the battles. She knew it was true because there was only her for him in this moment.

Andre kissed her and the tenderness brought tears burning in her eyes. He dropped his head back to the mattress but kept his eyes locked with hers.

"You belong to me, *csitri*, for now and all eternity. Thank you for giving yourself to me."

That set off a million butterflies in her stomach. Eternity sounded like a long time. She had a month, and then she would have to go home. She needed to find a way to tell her sisters that Grandma Trixie wasn't insane without them wanting to lock her up as well.

A shadow crossed his face. The cave filled with a kind of intense heat. She sucked in her breath. His eyes went from a beautiful burning blue flame to a beautiful glacier blue in seconds.

"We need to get you in the hot water so you will not be sore," he said.

Yeah. She was in trouble. She had a penchant for getting in trouble. Her sisters were always so good, following the rules. Going to church. Singing gospel music. She sang old love songs, and if she had to say it herself, she sang them very well. Perfect pitch. Her grandmother would have been happier if she'd joined the church choir like her sisters. Unfortunately, she skipped church more often than not, and she never followed rules if she could help it. Fortunately, she was extremely intelligent, which allowed her to outmaneuver most people. Not necessarily her grandmother, and probably not a man who could read her mind. But still, she had skills when needed.

"Andre." They needed to talk. The dreaded relationship talk. Men hated that. "We need to talk." That should do it right there. He should make excuses and run for the monastery.

He'd taken her virginity in a lovely, mind-blowing way. She would never be the same and no man was ever going to make her feel the way he did, but still, a month wasn't a lifetime. He certainly wasn't going to want her to think her vacation fantasy was real. Not when he was slinging words like *century* around. Right? She bit her lip again. She *had* to be right.

He slipped out of her and she nearly cried out with the loss of him. Involuntarily she caught at him, afraid he was going to disconnect immediately. Instantly she was embarrassed and ashamed. She wasn't a needy kind of girl. Or even high maintenance. She didn't need him to cuddle her after they'd had sex. She hadn't even known she would want it—but truly she didn't *need* it. There was a difference.

Andre stood up with casual ease, a fluid, almost catlike motion, and simply lifted her in his arms, cradling her close to his chest.

"You chatter at yourself, woman. Most of it is sheer non-sense. I like to touch you. I like my hands on you and my body as close to yours as possible. You are going to be sore if I do not get you into the hot springs."

"We didn't use protection," she blurted, horrified at herself. "I'm a modern girl. I might not have needed protection before you, Andre, but I certainly know all about it. I hadn't given it one single thought. Seriously, I'm my mother all over again. Oh, my God. I just had unprotected sex the one and only time

I've ever had sex and I'm probably pregnant. Seriously, I'm not trying to trap you. I'm fairly certain you won't want anything to do with me after I'm so reckless. How could you? Why would you want someone so completely irresponsible? I'll probably die in childbirth and Grandma Trixie will have to raise her *great*-granddaughter. The cycle could go generation after generation and that will be my legacy."

Andre's eye color went dark and intense, with just a shade of amusement.

She gave him her narrowed eyes. "There is nothing humorous about this situation, Andre. I wasn't being funny."

He shook his head, but she was fairly certain she could still feel laughter in his mind so she continued to glare at him.

"You will not get pregnant because you are not ovulating. If you did get pregnant, I would never leave you or the child. You are my lifemate. In your language you would say *wife*."

"Um. Andre. In order to be a wife, you have to get married. Take vows in front of a justice of the peace or minister or priest. There are papers to fill out. A lifemate isn't the same as a wife. Maybe a girlfriend? Or if it's more, a fiancée?"

Andre lowered her onto a smooth rock seat that even had a back on it. The hot water came up to her neck and felt wonderful. Soothing. She really hadn't known she was sore, she was still feeling far too good. He had to be the best lover in the world.

"How would you know if I was ovulating or not?" she asked curiously, allowing her head to fall back, noticing in a kind of offhand way that the rock seemed soft, seemed to have a little niche she could rest the back of her skull against. It was comfortable and in her dazed and sex-sated state, she was certain she wouldn't move again for a very long time. "I'm drained but perfectly happy right now. Especially if you're right and there's no chance of pregnancy. I really don't

188

want to be responsible for setting into motion a generational catastrophe for my family."

"I would think not," he answered.

She attempted a scowl, but the hot water combined with great sex made her too drowsy to give him a real glare. She subsided, idly pushing through the water with her fingers.

"You didn't answer me, Andre. Do you really know if I'm ovulating or not?"

"Yes. And you are not. I am going to make certain your body is not going to be sore. It will take a moment and you will feel heat."

She opened her eyes then—she *had* to. He was going to do his healing thing right down there. In the pertinent spot. "Um." She had to tell him. "That might be going a little too far. I'm not thinking about being absolutely naked or that I've just gone a little crazy in your arms. Or that I was a complete moron and forgot birth control. I'm just zoning out. If you're wandering around inside my body with your white healing light and moving around in my very happy spot I might ... um ... well ... um." She waved her hand, hoping he got the message.

His mouth twitched. "Happy spot?" he echoed.

She raised her eyebrow. "*Very* happy spot. Although technically, I'm happy all over, so I guess it isn't just one spot. Still, I wouldn't go messing around in there right now. You could set off an explosion or two."

The expression on his face was priceless. She figured he was getting the message, but really, she'd had to spell it out for him and that was highly embarrassing. It had to be a language thing. She was fairly articulate but not used to men who healed by going into other people's bodies. Which was cool, but still.

He shook his head. He looked good shaking his head. His gleaming long, thick hair was just plain beautiful falling

189

around him. She loved his face. She could get lost just looking at his face. He should be outlawed for his body alone, but then you put that together with his face and his hair and his eyes. Oh—and his mouth. No one could possibly be a better kisser. His kiss was something from another realm.

"Teagan."

She'd forgotten about his voice. Her belly did a familiar shiver and her breasts, beneath the hot water, tightened. She licked her lower lip and forced her gaze to his, trying to look innocent.

"You are doing it again, going off somewhere in your mind instead of out loud. But I can hear your thoughts. I appreciate that you think I am beautiful, but I am still going to check on you. I cannot imagine not repeating the experience with more enthusiasm, and I do not want you sore."

More enthusiasm? That sounded promising. Teagan nodded, speechless. She tried to curb her thoughts as well, because seriously, he was going to think she was insane if she kept it up. She just talked to herself whenever she was nervous. Okay, she talked. In general. To everyone. Whatever was in her head often came out her mouth.

Grandma Trixie had tried very hard to curb that particular failing. Her sisters had really tried to curb it, especially when they invited men—and that one woman—in the hopes she would find someone. They were pretty desperate . . .

"Teagan."

She bit her lip. "Sorry. I'm doing it again, aren't I?"

He smiled. A real smile. A full-on, perfect white teeth smile. He looked more handsome, more masculine than ever. Sort of like a wolf about to pounce. She brought herself up short and then couldn't help but laugh.

He didn't laugh, but his smile stayed more than one brief moment and his eyes went soft and incredibly beautiful.

"I love the sound of your laughter," he said.

She closed her eyes and laid her head back. He was going to blind her with his beauty or worse, cast his spell even deeper, and she couldn't afford that. She wasn't thinking sanely. She waved her hand. "All right. Get to it, healer. The *more* enthusiastically part sounds mag."

"Mag?"

She didn't open her eyes. "Yep. Totally mag. Magnificent."

He remained silent and she was tempted to open her eyes, but she wanted to be in his mind when he shed his body and became spirit. She didn't understand how he could do it and the healer in her was envious and totally blown away by his incredible talent. The truth was, she could fall for him just for that. Who had that kind of ability—that amazing gift?

She waited. Held her breath. He came into her and it was different than the feel of his mind pouring into hers. This was all about selfless healing. This wasn't his personality or his power. Simply his need to heal. It was beautiful like everything else about him. The light was bright and warm, hot in a completely different way than the heat generated when they had sex. His spirit warmed her. Soothed her. Eased every ache as he moved through her toward his goal.

She thought she'd be embarrassed. She'd felt blood and seed trickling together down the inside of her thighs when he'd carried her to the hot spring. He was so caring and gentle she'd been able to put it out of her mind. Now, because he was pure spirit, there was no way to be mortified.

If she was being strictly honest with herself, she was very tender. She thought maybe she had skid marks inside of her. The water helped, but the heat he applied deep inside her was wonderful and in a matter of minutes the ache was gone.

She opened her eyes to watch him come back to his body. It was there in his eyes. One moment his body dead, an empty

191

shell. She couldn't hear his heartbeat or see him breathing. His eyes were flat, unseeing. Then he was there, vital. Alive. Larger than life and giving off an aura of danger. He carried that with him, a supreme confidence that bordered sometimes on arrogance, as well as the feeling that he could be utterly dangerous.

"When you heal people or yourself, it's risky to you, isn't it?" She slid her hand over his arm. "You have to leave your body unprotected." She felt his instant shock.

Andre nodded slowly. "Yes."

"But you still do it."

"Of course. Especially if it is you."

She sighed. She had no choice. They had to have the talk. "Andre, you know I live in the United States. I'm here for a few weeks, that's all. I have to return home. The truth is, my grandmother isn't nearly as crazy as we all thought she was. There really are vampires in the world. I can't let doctors put her on medication, or have my sisters think she's losing her mind. That wouldn't be fair to her. So I can't stay."

Her confession was met with absolute silence. He was suddenly gone from her mind. She was no longer in his. She couldn't read his expression, but she had the feeling whatever he was thinking wasn't good.

"It's not that I want to leave you," she added in a little rush. "I don't. I really don't. I'm not leading you on. I'm really not like that. I didn't expect to meet someone like you or fall so hard. But I can't stay."

"Teagan."

Her name again. He wrapped her in black velvet when he spoke in that tone. A sorcerer's spell, and she kept falling deeper into it. Willingly. That was the worst part. She shook her head. "I don't have a choice."

"No, you do not have a choice," he agreed.

Okay, that hurt. She needed to hear him agree with her, but

still, there was a part of her—a big part of her—that wanted him to protest and say she couldn't leave him or he'd die of a broken heart.

"Okay then. You get it. That's good. That's a good thing." Her throat felt clogged. She hated that. Hated the burn behind her eyes so she closed them tight and kept her head back, resting against the rock.

"I get what has happened between us, Teagan, but you do not."

Her stomach clenched. Hard. Her heart stuttered. It was the *way* he said it. She opened her eyes again and looked at him. Yeah, there was trouble there. She just didn't know what it was or why. She bit her lip. Something was different about him. Something *more*. Predatory. He was just a little bit scary, and she didn't even know why.

"Andre? You're just a little scary right now. You aren't angry with me, are you? I mean, you know about visas, right? I can only stay so long legally."

"I have told you that you are safe with me."

He made it a flat statement and she had the feeling he didn't like repeating himself. Well, okay then. He shouldn't scare her like that if he didn't want to repeat himself. She made a little face at him just to show him she wasn't all that intimidated by him, although she kind of was. But he wasn't in her head anymore so she figured she probably could get away with it.

"What did you mean, by saying you get it, but I don't? I'm the one explaining it to you. I have to leave. I'm trying to be honest with you."

He nodded his head slowly. "I get that you think you are being honest." He held out his hand. "You need to have something warm in your stomach. I will make the tea and we can talk about this."

193

"Well, if I'm being strictly honest," Teagan said, taking his hand and standing up carefully, "I don't think tea is going to agree with me right now. Just the thought of it makes me feel a little queasy and since you're certain I'm not pregnant, then I'd just better not risk it. In any case, if I'm really caught in some very strange hallucinatory dream state, I'm definitely not having another cup of tea. The tea is the only thing I can think of that might have been drugged. But then that would make you a huge delusion as well and you're the one who made me the tea in the first place."

His hands spanned her waist and he lifted her easily out of the steaming water. At once he enveloped her in a towel.

"I am a delusion?"

"Actually, I don't think so, but you have to admit, it could be a possibility, since there's no one like you in the world, but I don't think I could make you up. Especially not the sex. I couldn't have made that up."

He rubbed the towel over her body, gentle, massaging strokes that soaked up the beads of water and left her a little breathless and definitely aroused. She couldn't help but love the way he touched her so gently.

She glanced up at his face. He wore a strange look that didn't bode well for her and she wanted to avoid finding out what it meant, because he really did look dangerous. He really could look scary—like a predator—and she was alone in the cave with him. She was avoiding the word *lair* at all costs, but it floated into her mind all by itself.

"I don't have many clothes left," she said into the silence. "I'll have to make a trip into town and pick a couple of shirts up."

"That will not be necessary, Teagan. I can provide clothing for you."

Her heart thudded. She bit her lip. "My grandmother

194

expects me to be in touch with her once a week. I'm due anyway. I'll just pick up the shirts and call her at the same time."

He caught her chin. "I do not like that you scare yourself like this. You have a vivid imagination for a woman who travels as much as you do."

"I know. I've always been afraid of everything. When I was a child I was certain there were monsters under my bed and in my closet. Most nights I'd go crawl in bed with my grandmother, but sometimes I couldn't make myself leave my bed and put my feet on the floor so I'd yell for her at the top of my lungs. I'd wake up the entire household. My sisters were in school so they weren't happy about it, but they always comforted me."

Andre removed the towel and held out a large men's button-down shirt. It was his size, but nothing like she thought he'd ever wear. Still, when she inhaled deeply, the material held his scent. He seemed the type to wear skintight shirts that clung to his muscles and blue jeans that cupped his very nice butt lovingly and only made him look sexier than ever. Or a really classy, elegant suit. Black and white. He'd look spectacular with his wide shoulders and ice-blue eyes.

Andre shook his head and reached his arms around her so she was caged against his body. He did up her buttons, pulling a little on the shirt so she leaned back, pressing her back into his front. Somewhere along the line, while he was drying her off, he'd gotten dressed. Yeah. Skintight shirt, soft material, blue to match his eyes, every muscle rippling so amazingly. She licked her lips and tried not to stare.

He'd brought her to two screaming orgasms and it had been her first time *ever*. She knew it wasn't always that good for virgins, but he'd made it good. No, he'd made it great. Spectacular.

"Teagan. You are doing it again. Going off somewhere. We need to straighten things out between us. You have tried to be honest. I am trying as well. I need you to focus. Keep your imagination under control for just one moment."

She was a little hurt. She'd shared a traumatic, recurring event from her childhood, which, okay, didn't exactly match the raging vampire who had punched holes in his body and tore long strips of skin off of him, but really, she'd shared.

"I'm focusing," she said quietly. She might as well get it over. They couldn't be together, and if they needed to end things right then, she could be grown-up and understand. She looked him in the eyes. His beautiful eyes that made her tummy flutter. "Really, Andre. I'm entirely focused on what you have to say."

And she meant it. She was absolutely finished with avoidance. It was going to hurt like hell when he said his piece, but he deserved her full attention when he did it. He'd been wonderful and he had saved her life and given her two orgasms, after all.

11

A ndre gestured toward the chairs. "Come sit down."
Teagan walked silently to the chairs. They were
positioned side by side and were deep and comfortable. She dropped into the nearest one and drew her legs up to rest her chin on her knees. The shirt was more like a dress, so she knew she was decent. Andre sank into the chair beside hers and reached for her hand. He enveloped her fingers and brought her palm to his thigh, his hand covering hers.

Her heart did a little stutter and butterflies took wing in her stomach all over again. It was the little things he did that got to her, she decided. The sweet, intimate gestures, so gentle and yet burning with an intensity only he seemed to be able to generate with her.

"You know I am not quite human, Teagan," he said softly.

This time her heart stood still and then began to thud. She closed her eyes for a moment, not wanting to face the

197

superhuman thing. Flying. Clothes appearing. The memories she saw in his head. It was best to remain ignorant.

She moistened her lips. "I'm not certain I'm ready for this talk. I thought we were going to talk about my having to leave and why you think I'm not 'getting' it."

"We are going to talk about it." His hand tightened around her fingers. "I am Carpathian. We are an ancient race. There are very few of us left. For us, we have only one chance to find the woman who is our other half."

This time her heart *and* her stomach fluttered. She couldn't help it, she liked the idea of being his other half. She really did, whether or not she had to leave. She would never find another man. She knew that already. Just the thought of being apart from Andre was terrifying. She didn't know how she was going to let him go. And she didn't know how she had fallen so hard so fast, so she closed her mind, refusing to deal with the consequences until she had to.

"That woman, for me, Teagan, is you. Carpathian males are born imprinted with the ritual binding words. I suppose it is necessary in order to ensure our males are safe from the gathering darkness in us. In any case, when we find our other half, we bind the woman to us." Andre spoke gently but matter-of-factly.

He wasn't joking with her. She could hear it in his voice. She could see it on his face. His eyes had gone almost liquid with intensity. She cleared her throat. "Are you saying that you can bind a woman to you *without her consent*?"

"Yes." He watched her closely.

Teagan tried to pull her hand off of his thigh. Her hand remained exactly where it was, pressed tight against the column of pure muscle, his fingers tightly wrapped around hers.

"You didn't do that to me." She made it a statement because, well, he'd better not have done it to her.

"Yes."

She narrowed her eyes at him. Glared. Gave another tug at her hand. It was hard to deliver a blistering lecture on women's rights when her hand was pinned against his hard, very muscular thigh. "You're saying you said these ritual binding words to me and somehow, now, I'm tied to you."

"That is exactly what I did. I waited long for you. I would never take a chance on losing you. Of course I bound you to me."

There was no remorse whatsoever in his tone. Not even a little tiny bit. Her breath hissed out of her throat. "Well, you can just undo it. You have no right to do that to me without my consent."

"There is no undoing it. It is impossible."

She couldn't help it. She jerked out of the chair and tugged at her hand. When he didn't let her go, she gave him her most fierce, scary glare. It didn't seem to have any effect at all. "Let go. I need to pace. I think better when I pace."

He shook his head. "Teagan. You have to take me seriously. I know this is a lot for you to take in, but you have to know the truth."

"I *am* taking you seriously," she snapped.

Without releasing the hand at his thigh, his other arm wrapped around her waist and guided her gently back to the chair. "Then sit down. You have to hear all of it."

Her heart went back to thudding and her body went still. There was more? She knew he had done something to bind them together, as crazy as that sounded, because she absolutely didn't want to be away from him. She'd worked hard to be an independent woman. She really had been afraid of everything and she had been determined to overcome her fears—not allow them to dictate her life to her. Now she was *bound* to a man she barely knew and really didn't want to know any more about that.

She subsided back onto the chair, pulling her knees up for protection. "Andre, what does this binding entail? Maybe we can find a way to undo it. You can leave your body. I can tune to the exact ..."

Andre's face darkened. If thunder took on a persona it would definitely be Andre. Teagan bit her lip. He was difficult to figure out. She wasn't even certain what she was dealing with and she'd just made love to him. She'd let him do all sorts of things to her body and her mind.

Before she could open her mouth and protest that he shouldn't be angry, *she* should, his fingers bit into her arms. He dragged her right off her chair and onto his lap. Close. Closer still, until her body was so tight against his, she couldn't tell where he started and she let off. Worse, she melted into him. The moment her body felt the heat of his, she went boneless.

Teagan tilted her head and looked into his eyes. Hot. A virtual blaze. He didn't look angry anymore, but the intensity burning in his eyes both scared and thrilled her. He dragged her closer and his mouth came down hard on hers.

His kiss was hotter than any he'd ever given her, his mouth demanding. No longer sweet and gentle. Taking rather than asking. It didn't matter in the least. Her body went weak, he had to breathe for her because she lost all breath, and her arms, of their own volition, slid around his neck. Honestly. She didn't do that, it just happened. She couldn't get any closer to him, he had her crushed against him, but still, she wanted to be right where she was. She wanted to crawl inside of him and stay there forever.

She wanted his kisses, long, drugging kisses she could never get enough of. She didn't understand why the moment he touched her, her body was no longer her own, but belonged to him. She really didn't understand why she felt his body was hers. She knew, as long as she lived, no one else would ever make her feel the way he did. Beautiful. Sexy. The only woman in the world.

You are the only woman in my world.

What man said things like that? Teagan had never heard anyone say such things to a woman. He began to lift his head and she chased him, tightening her hold on his neck and bringing her mouth back to his like a starving woman. She loved his taste. She loved the way he always took such firm control and his every touch was a flame on her skin. She kissed him over and over and then drowned again in his kisses.

Andre pulled back again, but this time, only far enough to press his forehead to hers. "There is no going back for us, Teagan. Even if there was a way to undo what I have done, I would not. You are mine. You are the keeper of my heart. Of my soul. My body belongs to you. All of me. I cannot survive without you."

Her entire body reacted to his words. To his tone. His black velvet voice slid over and into her. How could she not want to be that woman for him? She was a healer—an empath. She felt every word he said. Every single one. He meant them. For him, it was the absolute truth.

She moistened her lips. "Andre, I'm a modern woman. I don't like being told what to do. I don't like orders of any kind. How would we work? Visas aside. How could we possibly work? You have to know you're kind of bossy."

He shook his head. "That is untrue, Teagan. I do not tell you what to do unless it has to do with your safety."

"You can't tell me what to do at all, Andre. I have to make my own decisions. I'm all grown up."

"You left the safety of the cave, and you were nearly taken by a vampire."

201

Everything in her went still at the sound of his voice. Her gaze jumped to his. Her heart accelerated all over again. His expression was darker than ever. He looked seriously angry and she didn't want to wave a red flag in front of him, but he had to get what she was saying.

She licked her lips carefully, trying to moisten her sudden dry mouth. "That still has to be my choice, Andre," she said quietly. Firmly. Even though inside she had begun to shake. "It's called free will."

He shook his head. "Not in my world, Teagan. In my world there are rules we all live by. I hunt vampires, and they run in packs now. It is too dangerous to have an unprotected woman running around drawing their attention."

"You aren't getting it. This isn't about vampires, this is about you making decisions for me. That isn't acceptable."

He shrugged. Casually. Her head nearly exploded. She gritted her teeth to keep from shrieking at him like a shrew, even though he totally deserved it.

"What does that mean?"

"That means I refuse to argue about this. I will not allow you to place yourself in danger. *Te avio päläfertiilam*. You are my lifemate. My wedded wife. The keeper of my heart and soul. Without my soul, I will be the undead, a curse on the world. There is no question that I would take such a risk."

She opened her mouth to blast him, but at his explanation, she closed it. She was very confused. Andre seemed to believe every word he said, and if it was the truth, that meant he could become a vampire. She wanted to tear her fingers through her hair, but it had taken hours to put all those braids in for her journey.

She took a deep breath. "I'm really intelligent, Andre, but I'm not getting this. You met me, and just like that you knew I was the one you wanted to bind yourself to?"

He nodded slowly. "The males of my people lose their emotions and the ability to see in color after the first two hundred years."

She closed her eyes briefly. She couldn't deal with the time thing right then. There were too many other issues. They'd have to come back to that one.

"We live long lives but the living is barren and cold. Brutal. When a man has nothing but violence, brutal and ugly in his life and he finds beauty, sweet, funny and vibrant color, believe me, *csitri*, he will do anything he can to hold on to it. He will fight, kill if necessary and he will protect, even if that woman thinks she is capable of protecting herself."

He was killing her with his words. She understood. Okay, maybe not really, because how could anyone comprehend what he was telling her? If she hadn't seen him kill the vampire, hadn't experienced flying or any of the other things he'd done, she would be certain he was absolutely out of his mind.

He made her feel special and beautiful and the way he looked at her with his gaze so focused and intent on her, she could easily believe she was the only woman in his world. She took a breath and opened her mouth to speak.

He got there first. "*Sivamet*, seriously, you scared me. Terrified me."

Teagan studied his face. God. He was beautiful. Masculine. Strong. Alone. She shook her head.

He placed his hands on either side of her head. "Open your mind to me. See me. I was *terrified* for you. For me. For the world. See me, Teagan. You have to know."

She was fairly certain she didn't want to know any more, but it was too late to protest. Already he was pouring into her mind, and this time he opened himself to her fully. She thought she knew fear, but even the terror of the vampire's attack didn't compare with the sheer naked horror of that moment for Andre.

The terror wasn't for Andre, but for her and what the vampire would do to her. The horror she would experience before she died. And she would die hard. And then fear that if he didn't reach her, he would lose his honor. He would become the very thing he had hunted and destroyed to keep the world safe.

She felt sick, her stomach churning. Her body shut down, frozen with the knowledge that this man had gone through such trauma on her behalf. she would never fully comprehend it.

"Andre," she whispered, and trailed kisses to his jaw and back up to the corner of his mouth, as if that could somehow erase what had happened between them.

"You have to understand, Teagan. I know it is difficult for you, the transition into my world. I wanted to bring you in gently. To court you in the way you deserve. But you do not listen. You are of the modern world and you cannot comprehend the dangers of my world. *Te avio päläfertiilam.* You are my lifemate and you must live in my world with me. We no longer can be apart."

His knuckles stroked down her face in a gentle caress. "I know that frightens you, Teagan, but there is no need."

"Are you kidding, Andre? You have vampires in your world."

"They were in your world as well. The difference is, you know about them now. You know they are difficult to kill and someone has to do it. I just have to make certain you are safe when I do so."

She took a deep breath. He was holding her so close. So lovingly. She was surrounded completely by his warmth. She could still feel the evidence of him inside of her, a thick, beautiful invasion that made her feel complete and perfect. The way he touched her, everything about him.

"Tell me what living in the rules of your world means." She didn't do bossy well. She knew that, but maybe for him, she could find a balance. She couldn't help the little tremor that ran through her at the enormity of what she was considering. "You took my blood in the way a vampire would. Why? How?" Her gaze jumped to his mouth. He had perfect teeth, not fangs.

"I am Carpathian. We exist on blood. We do not kill. We are careful to be respectful and to ensure those who supply us do not remember."

"But not me."

"You are entering my world. It will be necessary for you to accept the fact that we have no choice. We must have blood to survive."

She shook her head. The taste of him was suddenly in her mouth. Her eyes widened. "Wait a minute. Don't say anything else. Not another word." She tried to break free of him, of the iron band of his arms and his mind. Suddenly other things were coming back to her. A dream world with her mouth on Andre's neck.

"Oh, God. No. No. No, no, no." She shook her head, panic filling her. "I didn't. Tell me right now, I didn't take your blood."

"Be calm, Teagan," Andre advised. "You need to be calm and accept what I am telling you. It simply is. There is no good or bad. It just is. This is my life. Now our life."

She shook her head. "Not mine. I do not drink blood. Are you kidding me?" Her voice was swinging out of control. "I drank your blood once?" Her stomach lurched and she pressed a hand tightly against it.

"Twice," he said calmly. "It takes three blood exchanges for you to come fully into my world."

This couldn't be happening. She really was batty. Completely around the bend. Grandma Trixie had infected her with some brain disease. They were all crazy. She belonged in a hospital. She tried again to pull away from Andre, but he held her firmly.

"Breathe. You need to breathe, *sivamet*. It is simply a fact of our lives."

"Not *my* life," she corrected. "Let go of me. I'm getting out of here. And don't you try to follow me. You had no right."

"I had every right," he returned. "Calm down."

"You be calm. I'm going to scream my head off if you try to keep me here. Blood? I ingested blood *twice*?" She touched her lips with trembling fingers.

The worst of it all was that she remembered now. She remembered his exquisite taste. Addictive. She craved it again. Just the mere thought of taking his blood sent tingles through her body—sent heat rushing through her veins, and her sex actually spasmed. She was crazy. Insane. And he'd made her that way.

Andre sighed. "*Csitri*, I would not hurt you for the world. Not physically and not emotionally. I cannot do anything about this situation you find yourself in. You are my lifemate. I see in colors. My emotions have returned and with them, when you placed yourself in danger, came terror. Absolute terror. I have spent centuries keeping this world safe from the undead, but throughout, the whisper of temptation was always with me. Crouched so close I could hear darkness breathing in my ear."

Teagan went still again. There was something in his voice that told her what he was saying was extremely important. Something huge. A gift that he was giving her. This wasn't a man who enjoyed having heart-to-hearts. She knew that instinctively. She knew he was hurting because she felt it. He was hurting for her. His resolve remained implacable, but that didn't stop him from having compassion for her.

She wanted to be a woman who was understanding when her man was upset and behaving irrationally, but seriously, *drinking blood*? She was human. It was probably going to make her sick. And if her grandmother ever found out, she might use her Internet vampire-hunting kit on her.

Andre sighed. "You do not understand, Teagan. I have only tasted that kind of fear one other time in my entire existence. I have faced multiple vampires and deadly armies of humans. I have never felt fear. Or terror. The one other time ended far differently than this one did."

She didn't want to hear this. Or see it, but already images were in his head. Strangely, his memories were vague and always colored in gray. She found few memories of his childhood, and she'd actually looked because she wanted to see what he'd been like as a boy. But there was nothing. Not even a memory of his mother and father. She didn't even know if he had siblings.

He was a confusing man. Monk. Bounty hunter. Vampire hunter. Now Carpathian. Who knew? But this ... this memory was vivid, not in color, as if he were color-blind, and maybe he was. She shook her head and tried to pull out of his mind.

"I don't want to see this, Andre. I'm too ... " What could she say? *Sensitive?* He'd actually gone through the experience—the one time he'd been terrified just like this time. She sounded self-centered saying she was too sensitive, but truthfully, she was an empath and she already knew she wouldn't be able to take what he was about to show her—as well as tell her.

"You have to know, *csitri*. I am not a dictator. I do not want things all my way. I meant it when I bound us together and said your happiness would be put before my own."

Uh-oh. Bound them together? She liked the part about putting her happiness before his own. She was willing to do the same, but the binding them together only made her see red all over again. Where was free will in his world?

Fear cruised down her spine because the way was all too familiar now. Binding. Blood taking. Flying. Things were getting out of hand, and all Andre seemed to have to do was kiss her silly and she just succumbed. Went under his spell willingly. Drowned in him.

Teagan bit her lip. "Um. Seriously, Andre, we need to talk more about this binding and other things." She didn't want to talk about them. That was the last thing she wanted to do. His eyebrows drew together and he looked as if he was getting upset all over again.

She laid her hand over his mouth. "Wait. I've changed my mind, Andre. If you tell me you sleep in the ground, then I'll have no choice but to stake you. There's no staking a man as gorgeous as you. It would be a sin. A mortal sin. Like I'd be eternally damned or something. You already had one hole in your chest and honestly, it wasn't that good of a look, even for someone as hot as you."

She chewed on her lip for another moment and then, she couldn't help herself, she ran her fingers lightly down his face, right where he should have had scars from the vampire. "I couldn't do it, you know. If you're really a vampire, if Carpathian is just a really nice word for *vampire*, you need to tell me and just get it over with. I'd have to let you kill me. I just couldn't even try to destroy you. You don't feel evil. You feel like a man who has more integrity and honor than any other man in the world."

She was rambling, blurting out anything that came into her head in order not to think about the things he'd said or was going to say. She couldn't process it all. Drinking blood? Oh. My. God.

Andre made a single sound deep in his throat. He caught her fingers and brought them to his mouth, brushing kisses over them. His eyes had gone from thunder to warmth. From glacier to tropical. He was so beautiful she ached.

"Tet vigyázam."

He whispered the words in his own language. Soft. Sweet. Husky. Like he meant them. Her heart turned over. Whatever he said, it meant something big. Something she needed to know. Something huge.

"You will not have to stake me," he assured her in that silky, smooth voice. "Still, you need to know why I must proceed with this course of action. I do not, as a rule, explain myself. I have never done so, not that I can remember. I say this so you know how much you matter to me. How much your peace of mind matters to me."

She swallowed hard. He was going to tell her about the one memory that had never faded. The one time he had been terrified. She had tried to distract him, although she'd meant exactly what she'd said.

"Andre." She tried to dissuade him, but already, she could see the memories in his mind. She could feel the way he felt that day, so long ago.

He was young. Seventeen. A mere babe in the eyes of his people. The night was beautiful, with a thousand stars spreading like diamonds overhead. She could see him moving through a thick forest, using long strides, his manner utterly confident, although she knew as Andre walked along the narrow deer path there were wild animals close by. Predators. Bears. A wolf pack. Much more than she thought possible in a forest.

Even the mountains looked different. She wasn't certain where in the Carpathian Mountains he was. The forest was dense, the trees lush with vegetation. An abundance of wildlife was everywhere. Andre's memory was so vivid she could actually smell the various animals each time the wind shifted even minutely. For some reason, looking into his memory, when it should have been carefree and happy, she felt a sense of dread. Of something evil creeping through the forest and moving toward the young Andre. She wanted to call out a warning. Instead she tightened her hold on the man whose arms locked her so close.

"This isn't necessary, Andre. There's no need to relive this."

"It is necessary, Teagan, for you to understand. I have lived this nightmare for centuries. You are the only one I have shared it with."

Centuries. Oh no. There it was again. Those little slipups she was afraid weren't real slipups. She knew Andre was deliberately slipping them into the conversation, getting her used to the idea that he had actually lived centuries. He was a man who didn't make mistakes. She wanted to childishly put her hands over her ears and sing *la la la* until he stopped talking. She wanted to be a coward, but she was looking into his beautiful blue eyes and once again she was lost.

If this was Andre's only memory left from his childhood, and the only time he could remember experiencing fear, she knew it was going to be bad. On the other hand, she liked the idea that she was the only one he shared this life-changing experience with. She did want to be that woman for him. She just didn't want the blood drinking. Or anything else weird.

Andre pulled her stiff body onto his lap and nuzzled her neck. "I need to share this with you, Teagan. Do this for me, but I will not force it on you. It is a memory, nothing more."

She turned her head to look at him over her shoulder, her eyes wide. "That's the first time you've ever lied to me. I can feel that it's a lie. It isn't just a memory, it's so much more than that."

"Perhaps, but nevertheless, it is a memory. In the past."

She had to make a decision. He had lived with this terrible memory possibly for centuries. She still wasn't ready to go there all the way with him, but this—this was different. She was a healer and this was a terrible raw wound that had never closed. She knew she would do almost anything for him, even if it was going to hurt. Instinctively she knew whatever he was going to tell her was going to affect her for the rest of her life. Like Andre, she would never forget it.

Teagan relaxed into him. No matter what. No matter what he was or how angry he made her, Andre was hers. He belonged to her, and the rightness of that couldn't be denied. She *had* to share this memory with him. She turned slightly so she could lift a hand to his face and cup his jaw.

"Let me see, then." Teagan gave the invitation softly. She didn't try to hide that she wanted to be there for him. That she felt he did belong to her and she to him. They were already in each other's mind. He would know she was feeling all soft and loving toward him in spite of everything.

She couldn't help herself. It wasn't just his "binding" them together, because she still wasn't sure about how that worked, or how real it was. No, this was all Teagan. Her compassion and empathy for others, but especially him. This was a gift and she was taking it.

She used the pads of her fingers to smooth over his jaw. She loved the line of him, masculine and tough with a permanent five-o'clock shadow that made him look even more handsome than ever.

Her heart went out to him. At times he seemed so absolutely alone. She knew what that was like—clearly not on the same scale as he did, but still, she ached for him.

"I want to be your woman, Andre," she murmured, and leaned in to brush a kiss across his lips. "I just think maybe—sadly—you got it wrong. I don't know if I'm the woman you need and want. I'm very modern and I really, really have trouble with anyone telling me what to do and making decisions for me."

His hand moved up to her hair. She knew instantly he would have preferred it down. He liked the idea of feeling it in his hands. He'd fantasized how it would feel sliding over his body, but he didn't say anything. He didn't try to take out the intricate braid work.

"I know you, Teagan," he replied softly. "I see who you are. You are the woman for me. You brought me out of the darkness and into the light. There is no other."

She leaned in and nuzzled his throat, inhaling the scent of him into her lungs. Sorrow clung to him. Deep. As if whatever happened all those years ago, he felt it just as if it had happened that very day.

"My emotions have returned. They are ... overwhelming at times. I am working to get them under control."

The admission coupled with his fingers massaging the nape of her neck sent little flutters of awareness down her spine. She did what she always did when she needed time to process. She ignored all the things she didn't want to think about and went with her heart.

"Tell me, Andre. I want to know."

He leaned into her and very gently took her face between his hands, his gaze capturing hers for a long minute. She felt herself falling into his eyes. He brushed his mouth over hers with infinite gentleness.

"Thank you, *sivamet*. You have already lightened my heart."

He settled her more comfortably on his lap, wrapping his arms around her. She didn't know if he was comforting her, or needed the comfort himself.

"In those days, life was very different. There were much

fewer people in the area where I grew up. I had no other siblings. My mother hadn't been able to have children and when she had me, something went wrong with her mind. Maybe something had always been wrong with her, I do not really know. According to those who knew her, she really withdrew from the world after that difficult birth. There was only my father for her. No one else could reach her."

His hand found hers and he pulled it close to him, his fingers tight around hers. "I felt like the ghost they always call me. I was there, but not. She didn't see me or acknowledge me in any way. My father was very occupied with her, so most of the time, I was a ghost to him as well."

Teagan detested that. Her childhood had been one of love and laughter. She hadn't known anyone called him "Ghost." That bothered her, too. But mostly it was the way Andre spoke, as if none of it mattered to him. That wasn't the cause of his sorrow. He didn't reflect on his childhood as bad or good. It simply was.

"There were a lot of wars back then. Carpathians stayed out of them as much as possible. We had no interest in politics, but sometimes the fighting spilled over to our homes even though we were so remote."

She listened intently. At least he hadn't said "centuries ago," which helped her concentrate on the story and keep everything else at bay.

"I was alone a lot. I wandered around on my own most of the time, but eventually I met a human family—the Boroi family."

She pushed down her shock. Andre had introduced himself with that surname. She stayed quiet, wanting more now, needing to share his past.

"They lived in a little hut hidden deep in the forest. They had a few animals and not much else, but they were family."

His hand slipped from hers to span her rib cage, just below her breasts. His chin nuzzled the top of her head.

"Much like the family you grew up with," he added, "they loved one another fiercely. They were the closest I'd ever gotten to knowing what a family should be. I met their son, Euard, first. He was my age. His little sister, Elena, was a bit younger, and we all became good friends. They would come out at night and roam the forest with me. I was careful not to be anything but human. I protected our people, but Euard and Elena became my family."

"What were they like?" Teagan asked gently, wanting him to remember something other than the horror of his only childhood memory—something warm and loving. His voice was very wooden, as if he was reaching to find the good part of his childhood.

He was silent a moment. She was in his mind and she felt him searching. Reaching. Trying to find those recollections. His fingers began a slow massage over her ribs. She felt them trailing absently to her belly button and back up to the undersides of her breasts. She knew he was completely absorbed in trying to remember his childhood friends and not paying any attention to his hands. She liked that he was using her as his anchor.

"Elena was beautiful and sweet. She laughed all the time. She liked to spin in circles with her arms out. I remember she would call to me and tell me to spin with her. Euard would shake his head like he thought she was crazy, but he'd spin with her just as I would. She brought joy to her parents and Euard. I knew because their faces lit up the moment she came into a room."

His voice was soft and she could actually see Elena with him. She had long, dark hair and gleaming brown eyes. She was young, no more than ten or eleven. With her was a boy of about sixteen or seventeen.

The two memories came alive in Andre's mind and instantly she felt, not joy, but intense sorrow. Overwhelming sorrow. Anger. Guilt. The emotions poured into him and she felt his body tense. Deliberately she relaxed and breathed deep, in and out, using her meditative breathing in the hopes his breathing would follow hers. She circled his neck with her arms and fit her face into his shoulder, trying to comfort him.

Already, her compassion and empathy for him had her close to tears. She had to hold it together. She knew the moment she fell apart, Andre would stop sharing. He was like that. If she was making a list of the reasons why she was so completely enamored with him, that would be one of the many reasons. She smoothed his hair and pressed a kiss to his throat before settling once again.

"She sounds beautiful."

"She was like her mother. Dorina." There was wonder in his voice. "I did not ever think I would forget her. I had never seen sunshine, but I knew, if I did, it would be like Dorina Boroi. She worked hard, the little tiny hut was clean and always smelled of good things. More than anything I can remember the smells. She must have known Euard and Elena were sneaking out at night because she followed them. She invited me home right away. Her husband, Ion, was just as wonderful to me as they were, although gruff and offhand, like I didn't matter, but I did. I could tell. They all saw me."

He rubbed the bridge of his nose. "I think she even knew I wasn't human, but she welcomed me into her home and she made me one of them. She loved her children. She loved her husband. She came to love me. I could feel it every time I was in her home. She made me one of her children."

His voice had gone soft and Teagan knew he loved Ion, Dorina, Euard and Elena as if they were his own family. That was why the memory was the only one he had left. The human

215

family that "saw" him was far more real to him than the Carpathian couple he was only a ghost to. Her heart turned over for him. He had known love, he just hadn't remembered until this moment. With her. He'd shared something personal and beautiful with her and she would always treasure that gift.

12

That night, I could not wait to go see them," Andre continued. "My mother had wandered farther down a path that was far from even my father. He told me it was time he took her to another realm where they could be together again. He said I would be fine, that other couples would look out for me. He had made arrangements."

Teagan pressed her lips together to keep from blurting anything out. She couldn't imagine her grandmother ever treating her or her sisters that way. She felt the burn of tears and blinked rapidly, grateful her face was pressed against his shoulder and he couldn't see her face.

"Csitri."

There was that voice. All silk and velvet, brushing over her like his mouth might do. She shivered and burrowed closer, her stomach turning a little somersault and a melting sensation around her heart.

His arms tightened. "You are in my mind and I am in

yours. Do not try to hide your tears from me. It was all a long time ago."

But it wasn't. Not for Andre. It was yesterday. An hour ago. It was that moment. She knew the wound was raw and had never healed. A little sound escaped her throat but she nodded, trying to blink a lot to hold back tears.

"The Boroi family were wonderful people."

"Yes. They took me into their hearts, and I brought them pain and death. Excruciating pain."

His sorrow pressed down on her in waves. She breathed through it, determined to share his worst nightmare.

"What did you mean, your father was taking your mother to another realm? What does that mean?"

"Every healer we knew tried to help her. She was bound to my father so he was the only one able to reach her, to talk to her. No one else. I cannot remember a single word she ever spoke to me. She would walk right past me, even if I stood in front of her, talking to her, trying to get her to see me, but she never did. My father walked with her into the sun."

She closed her eyes. Clearly his father had killed his mother and then committed suicide. How terrible. She couldn't imagine having her grandmother calmly tell her that she intended to kill a loved one and then herself. She stayed quiet, trying to surround him with as much comfort as she could give him.

"I knew it was coming," Andre admitted. "I just did not expect it so soon. I left the house because I knew I could not talk my father out of it and it was difficult to face the fact that I was already a ghost to him as well. Over the last few years, he had distanced himself from me as well. That was why I clung to Dorina, Ion and their children. I needed them that night."

She understood. There were no authorities that could

possibly stop his father. No one could, she saw that in his mind. He didn't have the ability either. Not physically and not verbally. He saw himself as a ghost in his home. He could argue and try to talk his father out of it, but he knew they wouldn't hear him. No one would hear him. Teagan pushed her finger into her mouth and bit down to keep from crying. She would hear this. He had gone through it and he needed to know she was strong enough to hear what had shaped his life and made him who he was.

Teagan pushed deeper into his mind and was surprised that she could. She had a vague notion that she could protect him from the horror of whatever it was that happened—and she knew there was far more than his father telling him he was going to kill his mother and then himself. Much more.

She was a healer, and she knew something about shields. She wished she had some healing stones with her, but she hadn't brought them. Only the one she wore around her neck. She wrapped one hand around the stone and let him take her with him into the deep forest.

She smelled wildflowers. Fox. She knew there were kits, snuggled with their mother in a den close to the narrow deer path Andre traveled on. She heard the music in the silver leaves of the trees. Still, in spite of the beauty of the night, the blanket of stars overhead, sorrow pressed deep.

Andre needed the sound of Elena's laughter. He wanted to see her face light up with joy when he arrived. He needed Dorina to ease the terrible ache inside of him—to welcome him the way she always did with a quick hug. Ion ruffled his hair and always clapped a hand to his shoulder and gave him a welcoming shake. Euard would try to hand him food. He always did, although Andre never took it. Never once had Andre used a single family member for sustenance. They were far too precious to him and he never wanted to put them at risk.

He quickened his pace, fighting back the sorrow pushing deep at him. His chest was heavy, the pressure burning. He tried to think about how Elena sounded when she spun in circles, her arms outstretched to the sky, her hands graceful, and her fingers fluttering. Sometimes the moonlight spilled over her and she looked ethereal. Other times she was laughing so much she looked the child she was, bright and beautiful and happy. Andre tried to remember, as he hurried toward their hut, the times when Euard spun with her and even Dorina and Andre joined them.

The smell hit him first because the wind shifted again, and the scent of burning flesh drifted through the trees. He stopped, his breath catching in his throat. Then the faint, terror-filled screams followed on the next gust. He recognized Dorina's voice. Something terrible had happened.

He forgot everything else and sped toward them, no longer pretending to be human or caring that he might get caught. He used the preternatural speed of his kind, streaking toward the small hut as quickly as possible. He saw Ion first. There in the front of the house. He was lying on the ground, his face turned toward Andre as he settled to earth and emerged from the trees.

Andre had never seen such pain on a man's face. Ion lay under a mountain of stones and they were clearly crushing him. Andre rushed toward him, but Ion shook his head, at least he tried to, his eyes frantic. He opened his mouth as if to try to warn him, but there was no sound, only deep red blood bubbling out.

Teagan's stomach lurched. She could see clearly that Ion was suffering terribly. The massive pile of stones heaped over Euard and Elena's father was enormous and the stones were huge. The blood coming from his mouth clearly meant it was far too late to save him, but the shocked boy racing out of the tree line to drop to his knees beside his friend clearly hadn't comprehended that yet.

Andre waved his hands, trying to move the stones. How they had gotten on Ion there in the forest was a mystery, but he had to move them before they crushed Ion to death. He was only just learning to control levitation. He had been moving small objects since he was a toddler, but nothing of this magnitude.

Ion turned his head one last time, drawing Andre's attention back to him. The boy froze. Ion's neck was torn and bloody. Comprehension dawned, and with it, fear. The undead had done this. He knew then, that Ion was already dead. There was no hope for him, but the others . . . Dorina. Euard. Elena. Sweet little Elena.

Ion made a sound, a rattling in his throat. A gasp. His eyes were frantic. Andre recognized the warning. Ion was trying to save him. He wanted Andre to run. He didn't understand Andre had nothing—no one—to run to. Everyone he had was right there.

Andre brushed a kiss over Ion's forehead, then was up and running around to the back of the hut. As he ran, he reached for his father on the private telepathic path that connected them. He found only a dark void. His stomach lurched. His father hadn't waited for the dawn. He was already gone and he'd taken Andre's mother with him.

The terrible weight in his chest grew as he rounded the corner, his mind reaching for the common Carpathian telepathic link they all had. He called for help as he ran, knowing it was too late, but if a hunter came, this family would be avenged. He had no experience. He was considered a child in Carpathian years and he had no formal training and lacked the skills and power needed to face a full-fledged vampire, but it didn't matter to him. This was his family and he would save it if he could.

221

Teagan wanted to scream at the boy Andre to stop. Dread filled her. Filled him. He skidded to halt when he rounded the corner of the hut. Euard was writhing, pinned to the back of the house by four stakes. Two through his shoulders and two lower, down near his ribs. Blood flowed freely from the holes the stakes made. His feet were off the ground and his body weight pulled against the stakes, making every move sheer agony.

Bile rose in Teagan's throat. She was far too sensitive to see and feel this, but she refused to pull out of his head. Andre had faced this and she would, too. She recognized the pattern of the stakes. Two at the shoulders. Two at the ribs. Those, round circular scars so prominent on Andre's body.

A monster stood over Elena, his bony fingers wrapped around her throat. He was large and powerful looking. His hair was in mats and hung dank and dirty around him, flowing down his back like a rat's tail. His turned his head slowly toward Andre. Blood was smeared over his face and dripped down his chin. His lips and teeth were stained red. His fingers tightened around Elena's throat, one talon digging into her neck so that small ruby red beads flowed down her skin.

"Ciprian." Andre breathed his name.

His uncle. His mother's only brother. He had disappeared when Andre was seven or eight and yet now he had returned. Why? He was vampire. The undead. He had chosen to give up his soul to feel the rush of the adrenaline-based blood of a kill.

"The little ghost. Come join me. Feast, my boy."

The vampire was high. The fear-based blood rushed through his system. His eyes burned red and hideous. His mouth stretched into a parody of a smile. He continued to force Elena's head forward. To Andre's horror, he realized Ciprian was insisting Elena drink her brother's blood.

Her wide, shocked eyes leapt to Andre. He saw the terror

there. The shame. The humiliation. Her eyes darted to the side and Andre followed her gaze. His heart stopped beating in his chest. His breath stilled in his lungs. Dorina, beautiful, vibrant Dorina, so full of love and laughter, so generous, lay like a broken doll on the ground, flung away from the undead after he'd tortured her, and taken her blood.

She wasn't dead. Ciprian hadn't even given her that final mercy. She lay dying, her last sight that of the vampire forcing her beloved youngest child to drink the blood of her son as he suffered, staked to the wall.

"You brought me here, boy. I followed your scent right to them." Ciprian threw back his head and laughed, the sound more of a shriek. Ciprian who, like his sister, had looked right through Andre when he was a boy, now wanted him to feel guilt.

Teagan gasped. The blow to Andre was so gruesome, so brutal, Teagan knew she was going to vomit. She tore herself out of Andre's arms, leapt off his lap and raced for the next chamber. She wasn't going to throw up in front of him. How had he survived such a thing? How? Tears blinded her and she nearly ran into the walls of the cave. She went to her knees, gagging and wretching up bile.

How? It wasn't possible to survive something like that. Not whole. Not intact. She wanted to scream and throw things. She wanted to wrap her arms around Andre and keep him safe. She wanted this terrible, hideous memory wiped from him for all time, but she knew—she absolutely knew—that wasn't going to happen.

"Teagan."

Her heart fluttered. Melted. She knelt on the floor, the back of her hand pressed tight against her mouth, desperate to stop what she couldn't stop. It wasn't over. She had to know everything. He would want to stop. She already felt it in her mind, but there were those four scars on him, when even a vampire punching a hole in his chest didn't scar him. Those scars had come from somewhere, just as the ones in his mind did.

"I'm all right, Andre. Just give me a minute. I need my toothbrush. And water. I need water to rinse out my mouth." She didn't look at him. She didn't want to see compassion on his face. Not for her. Not after what had happened to him. Not when the wound was still so bloody and raw.

"I should never have exposed you to such brutality. You are far too sensitive, *csitri*. I can remove the memory from your mind."

The gentleness, the sweetness in his voice, brought a choking lump to her throat. How had he become such a beautiful man when he'd gone through so much? He should be damaged beyond fixing, and yet he was so careful with her.

"Don't. I don't want you to erase anything from my mind, Andre," she protested. "As long as you remember this, I will remember it, too. And I want all of it. Not just this part. As soon as my teeth are brushed, you give me the rest."

His hands spanned her waist and he lifted her onto her feet. "No."

She turned in his arms, caught the front of his shirt in her fist and gave the material a little shake. "You don't get to say no to me. Not over something this important. If you mean what you said, and I'm your lifemate or whatever you said in your language, then you don't get to say no to me. This is important to both of us, not just you."

He touched her face gently, his fingers following the trail of her tears. He lifted his hand away and looked at the wet pads of his fingers.

"It isn't for them," Teagan whispered. "I feel terrible for them, but it was a long time ago and they're somewhere they can't hurt anymore."

His blue eyes searched her dark ones. "For me? These are for me?"

She nodded. "I wish I was a better healer, Andre. I'd take the pain and sorrow away. I'm sorry I'm not."

He shook his head, staring down at her broodingly for what seemed an eternity, his beautiful, deep blue eyes drifting over her face with a hint of possession in them. "Go brush your teeth, then, Teagan. Be certain this is what you want."

He was what she wanted, and this terrible event had been the defining moment of his life. She needed to know, to share it with him, no matter the cost to her. She lifted her gaze to his, held it. "I am absolutely certain."

He pushed a hand through his hair and then gripped the back of his neck as if it ached. "Teagan."

Her name again. He did that a lot, mostly when he was exasperated with her. Or she'd done something he couldn't quite get.

She held up her hand. "If what you said to me is the truth, Andre, and you belong to me, then this is my right. I need to understand. We're very different. If we're going to work, I need this information or I'm going to be stepping all over you without knowing it. Are you mine?"

He nodded his head slowly, his eyes suddenly soft. Just that look alone sent her heart tumbling and the butterflies fluttering.

"Well then, it's settled," she said firmly. She looked around for her backpack. She needed a small time-out so she could gather herself. Her legs were shaky and her eyes burned like hell, but she could do this. She *would* do this, no matter the cost to herself, because someone had to be in his life. Someone had to love him and care for him. Most of all, someone had to "see" him.

She looked over her shoulder at him as she removed her

toothbrush and toothpaste from her pack. "You're not a ghost, Andre. Not to me. Never to me. I do see you and I'll always see you."

Because she was his woman and she was going to make this work. Somehow. Blood-taking aside, she'd make it work. Andre needed her, and deep down, where she kept all her secrets, she knew she needed him as well. She turned away from him. "I need water for rinsing out my mouth. This is just gross."

Andre stood there just watching Teagan, his body utterly still. She had cried for him. *Cried.* Real tears. For him. He could love her for that alone. *Are you mine?* Such a simple question, but it meant everything to him. She was giving herself to him. *I do see you. I'll always see you.* He had no idea a woman could wrap herself so tight inside a man that he couldn't find breath without her. *You're not a ghost.* He closed his eyes briefly just to savor the soft sound of her voice breathing life into him.

He wrapped his arm around her from behind, a cup of water in his fist. She took it and gave him a small smile over her shoulder. Just a flash of her rich, dark chocolate eyes. A deep, melting brown. Liquid. She tried to look stern at times, or tough, he was never quite certain what look she was going for because to him everything she did, every expression, was adorable. Cute. Beautiful.

"Thanks, Andre. I'll be finished in a minute."

He heard the warning in her voice as she turned back to rinse her mouth and brush her teeth. She was determined to see this through. He didn't want that for her. She really was too sensitive. He needed her to know why he had to make the decisions he made, but he didn't want her traumatized for life. Still, she was determined and she was impressive in her determination.

His woman. Teagan. He breathed her name in his mind. Beautiful, sweet Teagan. Her light shone bright even in the darkest of times. He had never thought to relive his worst day and yet he had when he clawed his way from Carpathian paralysis knowing Teagan was so close to a vampire's lair. He hadn't been able to breathe. He could barely think, his mind swamped with images of the loss of his human family.

Sweet, beautiful Teagan who commanded the light and could find humor in anything. He had vowed if he saved her, if he reached her in time, he would never allow her to be in such a precarious position again.

He'd faced countless battles and had suffered horrendous wounds. Nothing had ever threatened to break him—to shatter him—after the death of his human family. Not once in all the centuries of his existence, until he thought he might lose Teagan.

He found the way she brushed her teeth with such enthusiasm fascinating. He found everything about her fascinating. He liked the way she walked, the soft sway to her hips. He liked that she was small and he could practically surround her waist with his hands. Her muscles were small as well, but firm and tight, a climber's muscles.

She had cried for him. His own mother had never looked at him with soft eyes or wet ones. Only Dorina, his human mother who had died far too soon and in such a brutal way. No one else ever had. Until Teagan. Every moment he spent with her, he was aware he was falling deeper under her spell. He knew the lifemate bond was strong, unbreakable even, but he hadn't known his feelings for her would be equally as strong and unbreakable.

He was having a much more difficult time with his emotions being so new and raw and overwhelming. He felt everything and when the memories closed in, the sorrow was all too real and impossible to ignore.

He felt her then, pouring into his mind. Strong. Unbelievably strong. Her ability shocked him when few things in the world did anymore. She was a powerful psychic and with the enhancement of his blood, she was growing even more in strength. He didn't know if it was her particular gift or not, but she was definitely already partway in the Carpathian world.

He took her hand, locking their fingers together as he drew her back to the chairs he'd manufactured for her. She had a long way to go before she learned all that was in store for her with her new life, but everything she saw, even his memories, would help to prepare her.

She settled into the smaller of the two chairs, drawing up her knees almost protectively, although he knew she wasn't aware that was what she was doing. Andre couldn't have that. He reached over and lifted her right out of the chair and into his lap.

"What are you doing? This lap thing is becoming a habit, and I'm not the kind of girl to sit in men's laps," Teagan declared, but she wrapped her arms around his neck.

"You might want to rethink your position on that," Andre said. "I like having you close." He paused, nuzzling the top of her head, wishing again that her long hair was out of the braids so he could bury his hands in all its richness. "I need you this close to me."

Teagan leaned into Andre, allowing herself to breathe him in. She was already rethinking her position on laps. He was so warm, and he felt as good as he looked. More, his arms were strong and that made her safe. Well ... she *loved* the way he smelled. Really loved it. Mostly, if he was going to relive the rest of his nightmare, she wanted to be close. She wanted to be holding him so he knew he wasn't alone.

"I'll rethink," she said, and brushed a kiss along his jaw. "Share the rest of it with me, Andre. Let me all the way in."

She hoped she was strong enough to be the woman he needed. The moment he reached for the memory, sorrow pressed in; not a blanket of it, more like a weighty stone. Grief was so acute she felt she was drowning in it. She took a breath and let herself go, gave herself to Andre. He needed her more than anyone else ever could.

She inhaled and smelled blood. She didn't know fear had an odor, but it did. Fear permeated the entire area between the house and the forest. She couldn't see Ion, but she knew it was impossible to save him. Euard was pinned by the four stakes through his shoulders and ribs. The hideous vampire gripped Elena—sweet young Elena—forcing her face toward the blood flowing from her brother's body. A few feet away lay Dorina, looking like a broken doll, her neck torn, her legs and arms twisted in macabre ways.

Andre rushed the vampire. Only a boy. No experience. His uncle was a big man, much like Andre fully grown. Clearly he had a *lot* of experience. Teagan wanted to close her eyes, just like she did if she inadvertently went into the room when her sisters were watching horror movies, but she couldn't. The scene played out in her mind—in Andre's mind—and she wasn't going to pull away and leave him alone. Still, she knew.

Ciprian laughed as he dropped the child to the ground and caught Andre as the boy tried to slam his fist through the vampire's chest.

"That is not the way, ghost," Ciprian said. "Join me. You led me here, now join me in the feast."

"Never," Andre declared, struggling against the power and strength of the larger man.

Ciprian caught Andre in his bony hands, his terrible talons digging deep into Andre's flesh. He bent his head and sank his teeth into Andre's neck, gulping at the rich blood. He didn't rend and tear as he'd done with the humans. He was more careful. Clearly he enjoyed watching Andre squirm. When he'd fed on Andre's blood, he flung the boy to the ground, deliberately aiming for Dorina's body.

"Even your blood is not strong yet," Ciprian said with derision. "You are a child playing at being a warrior. Join me or you will die with them." Contempt twisted his face, and he dismissed the boy, turning back to Elena, dragging her by her hair, off the ground where she'd crumpled at her brother's feet.

Andre landed almost on top of Dorina, on his back, the wind knocked out of him so that he lay there, his lungs burning, his face turned toward the only woman who had ever really showed him kindness. She was dying. He could see that, but still, her eyes, when she looked at him, were soft with love and fear for him. He touched her hand. He might not be able to save her, but he was determined to save her daughter at least.

The boy gathered himself, and this time he used his limited abilities to weave together a weapon. His uncle, completely absorbed in terrorizing the two human children, didn't bother to look at him a second time, certain Andre was no threat to him.

Andre moved fast, with blurring speed, and slammed the long spear through Ciprian's body, using his combined speed and weight for the force necessary to drive the wood through his back toward the vampire's heart. Ciprian screamed and flung Elena from him, whirling around as black blood splattered in a circle. He caught Andre by the throat with one hand.

"I am going to tear out your heart and eat it," he declared. A crafty look came into his eyes. "But first, you can wait while I kill the others." He waved his free hand and lifted Andre by his throat and drove him backward to the side of the house, right beside Euard.

Four stakes appeared anchored into the house, a good two inches around, the points razor-sharp. Ciprian slammed Andre's body right against the house itself, so that the stakes went through his shoulders and ribs, pinning him just like Euard. The tips came out the front so that his entire weight was suspended there.

The pain was excruciating, but it was nothing like the agony Andre suffered as he watched helplessly while his uncle tortured and killed both Elena and Euard. He wanted to die. He welcomed death. Not because of the physical pain, that didn't matter. In one long night he'd lost his birth parents. He had lost his uncle long ago, and now this human family—the one he loved—was dead. Ion. Dorina. Euard. Elena. All because of him. Because he'd sought them out and left a trail to them. He hadn't been strong enough to save them.

After what seemed hours, but couldn't have been, Ciprian turned toward Andre, smeared with the bright red blood of his victims and covered in his own black blood. The spear still protruded from his body as if he couldn't be bothered with such a paltry inconvenience as removing the weapon while he feasted.

Wind hit the building hard. Dark clouds roiled overhead. Ciprian whirled around, and out of the forest came another man. He was tall. Powerful. His slashing eyes took in the scene immediately and he was on Ciprian before the vampire could move. With the spear already through his body, just below his heart, the undead had little maneuvering room.

"Roman," Andre whispered, barely lifting his head. Blood streamed from around the stakes. He had struggled while Ciprian tortured and killed his friends, but now he didn't move. He didn't want to survive.

Roman Daratrazanoff slammed his fist deep into the undead with one hand while the other began a slow withdrawal of the spear. Teagan saw why the vampire hadn't removed the weapon. Black blood poured out of his body. He screamed and shrieked hideously, his terrible talons swiping at Roman's face and body. He couldn't quite reach the Carpathian hunter because Roman controlled his movements using the spear. All the while he kept digging through Ciprian's chest until he found the heart.

Andre abruptly closed off his mind to her. "Their deaths were my fault. I learned a valuable lesson that night. I stayed away from humans as much as possible. Unless I had to rescue them or use them to stay alive, I didn't go near them."

Teagan was still reeling from that nightmare memory that refused to leave him. She rubbed her palm up and down his chest soothingly. "It wasn't your fault and you know it. Maybe as a teenager you took that blame, but Ciprian wanted you to feel it. That was part of his whole high—to see your guilt and sorrow. He needed that to make himself feel something."

She felt Andre startle and knew she had judged the vampire's motives correctly. Andre's hand came up to her hair and once again she got the impression he wanted her braids out. She wanted to give him everything in that moment. He needed someone to give him everything.

She turned her face up to his throat and nuzzled him. "Baby, if you want my hair down, I'll take it down for you, but we're in the mountains far from a shower and I have a lot of hair. I sort of inherited it from both my mother and father, so it's thick and wild and very long. I keep it braided when I go hiking."

"Let me."

Andre sounded gruff, as if her offer meant a lot to him. As

232

in a *lot*. Her stomach did a little flutter and her heart felt as if it melted right there in her chest.

"What happened to you after that?"

"I lived with another family of Carpathians. They had three sons, triplets. Mataias, Lojos and Tomas. Over the centuries, like many siblings, they were never far from one another. They come from a long line of famous warriors, a respected family that always produced multiple children, yet rarely gave birth."

Andre sighed. "Two daughters were born to the family after the triplets, but neither lived beyond their second year. A master vampire claimed their mother when she was pregnant with another set of triplets. Of course their father followed his lifemate. I helped them hunt the vampire across two continents. We did not stop until we destroyed the undead, exacting justice. The triplets are younger than me by a few years. I stayed with their family, but I began to lose the ability to see in color nearly right away and then my emotions began to fade before I was fifty. I spent most of my time learning the skills needed to kill vampires. Because I did, the triplets did as well. I did not talk much, but they never seemed to mind."

"Are they still alive?"

"Yes. They went to the United States. I was supposed to go with them, but I stayed behind because I ran across the trail of a master vampire and his followers." He brushed a kiss over the top of her head. "If I had not done so, I would not have discovered my lifemate."

"Who was the man who came to save you?"

Andre sighed. "Roman Daratrazanoff. He was second-in-command to the prince of our people. He came too late."

"I'm so sorry, Andre." Teagan felt the weight of her hair as it slid from the braids as if by magic. His fingers were already diving deep, as if he had found a treasure. "That's where you got those scars."

"I kept them. Roman was a great healer. He made certain I stayed alive, but I kept the scars to remind me."

She tilted her head to look at him. There were drops of blood tracking down his face. She wiped at them with her thumb, unable to determine where they came from. "You have a memory that has refused to go away, Andre. You're already scarred. You didn't need to keep them."

"Four of them."

"I don't understand."

"One for each of them." He touched his left shoulder. "Ion." His right shoulder. "Dorina." The left side of his rib cage. "Euard." The right side. "Elena."

Her throat closed, clogged with tears. "Of course," she whispered. "I'm so sorry, Andre." She recognized that the four scars were his tribute to the family he'd loved.

"Then you will understand why I have to do this."

Her heart jumped. She bit her lip. His fists tightened in her hair. "Do what?"

"Make you wholly mine."

"You've already done that, Andre. I told you I wasn't going anywhere. I just want to make it clear I'm not okay with the blood thing. You can take my blood. It's sort of sexy, but no way am I taking yours."

She looked up at him. Met his eyes so he would understand she was laying down the rules of their relationship. She could accept what he was, but she definitely drew the line at ingesting his blood. That was just plain *eww* and she wasn't going there.

"You still do not understand. I slept with you aboveground, Teagan, but I cannot continue to do that on a regular basis. The soil heals and rejuvenates me. I must go to ground, especially after I have been wounded. If I do not, it weakens me. I cannot protect you when I am in the Carpathian sleep. You wandered off and put yourself in danger."

She swallowed hard. She'd known. It wasn't as if this came as a shock. She'd already suspected that he slept in the ground. She just didn't want to think of him as a vampire. Clearly he wasn't, but he definitely wasn't human either.

"I learned my lesson. I'm not going out on my own. I'll hang right next to you, wherever you're sleeping. *Above*ground, but still, very close to you."

Andre buried his face in her hair. "You know that will not work. We cannot be separated. Already your mind turns to mine. Once you cannot reach me, you will believe I am dead and that will be dangerous as well."

Now she didn't understand. She was a perfectly logical person. If she saw him sleeping in the ground she would know exactly what he was doing, right? "Andre, I'm totally committed to this relationship and you have to know that's huge for me. I've never heard of Carpathians and I always thought vampires were a myth. I'm taking in a lot right now."

"I know that, Teagan. I am well aware of the fact that I have had to push you faster and much further than I ever wanted to."

"Tell me about your people. That will help me feel like I'm not completely crazy. I actually considered that my grandmother might need to go to a hospital or at the very least, go on medication, and all this time she was right. Maybe if I know what's going on, I can convince my sisters ... "

"No. Our people cannot ever be known to humans. You know why, Teagan. We are nearly extinct as it is. There is a group, probably the one your grandmother is involved with, who hunt and kill everyone they consider vampire. They cannot tell the difference between Carpathian and the

235

undead. They sometimes even kill humans they just do not like."

Teagan could understand why he didn't want anyone to know about his species. Still. Her grandmother wasn't crazy, and Andre was living proof of that. "Okay, I'll find another way to convince my family. But please tell me about Carpathians so I understand you better."

"We have existed for centuries. We have longevity, so long it seems that we are immortal, but we can be killed. We must have blood to survive, but we are very careful of our suppliers. They are treated with respect and never frightened. We do not, of course, allow them to remember anything."

"You took my blood that first time and I didn't remember." But she did. She just thought it was an erotic dream. She put her hand over the pulse beating in her neck. Holding him to her. That's what it felt like, as if she were holding him to her.

"Yes, *sivamet*, I took your blood. I *have* to take your blood. It is erotic to me as well."

Teagan sucked in her breath. For the first time in her life she experienced jealousy. It wasn't pretty and it wasn't comfortable. "I'm not certain I like that at all, you taking pleasure from some other person's blood."

13

"**T**eagan."

There it was again, his voice that caressed her skin and sent hungry little flames dancing through her body so she went damp and needy.

"Not with others. I feel nothing at all when I take blood from others." There was a small smile in his voice. "I do not feel anything for other women, let alone when I am feeding, Teagan. I never have. There is only you."

Teagan let her breath out slowly. "Good to know. I'm the type of woman who might get very inventive if I ever found out my man was cheating on me."

"Inventive?"

"I might have an accident with a pair of scissors."

"I see."

He lifted her hair from her neck and nuzzled the soft skin there. A shiver went down her spine. His teeth nipped and scraped and his tongue teased. She closed her eyes. He was

237

hot. Just plain hot. And she was weak. He wouldn't have any arguments from her if he kept that up.

"I like the sound of your voice, Teagan. I like the way you laugh. You are a breath of fresh air. There were times I felt I could not breathe. There was no air left for me on this planet and then you came along and turned my world to color. You breathe for me. Did you know that?"

His mouth was at her hair, licking behind it, teeth tugging on her earlobe. Her stomach did a flip. Her breasts ached. The area between her legs grew hotter. Who said things like that? Was there a man on earth who could make his woman feel more beautiful or special? If there was, she'd never met him.

"Look at me, *sivamet*. I need your mouth right now."

She forgot all about learning about his people. No one kissed like him either, and she wanted to taste him. She was almost desperate for his kisses and he'd barely touched her. She liked the way he said that—that he *needed* her mouth— because she was fairly certain she needed his as well.

Teagan turned her face up to his. His eyes drifted over her face possessively. No doubt about it, there was total possession in all that darkening blue. Her stomach somersaulted. She knew that change in color. The way his eyes went from ice to warm, to melting, straight to liquid, and his were way past that already. She might be a modern woman, well versed in how men didn't own a woman, but she liked that look of possession. Call her primitive, she didn't care. She liked that he said she belonged to him—and he to her. It was sexy. Thrilling. Somehow safe.

"There are no words to describe what I feel for you," he murmured softly.

She smoothed her palm over his chest up to his shoulder, feeling the ridged scar there beneath his shirt. "I feel the same way," she admitted. "Stop talking and kiss me."

The faintest bit of humor slipped into his eyes and then his mouth was on hers. Destroying her for anyone else. No one could kiss like Andre. No one could make her body melt like his did. He kissed her over and over, barely letting her come up for air, but then she didn't want air. She wanted him. His hand slipped down the column of her throat and circled there, so that her pulse pounded into his palm.

His gentle kiss grew aggressive, rougher, hotter, definitely in command. She didn't know what she was doing, but it didn't matter, she followed his lead. She was determined to be good at this. She wanted to be everything for him, including very good at kissing.

He kissed his way down to her chin and nipped her there. The sharp little sting sent an arrow of fire straight to her sex. She heard a soft little moan escape despite how hard she tried to suppress it. Instantly she buried her face in his neck, knowing the color swept up her body.

"Teagan, I like to hear you. I want to hear you. You can never be embarrassed or ashamed with me. I am your lifemate."

"But I don't even know how to kiss you properly. And you're so good at it. I mean like off-the-planet good. I don't know how to touch you, or . . . or anything."

"I like teaching you things. I had centuries to prepare for my woman. Carpathian males believe in being prepared. It is up to us to make sex good for our lifemate so we study. We acquire knowledge. We learn. We need things to occupy our minds, so although we do not feel, we study."

She made a face. "Are you telling me you've been a hound dog for centuries? Because I really don't want to hear that."

"No, *csitri*, I am telling you I studied an art and I acquired as much information about it as possible so I could please you. I told you, more than once, I cannot feel anything for another woman."

239

She found herself very happy with that. And she liked the idea that he'd acquired a great deal of knowledge just for her.

He leaned down and kissed her throat. His hand moved and her shirt and panties were gone, just like that. She thought that particular gift wasn't just magical, it was *way* practical. His hand came up to her breast, cupping the soft, slight weight, finger and thumb strumming gently on her nipple, sending another shiver through her body. Then he was grasping, tugging and rolling, and her veins turned hot and molten. The breath left her lungs in a mad rush and another sound escaped—another soft moan.

"Are you wet for me?" he murmured against her collarbone.

She swallowed hard. She wasn't just wet, she was *very* wet. If he kept using his fingers and tongue and teeth like that, she'd be soaked.

"Yes." She could barely get the word out. "For you."

He kissed her again. Long. Hard. Amazing. Perfect. When he lifted his head, his eyes glittered, dark with passion.

"Put your arms around my neck."

It was her only warning and then he was up with her cradled in his arms and floating them across the cave straight to the bed. She loved the feeling of moving through the air, clinging to him, holding him close. Neither wore clothes, and this time, she wanted to see him, to touch him. She'd been shy before and she still was a little intimidated, but he belonged to her. He made that very clear and she felt it was true with every breath she took.

She felt the mattress at her back, her legs and arms sprawled out, and before she could move, he was on her, blanketing her. He was big and his weight should have suffocated her, but she only felt his hard, strong body over hers. His heat. His muscles. His very heavy erection. That sent another rush of dampness to the junction of her legs.

"I love that you are ready for me. I love that my woman welcomes me."

"You kissed me," she pointed out.

His hands framed either side of her head. His blue eyes drifted over her face, his gaze hot. Intense. Possessive. Filled with lust. Oh. My. God. So blue she was reminded of the deepest arctic sea. Another rush of liquid. Her heart stuttered.

"Is that all it takes?"

"From you, yes." She was honest. "You get the same results looking at me. Or touching me. Holding my hand can do it. Just standing there looking gorgeous could—"

He kissed her, cutting her off. She was quite happy that he did. His fingers found hers, threaded through them and stretched her arms out on either side of her head as he kissed her until she forgot how to breathe without him. Until her body was on fire and there was no one else in the world but the two of them.

He kissed his way down to her chin and then was at her ear, teeth tugging on her earlobe before following a path along her collarbone. She had to gasp, to find a way for her lungs to work, her hands straining against his, wanting to feel him. Touch him.

"This isn't fair," she whispered.

He transferred both hands to one of his, keeping her arms stretched above her head, this time pinning both wrists to the mattress.

"Was I supposed to be fair about something?" he asked. "I am of the ancient world, not the modern world."

He was teasing her. Tormenting and teasing. She squirmed beneath him, but his body had her just as firmly pinned as his hand did.

"Andre." She gasped his name on one of those rare moments she could find air.

241

He pressed kisses down the slight slope of her breast and nuzzled her nipple. His tongue stroked. She felt the edge of his teeth. Her body nearly convulsed with pleasure.

"I need you in me."

"You will get me." His voice was lazy. Sexy.

He didn't look up, he was busy at her breasts, using his tongue, his teeth and his clever, wicked fingers. His mouth closed over her left breast and he suckled strongly.

"Andre." She cried out his name, arching into him. Her head went back, thrashing on the pillow.

"I love to hear my name when you get close. You are close. I feel it. I have not yet entered your body and you are already close." There was satisfaction in his voice. "I want you to give this to me, *sivamet*. I need this."

His whispered words were so sexy. The brush of his long hair against her skin fed the fire growing in her. She was burning up, and he was so perfectly in control. It wasn't fair. She needed to find a way to make him burn, but with her hands pinned, it was impossible. She could only lie beneath him, her hips bucking, her body coiling with tension, tighter and tighter.

His teeth suddenly sank into her, right above her breast, right on the swelling curve. She cried out, her body exploding, imploding, the orgasm crashing over her. He let go of her hands and she wrapped both arms around his head, cradling him to her while he fed. It was the most erotic, sensual thing she had ever experienced. The wave took her hard, rushing through her body like a tsunami. She loved the feel of his mouth on her, his hands sliding over her skin, moving down, down past her belly and cupping her sex. What little breath she had left was gone when he pushed a finger into her. Deep. Possessively.

Mine.

That sent another wave of heat rushing through her like a firestorm. Her tight muscles clamped down hard around his finger, trying to draw him deeper. She loved being his. She loved how strong he felt. She loved that he could pin her to a mattress with his powerful body and not squish her. She loved the way he pushed a second finger into her to join the first and her body began that amazing build all over again.

I love the way you taste. So addictive. I will never get my fill. Centuries. And I will never get my fill.

She wanted to be addictive. She wanted it so much she closed her ears to the word *centuries*. The one he threw around so casually.

His tongue licked at the curve of her breast and then he was kissing his way down her stomach. Her fists found his hair. He was on a mission, leaving a trail of fire behind him. His large hands wrapped around her thighs and parted them. She gasped and tried to come off the mattress. He planted one hand on her belly, his head coming up.

Her heart nearly stopped at the look in his eyes. She'd never seen that particular look and, truthfully, it was a little bit scary. Hot. Predatory. Intense. Possessive. Definitely lust. Something else that made her subside. A demand. He could do that. Make her weak. Modern or not. Especially when he dropped his head and his mouth was on her—there, between her legs—and she came apart a second time.

It happened so fast. So unexpectedly. Sneaking up on her and taking possession of her before she could catch her breath. He didn't stop. His tongue and his teeth and his fingers continued to move in her. Press into her. Stroke that sweet, wonderful spot that sent tremors through her body, sent walls of flame dancing through her and shocks that rocked her over and over.

"Andre." She whispered his name. Moaned it. "It's too much."

Again. More. I need more. Give it to me again. You taste like nectar. So perfect. Give me more, sivamet.

He was driving her up again. Hard. Fast. Relentless. Ruthless even. His mouth was pure sin. His tongue wicked. His fingers clever and demanding. This time the tsunami took her with such strength, spreading up to her breasts and down to her thighs, so strong her body shuddered and she felt tears burning her eyes at the sheer miracle of such sensation.

He lifted his head and was on her again, rolling them so he was on the bottom and she was on the top. He lifted her by the waist, straight up in the air.

"Straddle me, *csitri*. Legs on either side of my hips. Take me in your hand."

She did what he said, wrapping her fist around the hot thickness of his shaft. He all but slammed her down right over him, impaling her, forcing her to remove her hand, to fight for air while fire streaked through her body and rushed through her veins.

His fingers bit deep into her as he urged her to move, to ride him. He filled her completely, so thick and hard she felt stretched and full. It was exquisite. Beautiful. Perfect.

His hands slid around to her bottom. Slid up her back and began to apply pressure until she was lying against his chest, his body moving in hers. Controlling the rhythm. His hands went to her hair, fingers sliding through the length of it.

"Avio päläfertiilam, come into my world with me," he murmured softly. He tugged her head up and leaned up to kiss her.

His kisses were extraordinary. She felt light-headed. Dazed. In love. The movement of his hips, his body moving in hers was delicious.

"Find the rhythm, *päläfertiilam*, find my heart. Hear my pulse? The blood in my veins calls to you. Kiss me."

Teagan kissed him. She found she could kiss much better than she thought she could. She burned. Deep inside. In her mind. She needed. She craved his taste. There, on her tongue, she was addicted to his taste. She had to have more. She kissed her way along his strong jaw, down his throat. She licked at his flat nipple and nipped at his skin with her teeth.

His hand came up between her mouth and his skin. Between that strong, dark pulse beckoning to her. His hand was gone and then was back to shaping her skull, urging her mouth against him once more. She licked at skin and there it was. That delicious, addictive taste. Every cell in her body went wild. Out of control. Her muscles clamped down hard around him, holding him to her as he rocked her body with more force, sending streaks of fire through her.

She lapped at his skin and then clamped her mouth on him, suckling, drawing the hot, spicy masculine taste that was all Andre into her mouth and down her throat. Flames spread from her throat to her every organ. Every cell. She could feel the fire building and building and it wasn't enough.

She heard Andre groan. Sexy. She felt him swell in her, stretching her even more. His hips went wild, surging into her over and over. Faster. Harder. She ground down on him, needing the fire now. Needing his taste. Needing to be complete. Needing. Just plain needing.

Tell me you are mine.

You know I am. And she was. Her beautiful, extraordinary man who could give her three orgasms before he was even inside of her. Who could show her such beauty and make her feel extraordinary as well.

His hand was back, pushing between her mouth and his chest. He was gentle, but adamant, even when she protested. *You can have as much as you want later, Teagan. Right now, I want something else.*

The way his voice brushed on the insides of her mind was just plain thrilling. His hands bit once more into her waist and she was lifted off of him. She cried out and tried to catch at him, but he rolled her onto her stomach, caught her hips and yanked them up, one hand on the nape of her neck, pressing her face down so that her bottom was high.

He entered her in one swift thrust. She screamed. Loud. The friction was incredible. He was scorching hot. Deeper than he'd ever been. Perfect. Amazing. She wanted more.

"Harder, Andre," she whispered.

She turned her head to the side, closing her eyes to feel every stroke. She gripped the cover in both fists, holding on tight while he slammed into her over and over, jolting her body with each thrust. She could have sworn lightning streaked through her, great white-hot bolts that forked out and spread through her entire body.

Andre went harder. Rougher. Driving into her with such power he rocked the bed beneath her. She felt the building of a tidal wave deep inside. It started in her breasts. Crept up her thighs. Coiled tighter. Centered there in her sex. Her body shuddered. She gripped the cover tighter.

Let go. I feel it. Give me what is mine. So beautiful, Teagan. So beautiful.

His voice was her undoing. The velvet, sensual pitch that caressed her skin and took her right over the edge. Her body seized. Held there. He pounded hard, sending streaks of lightning burning through her. Her feminine channel clamped down. Convulsed. Held him in a strangling grip. Then she was gone, clawing at the bed to stay anchored, her body slamming back into his, as the orgasm went on, seemingly endless.

She felt him swelling, stretching her more. He groaned her name. *Teagan.* Soft. Velvet. Silky. Perfect. She felt every bit of hot seed pouring into her. That triggered another long orgasm. He stayed in her. She didn't want to move, breathing hard into the mattress.

His hands slid over her back, a soothing caress. Both hands went to her buttocks, massaging, smoothing. Then he was pressed up against her, his front to her back, kissing his way up her spine until he reached the nape of her neck. He pushed her hair aside and kissed her there, too.

She would have collapsed if he hadn't had his arm firmly around her waist. She didn't want to lose him, but she needed to fall forward. Right on her face.

"Are you all right?"

"*Mmm.*" She couldn't form a single word. With his every movement there were more aftershocks. Big ones. Delicious ones.

"*Csitri.*" His hands were gentle as he slipped out of her and turned her into his arms. She found herself on her side, her body tight against his, his arm locked around her waist, one thigh between hers. His hand smoothed over her hair. "*Mmm* is not a word."

She ran her hand over his arm. "It is now. You're yummy, Andre, so *mmm* is definitely a word."

He laughed softly. His hand moved up her rib cage to cup the slight weight of her breast. She shivered when his thumb stroked her nipple. Her womb gave a little spasm and had another delightful aftershock.

"Your breasts are so sensitive."

"Small. I've always wanted to have bigger breasts. I contemplated surgery for a while. Nothing fits right. Clothes, I mean."

"Surgery?"

She turned her face to look at him over her shoulder, wanting to see his reaction. He *felt* puzzled. "Yes. Surgery. Implants. To be bigger."

"Why?" Now he looked horrified.

"So I'd look like a woman instead of a boy."

His eyes went soft. "Teagan. You are the most beautiful woman I have ever seen. I love your breasts." His palm cupped over her, swallowing her. "I love the way you feel in my hands. I especially love how sensitive you are. Never think about such a thing again."

He meant it, too. Teagan could tell. He was shocked and more than horrified. His palm cupped her breast. Held it to him like something precious, as if she were going to disfigure herself and he had to stop her. She found herself relaxing into him. He had no idea how much his reaction meant to her. She had always, for as long as she could remember, equated beauty with her sisters. All of them were simply stunning. All of them had real curves. Lots of curves. More than once they'd walked into a roomful of people together and the room fell silent. Teagan was so proud of them. They weren't only beautiful, but they were nice as well.

She had a Caucasian father—one who had left as soon as he realized his partner was pregnant. Her mother had died giving birth to her. Teagan was ten years younger than her closest sister and looked very different from all of them—short—slight—very little curves—and wild hair that was more silk than hair and impossible to tame. She was a brain, had no real social skills, but her sisters loved her with everything in them.

"Teagan. I would not like such a thing."

She tried not to smile. No matter how sweet Andre was, he often sounded as if he was issuing an order. Nicely. But still, an order.

"Do you remember when I told you I had real problems with authority figures? Bossy ones. Especially men." She thought a reminder might be just the thing. They were starting their relationship, and she might as well lay it on the line for him. "I'm not exactly a pushover, Andre. I have a temper."

"*Sivamet.*"

Just that. The sound of that word coupled with his silky accent sent a little tremor right through her entire body. He'd just made crazy, wild love to her and given her like a million orgasms, but her body forgot that and reacted all over again. *Sheesh*. She had no idea she was going to turn into a sex machine.

"What does that mean exactly?" The language was so beautiful and had so many meanings, she loved to hear his translations.

He was silent a moment, clearly trying to translate the word into English for her. She could feel his chin nuzzling the top of her head. She even loved that. His body was curved around her protectively and she loved that he cuddled her close. She could get used to that.

"Of my heart. My love. An endearment in my language that means something more. I cannot explain it better than that."

She liked that. She liked being of his heart. "That's nice. It makes me feel special." She bit at her lower lip for a moment. "Um, Andre?"

"Do not hesitate to ask me anything, Teagan. You are my other half."

"I like this. You holding me like this. Would it be too much trouble, before you have to go sleep in the ground, however you do that and please tell me coffins are not involved . . ."

"No coffins."

There was a trace of amusement in his voice. She liked that she put that there. He wasn't a man who laughed or found amusement in many things. She'd been in his mind. She knew that, yet he seemed to be on the verge of laughter a lot around her. She was grateful she could give that to him.

"Since we can't sleep together at night, would you be able to hold me like this until I fall asleep?" She felt a little silly asking, but it was the most amazing feeling. She'd never felt so safe in her life. Andre made her feel as if he'd walk on water for her.

"I sleep during the day, Teagan. You will, too."

"Some of the time," she agreed. "Because, of course, I want to spend most of my time with you, but there are things that can't be done at night."

He sighed and brushed his mouth over her hair. "*Csitri*, did you not hear me when I said you cannot go anywhere without me?"

She stiffened. "No. I heard you say not to leave this cave and your protection, but we aren't living here." She took a breath. "Are we? Permanently? I mean, we'll have a home. A house. Somewhere my family can come and visit." She was beginning to panic. "I don't know where I got the impression that you wouldn't mind living in the States if it was important to me."

"If something is important to you, Teagan, then we will do it. Mataias, Lojos and Tomas are in the States and I like to keep my eye on them. Knowing I found you will allow them to hold on a little longer. I have been a nomad for centuries, but we can have a home base if that is important to you as well."

She winced. There was that word *centuries* again. She was beginning to accept that he really was from another race and that he'd lived centuries, but still, it was difficult to process. Nearly immortal he'd said.

"When I grow old and die, what do you do then? You said there would be no other woman. In terms of your time, even if I live long, say, to ninety, that isn't long in your years."

"You will not grow old."

She turned in his arms to look up at his face. "Of course I will. Even you can't stop that, Andre."

She pressed her hand to her stomach. She hadn't eaten anything all night, which should have been her day. The thought of food made her sick, but her stomach was definitely hurting and getting worse by the moment.

"Honey, I think I'm going to get sick. I don't feel so good."

She tried to roll away from him, afraid of getting him sick, but his arm turned to iron. It was coming on fast. Her stomach felt as if she had a thousand razor blades cutting through her insides. Her hair was everywhere, a terrible mess and heavy on her head, pulling at her scalp. Her eyes burned. Her skin went hot. Not just hot, but so hot she began to sweat.

"Seriously, Andre, this isn't good. I'm really sick and I don't want you to get this."

"You are not ill, Teagan," he said.

The gentleness in his voice warned her something was off. He knew something she didn't. He was also very calm about her feeling so awful. She'd come to think of him as protective about everything—even something so mundane as her getting sick.

She licked at her suddenly very dry lips. They were already cracked as if she'd been running a high fever for days. Her stomach cramped and she bent nearly double.

"You can't touch me. Everything feels too heavy and too hot. My hair is driving me crazy." She was beginning to panic. They were far from medical aid. She had to have contracted some foreign bug. A nasty one.

Immediately her hair was back in the braids, not as intricate, but still, off her face, shoulders and back. A cool breeze swirled through the chamber. He sat up, a cool, wet cloth in his hands.

251

"I'm ill. I need a doctor." She tried to push his hand away. He *had* to get away from her before she infected him.

"You are going through the transition."

The explanation barely penetrated. Her brain even hurt. Her entire body cramped, every single muscle. She cried out, unable to stand the pain without an outlet. She'd never hurt so bad in her entire life.

"I don't understand."

"Teagan, look at me. Follow my breathing. Get on top of the pain."

"I'm not having a baby," she hissed.

But the pain came in a huge wave, overpowering her. Her body convulsed, her bones threatening to snap under the pressure. The convulsions were so severe she nearly came off the bed. Only Andre's strong arms kept her from rolling to the floor.

"I know. You are going through the transition. The change. From your life to mine. Your body is getting rid of toxins and reshaping organs. I can take the edge off the pain, but I cannot bear it for you, as much as I would like."

Her breath hissed out of her lungs. "I'm what?" She tried not to shout. Maybe she'd heard him wrong. Especially since he'd delivered the news in such a matter-of-fact voice, like she wasn't convulsing and her bones nearly breaking into pieces. It hurt. It hurt *so* bad.

She didn't want him looking at her. Witnessing this. She didn't want to look at him, not when he was looking so remote. So removed. She wanted to cry, but she couldn't spare the energy. Another wave was coming. She felt it swell through her insides, cutting her like jagged glass. She tried to relax and breathe, just like Andre had told her, but it was impossible. Her lungs felt cut up, raw, burning with every breath she tried to take.

Her body contorted and bile rose. She knew she was going to get sick and she tried again to roll off the bed, to get away from Andre, to crawl out of her own skin and disappear. Andre caught her in his strong arms and took them both to the floor of the cave, away from their bed. As he wrapped her up in his arms, to keep her body from slamming hard on the floor, the wave receded.

Teagan glanced up at his face. Pure stone. A mask. His eyes glacier blue. Nothing but ice. A muscle ticked in his jaw. His hands were gentle. He murmured soothingly to her in his own language, but his body was rigid, just like his face.

"What's happening to me?" she asked again, needing clarification. "Hurry. It's going to come back."

"It takes three full blood exchanges to bring another into our world. They must have a psychic gift in order for the conversion to be successful."

Her eyes widened. "Are you saying that when this is done, I'm going to be like you? I'll need blood to survive? The blood of others? I'll have to sleep in the ground?"

Already the next wave was on her. This was far worse than the others, and she turned from him, vomiting, over and over, her body rejecting everything in her that was human. Her throat felt raw and bloody. Her skin didn't feel right, and even her scalp hurt. The worst was her midsection. A blowtorch had been added to the jagged glass and razor blades slashing her up.

Andre knelt with her, holding her up, cleaning her mouth with a cool wet cloth. Somehow he managed to pin her thick braids to the top of her head, and get rid of the mess she'd just made. Still, she *detested* him.

You planned this, she accused. *You did this to me.*

You gave me no choice. I will never see you put yourself in such a dangerous position again.

253

You had no right.

I have every right. Not only is it my right, it is my duty to see to your protection.

She couldn't even scream in frustration, not with her throat so raw. She could only push at the wall of his chest, rejecting him physically while trying to oust him out of her mind. He wouldn't go. In fact, his arms tightened and he seemed to surround her, not so much with his body, although she could feel him close, but with his strength and power.

She was too weak to fight him. The next wave came, overtaking her before she was ready, the convulsions almost tearing her body out of his arms, but he held her safe from slamming to the floor. She didn't want to be safe. She wanted to be alone.

Leave me, Andre. God. Why wouldn't he just *go*?

When the pain eased enough for her to catch her breath, she looked up at his face. There was blood tracking down it. Drops of blood leaking from his eyes. She felt one splash on her sternum and run down the slope of her breast.

For the first time, she caught him looking upset. Not just upset. Devastated. The moment he realized her gaze was on his face, his features settled into a carved, stone mask.

You didn't know.

He bent over her, just for a moment and she caught the sorrow, not in his eyes, but in his mind.

I should have researched before I subjected you to this. Not knowing is no excuse.

Not knowing wasn't an excuse, but it was something. She could see he was holding himself together to try to help her get through. She even realized he was shouldering as much of the pain as possible.

The next wave was worse than the last one, jerking her body until it was stiff, contorting it and then slamming it

254

toward the floor of the cave. Andre was there, cushioning her, surrounding her with his presence. She could hear him, far off, speaking in his language, his voice like velvet and silk.

Sleep now, Teagan. I will hold you close.

She'd asked for that, Andre holding her close. At first she'd wanted to just move away from him; now nothing mattered but escape. The blowtorch in her stomach was still there, but the intensity wasn't the same.

Let go for me. Sleep now.

The command was stronger. She actually felt the "push" behind his sensual voice. Teagan obeyed him and let herself fall under whatever spell he'd conceived in order to stop her suffering.

14

Teagan became aware of a breeze first. Cooling. On her body. Her naked body. Next she became aware of Andre wrapped around her. Holding her tight against him. His arm was draped around her waist and his thigh was between hers. She lay still, trying to figure out if she'd had a terrible nightmare—which was understandable after the horrific memories from his childhood Andre had shown her. She'd also had an encounter with an honest to God vampire. That would give anyone nightmares.

She took stock of her surroundings. Yep. Still in the cave. She could see though—see as well as if it was broad daylight—and she was in a cave. She'd been able to see a bit before, enough that it worried her, but this was incredible. Someone might as well have turned the lights on. It should have been a good thing because it was very cool, but it wasn't. It really, really wasn't.

She touched the mattress beneath her and let her breath out

slowly. She was in a bed, not buried in the ground. She felt absolutely fine. No pain. No cramps. No convulsions. Even her throat didn't hurt. Still, she felt that little bit *too* good.

She turned her head to look over her shoulder at the man lying curled around her. Protecting her. His eyes were open and he was looking down at her. His eyes, in that unguarded moment, were a soft blue of the deepest sea. Her heart contracted. Her sex spasmed. Even her breasts reacted, feeling suddenly swollen and achy. Just by looking into his eyes. She was in trouble.

"You are awake."

He shifted. Bent to brush her mouth with his. Gentle. No demand. That wasn't good, either. Because Andre was the type of man who would want morning sex. He'd want afternoon sex. He'd want night sex. He wasn't being in the least bit sexual, unless you counted the heavy erection pressing tight against her bottom.

"It isn't morning, is it?" That was all she could get out. Her mouth had suddenly gone dry. She *knew* the sun had set. She knew it was already evening. She was in a cave she could see perfectly in, but she knew it was early evening outside.

"No, the sun set about a half hour ago."

"Did I sleep here?"

"Teagan."

She closed her eyes and turned her face away from him. Even so, with the sinking feeling in the pit of her stomach, her body responded to his voice. All that silk and velvet. So rich. So perfect.

"I find it necessary to inform you, Andre, that you're not so perfect." She sat up, wishing she had a shirt to cover her body. "I already told you how gorgeous and sweet you are, which clearly was a mistake. It went to your head or something and convinced you that you could get away with anything." She leveled her gaze at him. "Which you cannot." She at least needed one of his shirts. "I think you need to know you aren't perfect and you just dropped *way* down on the boyfriend scale. Like hitting the bottom."

She stood. It was difficult to walk away with great dignity when she was absolutely naked. She really, *really* needed that shirt. Instantly she was wrapped in warmth. In his shirt. A button-down flannel that was warm, soft and more than comfortable. It came all the way to her knees, covering her completely.

Her breath left her lungs in a little rush. "Thank you." Because that was mega-cool and the shirt made her feel as if she had a little of her own power back.

"I did not give you the shirt. You did."

She swung around to stare at him. "I did not. I can't do that sort of thing."

"Is it the garment you pictured in your head?"

She nodded slowly, her hands clutching at the lapels of the shirt. "How?"

"You are fully in my world," Andre said. "The conversion was completed two risings ago."

There it was. Confirmation. She closed her eyes briefly, her mind shutting down for a moment. When she lifted her lashes, Andre was in front of her, wearing nothing but a pair of soft jeans. They clung to his superb body, rode low on his hips and cupped his very fine butt. She could see the two circular scars on his wide shoulders, his thick, heavily muscled *bare* chest and two more circular scars on either side of his ribs. It had to be said, but not out loud, that he truly was gorgeous.

His hand came out to settle in her hair, his thumb sliding gently over her face. "I am glad you think so, *sivamet*."

She glared out him. "What part of *not out loud* do you

not get? You are a bastard. A rat bastard, as my good friend Cheryl would say." She pointed her finger at his chest for emphasis. "A *huge* rat bastard. That, in case you don't get the translation correctly, is *not* a good thing."

He crowded her, moving into her space, and he was a big man. More than a foot taller than her, he outweighed her by over a hundred pounds, but she didn't care. She thumped his chest with the flat of her hand, because if he was getting in her space he could just pay the consequences. She smacked him again for good measure and then her temper went up a notch because he didn't seem to notice. He just kept looking down at her with those eyes of his.

"I get that maybe you didn't realize I would suffer the agonies of hell, but I don't want this. I was going to live my life with you, give up most days to be with you and then die a quiet, nondramatic death with no vampires involved. No ground. No blood, just a plain ordinary *human* death."

"Teagan."

Her heart turned over. She smacked him again. "Don't you *Teagan* me. What you are going to do, and you're doing it this minute, is take the hoodoo off me and put me back to normal. Cool shirt and seeing in the dark aside—because they are definite pros—the blood and the dirt thingies are *way* not cool and I don't want this."

"Teagan."

"If you say my name again in that particular tone, I swear, Andre, my head is going to explode. Seeing as how you saw fit to make momentous, life-changing decisions for me that I don't want, you can just undo it. Right. Now."

She crossed her arms over her chest and looked him straight in the eye to let him know she wasn't kidding around. He needed to take it back right away. That minute. Their gazes locked. Held. The bottom went out of her stomach, and she felt fear first and then terror crept in. She could see the answer in his eyes.

Her tongue touched her lower lip. "There's no taking this back, is there?"

He reached for her.

She stepped back, eluding him, holding up her hand to ward him off. "Is there, Andre?"

He shook his head slowly and took another step toward her.

Teagan retreated two steps, trying to catch her breath. Why couldn't she just faint and get out of the situation? Terror was clawing at her. Sheer terror.

"What you did was wrong, Andre. You understand that, don't you? I have the right to make up my own mind about something this huge. You can't do that kind of thing."

"It is not wrong in my world, Teagan. There are reasons the binding words are imprinted on the male of my species before birth. We *must* bind our lifemate to us. Without her, we can become the undead. A horrific monster with no soul, one who only seeks to inflict as much pain and death on everyone as possible."

She put her hands over her ears and shook her head. "Stop it. I mean it. You aren't even sorry you did this."

"I am sorry you suffered because of my actions," Andre said.

His voice, silk and velvet, penetrated right through her hands to her ears and managed to enter her body that way. She couldn't breathe. She couldn't even think. All along, she'd believed he could do anything—even reverse what he'd done. She wanted to scream.

"Do you even know what you've done to me? Without asking? Without my permission. I wasn't born in the century you were born in." She wanted to run. She was going to run, to outrun what she'd become. "I'm not what you obviously need or want. My man doesn't make decisions for me. Certainly not one like this."

He kept coming no matter how far she backed up, so she did the only thing left to her—she ducked under his arm and sprinted across the cave floor. She'd never moved so fast in her life. She actually ran with blurring speed. Phenomenal speed. She'd always been dismal at running, although she did it to stay in shape, but still, this was lightning fast.

Even her speed didn't save her. Andre hooked his arm around her waist, bringing her to an abrupt halt. She kicked him as hard as she could in the shins, connecting. Pain raced through her foot right up her own shin. Andre retaliated by swinging her off her feet and cradling her against his chest. She absolutely refused to be so undignified as to claw him in the face, even though she wanted to.

"Calm down. I am not going to allow you to hurt yourself."

"Don't say *allow*. Haven't you heard one single thing I've said to you?" She wanted to cry. The lump in her throat choked her but she wasn't going to cry in front of him. "I'm over this relationship. I mean it, Andre. I'm *so* breaking up with you. You aren't at all the man I thought you were."

He winced at that. Not physically, but she knew she'd scored when he flinched in his mind.

"I realize this is extremely difficult for you to process . . . "

"You think? Put me down. I'm totally serious, Andre. We are over. You go your way, I'll go mine. I just hope Grandma Trixie doesn't stake me before I can explain to her why I need to drink her blood and sleep in the basement." She glared at him. "And just who is responsible."

"No one is going to stake you, *csitri*."

There was his voice again. Soft. Gentle. Tender even. Mixed with just a little amusement, which fired her temper all over again.

"Don't you dare laugh at me. God, Andre, don't you see what you've done? I'm not me anymore. I don't want this. I would have stayed with you, given you everything, and that was a gift to you. I gave myself to you. You took something you shouldn't have and it's no longer a gift."

He set her on her feet against the far wall, caging her in with his larger frame and his hands on either side of her so there was no escape.

"You did give yourself to me. You put yourself into my keeping. I told you I would protect you, Teagan. It is impossible to protect you when I am in the ground and you are running around. Anything can happen to you. I would not survive your loss."

"You didn't have the right," she whispered. "I can't accept this. I can't. You can't take away my freedom."

"You do not understand the concept of lifemates. We are bound together. Your soul is the other half of mine and we're one now. Complete." He cupped her chin in his hand, leaning into her so there was no possibility of her moving away from him. His thumb caressed the soft skin of her face. "I tried to explain as best I could, Teagan. I showed you what I have never shared with any other. You needed to know who I am and why I do the things I do."

"That's well and good for you, Andre, but it's still selfish. You took away my decisions and you didn't care how I would feel."

"Is that what you really think, *sivamet?*" His eyes blazed down into hers. "You are always my first thought. *Always.* I am telling you and I want you in my mind. I want you to hear what I say and feel it and know it is the truth. It is *impossible* for me to allow you to put yourself in danger. Physically, mentally and emotionally impossible. I am not a modern man. I do not know the rules of your world." *Nor do I want to.* "I live in my world, and it is a dangerous one."

262

Nor do I want to. She caught that fleeting thought and jerked her head away from the warmth of his caressing hand. She shoved at his chest. "I caught that. You don't want to know the rules of my world. The one I lived in. Grew up in. Have family that means the world to me. I've traveled all over the world by myself or with a few girlfriends, hiking and climbing and making my own decisions."

"Decisions that led you to a serial killer and a vampire. I do not think this is your best argument, *csitri.*"

There was the faint humor again that made her head want to spin around three times on her neck and have demon sounds come out of her mouth. When that didn't happen she settled for thumping his chest with her fist. She struggled to get herself under control. When she was fairly certain she had a handle on her temper and fear, she took a deep breath and looked up at his face.

"Andre, I need you to step back. I'm going to get dressed, pack my things and go home. I need to come to terms with this and I want to do it at home, surrounded by people who love me. People who will listen to me when I talk to them."

His fingers curled around the nape of her neck. "You are going to stay right here with me and talk to me. I will listen to you and we will work this out between us. You are my heart and soul. No one else loves or needs you in the way I do. No one. Not your grandmother. Not your sisters."

"See. Right there. That's *not* listening," she was compelled to point out.

"I listened, Teagan. I heard every word you said. You are not listening to *me*. I get that you are afraid. Everything about my world is frightening and new to you. Your grandmother and sisters cannot answer your questions or help you adjust."

He wasn't going to let her leave. She could see the resolve on his face. This man, this beautiful man, had trapped her in a body that wasn't hers. The worst part about it was that she actually understood his reasoning. She didn't agree with it, but she had seen his terrible childhood tragedy. He'd been terrified for her when she'd climbed the boulder and somehow disturbed the vampire in his lair. He'd had his lures out, just like a spider, and she'd nearly been trapped in his web.

Apparently in Andre's world, men could dictate. That was *not* going to happen. It just wasn't. She took a breath and let it out.

"Andre, you say lifemates are predestined. That there is only one and she is your other half. We're so different. I am modern and was raised to speak my mind, have my own opinions and make my own decisions. Clearly in your world, women do what men tell them to do ..."

He laughed. Out loud. He actually threw his head back and laughed. The sound was amazing. Beautiful. He was beautiful when he laughed. She'd never heard him laugh wholeheart-edly and the sound was pure music. His eyes lit up and his face had gone softer.

"What?" She tried to inject temper into the demand, but watching him laugh was mesmerizing and she failed completely.

"The women in my world do not do what their men tell them. Not one that I can see, unless it has something to do with safety. I would say they obey because they choose to obey and know their men take their safety seriously. They aren't stupid. They want to be safe from the dangers in our world."

She narrowed her eyes at him. "Are you implying I'm stupid?"

His fingers tightened on the nape of her neck. "Teagan. Seriously. You have every reason to be upset and hurt by what I did, but do not look for other reasons. We need to deal with this issue."

Her head really was going to explode. She didn't care if his fingers massaging the tension from her neck felt great, or that he was the hottest man on the planet. Or that his voice slipped inside her every single time and turned her insides to a melted puddle of scorching hot need.

"You do realize," she bit out between her teeth, warning him. Because *seriously*, he needed to be warned. "Standing this close to me, when I detonate and go up in a fiery flaming bomb, you are going to get caught in the blast. For your own safety, Andre, just step back and let this happen."

He leaned into her, one hand still at the nape of her neck, the other on her belly, fingers spread wide pushing her slightly so that she was up against the wall. His head descended and she quickly turned her face away from his, knowing if he kissed her, she might just give in, and she wasn't going to. Not over this. It was too important.

Kiss me, Teagan. His mouth followed hers.

She clamped her lips together and shook her head. His hand went from her belly to her jaw, controlling her head.

His mouth rubbed gently over hers, his tongue tracing her lower lip and then the seam of her mouth.

Teagan shook her head, glaring at him. With her lips clamped shut, she still told him off. *Your listening skills need serious work.*

Sivamet, kiss me.

His tongue lapped at her lips. His mouth brushed across hers, sending little darts of fire straight to her bloodstream where they rushed like a fireball to her sex. She thought to resist. She really, really did. But maybe she needed to be kissed. She needed something. She was so scared of what she was that she wanted comfort.

She opened her mouth and was instantly lost in him. His kisses left her breathless. On fire. But more, they swept her away to another realm altogether where she couldn't think. Only feel.

The moment she began to return his kiss, Andre yanked her to him, his arms strong, powerful even. He deepened the kiss, devouring her. She met his hunger with her own.

Arms around my neck, sivamet.

There was that beautiful voice. Velvet. Silk. A new rasp that sent tingles down her spine and liquid fire spilling from her sex. His mouth never left hers, and it felt like he poured himself into her, down her throat. All of him. Who he was. What he was. How he felt. How much he felt.

It was intense. So intense her eyes burned with tears for both of them. She slid her hands up his chest to his shoulders and then circled his neck with her arms. The moment she did, he lifted her. Easily. So easily. Instead of making her feel vulnerable, she felt safe. Cherished. Cared for.

He kept kissing her, even when she had to breathe, and then he simply breathed for her. His bare chest pressed against her bare front. Her shirt was gone as easily as it had come. Like magic. She didn't know if she had done it or if he had, but it didn't matter. All that mattered to her was his fiery mouth and his hands cupping her bare bottom.

Hurry, Andre. I can't wait.

Her breathy admission was the truth. Her body was already coiled too tight. The tension built fast, just from his kisses. Just from her nipples sliding over his chest. From the way his fingers sank into the firm muscle of her buttocks. Her blood was too hot in her veins. She could hear his heart beating, accelerating like her own. She needed him inside her.

My impatient woman. Are you ready for me?

Yes. Hurry.

Wrap your legs around me. Open for me.

She hadn't done that. She'd pushed on the strong column

of his thigh with her feet, not thinking. Not knowing and she should have. She did what he said instantly, wrapping her legs around him. Instantly she felt his perfect, beautiful crest pressing tight at the entrance to her sex.

So hot. So perfect. Every time. No matter how he took her, she felt the fire raging through her and she let herself burn. She welcomed it. There was no fear this time because she was already so far gone with fear, she couldn't process it. She strained toward him, needing to impale herself on him. Connect them.

Andre. Frustrated, she caught his hair in one fist, her fingers sliding through the silk in a little caress. She moved against him. *You aren't listening again.*

I am listening. Still, he held her there, that hot spike pressing into her, but not giving her what she needed.

His mouth left hers and he kissed his way to her neck. Her throat. That was beautiful, too, but it only made her hotter.

What are you waiting for? she demanded.

You, päläfertiilam, I am waiting for you.

Teagan froze. There it was. She was in his mind. She knew what he needed—her acceptance of him—of his world. She was naked. In his arms. Burning from his kisses. Her body out of control, hips writhing and him pressing into her entrance, just enough that she felt his scorching heat, that burning stretch that felt so good and made her desperate for more.

She bit down on his shoulder, closing her eyes. It was done. There was no taking it back. Would she be able to live without him? Did she even want to? But was she the type of woman who could be dictated to? No way. And he was using sex to get his way—that was her prerogative, wasn't it?

Andre pressed her down slowly, another inch of him filling her, stretching those tight muscles until she moaned his name against his shoulder.

Tet vigyázam avio päläfertiilam.

He whispered the words in that voice. The one she couldn't resist. With that accent. She closed her eyes and nuzzled his chest.

I don't know what that means.

Look at me. I want to see your eyes.

She took a breath, knowing she'd need one, and raised her eyes to his. Oh God. She was in *so* much trouble. There was love there. Real love. Intense love. The kind of love there was no way to resist. She melted inside.

"It means I love you, my lifemate. It means I will cherish you for all time, for eternity. It means you will be safe in my care," he whispered, holding her gaze captive. "It means I am going to make a mess of things and you will take me to task and forgive me. It means all that, Teagan. Forgive me. Be mine. Give yourself to me and allow me the privilege of cherishing you for all time."

Teagan knew it wasn't the sex. It was the sincerity in his voice. The love in his eyes. Mostly it was the intensity of his emotion in his mind. She was everything to him. His entire world. His entire focus. He was telling the absolute truth—there would be no other woman for him. She might not understand it, but there was no other woman in the entire world, and there hadn't been all those long centuries. How in the world could she turn her back on him? And the truth was—she didn't want to.

"I love you, too, Andre," she conceded, looking him straight in the eyes.

His eyes went so dark blue and liquid she wanted to melt right into him. He kissed her. Hard. Rough. Hungry. His hands went to her hips and slammed her down hard over his cock, surging up at the same time. He tipped her back against the wall and drove into her hard.

268

It was wild and out of control. It was perfect. Beautiful. She bit her lip. *Harder. More. Give me more.*

He took them to the ground, only of course, because it was Andre, there was a blanket beneath her body. Still, the hard ground had no give and with her legs wrapped around his hips he could drive into her with hard, satisfying strokes that jolted her body and sent flames crashing through them both.

She reached for him, feeling the fire stealing over him. Threatening to consume him—consume them both. She moved to meet him. Moved to increase the wonderful friction, her body grasping and pulling to keep him in her. His stretching her, filling her, invading her, trying to go as deep as he could get. She felt the flames rising in him. The tidal wave threatening to engulf him. She actually felt it start in his toes and work up the strong columns of his legs.

Let go, he demanded.

Teagan looked up at him, at his face. He was watching her, his gaze devouring her. Hungry for something. *With you,* she told him.

He shook his head. *I need to watch you. I love the way you look when I give this to you. For me, sivamet. Give this to me now.*

He thrust hard. Once. Twice. A third time. He was so close. She felt the fire in his sac, boiling, roaring. Still he waited. Her own body was just as close. She just had to let go and let it take her. Give that to him. Staring into his eyes, she did. She gave him what he wanted.

Her orgasm roared through her, taking her over fast, rushing down her thighs and up to her breasts, into her stomach and sending strong quakes through her feminine channel. Her tight muscles constricted around Andre's shaft, clamping down, gripping hard. All the while he watched her face.

Beautiful, he breathed into her mind. *The most beautiful thing I have ever seen.*

He surged into her, strong. Hard. Deep. Over and over, powering through her tight muscles, prolonging her orgasm, until she took him with her. He groaned softly in her ear, with one last thrust burying himself all the way, as deeply as possible. He lay over her, their hearts pounding, both trying to catch their breath.

Andre lay on top of her, his body nearly crushing hers, making it difficult for her to breathe. He was holding her tight, his arms around her, his face buried in her neck, still deep inside of her. It was the first time he'd ever done that—not lightened his weight—and she slipped her arms around him, holding him to her, feeling completely surrounded—and taken—by him.

His hands slid up her body to her hair, fingers sinking into the braids. He lifted his head and only then did his body weight change. She sucked in a breath, but something in his eyes kept her from complaining. He looked at her as if he'd nearly lost his world and she'd given it back to him.

She was terrified to face the change in her, and she was still angry with him that he'd made such a momentous decision without even consulting her, but she honestly didn't know if she really could have left him. The lifemate bond aside, because she didn't fully understand that, she knew she was in love with Andre.

It was all the little things he did that made her feel special and beautiful. She couldn't work up the energy to tell him she was still angry with him so instead, she took the opportunity to run her hands slowly down his back to feel the delicious muscles there. She let peace steal over her, the warmth of his body and the solid feel of him surrounding her gave her that.

Teagan had never felt at home anywhere other than with her grandmother and sisters. She just didn't fit. She liked people, but she never felt comfortable enough with them to share her body or soul. She was always on the fringe. She had friends, but even they didn't really know her, not even the ones she'd grown up with.

Andre was in her mind. With her almost all the time. He knew her. The way she thought. What she thought. How she thought. He just knew. He *got* her.

"I will work very hard to fix this between us," Andre said softly. He brushed kisses along her throat and up her chin to the corner of her mouth.

"And we'll talk before making decisions. When we make them, we make them together," Teagan prompted.

He kissed her. Her stomach did a roller-coaster number on her and she felt her inner muscles tighten around him. Her heart melted. She found her arms circled his neck all on their own so she could bury her fingers in his hair.

When he lifted his head and looked down at her, she blinked up at him several times, feeling a little dazed and even mellower. She narrowed her eyes at him. "You're doing it again," she accused. Both hands went to his shoulders and she shoved at him.

"What am I doing?"

"Don't look innocent. You know very well what you're doing. You didn't answer me. I said *we'd* make decisions."

He rubbed his chin along her jaw. "*Sivamet.*"

"Oh no, you are not going to *sivamet* me in that voice or kiss me senseless. Get up, Andre. We're going to sort this out right now, and I need clothes and you off of me to do that."

"I kiss you senseless?" He smiled at her.

"You know very well you do, which is why you take every opportunity to kiss me when you want your way."

"I was not doing that, but it seems a good idea."

There was amusement back in his voice. She liked that too much. She pushed at him again and this time he slid out of

271

her and instantly she regretted insisting. He was up in one fluid motion, reaching down for her. He waved his hand and she was clean, refreshed and fully clothed in the softest jeans she'd ever had, faded and vintage blue. She loved them. Her top was a soft, fitted sweater in a cream color.

Okay, that was just plain cool. She wasn't a morning person. Without her preferred black tea she just wasn't moving. Being able to do this would save time and effort. She ran her hands down her thighs, feeling the material. Andre wore similar jeans and a shirt that stretched tightly across all the amazing muscles he had.

"I love the jeans, Andre, but I usually wear pants I can climb in easily." She had to say something because he looked gorgeous, and that was what got her in trouble in the first place. Who knew she was susceptible to cavemen?

His smile was faint, but there was amusement in his eyes. "Teagan. Seriously. You can fly. You can change your clothes with a wave of your hand and the image in your mind."

She bit her lip. That was seriously cool. "Andre, I'm not hungry at all. Maybe I won't need to take someone's blood." She said it hopefully because, really, she could get used to the cool aspects of being in his world.

"Before I woke you, I fed and then fed you," Andre said. All trace of amusement was gone and he was watching her closely. Very closely. His eyes hooded and a little possessive. "You told me you liked to be held, so I brought you out of the ground where you were healing and made certain you were completely healed before I woke you."

Her stomach lurched and she pressed a hand there. "I was in the ground?"

"You were in terrible pain, Teagan. The moment I knew it was safe to send you to sleep, I did. I put you in the ground to heal. You have been there for two risings."

She knew he meant the rising of the moon. Two nights. Forty-eight hours. He'd *fed* her. That meant he gave her blood. He'd brought her out of the ground. Cleaned her. Cuddled her. She bit her lip again. As much as it was *all* his fault, he'd still been thoughtful. She couldn't have faced all that. Not blood and dirt.

"Do bugs crawl all over us when we're in the ground?"

His eyebrow shot up. "Bugs?"

"Andre, I don't mind insects, but not crawling all over me."

"I will do my best to keep that from happening."

"And from now on we make decisions together," she pressed.

He was silent for a long moment. Too long. She went back to narrowing her eyes at him. He *so* deserved narrowed eyes *and* a black scowl. Her meanest one.

He sighed. "Lifemates cannot tell an untruth to each another. You are not always rational, Teagan, and I do not argue well."

She was outraged. "I am very rational."

He shook his head. "You are not. And you admitted already you have trouble with anyone telling you what to do. What happens when I issue an order and you do not obey?"

"You do *not* issue orders, Andre. I do *not* obey." Now, finally, she knew why people in books were sometimes described as "tearing their hair." Because she wanted to tear at hers. He was impossible. Standing there, looking all gorgeous from his *way* superior height and telling her she wasn't rational. *Whatever.*

"It was not rational to come here alone and go into the mountains with a serial killer who I will add was also a serial rapist."

She did grab her long braid and yank. "You *cannot* possibly use that as an example. I didn't know he was a serial killer."

273

He was silent. His blue eyes had that faint trace of amusement in them. She could never resist that. Still. She was entirely rational at all times. She didn't want to think about any of this right now. She needed to be normal, even if just for a short while. She'd *discuss* life-changing decisions with him when she wasn't so emotional, because she *was* rational. Feeling better, she took a breath and let it out.

"Thank you for this evening. The wake-up, I mean. That was very thoughtful of you to remove me from the ground and ... um ... feed me. I'm not ready for reality yet."

"I am aware of that, *sivamet*. I am happy to take care of those things for you. You will be ready in time, but for now, I enjoy taking care of you. The idea of you taking blood from another man does not sit well with me. We both have things to learn."

That released about a million butterflies in her stomach. She lifted her gaze to his, trying for rational and practical. "I'm going into that little town to report that Armend Jashari is dead and someone needs to come up and get his body. Then I need to talk to the village police or whatever and tell them about the women he killed. After that I have to call Grandma Trixie and tell her I met someone."

She could see, by the way his face darkened and his eyes went ice-cold, that once again he didn't think she was being the least bit rational or practical.

15

Andre stood outside the entrance to the cave, looking up at the night sky. Gray and misty, not even the clouds could be seen. "A storm is coming in," he announced. "A real one."

"As opposed to a fake one?" Teagan asked, smiling up at him.

Teagan was full of smiles, he knew, because she was getting her way. It wasn't rational or practical. He'd explained to her that it wasn't a good idea for Carpathians to draw attention to themselves. He'd stupidly mentioned that he could easily get someone to come up the mountain, find the body and eventually discover the bodies of the women Armend Jashari had killed.

She had jumped all over that and argued if he could do that, he could protect her in a village with so few people. So she was making him just as irrational as she was—because he couldn't say no to her. Not when he felt her need to do

275

something normal, something human. Not when he could tell she'd buried her fear, but it was there. She was terrified and still holding it together. Mostly he couldn't tell her no because he loved her and he wanted to give her everything she wanted and he couldn't give her what she wanted most.

Not just couldn't. If he was honest, he would never give her that, never take back that he'd brought her fully into his world even if it was possible—which it wasn't. He hadn't known she'd suffer the way she had, but still, it was done. She was his. She would get over being angry—and he could admit her anger was justifiable—but she wasn't the type of woman to hold on to anger.

He'd said she wasn't practical, but she was. She knew they couldn't reverse the conversion. Because she couldn't deal with it, she buried it along with her fears and turned to human normal. She would let him deal with Jashari's death and the bodies on the mountain, but she just wanted to walk through the streets and look into store windows. Normal.

Andre shook his head and reached out to take her hand. She was trembling, but she didn't hesitate. He needed to give her something else. Teagan admitted she was afraid of everything but she didn't want to allow fear to rule her. She would accept the challenge of her new life. He had to give her time.

He closed his hand around hers and drew her to him. "Do you want to fly? By yourself, I mean. You doing it, not me."

Her breath came out in a rush of white vapor. She shivered. He brought his hand up to the nape of her neck to ease the tension out of her.

"First, I want you to learn to control your body temperature. When you get cold or hot, you can regulate it to be comfortable."

Her eyes went wide. Surprise. Shock. Like he was giving

her a gift. His fingers tightened on her neck and he brought her closer to the shelter of his body. She had a way of looking at him that made him feel as if he was the only man she ever saw. Or would see. He liked that a lot. He had never considered what the reality of having a lifemate would be like, but he was learning. Emotions got in the way of rational thought.

"I can fly. By myself?"

He nodded. "There are a lot of ways to do it, but the easiest is to take the form of a bird. We use owls at night because they are more common. Owls are found anywhere. As long as you know which species is native to the area, no one will ever know you are even in their neighborhood."

Her eyes were shining up at him. He couldn't stop himself. He wrapped her up in one arm and pulled her tight against him, fitting her into his side. With his other hand he tipped up her face and brushed a kiss over her mouth. He couldn't stop there, not once he got the taste of her. She was so addictive. He didn't want to go into a village full of humans with her. He wanted to spend a few risings in bed with her. He poured that into his kisses, letting her know without words just how he felt.

Teagan blinked at him when he lifted his head, making him want to groan in frustration. Another thing that happened with emotion was the loss of his great control over his anatomy. She seemed more in control of his body than he was. The moment he pulled her close, or she got that dazed, confused, sexy look on her face, his body went as hard as a rock.

"I love when you look at me like that," he admitted.

She smiled at him and touched the pad of her finger to his mouth. "I think your lips should be bronzed or something. Really, Andre. You're smiling, but you have no idea."

He had an idea because he felt the same way about her mouth—her entire body—but especially her mind. He loved

277

the crazy way her mind worked. He never knew what she was going to say, or think, next. She made him laugh. He'd lived centuries and he hadn't known he *could* laugh. She'd given that to him. That gift. So many gifts and she still had no idea what she was to him. What she meant to him.

He would guard her, protect her and the only way he could do that was to make certain she was with him at all times. He couldn't chance her running around the mountain in the daytime when anything could happen to her and he couldn't save her. She would come to understand the need once she'd spent time in his world and had come to terms with it. Right now, he knew, she couldn't help feeling he'd betrayed her.

Kissing him the way she did, even knowing she was upset, that she was afraid and felt he had deceived her, was a miracle in itself. He was a man who had given up on miracles. He'd given up on life. He'd thought to die with honor, and in that moment of absolute despair that he would have to continue, she had come to him with her laughter and kisses and a bright, bright light that shone from her soul.

"So how? How do I go from this . . . " Teagan swept a hand down her body. "To that?" She pointed to the sky.

"I will show you first. And then I will talk you through the steps."

She nodded, her lower lip caught between her teeth. He could see the flash of fear in her eyes, feel it in her mind, but she wanted to know how to fly. She wasn't about to allow fear to stop her from learning. Andre felt his heart flutter and the knots in his belly he'd had since he'd risen loosened a little. Teagan faced life head-on. *His* Teagan.

He brought her hand up to his mouth and pressed a kiss to her knuckle because if he kissed her mouth they wouldn't be going anywhere other than back inside the cave. Dropping her hand, he stepped back, giving himself room and her space. He didn't want her to panic when he shifted form.

"The change always starts in your mind, Teagan. Stay in mine and see the image I project. It can be anything from putting clothes on to taking them off. Shifting is more difficult in the beginning because you have to have your image in perfect detail. You will learn how to do that and it will become second nature. You will no longer have to think about it, your body will just do it."

She nodded, but she took another step back. He didn't like that, but gave her the space.

"*Sivamet*, if this is too soon, there is no need to start yet. I can take you to the village. You will enjoy that as well."

She took a breath. "I want to learn. This is something that would go on the pro side of being like you. I have to have a lot of pros right now, Andre."

He smiled at her. He couldn't help it. She was so adorable. So determined. He didn't think a man could love a woman more than he did Teagan in that moment. He didn't wait, because she only had so much courage and she'd already faced so much.

Andre deliberately pictured the owl in his mind. He chose the medium to large Ural owl because he was certain Teagan would have seen it numerous times. Grayish feathers, dark eyes, no ear tufts, chest heavily streaked in gray and white. A good four-foot wingspan. Fierce. Free. Beautiful in flight or sitting quite still, waiting for prey. They punched with their talons and protected their territories, nests and owlets with a ferocious and very aggressive single mind.

He gave her the information as well as showing her the feather structure and detail. As he did, he reached for the change, the shift to that amazing creature's form. He was lightning fast as a rule. He could shift in midair in the blink of an eye. He'd been shifting for centuries and it was second nature to him, but he did this one slow so she could see it happening.

Teagan's gasp nearly made him stop midchange, but she stepped closer to the forming bird, her eyes wide with shock and wonder. Her entire face lit up. He stayed firmly in her mind.

While you are shifting, it will feel strange to you, but you must keep only the image that you want to be in your head the entire time.

"What will happen if I mess up?"

Even in the owl's body, he heard the trepidation in her voice. *I will be with you and can guide you back. Keep your mind in mine. Focus on the image of the owl. Study my form before you attempt it. Have no fears, Teagan, I will not allow anything to happen to you.*

Teagan took a deep breath and walked around the owl. It was a powerful creature. Intelligent and, she could see, fierce, just as Andre had described it. Its facial disc was prominent and mostly a grayish color. There was a rim around the disc that had beautiful, pearl-like spots in light and dark. The head was round and the tail, with its wedge-shaped tip, was long.

She wanted to make the change. She had watched him do it. Andre, going from his tall, broad-shouldered, thick-chested frame to that of an owl had been unbelievable. She'd seen it with her own eyes and still couldn't believe it. To think she might be able to do that was ... well ... extraordinary.

She licked her suddenly dry lips. She *had* to do this. It might be more thrilling than climbing a V13, which was crazy difficult but utterly mind-consuming and absolutely satisfying.

"Shifting starts in the mind," she murmured softly.

Determined. She could do this. Andre had brought her into his world because he'd been too afraid to allow her to remain in hers. She didn't have to worry that he would ever want her to do anything he considered dangerous to her. That gave her confidence. *He* gave her confidence, because in spite of everything, she knew, without a shadow of a doubt, that Andre would never let anything happen to her.

She took another deep breath, held the image of the owl in her mind and willed her body to shift. The moment she felt the pull on her skin she startled, but she felt Andre there with her. He was warm and strong in her mind. Steady. Calm. So calm, as if this was an everyday event, not the monumental phenomenon it truly was.

His calm spread to her. Her heart followed the steady beat of his. Her lungs followed his. She held the image firmly. Held to the command, willing her body to cooperate.

When it happened she was so shocked the female owl nearly fell over. She hadn't really believed it was possible for *her*. Andre, yes. He could do anything. She wouldn't be surprised if he moved a mountain. But for her to shift. To feel her body changing. Reforming. The sheer exhilaration was alarming because it meant she was already accepting there were good—no—*great* things about being in Andre's world.

I did it, Andre! Look, I really did it. This is the most amazing thing in the entire world. The best. Well, she hedged. *That's not strictly the truth because kissing you is the best. Umm. Okay, that's almost the best. Making love with you is the ultimate, but this really, really ranks right up there. But not as good. Just cool. Maybe cooler.*

She felt his laughter. Right there in her mind even though she was an owl. *She was an owl!* She wished her sisters were around. Not Grandma Trixie, because she'd stake her with that vampire-hunting kit she bought off the Internet, but she was fairly certain her sisters would think it was cool that she was an owl.

Um. Andre. Can we go to church? Because Grandma Trixie is big on church. If I melt or go up in smoke inside a church, she isn't going to be happy with me. I'm already in danger of being staked by her.

The male owl shook his head as if she was being crazy, but it was all the truth. *The church question is absolutely legit. Have you been inside a church, like ever, since you've been this way?*

I was born this way. Spread your wings, csitri. Get used to moving in the owl's body. And no, I do not go to church, but Ivory and Razvan and Mikhail and Raven do. I know both couples very well. Neither has ever gone up in smoke in a church, although all four of them could easily become smoke if they wished.

She flapped her wings like a wild bird, very enthusiastically. It was totally awesome. *Can I become smoke?* She could scare the pants off her nephews with shifting. How cool would that be?

I think you should try flying first. Smoke is more complicated. Take a few hops. You will have to land. And, Teagan, I know this feels amazing to you, but you have to stay in control. Stay close to me at all times. There are vampires close by. We do not want them to know we are anywhere close. I believe they are still nursing their wounds, and gathering strength, but they must feed, and that means they will come out each rising to do so.

Do they know you killed their friend? She continued to flap her wings and hop around on her taloned feet. So cool. The best—except for kissing and sex with Andre, of course.

Vampires do not have friends. In the old days, if they met one another, they fought to the death to keep territory. Now a master vampire will find fledglings, those who have just turned, and he uses them as his pawns.

She couldn't help but notice the contempt in his voice. He

282

had such a sense of what was honorable in battle that he found the practice appalling. She opened her beak in a semblance of a smile.

The vampire will have connected all of his pawns. They all are aware I defeated the undead in battle. He did not return to his master with a victim to feed from.

She went still. She stopped hopping around and folded her wings. *Are you telling me that he would have taken me back to his master so his master could feed off of me?*

Each of the pawns will be sent out to bring back a victim for their master. He was wounded far worse than the others in our battle. Had they not come to his rescue, I would have killed him.

You fought him, and that's why you were wounded when I found you.

I was in bad shape, he admitted. *I could not open the earth enough to crawl in. I was that weak. Fortunately, I was able to open it just enough that the nutrients in the soil helped to rejuvenate me enough that I could eventually heal myself.*

I would have healed you, she said quietly. *Not like you can do it, but I really can heal people tuning crystals to them and centering on the problem.* She had wanted to heal him. That had been important to her, but when she saw his gift—it had been so much more than hers.

Not so much more, sívamet. Different. Move to the top of that little mound of dirt just above the drop off.

Do you think they have found another victim to bring to their master instead of me? She couldn't help the tremble in her voice. She couldn't imagine how it would have felt to be taken to someone worse than the vampire she'd encountered.

I do not know. I will hunt him, but if he has someone with him, csitri, it is already too late.

The gentleness in his voice turned her heart over. She even

283

felt a caress *inside* her mind. How was that even possible, and yet he soothed her with his nonphysical touch.

He would kill them immediately?

He hesitated, and her stomach churned. She wasn't certain she wanted the answer, not if he was hesitant about revealing what a master vampire would do to his victim.

There is no way of knowing. I doubt it. He would want to feed as long as possible on his victim while he heals. He knows I am hunting. He will not wish to move until he thinks it is safe.

That said volumes. Teagan realized the master vampire had to be afraid of Andre. He had taken on the master vampire and several of his pawns. She couldn't help the little surge of pride she had in him as well as the fear for him. She wanted him to stop the vampires from taking any more victims, but at the same time, she didn't want him hurt. Not one scratch.

Stop thinking about vampires, Teagan. This will require complete concentration. You have to allow your owl to take flight. You will need to recede into the background enough that whatever form you take can behave naturally with you present enough to guide it. Do not try anything else. One skill at a time.

He didn't have to remind her of that. She was a climber and she was terrified of heights. She knew how to focus her entire brain on a single problem, especially when she was afraid. She was about to try to fly. She didn't risk looking at the sky, because she considered the sky pretty much as high up there as she was ever going to get.

Um, Andre. Her heart began to hammer. She heard it. The birds heard it, and so did he. *There's something you should know about me.*

Tell me.

I often, as in every time, completely fall apart when I'm around fifty feet up. I freeze. I always cry. It's a total panic thing. I can't stop it. I talk myself out of it, or my climbing partner does, but no matter how often I climb—and it's a lot, both bouldering, and with ropes on the higher trad climbs—I always panic.

Teagan.

Her heart turned over. No contempt. No arguing. No telling her not to do this. Just her name. Tender. Sweet. Silk and velvet. His voice helped to settle her.

I will be with you. If you get too high and panic, I can talk you out of it. I will be right beside you. Look to me. I have got you, always.

She believed him. That calm, absolutely confident man wouldn't allow anything to happen to her. He didn't seem to mind that she needed reassurance, or that she confessed she panicked. He was there, right next to her, and she sensed that he was proud of her, whether or not she actually got into the air.

You are allowing me to show you my world, csitri, and I am honored and privileged to do so.

He was so formal. So gallant. She so wanted Grandma Trixie to meet him. She knew her grandmother would love him. So would her sisters. Unless of course, Grandma Trixie didn't take the time to know him and staked him instantly.

Teagan. Keep your mind on flying. You are distracting yourself.

Of course she was. She was about to take a leap of faith and throw herself off a very high cliff. She'd looked down, and it wasn't pretty. Rocks. Below that, trees. She needed a minute, but if she didn't just close her eyes and go, she might never experience flying on her own.

She deliberately retreated in her mind, sliding back to allow the owl to the front. Instantly the bird spread its wings and took flight. No hesitation. She was in the air. Almost immediately she was aware of the night. The mist on her. The way her down feathers trapped air and provided insulation. The fringe on her primary wing feathers actually broke down

285

the turbulence from air rushing over the surface of the wing. She realized that was the reason the owl was silent as it flew across the sky.

She was flying. Teagan Joanes, flying. Crazy cool. If she didn't let herself look down—let the owl do it—she would be fine. Perfect. The sensation of the air moving through her and over her was amazing.

You have to guide the owl. You are the owl, and yet you are not. I am right beside you. Nothing will happen if you look down. Seeing through the eyes of an owl is wonderful and not to be missed.

That's total bribery. If she was being honest, bribery was working. She wanted to see through the eyes of the owl. Fear shimmered through her. *I don't want you to see me in panic mode. You already think I'm irrational. I don't need you thinking I'm unreasonable as well.*

I do not think you are unreasonable, Teagan.

That's because you haven't seen me in full panic. I am unreasonable. It takes me forever to get myself under control.

Open your eyes and let yourself see. I am guiding both owls and you are perfectly safe. I will not let you fall.

Teagan had spent years learning to meditate and doing deep breathing to remain calm when her fears got the best of her. She wasn't in the least prepared for this situation. He didn't understand, and she was a bit ashamed to confess.

I boulder, Andre. I can trad or sport climb using a rope, but I prefer bouldering.

And this means? he prompted.

She hadn't realized his opinion of her meant so much. She had never much cared what others thought of her. She went her own way and did her own thing. But it mattered what Andre thought of her.

Bouldering is just me figuring out a problem. Controlling the climb. If I climb with a rope, I'm relying on someone else to save

286

me if I'm in trouble. It shamed her, that she didn't have enough trust in her that she could allow a climbing partner to belay her properly. She'd never been able to get past that one fear—placing her life in the hands of another without falling apart.

Teagan.

His voice brushed over her. *Through* her. So much silk and velvet. Inside the owl, she shivered, unable to stop her reaction to his mesmerizing voice. She'd never liked her name so much as when he said it in that tone.

You have placed your life in my hands repeatedly. You have great courage facing my world whether you think so or not. The idea of shifting has to be frightening, yet you followed my instructions and were successful.

She hadn't considered that she trusted him to get her out of a bad situation if she messed up. The idea of shifting had been incredibly fascinating. She had been determined to learn how. Yes, she'd been scared, but she could feel Andre there in her mind. His presence, even without his physical body, was so incredibly large and powerful—so *steady*. Like a rock.

How could she possibly trust him with her life—almost a stranger who had forced her into a world she wanted nothing to do with—and yet not trust the people she knew for years? While astonishing, she realized it was the absolute truth.

I am in your mind, csitri. You are in mine. You know I will protect you with my last breath. You know that. No matter what I have done to displease you, that will always and forever be a constant you know you can rely on.

Don't remind me you have displeased me. And displeased is a very mild word to describe how I feel when I think about what you did.

Then I regret bringing it up.

But there was no remorse. She kept waiting for Andre to feel remorse or guilt. She found neither in his mind, only the sorrow and regret that she suffered. He hadn't known how hard the conversion was on a human psychic and he wished he'd researched more carefully and thoroughly, but she knew, without a doubt, he still would have converted her. His culture and her culture were very much opposites when it came to what men were allowed to do with their women.

She understood him more after seeing what he'd gone through as a child and the trauma he'd suffered. She could see the reason in his mind that he had held on with honor for centuries and if he didn't bind them together, he was at risk because he was already so close to the darkness of his species. Truthfully, she didn't fully understand that, but she knew it was real enough. Both those reasons were the only things that kept her from fighting for a freedom she wasn't certain she really wanted.

Teagan, let yourself look. Guide the owl. Stay beneath my wing. I will have you in my mind. Nothing bad will happen to you.

She believed him. He was calm. A rock. Steady. There was something so powerful and invincible about Andre that there simply were no doubts. She was safe. She took a deep breath, feeling it inside the owl's body, and opened her vision behind the owl's eyes. For a moment she was disoriented. The owl could see greater distances due to the shape of its eyes and its ability to turn its head. It took just a moment to adjust to that. The ground wasn't as far as she thought it might be, and the owl could see everything, spotting the smallest movement in the vegetation as they moved overhead.

From above, the trees looked beautiful. Breathtaking. She had never thought to see the tops of the canopies like she could from a bird's perspective. Andre was really the guide, keeping the coordinates in her mind so her female owl responded and flew away from the mountain toward the village in the distance. Still, it was exhilarating to see the beauty of the land from her position in the sky and to feel as if she was navigating, even if by Andre's instruction.

So beautiful, Andre. Truly beautiful. There was wonder in her voice and she didn't try to hide it from him. She knew he was giving her gifts from his world in order to combat the things she considered negative.

She felt that he was pleased. More, she felt she was giving him the same gift that he had given her. For the first time in centuries, he was experiencing something he took for granted with fresh eyes—her eyes.

It is beautiful, he agreed.

There was something in his voice that took her breath away. That sent little darts of fire licking down her spine and into her body, despite the fact that she wasn't in her natural form. She understood then that she was still present, and her attraction to him, her responses, started in her mind and moved through her body. In her mind, she still had her body and always would have. She was there, she'd simply mixed up the molecules and made her form something else. She still felt and thought and reasoned as Teagan.

Addictive, Andre. Flying is addictive. Like bouldering. Like you. She didn't care if she admitted it to him. He already knew she thought he was absolutely the best. She could still be angry at him and tell the truth. *Okay, honey, maybe anger is fading. Maybe it's all about fear at the things you'll expect from me.*

Sivamet.

The tenderness in his voice turned her heart over.

Teagan, I do not expect you to go to ground with awareness. There is no reason you ever have to be aware of it. I can wrap my body around yours and wait for you to fall asleep, make certain you are out for the night and put you in the earth where you will be rejuvenated. I can wake before you, feed you and make certain you are refreshed and in bed again with me before you wake. I have told you, whatever makes you happy and comfortable in our world is what I want to do for you.

She knew he meant that as well. It was impossible to miss the sincerity in his voice or his mind. But still, Teagan's brain played the "what if" game that she always played when she was climbing with others. She always considered herself the weak link. If someone fell or was injured and they were up four or five hundred feet, even in a harness, she would have to bring them down. Of course she'd trained for it. She'd even practiced it repeatedly, but she always wondered if she would panic.

There it was. Panic and fear, her old nemeses. If Andre fought off a master vampire or a pack of vampires, he would be injured. He would need her. Just as her climbing partners would need her in an emergency. She didn't know, even if he trained her, if she could open up the earth and put them both in it.

There is no need to worry about such things, Teagan.

Of course there is. It could happen. It's even likely to happen.

Teagan, you are my lifemate. We share the same soul. You are in my mind and you can pull out information on anything I have done. You would protect me with the same fierce determination that I would use to protect you. It will never matter what you have to do—you will simply do it.

How do you know?

You have great courage. You always have. You are already bound to me, not only our souls, but in your heart as well. It is in your nature to take care of those you love.

You can't know that.

Teagan.

Her stomach plummeted and rolled at the silk and velvet brushing through her mind so intimately.

I am there. In your thoughts. In your memories. You traveled all

the way to these mountains alone, determined to heal your grand-
mother's mental illness. If you could not help her, you planned to
move back in with her and take care of her. You are a woman of
great courage who will do whatever it takes to care for those you
love.

It was absolutely true that she would have moved in with
Grandma Trixie and taken care of her rather than see her in
a hospital. She would have consulted with the best doctors
to learn how to care for her. But she would never, under any
circumstances, abandon her. Grandma Trixie had taught her
that.

Unconditional love. She'd known that always, her entire
life. She'd always had that from her sisters and her grandmother. They didn't mind when she panicked, but it was a
weakness—a character flaw—and she'd never been able to
overcome it.

She took another breath and stared down at the ground
below her. It was far, far below her. She felt the first wave of
uneasiness, the tightening that heralded the full-blown panic.
She hated being out of control. *Hated* it.

She forced herself to scan the ground below them, seeking
beauty, seeing the landscape from a different perspective. Too
far down. So far down. She hated heights. Flying was very
cool. Maybe the coolest, but it wasn't her thing. She couldn't
be up·this high without her stomach lurching and her mind
freezing.

Do you know what I would like to do with you right now? You
brought the beauty of shifting and flying back to me. You are magic,
Teagan, my magic. Still, with all this beauty, all I can think about
is kissing you. Being inside of you. That is the most beautiful of all
places. You are so perfect.

Her mind and body went from frozen to melting, just that
fast. His voice, soft, sensual, mesmerizing.

I especially love your breasts. Your nipples are perfect. I love how sensitive they are. I love how wet you get for me, so ready, and you never hold back. You give yourself to me all the way. You put everything out there for me. So sweet, sivamet. So beautiful.

The terrible panic was gone. She was hot and wanting him, but thankfully she wasn't screaming hysterically.

Wow. She sent the word into his mind when she could find a breath. *Not a single one of my climbing friends ever thought to say that to me when I was freaking out. I think it was quite successful.*

And true.

There was a trace of humor in his voice. Mostly it was all velvet and silk. She felt his pride in her and didn't really understand why. *You know it doesn't make any sense at all that you feel that way about me.* Teagan really felt compelled to tell him the exact truth.

I see you, Teagan. The real you. That is the one I have fallen so hard for.

Her heart stuttered. She knew her reaction to him wasn't strictly physical. She knew it was impossible to fall in love with someone so fast. She couldn't love him. Could she? She knew him better than she knew any other person on the face of the earth, including her family members. She was in his mind and he was right, it was impossible to stop the flow of information back and forth.

She could see his honor and integrity. For him, she really was the only woman in the world and he would do whatever it took to make her happy. Of course, he was arrogant and bossy, but she supposed with his past, his abilities and the longevity of his life, he'd earned the right to a little arrogance.

He was gentle and kind and compassionate. He didn't complain about his life. He accepted the centuries of hunting the vampire. He accepted the terrible wounds and the loneliness that came with that. He accepted her for exactly who she was and with all her failings, with every fault, she was still the only one. His. That made her happy in spite of being so afraid of the future. Very happy.

16

The small village was nestled next to the mountains, sitting in close as if for shelter. It was fully dark by the time the two owls made their way to the outskirts. The rain was falling softly, more than a mist, but not quite raindrops.

They shifted on the very edges, out of sight, clothing themselves. Andre had provided the clothes for her, but Teagan insisted on creating her own very cool designer boots. She'd never been able to afford them, but she certainly had studied them often enough and she could replicate them, so she did.

Teagan turned her face up to the moisture, letting it wash over her face, the feeling against her skin wonderful. Exhilarating even.

"Teagan," Andre said softly. "This is dangerous. You are no longer human. There are people who would murder you just for being different."

Like her own grandmother. *Like her own grandmother.* The thought of it had a lump in her throat, choking her.

Andre swept his arm around her waist and pulled her beneath the protection of his shoulder. "Your hearing is more acute. Turn the volume down if it gets too much, but listen to conversations. We need information, whether or not Jashari's body was found and who his friends are. It is essential we keep a low profile. That is going to be difficult because you are a beautiful woman and a stranger here."

You are a beautiful woman. That made her glow. "Andre, I hate to have to break this news to you, as much as I want you to believe that, but you're the only one in the world who thinks I'm beautiful."

She slipped her arm around his waist because she liked being so close to him. His arm circled around her. Her arm made it halfway and the angle was awkward. He was way taller than she was. She settled for slipping her fingers into his back pocket. The moment she did, the intimacy of the action moved through her like a soft shimmering fire. She had never wanted—or dared—to do such a thing and yet now, it seemed the most natural thing in the world.

He leaned down. Close. His lips brushing her ear. She swore his tongue touched that sensitive spot just behind her ear. "I have a little bit of news for you, *csitri*. Men find you attractive. Very attractive."

"You can't know that. We've never been together around other men, unless you call that horrible vampire a man." She gave a delicate little shudder and moved closer to Andre's side. He made her feel safe.

"I read minds. You have memories, and the men are in your memories."

"But they're *my* memories and I never once thought a man was really attracted to me. So you'd only see that. Right?"

He shook his head.

She stiffened. One hand went to his flat, hard belly. "You can't really do that. Can you? Andre, can you really do that?"

"Yes."

"But that's incredible. How? That doesn't make any sense. Just by seeing other men in my memories you can read them?"

"I told you, I am a ghost. I can get into heads and see everything. I have always been able to do so. Still, I do not think most Carpathians have that ability."

"You didn't tell me that." She felt nearly breathless with the wonder of Andre. He'd given her a gift by teaching her how to shift and then to fly. More, he gave her the gift of not panicking when she always did. But mostly, he'd given her the gift of acceptance. He really didn't care if she panicked. She felt his love for her. It enfolded her. Surrounded her. Wrapped her up until she felt she belonged.

"Andre." She looked up at him. "You aren't a ghost. Don't think that of yourself."

"Everyone else thinks it."

"I'm not everyone else. I see you. I'll always see you."

"Even when you are really angry with me?"

She looked up at his face. It was a beautiful face. Some great sculptor should carve his face in marble. Up so close to him, she could see his dark, thick lashes and the marvelous color of his eyes. So unusual and always changing.

"Teagan."

Her stomach did the familiar flip at the way he said her name. She smiled up at him as they walked along the main street of the village. She knew he was scanning the entire area, taking in everything around them, searching out any danger that could possibly be coming their way. Still, even knowing that, because she was in his mind, she still felt as if his entire focus was on her.

296

He didn't miss one single thing about her. He was aware of the way she moved, her body brushing against his with every step. He was aware of her hair, down, in the way he liked it, cascading down her back and around her face.

Andre liked the sway of her hips and the way her breasts pushed against the material of her top—the one he'd created for her. It fit close, accentuating her narrow rib cage and tucked-in waist. She didn't really need the lacy bra she was wearing—she really was that small—but he insisted and she suspected she knew why. With every movement of her body, the lace teased her sensitive nipples. It felt delicious and a little bit naughty. The sensation also kept her very aware of Andre and wishing they were back in their cave and alone.

"*Sivamet*, answer me. Your answer is important to me."

She heard the sincerity in his voice. She was going to have to let go of her anger at him, which wasn't nearly as difficult as she wanted it to be. She sent him a quelling look from under her lashes. "I'm not turning into one of those women who give in to their man just because he's amazing in bed."

His eyebrows shot up. "That has something to do with your answer?"

"Yes." She nearly snapped the affirmative at him. "Of course it does. You cannot make me angry and then flirt and be all gorgeous and sexy. That's definitely in the rule books. When I'm angry you can be suitably cowed."

If it was possible, his eyebrows went higher. His lips twitched, drawing her attention to his beautiful *perfect* mouth, which immediately made her hungry for his kisses.

"Cowed?"

He repeated the word as if he didn't quite understand it, and maybe he didn't because he wasn't only a different nationality, he was a different species. He managed in his utter astonishment to look even sexier than usual. She sighed.

"Clearly"—she injected sarcasm into her voice—"you are not getting the concept. Don't talk anymore. It's just better than way."

"*Csitri.*"

She closed her eyes. He said that word so softly, his accent twisting the sound of each individual consonant and vowel separately, so the word was musical. The notes slid inside of her. Softly. Gently. Just slipped in and melted her. Her fingers tightened on his back pocket. He was hers. This amazingly beautiful man belonged to her.

"I need an answer. Can you still see me even when you are angry with me?"

He asked the question gently. Softly. Just as melodically as when he'd called her *baby* or *little one* in his own language. She knew that, not because he told her, but because the translation was there in his mind.

Teagan looked up at him, her eyes meeting his. What she saw there took her breath away. He looked at her as if there was no one else in his world. As if he wanted to swing her up in his arms and take her back to the cave and have wild, crazy sex with her and then make love to her slowly.

She blushed. She was reading his mind again, not just the telling look in his eyes. "I see you all the time, Andre. *Especially* when I'm angry with you. You're too sexy for your own good. Well. For *my* good." Scowling, she clapped a hand over her mouth, as if trying to push the words back inside. "Seriously, I have to learn to keep my mouth shut. You're already as arrogant as a man could possibly be, which ... " She glared up at him, uncaring that her voice was muffled behind her palm. "It is *not* a compliment."

His fingers settled over hers, gently pulled her hand away from her mouth, kissed her palm—which sent a million butterflies winging through her stomach—and placed her palm on his flat belly again, his hand covering hers. The butterflies just kept fluttering.

"It sounded like a compliment," he said softly.

She loved his voice. Plain and simple. There it was. Her entire problem. His voice was sexy no matter what he was saying. Okay. If she was being strictly honest, his voice wasn't her *entire* problem. There was his really masculine, manly, gorgeous face and his rock-hard, muscles-everywhere body. That was a good part of her problem right there—and the fact that he knew how to use his body. His mouth. His fingers. His . . . well . . . *everything*. And then of course, he was a kickass vampire hunter. That was pretty cool. And mostly, he looked at her with that look, the one that said she was his world. Teagan sighed. He had every reason to be all arrogant and confident. She was falling like a ton of bricks.

For the first time she noticed the rain had begun to fall much faster. No longer mist, it should have soaked both of them, but it didn't. They strolled through the drops without really getting any wetter than if it was still mist.

"Is it really so bad?"

"What?" She was too absorbed in the minor miracle that she wasn't completely soaking wet.

"The way you feel about me. Is it really that bad? You know I feel the same way about you."

She stopped right there with the rain coming down and darkness surrounding them. Teagan shook her head. "It's not the same way, Andre. The way I feel about you is fierce and intense, so much so, that against my better judgment I'm still with you. You feel for me, yes, but you can say no to me very easily. You refuse to get the concept that I wasn't born in your century. I'm going to have to live with that, and it will be difficult for me."

"Is that what you think?" Andre's arm tightened around her. "Teagan, against my better judgment, we are here, in this village."

She bit down on her lip. She had forgotten he'd objected strenuously to coming here. He didn't mix with humans, not if he could help it. She understood part of his reason, but what was the harm of walking down the street and feeling normal for a few minutes? Well, her normal.

"I need this."

His hand moved up her back to the nape of her neck. "I know you do, Teagan. That is why we are here. Just remember, it is imperative to keep a low profile. Stay close to me and always keep your eyes open. This is the nearest hunting ground for vampires."

Her throat closed for a moment. She hadn't thought of that. Of course the undead would hunt in the village. The next closest humans were many miles away.

"You're going to go after them, aren't you?"

"It is what I do. First, I want you safe and happy. I need to know you have my back on this before I go out. It is necessary that you are comfortable with your new life."

She pressed her lips together and then decided the best thing to do was just tell the truth. She was who she was. "I'm scared, Andre."

"Teagan." That soft loving tone. "I know you are."

"No. I mean all the time. Every minute of every day. I'm so used to being afraid that it's a part of me, of who I am. Fear is inside me. In my skin. In my blood."

They were coming up to a building that looked like it could be a modern day Internet café, when everything else around them looked a little old world to her. He stopped right in front of the wide windows and turned her to him, his arms settling around her back, drawing her close to him, her front pressed to his. Everything else dropped away but the awareness of his hard body tight against her soft one.

"I am well aware of your fears, Teagan, but you are not afraid when you are with me. Not even when you shifted and took flight. You trusted me to look after you. You gave yourself to me and I take that seriously. You are safe with me. You always will be."

His lips brushed the top of her hair and she felt the sensation go all the way to her toes. She wasn't *as* afraid, which was kind of shocking because she hadn't known him that long. But she knew absolutely he would lay down his life for her, this man who had spent centuries alone.

"Don't ever let yourself be fooled, Andre, I can freeze in a heartbeat and dissolve into hysterical tears."

"I have seen this in your memories."

He didn't sound in the least perturbed. Instead, he used that low, sexy voice that tended to slip inside her skin and wrap around her heart.

"But, Teagan, you always, *always* recover quickly and finish whatever you are doing. You overcome your fears."

She shook her head. "The fear is there, I overcome the panic." She felt compelled to tell the strict truth even though his statement sent a rush of warmth through her veins.

Andre tipped her chin up so her eyes met his. "And that is just another beautiful, courageous trait I love in you."

He dipped his head to hers, brushed his lips over hers gently. Tenderly. She felt that touch almost as deeply as if he'd kissed her hard, with lots of tongue. Her entire body reacted. Her mind. Even her heart fluttered. She stared up at him a little dazed as he lifted his head.

"You belong to me, *csitri*, and that means every vow I made to you, I keep. That means I take care of you. No one hurts you. Not ever. Not physically and not emotionally. Now, call

301

your grandmother, Teagan. You need to tell her you have met someone. Tell her you will be bringing me home."

She didn't like anyone telling her what to do. Not ever. But having him declare with absolute honesty, with such conviction, that he would stand for her, protect her, *and she knew he would*, felt good. No. It felt great.

"When should I say we're coming home?" She couldn't believe he would actually move to the United States with her. She bit her lip. Maybe she was reading him wrong. Maybe it was a visit. She didn't want a visit. She wanted to be close to her grandmother and sisters. She wanted to see her nephews and nieces grow up. If she was now like Andre, did that mean her entire family, generation after generation, would grow old and die and she wouldn't?

Teagan raised her eyes to his once again, tears close. "I haven't asked you a lot of questions about what my future holds, mostly because I was so upset and I need time to process, but will I have the same longevity you have, Andre?"

His arm tightened around her waist, holding her even closer as if he could give her strength. "Yes, *sivamet*."

"My entire family will die?"

"That is the natural cycle of life, Teagan. Most likely you were going to lose your grandmother and sisters before you died. They are older than you."

She bit her lip harder, shaking her head. "But not the children. I'll have to see them die as well, won't I? And their children?" It was suddenly difficult to breathe. Her throat felt raw and her heart accelerated.

He didn't reply right away. She leaned into his strength. His warmth. His arms, surrounding her, felt good.

"Living in my world, there are really wonderful things as well as drawbacks. Just as there are in any world. I will see to your happiness, Teagan. Always. You will have the privilege of seeing future generations if you so wish. The descendants of your sisters. We will of course travel and have new identities every so many years, but you can go back when you need to in order to see your relatives."

She tried to push away the idea of her family members dying over and over and her having to watch it.

"How do you do it?"

"I am not human and I have never come to love humans after I lost those I considered family. The idea of leading a vampire to anyone I cared about was too soul-destroying, so it was easier to just avoid them."

She closed her eyes and leaned her head against his chest. She hadn't meant to bring up something that was so traumatic.

His hand cupped the back of her head, his fingers sliding into her hair. "*Csitri*, that was a long time ago, long before you were ever born."

"But I brought the sorrow back to you. The guilt you really don't deserve to feel. It's all new and raw just as if it happened yesterday." She tilted her face up to look at him. "I'm in your mind, too."

"I can shield you," he offered. "There is no need for you to feel the emotions from so long ago."

"Don't you dare, Andre. I know you protect me, but I want to give you the same thing back. If you're my man, then I have that right."

His eyebrow shot up and a slow frown darkened his face. A little shiver crept down her spine. He didn't look happy.

"*If? If* I am your man? You are not certain yet?"

She bit her lip. *Whoops.* That wasn't well thought out, not when he was the possessive type. "It's all new," she defended.

"New or not, you should be certain."

"I need to call my grandmother." Avoidance was the only real savior and she grasped at it immediately.

"So call."

Yep. Still not happy with her. She pulled out her cell phone, happy for international calling. She couldn't wait to call her grandmother. She needed to hear her voice. Already, she felt the eager anticipation she always got when she had been away from her grandmother for too long.

Andre didn't let her go. If anything, his arms tightened, holding her to him while the phone rang.

"Teagan?"

There it was. Her grandmother's voice. Her throat closed for a moment. She loved her *so* much. "Grandma Trixie? How are you? I miss you."

"I miss you, too, girl. I wish you were home. Your sisters come round every day getting into my business. Sometimes all of them. Whispering. Staring at me. They think I'm totally batty."

"You aren't, Grandma Trixie. I know you aren't. I'll be home in three weeks or so. I want to take in as much as I can. And . . ." She took a breath. "I've met someone."

There was a long silence. "Someone? As in a man?"

Andre's hands tightened around her belly, pulling her closer into him. There wasn't any room left, any place to go with the exception of his skin. She could just melt there and become part of him.

"Yes. A man. His name is Andre Boroi. He's amazing. He's going to come home with me so you can meet him."

Again there was silence.

"Grandma?"

"This isn't like you, Teagan. How did you meet him?"

"Remember Armend? He turned out to be not so nice. In fact it appears he's kind of . . . um . . . a serial killer," she said it fast. Really fast. Hoping her grandmother really didn't notice. "Andre sort of rescued me."

304

"A serial killer?"

Her grandmother screeched the words at the top of her lungs. Teagan held the phone away from her ear. Her hearing was acute enough as it was. There was no turning down the volume fast enough.

"You went into the mountains with a *serial killer?*" Grandma Trixie demanded.

"Well. Yes. But this time it wasn't my fault," she assured.

This time? Andre asked.

She tipped her head to scowl at him, hoping that would serve to shush him.

Grandma Trixie sighed. "Teagan, it's never your fault, but you always get into trouble and still, you insist on traveling all over the world where I can't get to you when you're in trouble."

"I'm not in trouble," she denied. "I don't get in trouble and if I do, I always get myself out."

Clearly you do get into trouble, Andre observed. *I should have been told about this or looked closer into your memories.*

She glared at him. Her most fierce, practiced glare. Andre didn't appear impressed.

Stay out of my memories and stop listening in on my conversation with my grandmother. I mean it, Andre. She hissed the order into his mind, using her famous "tone," the one that sent her brothers-in-law scurrying to the other room to avoid any confrontation with her. She had a very carefully cultivated reputation of being the best at verbal battle.

He didn't appear intimidated or impressed. She could have sworn his lips twitched, and for one moment amusement dared to light his eyes.

"Teagan, tell me about this serial killer right this instant," Grandma Trixie insisted, using her no-nonsense voice.

Are you laughing at me? she demanded. *Because I have enough*

305

to contend with trying to convince my grandmother I'm perfectly fine.

The trouble was, she wasn't perfectly fine. She had no idea what she'd gotten herself into this time, and she didn't think her grandmother could get her out of it. Why did things like this always happen to her? She knew Andre was monitoring her thoughts because he trailed kisses down the side of her face from the corner of her eye to the corner of her mouth and then back up to her ear.

She had to suck in her breath sharply and work to keep her wayward body under control when it wanted to melt into a puddle at his feet. As it was, she went fairly boneless and his hands at her belly held her upright.

"I told you I asked Armend, you remember him from college ... "

"I never met him, but you talked about him."

"I tutored him, Grandma. I went to school with him for three years. He grew up in a village near the highest peaks of the Carpathian Mountain range. I wanted to explore that region. You know I love to hike, so when I decided to head over here, I contacted him through the Internet. We occasionally had exchanged email just to keep up. He seemed nice enough."

"A serial killer?" Grandma Trixie repeated.

Teagan sighed. "At the time I agreed to tutor him I didn't know he was a serial killer. He dated all the time, just not me." She chewed on her lip for a moment. "I don't think he actually killed anyone then. I would have heard about it."

"Well thank heavens for small favors. What, you weren't his type?"

"Thanks, Grandma." She tried to keep the sarcasm from her voice, but really, her grandmother was implying she wasn't attractive enough to even get a serial killer interested.

She didn't mean that.

She tried another scowl, which was seriously difficult to do when his fingers were sliding through her hair and then dropping to the nape of her neck in a slow massage before returning to her hair—and that felt nice. Too nice. She was *so* susceptible to him and the way he touched her. Exasperated, she pushed at his hand.

"Teagan, you sound as if you wanted a serial killer to find you attractive."

She sighed. Her talk with her grandmother wasn't going at all in the direction she wanted it to go. Worse, Andre's hand had stopped moving, but remained wrapped around the nape of her neck. Her life was totally out of control.

"*Grandma Trixie*, take a breath. I don't want a serial killer to find me attractive. I don't think that much matters to them, although since he was a serial rapist as well, maybe he had a preference type."

Her grandmother shrieked, an ear-splitting shriek Teagan was fairly certain she heard straight from the States and *not* from her cell phone. Okay, another mistake. She blamed Andre, because right at the moment she began trying to explain, his fingers slid into her hair again and totally short-circuited her brain.

"A rapist? Teagan Jonelle Joanes, you come home right this minute. Now. Get on a plane or I swear, I'm coming out there to save you from yourself."

When her grandmother used all three of her names in that tone, she meant business. She opened her mouth to defend herself, but her grandmother wasn't finished.

"Whoever this man is, he is a total foreigner. He has a different culture, and those foreigners treat women different. He might lock you up in his harem or something. Lose him now and get home."

Teagan closed her eyes. Andre heard. Probably the people in the pub down the street heard. "He isn't from a place where they have harems," she defended lamely. "Grandma Trixie, you have to take a breath and just listen to me. He's dead. Armend is dead. There is no threat to me." Her voice kind of took a dive on that, because if you counted vampires and Armend's friends she might have been lying just a tiny bit to her grandmother.

A tiny bit?

Andre's laughter slid into her mind. Poured through her skin into her veins. It wasn't fair he was so damned sexy. She tried hard not smile. The situation was just plain out of hand. Everything she said only made it worse.

"Don't you lie to me, girl. You went right up into those mountains, and I warned you there are vampires wreaking havoc on the population."

"I'll watch out for them, Grandma Trixie," she assured, because she *would*. "The idea of encountering a vampire in my travels is very, very low on my to-do list."

"You take me seriously."

"I always take you seriously. I have to go now, but I'm all right. I'll check in again in a couple of days, and please stop worrying about me. Andre is perfectly capable of protecting me from anything or anyone who might want to harm me."

"You don't know this man, Teagan. Come home."

"I'm going to marry him, Grandma Trixie," she blurted out. "I'm very serious about him so don't get it in your head he's wrong for me. I've waited a long time to find the right man and he's the one. He's coming home with me, and I want you to make an effort with him."

There was a long silence. Teagan bit her lip hard. Her heart pounded. Andre leaned down, his lips against her ear.

Breathe, sivamet. She will learn to accept me. She wants to protect you, that is all. She loves you. You apparently get into a lot of trouble when you are out of her sight.

I do not. She was silent for a moment. She sighed. *Okay that's not exactly the truth, but really it isn't my fault. There was the time in Chile when the police—corrupt police—tried to take my passport and I refused to get back on the bus without it and they nearly shot me.* She chewed on her bottom lip. *There might have been a few incidents like that one, but I always get out of them.*

"Come home, Teagan. Bring him if you want, but don't do anything until we meet him. Just get away from those mountains. I have some friends who know all about that particular mountain range, especially around Romania."

"I'm not in Romania at the moment, Grandma Trixie," she pointed out. "I really have to go. I love you. Like crazy, I love you. To infinity and back."

"I love you, too, Teagan," her grandmother whispered. "Honey, come home."

Teagan didn't answer. She ended the call and turned in Andre's arms. "That went well."

"The police in Chile wanted to shoot you?"

"*Corrupt* police," she said. "They have a great black market for American passports. I managed to get my passport and get back on the bus in one piece."

"And Argentina?"

She gasped. "You looked into my memories."

"What were you thinking in Spain, confronting those two men who tried to put something in your drink?"

"Well, it was an outrageous thing to do and very disgusting. It happens to women all the time, but see, I noticed because I was paying attention."

"Why were you there in the first place with no one to look after you?"

He sounded genuinely puzzled as well as angry. Risking

309

a look at him—yeah—he was definitely not a happy camper. His eyes went glacier cold, like total blue ice, and at the same time, his face darkened. He looked—scary. Really scary. She took a deep breath and tried to step away from him, put a little space between them.

His arms turned into absolute steel. She couldn't move, not even a fraction of an inch.

"Andre." She pushed at his arms. "Modern day women travel all the time on their own. They go into bars and have a drink, not to pick anyone up, but just to wind down. I don't exactly look like the kind of woman men are going to get excited about. Maybe because I'm small, they thought I looked like a victim. I have a few self-defense moves. I can take care of myself."

His breath rushed out of him. "We will talk about this later. We need to hear as much as we can about Jashari and his friends. We need information. The best place to hear gossip and news is there." He indicated a rustic building just about a city block away. People were coming in and out of the door constantly. In fact, it seemed to be the only place where there was any activity.

"If a vampire is hunting, he will hunt there, or just outside. He can mask his appearance and force a compulsion on someone to accompany him outside."

"Do you have your identification on you?" she asked. "I carry my passport and ID in my jacket."

He lifted an eyebrow. "I have sent word to Josef, one of our boys well versed in modern technology, and he has built a full identity for when I travel with you to the United States, but I do not need anything here."

She didn't tell him he was mistaken. He slid his hand down her arm and threaded his fingers through hers, taking her with him down the street to a building where music, laughter and voices spilled out into the night. The rain had let up again so only a fine mist touched her face.

She noticed Andre was reaching out with senses, searching for something—or a lack of it. She stayed in his mind, trying to study what he did.

Vampires are so foul, nature shrinks from their presence. They try to disguise themselves by creating a space of nothing. No scent. No tracks. Nothing at all. That can give them away.

She liked that he shared. She liked that a lot. She especially liked walking beneath his shoulder, close to his body.

Did you spot anything?

"No. That does not necessarily mean we can relax our vigilance, but it is less likely one is close."

He reached around her to open the door. At once the noise assaulted her ears, forcing her to figure out how to turn the volume down. Immediately Teagan realized just why Andre didn't need an ID. She *felt* the exact moment he reached out and took control of the mind of the man at the door. They were waved through. He kept her close as they made their way to a table all the way at the back of the room.

The smell of alcohol nearly made her gag. She'd never had that reaction before, and she knew immediately she couldn't possibly have a drink. Still, the moment the waitress came over, Andre ordered two drinks. He leaned close to her, creating an intimate space. *Listen, sivamet. After a few minutes you will be able to process several conversations at the same time. Listen for Jashari's name.*

She nodded. She wanted to learn as much as she could from him and sitting at the small table listening to his quiet instruction made her feel as if he'd accepted her as a partner, instead of someone who had to be shielded at all times.

Water came first while they waited for their drinks. She sipped at the water, her eyes moving around the bar. It was packed. She was certain there wasn't much else to do in the evenings. Music blared and couples danced. Laughter broke out at a table a couple of feet from theirs. It was normal. Human. She took comfort in that. She was apart from them all, just as she'd always been, but now, she had Andre. She was with him. She fit with him. She belonged with him. And that was just plain awesome.

17

Andre's hand, still holding Teagan's, dropped beneath the table to rest on her thigh. He rubbed the back of his hand there. Up high. She was instantly aware of him. Acutely so. Every single cell in her body was aware of him, especially her sex. Damp. Hot. Inviting. How could he do that?

He was looking at her, but she was in his mind and he was searching the room for information. Still, he was all too aware of her, just as she was of him. He didn't miss anything about her, not from the nervous hand that came up to push her hair behind her ear to the fidgeting in her chair because—well—if she didn't fidget, she might just spontaneously combust. Or have an orgasm. Could a woman actually get an orgasm just from a man rubbing the back of his hand along her thigh while his fingers were tight around hers? If so, that was *definitely* going to happen. So who could concentrate on trying to hear information in the packed room?

313

"Teagan."

She did a full body shiver. There it was. Silk and velvet. But low and rough at the same time. Somewhere between a purr and a growl. She loved the way he said her name. *Loved* it.

She risked looking up at him, and it was a risk because he was gorgeous and he had those eyes she couldn't resist. She didn't try to answer him because nothing coherent was going to come out of her mouth. "Um ..." That was it. That was the best she could manage. *Um.* What was that? She cleared her throat and tried again. "Let's just go. I mean, what do we really need to find out that we don't already know? If we left now, we could get back to the cave and ..." She trailed off, blushing. The color swept right up her body, probably starting in the vicinity of her toes and ending at her face. A full body blush.

"*Sivamet*, we will get back to our base soon, I promise."

She swallowed hard and looked at the waitress as she plopped drinks on the table. Automatically Teagan reached for the money clip she kept inside her jacket pocket. Instantly, Andre's hand covered hers. Gently. Firmly. When she looked up at him, his eyes had gone totally glacier. He slid money across the table.

"Keep the rest."

The waitress stared at him with her mouth parted like she might gobble him up at any moment. Yeah, Andre was hot. He said not to draw attention, but every female eye in the place had noticed the moment he entered. She was certain the men recognized danger when they saw it. The crowd had parted for them as he'd led the way to the table he wanted. She had also noted that the table hadn't been empty until Andre looked at it and directed her there. The occupants got up and left abruptly when they were halfway to it.

The waitress smiled and slipped back into the crowd,

expertly keeping her round tray from hitting anyone in the head as she made her way back to the bar.

"I pay, Teagan. Not you."

Of course. Macho man from another century. She rolled her eyes, but she wasn't going to argue with him over drinks they weren't going to drink. "I didn't even know if you had money, Andre. There are a lot of things I don't know about you."

"When you live centuries, Teagan, it is easy enough to acquire wealth. We will not be hurting for money."

"I've got money put away as well. Not that much, but it will help."

"The triplets and I own oil reserves. And a couple of gold mines. We have the rights to other minerals as well. Our companies make millions." He paused. "Actually billions. I do not pay much attention. A couple of the others handle that kind of thing for us now. If we decided to move on, we would leave our shares to other Carpathians."

Her eyelashes fluttered. He sat there so casually telling her he was a billionaire. Who did that? She could see he didn't care in the least about the money.

"I do not need it. Or I have not needed it until now. I have never touched a penny beyond money I use when I go to a human village, which is exceedingly rare."

He was talking to her, giving her details of his life, yet all the while, he was listening to the conversations swirling around them. *There it is, csitri. The table in the corner. They are talking about Jashari and his father. The body was found by his friends and brought down the mountain. His father wants to organize a hunting party and wipe out the wolf pack.*

She gasped at the matter-of-fact way he announced the potential slaughter of wild, beautiful animals. *It's not that I want to get eaten by wolves . . .* She couldn't help the little shudder that ran through her body. *That would be a really bad way to go. I don't want anyone else eaten by them either, but really, Armend was a serial killer. Maybe if we locate the bodies of the women he killed, they'll leave the wolves alone.*

Andre smiled at her. *Do you have any idea how amazing you are?*

Because I don't want the father of a killer to destroy wolves? Anyone would feel the same way.

That is not so. People hunt for sport. It makes them feel powerful to take lives.

She bit her lip. She knew he'd spent centuries taking lives. "It must be hard for you, Andre," she whispered aloud.

He shook his head. "We do not feel, Teagan. Nothing at all. There is no compassion, mercy or remorse. I hunt evil. That is all. It is simple and it must be done."

"You said sometimes they were people you knew. Like your uncle. I know you didn't hunt him, the other Carpathian killed him, but you might have had to." She couldn't help herself, she cupped the side of his face in her palm and daringly stroked his jaw with her thumb.

He nodded slowly. "Yes, but without our lifemates, we do not feel anything at all. I could recognize that I should feel sadness, but the actual emotion escaped me."

"Until me."

He nodded again and sent her one of his heart-stopping smiles. "Overwhelming floodgates opened. Mostly though, I feel for you—everything there is possible to feel just for you."

She swallowed hard. He looked at her with such a hungry, possessive look, such a look of utter love that it hurt to see it. He didn't care about appearing vulnerable to her or to anyone else. It was there, stark on his face for the world to see—love. Adoration even. And she *so* didn't deserve it.

"Andre." She murmured his name. It came out husky. All wrong. She wasn't coming on to him, she was trying to tell him she had his back. She would find a way to embrace her new life with him and live in his world. She just needed time. She tried to pour all that into his name and failed miserably. She was the one who always chattered about anything and everything, but this one moment, when she needed the right words, when she wanted to give him something back, she couldn't think just how to put it. Embarrassed, she looked down at the table.

He covered her hand with his, holding her palm tight against the rough shadow on his jaw, his blue eyes burning intensely into hers.

"Dance with me, *sivamet*. I have the sudden desire to hold you in my arms."

She wanted that more than anything ... but ... She bit her lip. "I want to dance with you, but that could be risking everything we have."

His eyebrow shot up. "I cannot wait to hear this."

"Seriously. You have to take this very seriously, Andre." He was not of the modern world and he didn't understand everything. "There have been copious amounts of articles written on this subject and none of it bodes well for us. If we dance together, you're going to really see the problem."

He pulled her hand from his jaw, turned it over and pressed a kiss into the center of her palm. "I have no idea what you are talking about, Teagan."

She'd been afraid of that. "The difference in our heights. I'm short, and you're nearly a foot taller."

"I am a foot taller."

She glared at him and tugged at his hand. "There's no need to be arrogant. *Nearly* is a good enough description."

"But not accurate."

317

She blew out her breath in a sign of pure exasperation. "Sometimes, Andre, strict honesty is not always the best policy, especially when our future together is hanging in the balance."

His face darkened, his eyes going intense. Bluer than she'd ever seen. Ice-cold. Scary. "Tell me of these articles."

"Well, apparently people with real height differences don't have a chance of staying together for the long haul. The man has to hurt his back in order to kiss her or hold her, and the disparity really comes up when they dance together."

He leaned toward her, nibbling at the pads of her fingers. His teeth scraped gently back and forth over her skin and his gaze never left her face. "I am trying to follow the strange illogical and irrational path of your mind. You believe if we dance together I will have to break up with my lifemate, the only woman that can complete me, the one woman I looked for throughout the centuries of utter loneliness?"

She frowned. "Put like that it doesn't sound too logical, but really, Andre, there are several articles written on the subject and all of them say men don't like the height difference, especially while dancing, and I just thought, seeing as how when I morphed, I didn't get the breasts I wanted or a few inches more in the height department, that there might be a problem." There was the tiniest bit of accusation in her tone.

His lips twitched. He blinked. That did not amuse her in the least.

"I am not going to hide the fact that had I woken up with bigger breasts and was maybe at least five foot four or five that would have made up for a *lot*. Seriously, Andre, don't you dare laugh at me. Had I morphed into beauty queen or model status, that might have gone a long way to keeping me happy in my present weird state. Instead, I'm still me and now you're asking me to dance and you'll hurt your back and that will be a disaster." There. She warned him.

Andre smiled. Slow. Burning hot. Gorgeous. Holy cow. She was going to have an orgasm just sitting in the chair next to him. She really should be annoyed that he didn't take her warning seriously, but how could she be when just looking at him turned her into a melting puddle of absolute goo? He was forever going to get around her just by giving her his slow, sexy smile.

"I need to hold you in my arms, Teagan. Right now. Right here. I want to feel your body move against mine. Dancing is the only safe way to do this, so we shall try out your theory. If I suddenly get a backache, I will be certain to tell you."

She opened her mouth to protest because, really, he was totally mocking her when this was serious business, but he successfully stopped anything she had to say by leaning down and taking possession of her mouth. There was a fleeting thought—just one—and it really did fly away, but hadn't he said not to bring attention to them? And wasn't kissing in public bound to draw attention? Then it was gone and there was only Andre in her world.

Andre. His glorious, perfect mouth that poured golden fire down her throat and into her body so that it spread through her like a firestorm. A single sound escaped her throat that sounded mysteriously like a purr, but she didn't care. She slipped her arms around his neck and gave herself up to his kisses. Breathtaking. Earth-shattering.

Sivamet. Dance with me.

He didn't stop kissing her, but it was a clear command. That voice inside her mind, so intimate. Stroking her. Caressing her. Every bit as sensual as his mouth. She found herself moving up out of her chair, still kissing him, her arms sliding from his neck down his chest to circle his waist.

He lifted his head, his eyes moving possessively over her face. "I love the way you look at me with that expression you have right now."

She managed a laugh. "You mean dazed and confused."

His arm slipped around her. "Beautiful. Looking at me with that look is worth all the gold in the world. You are a gift, Teagan."

She didn't know about that, but she thought he was. She let him guide her through the crowd to the part of the bar where there was dancing. He was a force to be reckoned with. Tall. Muscular. His face as dangerously male as a face could get. The crowd parted without hesitation. She kept her hand in his back pocket, staying close to his body with every step.

He turned and drew her into his arms. Her arms slid around his waist and she rested her head in the niche between his rib cage. Perfect. She fit. His body pressed tight against hers. After two steps she felt the heat of his cock pressed tight against her. Growing. Hardening. Delicious. She loved that she was short enough to have his body rubbing against hers as they floated with the music, or it felt like floating. Like being in the clouds.

Her lashes drifted as she savored the heat of his body. The hardness. The hunger rising between them. She'd never had this in her life. A man holding her like she was his world. It really didn't matter that she was short and he was tall. He didn't bend down to her. He held her tight against his front, enjoying her body brushing against his. She suddenly didn't mind in the least that she was short or that her breasts were small. He fit. Perfectly. The feeling of him snuggled tight against her, so close to her mouth was exquisite.

Is this human enough for you, sivamet? I have never danced with a woman in my life.

The caress in his voice curled her toes. She loved that he'd never danced with another woman.

Or held her in my arms. I have never kissed another woman. You have to get over feeling as if you do not belong. There is one place you will always belong, csitri, and that is in my arms.

Oh God. Did he just say that? He made her weak, so much so that she was afraid her legs were going to give out. They needed to leave. Right now. This minute.

Andre. Let's go. She knew even in her mind, her voice was breathless with need.

His arms tightened. *I will take you back to the table. I have to speak to a couple of men. Then we will leave.*

She was a little disappointed. She was so aroused she could have stripped his clothes off right there if she could hide them from prying eyes.

It is possible. I could take you into the corner and make it so no one would see us, but I prefer to have you stretched out under me for a long time, showing you how I feel.

It was possible? Yikes. *Um. I think that was a "be careful what you wish for" moment. I like the idea of being stretched out under you and lots of time.* Just the thought sent a very pleasant pulse through her sex.

The music stopped and then started again into a fast number. Andre immediately moved her through the crowd back toward the table. This time, he kept her in front of him, one arm wrapped tightly around her waist, locking her to him. Once again, something in his eyes and the set of his jaw had the crowd parting. He did it smoothly, yet he didn't use his ability to "push" anyone to move—they just did.

He held her chair for her, but his gaze swept the room while he did it. Teagan sank into the seat and picked up her water glass. Both of the glasses holding alcohol were empty, as if they had already drank them. She knew Andre had done that, a slow lowering of the liquid, but she wasn't certain how.

"I will be back shortly," he murmured.

She blinked and he was already gone. Instantly she was uneasy. He moved with fluid grace through the crush of people and tables. She sat back and observed him. He was beautiful, and she wasn't the only woman in the room to think so. He walked right up to an older man who was sporting a full beard and wore rough clothes. He looked like he lived on the mountain and had for most of his life.

Andre clapped him on the back as if they were old friends. The bearded man turned to him and smiled, and they began an animated conversation. After a few minutes, Andre left the mountain man with a new drink and wandered over to a well-dressed man sitting at a table with a dark-haired woman—a woman whose eyes devoured Andre.

Teagan studied the woman. Curvy. Of course. As in *lots* of curves. She bit her lip. The woman looked confident and she was definitely trying to draw Andre's attention as he talked with her man. She leaned close, fiddled with her hair and showed cleavage. There weren't that many women in the room showing cleavage. It wasn't that kind of a bar. She had gone from looking seriously bored to animated the moment Andre approached their table.

She knew Andre was aware of the way the woman flirted, but he didn't pay attention. He spoke only to the man, looking friendly, acting like they were good friends. Again he bought drinks for the table and wandered away. The dark-haired woman looked miffed, and Teagan took a sip of water to hide her smile.

Andre's head turned and he looked right at her and smiled

that slow, sexy smile that sent fire racing through her veins. She *loved* her man. He made her feel like the only woman in the room.

Are you all right?

Absolutely. Do your thing.

She loved that she could talk to him telepathically. She could get used to some of the perks of being Carpathian. It was really, really nice that he took the time to check on her. She sent him a smile and gave a little wave of her fingers indicating he should get on with whatever he was doing.

Planting information in their heads. The missing women, how they were all last seen with Jashari and his boys. Possible locations of bodies. They will not be able to stop thinking about it and they will find those bodies.

Her heart stuttered and she pulled out of his mind abruptly. She drew in her breath and looked down at the table, pretending interest in the pattern of the wood. Andre knew where the bodies were, she was absolutely certain of it. She caught that information in his mind. He was giving that to those men. How could he know where the bodies were? How? She didn't know. Only Armend and his friends knew.

Oh God. What had she been thinking? How could he possibly know that? There was no way, not if he found Armend dead. He would have to know him. Know his friends. Dread filled her. Fear. She wanted to jump up and run out of the bar, but she didn't know where she would go or who she would trust. She could make her way to the ladies room and hope there was cell phone service. She could call her grandmother again and alert her to the fact that she was in danger. She hadn't told Grandma Trixie that Armend had sick friends.

Teagan. What is it?

Andre's voice slipped inside, right under her skin. Usually

that silk and velvet, rough and sensual and so beautiful voice could calm her churning stomach and keep fear at bay, but the knots tightened and a sense of dread filled her.

How could you know where the bodies are? Stupid. She'd tipped him off that she knew. Her fingers clenched the edge of the table until her knuckles turned white. *You knew him. How else could you know?*

I did not know him. He was alive when I got to him. We can discuss this when we are alone. I have one more person to talk to.

You lied to me. You said wolves killed him.

Wolves did kill him.

So go talk to your man so we can get out of here.

Are you good?

Yes. And that was a lie. She wanted to go home. To the comfort of her grandmother and sisters. The familiar. She didn't want to be Carpathian, flying through the sky in the form of an owl, no matter how cool it was. She just wanted to feel safe again, and she didn't feel that way.

She didn't know what to think. She bit down on her lip, trying to figure out why she felt so scared inside. She had deliberately touched Andre's mind again while he talked to her and he believed what he was saying. He sounded honest. He felt honest. He was always gentle and sweet with her—but—he had taken away her choices. Still, he could have killed her anytime he wanted. She really didn't believe he was a straight up killer. Maybe he'd had to defend himself against Armend. Maybe he'd really stumbled on the aftermath of the attack by wolves and tried to help him. She'd just panicked as usual. Still. That horrible feeling in her stomach persisted.

She sensed movement and glanced up, steeling herself, expecting Andre. Her beautiful Andre who had lied to her. Instead there were two men she'd never seen before.

One carried two drinks, the other one held his own. They must have slipped into the bar while she was dancing with Andre, because she'd really looked around when they first entered and would have noticed both men. Really good-looking.

She hadn't spotted either of them before. She could tell by their clothes and the flashy watch one of them wore that they either weren't from around there, or they were one of the few families with money. She knew instantly why she'd jumped to such stupid conclusions about Andre. She'd been feeling *them*. These two men. The dark dread in her stomach and moving through her body was all about them.

"A beautiful woman shouldn't be sitting alone," the one with two drinks announced with a smile. "I'm Giles, Giles Barabash. This is my brother Gerard." He set the drinks on the table, one in front of her, and both men pulled out chairs and sat down.

"I'm here with someone," Teagan blurted out, using English just as he had. She could tell by his heavy accent that English wasn't his first language, but he clearly could speak it easily.

Giles exchanged a glance with his brother. The look that passed between them made her uneasy. Giles shrugged. "He's not here at this moment. His loss."

"Seriously, he isn't going to be happy with you sitting here."

Giles pushed the drink toward her with two fingers, still smiling. His eyes were hard. "Drink it."

She smelled the drug with her heightened senses. "No, thank you."

Giles leaned close to her. "I wasn't asking, *Teagan*."

Two more men slid in on either side of her, trapping her between them. Her stomach did a steep pitch. She didn't doubt for one moment these men were Armend's friends. They knew who she was.

She refused to be intimidated. They were in a packed bar, and after all, Andre was there. She just needed to reach out to him. She didn't. Instead she looked from one newcomer to the other. "And you are? You look like brothers as well."

Giles snarled, lifting his lip and actually making a snarling sound, drawing her attention back to him. "Cousins," Giles snapped. "Keith and Kirt."

"So you're all related. Wow. You believe in keeping it in the family."

"Drink your fucking drink," Giles commanded.

Without warning, the bar went quiet. The air actually vibrated with a heavy sense of danger impossible not to feel. She sucked in her breath and lifted her chin so she could look over Giles's head. Her gaze collided with Andre's. Cold fingers crept down her spine. He was angry. Seriously angry. The walls of the bar couldn't possibly contain the wealth of anger pouring from him. His eyes were glacier blue and burned like a blue flame. She touched her tongue to her lips, unable to look away from him.

Andre looked like an ancient warrior out of a movie. His face was beautiful, carved of stone, totally masculine. His long hair flowed down his back. Her heart did some kind of melty thing and her stomach did a somersault. Hers. That man was hers. He certainly wasn't friends with Giles, his brother or cousins. And he really, *really* didn't like them sitting at her table.

"Teagan." Andre held out his hand to her. His eyes, total blue flames, totally hot, burned over Giles.

Teagan rose instantly, pushing back her chair and moving around Keith to take Andre's hand. He pulled her into his side. Close. Under the protection of his shoulder, and it was a broad shoulder. She slid her arm around his waist.

Andre didn't say a word to the four men, he simply turned

and made his way through the silent crowd toward the door. A woman pushed close, touched Teagan's hand.

"Be careful of them," she whispered. "They won't let this go." Her fingers slipped away and she melted into the crowd, clearly afraid of Giles and the others.

She delivered the warning in her native language, but Teagan caught the gist of it. She knew by the way Andre nodded at her. The nod was barely perceptible, but she saw the way the woman's face glowed, just for a moment.

That's nice, she whispered into his mind. *She caught that, and you're so gorgeous she can totally keep that going for months.*

Do not be adorable right now. Or funny. I am seriously angry with you.

Gulp. She had been trying hard to pretend he hadn't directed that anger at her, but there it was. No getting around it.

She lifted her chin and snuck a glance at his set jaw as they emerged into the night. The mist was once again thick, but this time, more of a dense, gray vapor that set her heart pounding—not as much as Andre's dark, angry features, but still, who knew what that fog held?

It isn't as if I invited those men to sit down with me, she told him in a snippy little voice. *Sheesh. That totally was not my fault. At all. And, just because, for only one teensy second, I entertained the idea that you might be a . . .* Yikes. Calling him a wacked-out killer wasn't going to get her out of trouble. *In my defense, you do know where the dead bodies are and I had no idea Armend was alive when you found him.*

Armend put bruises on you. He tried to rape you. He punched you. Did you think he would share the same air with you after that?

Oh. My. God. Her heart stopped and then began pounding. Hard. Hurting hard. *Andre, what are saying? You told me wolves killed him.*

327

His arm wrapped her up, locking her tightly against him. Behind them the door to the bar opened and then closed. She knew, without looking, that Giles and his crew were following them. They had convinced themselves it was four to one, clearly not counting her as a threat.

I told you the truth. I did not say I had not spoken with him. His mind was rotten and he enjoyed what he had done to those women, thinking of it often. He kept mementos in his home, the third drawer down in his private, locked desk. He takes them out at night and jerks off with the women's underwear surrounding him.

She stumbled. Armend had touched her. Sat with her for three years while she tutored him. They'd laughed together. She'd counted him as a friend. Bile rose and she pushed the back of her hand against her mouth. Her vision actually narrowed, threatened to turn black. She felt dizzy and weak. She stumbled again.

Andre swept her up into his arms. *I apologize, sivamet. I should not have shared that with you. Breathe. Take a deep breath.*

He didn't increase his speed. In fact, he went from walking in silence, to making noise, allowing the soles of his boots to hit the surface much harder than normal. Teagan took in great gulps of air, her hands clutching at his shoulders. He was luring them to him. Giles and the others. Andre deliberately was baiting them. Tempting them to come after him.

Don't, Andre. There's four of them. You might kill vampires, but you can't take on four killers. And you know they kill. Not all four at once.

They pry on helpless women. They beat up drunks. I am Carpathian. You are Carpathian. You have more strength in your little finger than all of them put together.

She blinked rapidly, trying to process that. *I do?* Wow. Now that was definitely on the pro side of the list for becoming Carpathian. She could be a real badass and kick butt if she had to. She liked that idea a lot.

Of course.

Still. Why are you getting them to follow you? Why don't we just leave?

I do not leave behind men who rape and murder women. They will follow us into the lower hills. I can dispatch them there.

Dispatch? She licked her lips. *I'm just guessing here, but I don't think you're using that word to mean a message, or post or something of that nature.*

As in mete out justice to them.

Um. Andre. You can't do that. It's against the law.

I am not human. Human laws do not apply to me. I am Carpathian and I am the wielder of justice in my world.

Yikes all over again. He wasn't kidding. He was planning on killing all four men. Maybe. "Can't . . ."

Sound carries. Stay quiet. Let them follow my footsteps.

They're human. Can't you leave them to the human law?

Humans haven't dealt with them. I will not allow them to torture and kill another woman. They have a taste for it, and Giles has declared himself the leader now. He gets off on hurting others. You should have known they were approaching and you should have read their intent.

Okay. Now they were getting to the anger part. He wasn't angry because she'd been idiot enough to think he might be Armend's friend. No, he was angry with her because she hadn't used her new very acute senses as a warning system.

And you did not reach out to me, Teagan. Immediately, when you knew you were in trouble, you did not call to me.

She hadn't. She didn't know why. But she hadn't, and he had every right to be angry over that.

I didn't, did I? That confused her. She felt safe with Andre.

329

She hadn't panicked. She was afraid, but fear lived and breathed in her all the time. She felt the coiling in his gut relax.

No, csitri, you did not alert me. Had I not been monitoring you at all times I would not have known you were in trouble.

He was monitoring her at all times? She liked that. She shouldn't. She was an independent modern woman who could handle herself in tough situations and had, many times. She didn't rely on others to fix her problems, especially when she was traveling. She relied on herself, which was probably why she hadn't thought to reach out to him.

From now on, you rely on me just as I will be relying on you. Always, always stay alert and scan your surrounding area, he counseled. *Read the minds of those around you.*

That is totally invading people's privacy.

The world you live in now, sivamet, is dangerous. Humans wish to kill us. Even your own grandmother would put a stake through our hearts if she knew what we are. You know that is true. You have to learn to be vigilant and you have to learn to rely on me. The moment you sense trouble, real or not, you reach out to me.

She bit her lip. He was right about her grandmother, with her Internet vampire-hunting kit. There was a special device that shot wooden stakes out of it, which was very cool by the way. She'd seen Grandma Trixie practicing on targets in her backyard. Teagan hadn't told her sisters, fearing they would lock her grandmother up before she could cure her mental illness.

She sighed. Now she had another problem. Her grandmother wasn't as crazy as they all thought, but she might have to convince her that she was.

Tell me you understand.

Teagan hesitated. She was beginning to realize the idea that she had of Andre being a sweet, gentle man was maybe just a tad off. He preferred to eliminate threats by *dispatching* them. As in killing them.

Teagan.

That was silk and velvet and rough, but it was a warning. He wasn't fooling around and being all sensual and sweet.

Um. Tell me whenever I am threatened you will not dispatch people. Promise me. She needed to at least bring him into the present century. *You are not a wild man, living in the caveman era.*

I cannot give such a promise. I am a Carpathian male. A hunter. And you are my lifemate. As your lifemate it is my duty and privilege to keep you from harm at all times.

She huffed out her breath. *Taming you is not going to be quite as easy as I envisioned. You are stubborn and maybe just a little too old. You know the old adage about teaching old dogs new tricks.*

There was a moment of silence. She glanced up at him. His blue eyes glittered down at her. She wasn't certain of his mood. One moment he'd been furious. Scary. Next he was luring not so innocent prey to him—and they were prey. He had targeted Giles and his crew and meant to *dispatch* them. Now he was looking at her as if he was torn between laughing or throwing her on the ground and having wild sex with her. If she had a choice, she'd take the wild sex *and* his laughter. Once in a while he smiled. He didn't laugh except that one time.

Teagan.

Her sex clenched at the sound of his voice sliding into her skin. They were out of the village. She could see the trees every once in a while as the fog swirled, opening a view and then closing it. He took her right into the forest and began to work his way to higher ground, using long, ground-eating strides. Still making noise. Breaking twigs on purpose. Not taking to the air. Still throwing out his lure. From the sounds behind them, the four men were taking the bait.

Are you calling me an old dog?

I would answer that, but anything I say could get me into trouble.

You have no idea.

His voice was that sound that took her breath and her bones. It was a promise, and she didn't know whether to try to run or to cling to him. Either way, her body was thrilled.

18

Andre climbed the mountain fast, taking a deer trail, one that was well-used and easy to navigate even in the fog. In his arms, Teagan shivered, but he knew it wasn't the cold. She didn't understand him or his ways. He got that. He got that she lived under a different set of rules, and his world was very scary to her. He didn't like her afraid, but there was little he could do about that at the moment.

They were in far worse trouble than any human could give them, even humans trained in the art of killing his species or vampires. He tasted the threat in the moisture. Felt it in the soft breeze blowing toward them. Smelled it in the faint stench rising through the trees. Vampire. The undead was hunting and he'd come down from the mountain, heading for the village.

Andre allowed his senses to flair out into the night, seeking more information, but much more carefully. He muffled the sound of his boots on the ground. Kept the snap of twigs and the rustle of leaves from the air surrounding them. That would leave only the noise of the humans as they hurried along the trail, occasionally cursing. One wanted to go back and track them in the morning. He protested over and over in a whiny voice. Even though he'd only heard the voices over a radio, he recognized the one called Keith.

What's wrong? Aside from the fact that you want to commit a felony. Maybe four of them, and I'll have to visit you in some forgotten, horrible prison filled with rats and sewage where they torture the occupants just for fun. She gave a delicate shudder. *What else are you preparing for?*

Teagan was very sensitive to him. She was already beginning to read not just his moods, but when he sensed danger. He wanted her to be able to do that herself.

Be still. Completely still. Close your eyes if you have to, but feel. Do not think. Just feel your surroundings. When you feel everything close to you, allow your senses to expand outside yourself. Outside the landscape close to you. Go above you. Below you and all around you.

Andre willed her to understand. For all her nonsense—the things she blurted out which he loved—she was highly intelligent. And sensitive. To him, before he'd ever brought her fully into his world, she felt as if she was already partway in it. He'd never heard from a single male who had a lifemate that they felt that. There was something a little different about Teagan. She was human through and through. She wasn't Jaguar, or Mage, or Lycan She was fully human. Yet her gift of healing was incredibly strong and so was that tuning fork of hers, she just needed to refine it a bit.

She didn't argue with him. That was another thing he was grateful for. It wouldn't have mattered if she did. When they were in danger, he would have covered it, stopped it immediately and taken over. That was his way, but he was glad he didn't have to. He was glad she'd listened to him when he'd laid down the rules of his world. He didn't want her to ever be afraid of him, but above all, her protection came first.

Her hands tightened on his shoulder, and when he glanced down, Teagan's eyes were closed. He was in her mind, a shadow, no more, monitoring her, making certain she was all right. He felt that reach. Tentative at first, but she'd been in his mind and she was already learning. She might not have identified what he was doing immediately, but she knew how to do it. She learned that fast. She sent her senses reaching out into the night.

Mistakenly, she concentrated on the threat that was coming up behind them. The four men following them had split, two working their way around to try to cut them off. The other two had gained on them because, before Andre felt the threat of the vampires, he wanted them to catch up.

Teagan found the location of all four men. She didn't stop there. He found himself smiling inwardly. She was afraid, just as she said she'd be, the fear inside of her, but that didn't stop her. She allowed herself a brief moment when she identified those following them and knew they were closer, but she continued to follow Andre's instructions, reaching out into the night.

Tell me what you know.

She gave a little shudder. *Belowground are insects and worms. A few ground squirrels. Not much in the way of animals. Giles and Gerard are behind us, maybe the distance of a football field. Their cousins are coming up on our right, almost parallel with us.*

He waited, his chin dropping down to nuzzle the top of her head. A part of him was still smoldering inside that she hadn't called out to him when she recognized she was in danger. He didn't like that and he intended to address the issue when they were in a safe place. He pushed that aside and let himself feel pride in her. She learned fast.

He knew the exact moment she allowed her senses to rise above them. Into the mist. Into that dense fog that pressed down on the forest and mountain. Her breath caught in her throat, and she clutched him tighter as she buried her face against his chest.

A vampire.

You missed one. There are two. I doubt either are the master. They are not covering their tracks. Both are on the way to the village. They are hunting victims.

He felt her fear. The panic rising. Her feeling of terror nearly overwhelmed him it was so strong, but along with it, he felt something else. Sheer, utter determination. A will of absolute steel.

We can't let them get to the village, Andre. They'll kill someone. Maybe more than one innocent person.

He had no intention of allowing the vampires to get to the village. He was a hunter. He sought out and destroyed the undead. That was who he was. What he was.

I am going to draw them to us. You will have to trust me, Teagan, and do everything I tell you. I am going to bring Giles and his friends to us as well.

Teagan went still. She had known, even before she said something, that Andre wouldn't allow the vampires to reach the village where they could kill any number of innocents. She bit her lip. This was certainly one of those moments to prove the old adage, *Be careful what you wish for.* Still . . .

I left my grandmother's off-the-Internet vampire-hunting kit in the States, so you might want to take them on all by yourself. Giles and his slimy friends, I can help with. In fact, I'm all about helping with them.

336

You are all about sitting quietly and waiting for your man to clean up the neighborhood.

Teagan bit her lip. She wasn't really all about that. She believed in pulling her own weight, and six to one weren't the greatest of odds. She didn't reply. Andre took it for granted that she would obey him. He did that a lot. She figured sooner or later he would catch on that she wasn't good with authority figures. He could deliver his commands in his low, sexy voice, but that didn't mean she would obey them.

Andre stopped under some trees where there was just a small clearing forming because a large tree had come down and hit another, dropping both to the forest floor.

Shift to an owl. I want you in that tree and very still.

Teagan blinked as Andre set her on her feet. She looked up the tall tree, at the thick branches. *You want me to hide away while you face all this alone, because I don't think I can do that.*

His hand slipped into her hair, bunched there, exerting pressure until her head tipped back. He kissed her. Hard. Long. Delicious. As if they had all the time in the world. Even as he kissed her, she knew he was still scanning the area around them and he knew the exact position of all six threats. She didn't bother to scan, she enjoyed the kiss. A lot.

Do what I say. I do not want to have to worry about you.

Well. She felt a lot more in the mood to do anything he said after that kiss. She had to admit to herself that she was maybe a *lot* bit of a pushover when it came to Andre and his sexy side.

She stepped away from him and held the image of the owl in her mind. She'd already done this once, so it wasn't nearly as difficult the second time. One moment she was Teagan and the next she was the owl, spreading her wings to get the feel of them.

Next time, instead of a bird, I'm going for sex kitten. Lots of curves.

You already are a sex kitten. Now get into that tree. Keith and Kirt are very close, Andre announced. *Get up in the thickest part of the tree and stay there.*

She liked that he thought she was already a sex kitten. Wow. She knew he was telling the truth because she was in his mind and he spoke matter-of-factly, as if his mind was elsewhere and he could only be honest.

Teagan.

She did a full body shiver right there inside the owl. Well, she'd definitely have a ringside seat. She took to the trees, rising fast, her wings silent. She found a branch that was slightly under several larger ones and she perched there, her talons gripping the bark so that she could peer down and see the little clearing and much of the surrounding trees.

Teagan could feel the vampires, much closer now. The air had turned foul. Oppressive. She could barely breathe. She was shocked that the human men couldn't feel the difference in the air. Each time she drew in a breath, her lungs hurt. Burned. Felt raw, almost as if they pushed the air out as fast as possible to avoid contamination.

From her vantage point she saw the two men creeping through the trees, trying to sneak up on Andre. He had his back to Kirt, and Keith approached from the front. Kirt was much closer, moving into position for the attack while his brother kept Andre's attention.

Andre, behind you.

No distractions. Do not help me.

He didn't turn around. He just barked orders at her. *Sheesh.* Try to do someone a favor and they just got mad. Kirt was nearly on him now, and she could see the knife in his fist. Keith broke through the brush right in front of Andre, also armed with a knife. Andre whirled around fast, slashing across Kirt's throat with his open hand, his nails long and sharp. Blood spurted. Andre spun again and met Keith as he rushed in, knife low, blade up, going for the softer parts of the body. Andre slapped the knife away with blurring speed, so fast Teagan couldn't actually see his palm hit Keith's wrist, but she heard the smack and saw the knife go flying. Andre's hand continued in motion, going from where he'd deflected the blade away from him, up to Keith's throat.

Teagan's heart stuttered to a halt. There was blood everywhere. Droplets hit the fog and she knew Andre was calling to the vampires, using their assailants as bait to bring in the undead, to draw them away from the village. With hunger clawing at them, the vampires would never be able to resist the lure of the scent of fresh blood.

Andre flowed around the two men, fluid and breathtaking, no wasted motion whatsoever. Teagan felt as if she watched a brutal dance of death, primitive and savage. She shouldn't have been caught up in the beauty of Andre's every move. She should have been horrified—and terrified. She wasn't.

There was no anger at all. He didn't hurt Keith and Kirt out of a personal vendetta. They came after him and after his woman. It was a logical conclusion. At the same time, he could use them to keep the vampires from invading the village and murdering an innocent. She knew all that because she was still in Andre's mind and she saw his strategy.

There was nobility in how Andre lived his life. He had honor and integrity. She saw the warrior, the true warrior, willing to put his life on the line for others—always. He was a fierce fighter yet absolutely cool and calm. She moved through his mind and couldn't find one single thing that might raise his blood pressure. No fear.

No fear. He had told her he hadn't felt fear in centuries. Not since he was a seventeen-year-old boy. He hadn't been exaggerating. He was telling a strict truth because he really didn't

339

feel fear. Not in battle. Not when he knew two vampires were coming—that he was luring them to him in order to keep them from a village of innocent men, women and children.

She could never have explained how she felt to anyone, not even her beloved grandmother, but the moment she saw Andre in action, moving so fast, his body in motion, as graceful as any ballet dancer and as lethal as any tiger in the wild, she knew she would always love him. The moment she realized she had been the one to bring fear to him after so long on earth, there was no way to resist him.

She fell hard. She would always crave him. Always belong to him. Always, always love him. Maybe it was wrong to be so madly in love with him, when he was killing someone, but it was the sheer poetry of it. She couldn't take her eyes from him. She almost didn't see the two men staggering around, or the blood running down their necks while Andre stood to one side, not looking at them, but keeping his attention on their surroundings.

Deep inside the body of the owl, she suddenly felt a pull. A tuning. A discordant note out of place. There was harmony in nature and at that moment she realized she was always aware of it, aware there was music, a symphony, everywhere she went. She needed that symphony and she sought it out, climbing and hiking around the world so her body became part of nature's orchestra.

Now, that jarring note hurt. Sickened her. She nearly shifted to her own form in order to press her hand to her stomach in an effort to fight the bile rising. She forced herself under control, but used the owl's superior range of vision to look around her. She saw nothing out of place. Not one thing, but the note became jangled. Insistent. The owl went utterly still. A strange clicking noise, one with an offbeat pattern began in the trees surrounding them as if the branches were rubbing together in the wind. She knew better. That clicking was the drumbeat to the harsh, inharmonious notes that jarred in the beauty of the symphony nature created.

She pushed further into Andre's mind, a gentle flow, conveying the information to him. He didn't look her way, but she felt him stroke a caress through her mind.

My woman. Looking out for me.

She would have bitten her lip if she had one. The words. The tone. That caress. She shivered. He still took the time to make her know she was his and he was watching over her. She didn't consider herself shy, but she couldn't find the words to answer him back. When it came to relationships, she didn't have the first clue, only that she was determined to have his back. She wanted him to know that. To feel it, just the way he made her know he would be there for her under any circumstances.

The branch the owl rested on shivered. Teagan's stomach did a somersault, and not in a good way. The large, very thick trunk shuddered. Sickness spread through the tree. She felt it—disease—as if some mutant parasite had entered through the roots and moved through the veins and arteries of the tree, spreading a dark acid through the sap. Branches trembled. Shuddered. A few leaves curled on the lower branches.

Now the note became several. The clacking noise continued, providing a jarring beat behind the malevolent notes. The musical symphony of the night—of the mountain itself—changed into something altogether different. Teagan tuned herself to the notes, separating the sounds until she knew there were two of the undead stalking the night. Now she simply had to trace the path back to them.

Do not.

She winced. That was nothing less than a command. *Seriously, Andre, I can help. Kirt and Keith may be bleeding profusely, but they're still alive and they could be dangerous to you. I can find the vampires and tell you exactly where they are.*

She ignored his warning, because it was the only thing she could do to help him. It might have sounded like she was joking when she told him he could handle the undead, but there was no way she was getting close to one of those creatures. Well, not unless it was a dire emergency.

Teagan stretched her senses, allowing them to flow out of her, listening to the music in her body. To the tone. To the . . .

Everything in her stilled. Inside the owl she went rigid. Paralyzed. She couldn't move. She couldn't reach out to Andre, let alone anyone else. Panic hit her hard. Something had taken over her mind. Shut her down. She couldn't shift. She couldn't scream. She couldn't warn Andre. The vampires had found her.

You are perfectly fine. Sit there quietly. The vampires have no idea of your existence and we are going to keep it that way.

Oh. My. God. Andre had totally shut her down. It was Andre controlling the situation. She couldn't help because *Andre* had decreed it. When he let her loose, if he was still alive, she was going to kill him. Make her own vampire-hunting kit and do him in while he slept. No. She wanted him to see it coming. She'd be the black widow and kiss him silly and then stake him.

Do not make me laugh. You are distracting me.

She couldn't reply, which made her all the angrier. But he was reading her thoughts and that meant she could *think* about what a rat bastard he was. Her best friend growing up, Cheryl, had it right. Cheryl decreed a lot of men were rat bastards, and now Teagan was hooked up with one.

The very branch she was on shook and then it expanded as if it couldn't contain the poisonous brew spreading through its main body. Instantly she saw Andre's head come up alertly, even as he faded into the trees, behind Keith, who was on the ground, on his hands and knees, knife gripped tight in his fist as blood continued to run down his throat to soak the front of his shirt. Kirt slumped a few feet from his brother, the slashes in his neck much deeper. He gasped over and over as if he couldn't get air.

The entire tree trunk quivered and then began to creak ominously. If she could have, Teagan knew she wouldn't have been able to stop the owl from flying off the groaning branch. Because she couldn't move, neither could the owl. She knew Andre saved her life. She could never have remained calm and still when insects surged up the tree, a black moving carpet, swarming over every leaf and twig, straight toward her.

Right before the insects reached the owl, the trunk of the tree began to split. Black sap erupted and rats and more insects poured out of the center as if the tree was giving birth to something malignant. The pile of rats fell to the ground, revealing the vampire. The rodents rushed toward Kirt as the vampire laughed hideously.

"What do we have here?" The creature's breath hissed out of him. "Did you two get in a knife fight? How very sad. Brothers, I see. I will end your suffering. Not right away, but I promise . . . eventually."

He waved his hand as the rats reached Kirt and began tearing at his body with sharp teeth. "My friends are hungry. That one is too far gone to have much fun with, but . . . " He smiled down at Keith, revealing his spiked, blackened teeth, stained with the blood of his victims. "You and I can have a great deal of fun before you die."

Everything about the vampire was hideous. His voice hurt Teagan's ears. His skin was drawn tight over his bones, so that he looked like a walking skeleton. Flesh seemed to slough off of him. His eyes appeared to be two burning holes in empty sockets. She didn't want to watch as he approached Keith, but as if a horror film was unfolding, she couldn't look away, even if Andre had released her from the paralysis.

Andre materialized out of thin air, his body between the vampire and his prey. The two came together hard, hunter and hunted. She saw Andre's fist hit dead over the heart, punching through the wall of flesh and bone to get to his target. He rocked the vampire with his enormous strength, with that punch that penetrated deep, so deep a good portion of Andre's arm disappeared as well.

The vampire threw back his head and howled. Spittle ran down his mouth. His eyes blazed fire. Black blood erupted around the hole in his chest and ran down his stomach and legs. Teagan also noted the thick goo that coated what she could see of Andre's forearm.

The vampire went wild, thrashing, slashing, biting at Andre, and calling to his rats for aid. He raised his voice loudly to the wind, calling his master and his brethren for help. To Teagan's horror, the rats abandoned Kirt and raced toward Andre.

Andre didn't flinch. He didn't even look at the rodents. He kept his gaze burning over the vampire's face, staring him right in the eye. There was a terrible sucking sound and Andre withdrew his hand, whirling away from the vampire to toss the blackened, wizened organ a distance from him. He raised his hand toward the sky and a whip of lightning sizzled and cracked, hitting the heart as it bounced and rolled along the ground trying to find its way back to its body.

The whip of lightning struck the heart, incinerating it. Instantly the vampire went down, falling in the middle of the rats that had stopped just as abruptly when the rotten heart had been destroyed. The white-hot whip hit the vampire's body, the flames jumping to the rodents.

Teagan felt her body tune to the second discordant note. It was much more muted, as if the vampire was aware it was being tracked—or if it was already stalking Andre. Her heart stammered. *Andre, another one.* She couldn't reach him on their shared telepathic path, but she knew he was in her mind. She concentrated on the jarring, jangled sound resonating inside of her. She could at least give Andre a direction.

Giles and Gerard burst out of the trees as the scent of foul burning flesh mingled with the odor of blood. Giles held a gun; Gerard, a knife. They took in the fact that Kirt was lying on the ground, blood all over his clothes and throat. Keith still clutched his knife but he was unmoving, his eyes wide with shock, his mouth stretched open, a look of utter terror on his face.

Giles already had the gun up and trained on Andre, who was wielding the whip of hot energy to clean the black acid from his arms. Giles fired straight at Andre. Teagan heard her own scream, deep inside the owl's body. She fought the paralysis gripping her, stark fear warring with Andre's command. Forcing herself not to panic, she followed the thread in Andre's mind back to the source of the command.

The first bullet took Andre in the arm, just below his forearm. The second skimmed his left bicep because he moved fast, whirling to one side to avoid the lead coming at him. At the same time, he snapped the lightning and the whip wrapped around Giles's neck, turning his body to ash. Gerard skidded to a halt, his mouth open as his brother dissolved into little curls of blackened soot right before his eyes.

He swore and backed up, right into the hands of the second vampire. The undead gripped him in bony hands and bent his head to sink his teeth into Gerard's neck, all the while keeping his gaze on Andre. He held the human in front of him as a shield.

"Take care not to be too greedy, Bacsa," Andre cautioned. "Your master needs his blood and he will be most unhappy with you if you bring back a dead feast. He likes his blood hot and fresh."

Bacsa was careful to close the wound on Gerard's neck. "I see you have your own messy feast." Deliberately he indicated Kirt and Keith.

Andre shrugged. The lightning whip sizzled.

Bacsa smirked, believing he was safe as long as he had the human shield. He lifted his head and scented the air. His gaze widened and a crafty expression crept over his face. "You have a woman. A lifemate. I can smell her on you."

"Where is he? Your master," Andre asked softly. "You know why he sent the two of you after his food. He knows he cannot defeat me and he sent you as his pawns, fodder to be killed while he slips away. You have been around long enough to know how it works. Where is he?"

Bacsa took two steps back, dragging Gerard with him. "You are wounded. You have a woman. Do not follow and I will allow you to live."

"I will not allow you to live, Bacsa. I am a hunter. I bring you the justice of our people."

Teagan went still. She realized right then that Andre didn't argue—not with anyone. Not a vampire. Not a human. Not with her. He explained things to her, but he didn't argue with her. He told her what he was going to do and the consequences if she didn't listen to him, and he followed through no matter what. It was a very good insight to have if she was going to spend a lifetime with him.

She knew what he was going to do and she wasn't at all shocked when the whip cracked, unfurled and wrapped around Bacsa and Gerard. The vampire screamed. Gerard disintegrated, the blackened ash falling away from the undead.

346

Bacsa's rotted flesh and clothes melted away, leaving him a hideous shell of bloody, burnt bones.

Andre dropped the whip and was on him in a flash, driving his fist deep into the chest cavity, seeking the heart of the vampire. Bacsa shrieked and fought, pummeling Andre's face with bony hands and then ripping at his throat and shoulders with sharp talons. He tried to shift, but Andre's fist was already too deep inside, his fingers grasping the shriveled heart.

Bacsa slammed his bony hand into the gunshot wound on Andre's arm. Teagan raged at her inability to move, to help. She could see Keith crawling across the ground toward Andre, knife still in his fist. His gaze was on Andre, not the vampire, his entire being focused on killing her man.

Teagan found the command keeping her still, right there in Andre's mind. His entire concentration was on taking Bacsa's heart. He blocked out all pain and everything else around him, determined to kill the undead. She fixed her focus on the command, reversing what he'd done. Instantly she felt freedom. She spread her wings and dropped down fast, straight at Keith's face, talons extended.

The talons raked his cheeks, her wings beating hard, striking him repeatedly. Keith fell back, swiping at the bird with his knife, sawing the air back and forth in an attempt to get the owl off of him. He struck the body of the bird on a frantic and very lucky slash. Bright red droplets of blood splattered in the air. At the same time, Andre withdrew the heart and stepped away from the vampire.

Bacsa turned his head toward the bird, his gaze desperate. He lunged and caught the faltering bird by one wing, dragging it to him. Even as he did, Teagan had presence of mind to rake her talons down Keith's face, ripping through flesh and bone, destroying his face as the vampire jerked her to

347

him. His teeth sank deep just as a bolt of lightning slammed into the heart Andre had tossed to the ground.

The moment the heart was incinerated, Bacsa's body shuddered. His bony fingers closed reflexively around the bird, his mouth opening wide in a silent scream. He fell hard, taking the owl with him, so that she landed beneath his toppling body. Teagan felt the dead weight of the vampire pressing her into the ground. The owl's neck was twisted funny and she couldn't move. Black blood dripped onto the feathers of her back, burning right through the flesh of the bird to the very bone.

Panic set in immediately. There was no air to shift back to her normal form. She couldn't even form a picture in her mind she was so afraid the heavy body was smothering her. Abruptly the vampire was lifted from her. She saw the bright flash as the whip of lightning incinerated first the vampire and then Keith as he crawled blindly along the ground, his knife still clutched tight.

Shift. The command came in a tight, hard voice.

The sound was shocking to her, enough so that it snapped her out of her panic. Air rushed back into her lungs. *I just saved you and you're angry at me again. I can't believe you. This was terrifying, and in case you haven't noticed, there are dead people everywhere. Dead people and dead things. I'm having a very bad night.*

Shift. Now. I am holding the image in your mind for you.

His voice was unrelenting, and Teagan shivered. She was reluctant to face him in human form. Her body hurt and she knew she was bleeding. She had vampire teeth marks in her back, up high where Bacsa had driven his teeth deep. She didn't want to see what her belly looked like and more than anything, she didn't want to face Andre's steely wrath. Not now, not with dead people's ashes floating in the air around her.

Teagan, if you do not obey me, I will force the shift.

Oh, yeah, he was angry with her. And unrelenting. She sighed and complied. She didn't like the idea of him taking control of her that way and she knew him well enough now to know there wouldn't be a second warning.

She found herself crouched beside him, no clothes, because she'd forgotten them. Shivering, she tried to think how to do the clothes, but he waved his hand and she was dressed in the same attire she'd worn all evening—minus her shirt.

Andre caught her wrists and pulled her up and to him. He had already removed the vampire's blood from his arms and chest. Her heart began thudding when she heard the sizzle of the whip. Her entire body began to shake. The sound of that white-hot energy bolt was worse than the black acid burning through the skin of her back and shoulders. Instinctively she tried to struggle, to get out of Andre's hold.

"Quiet, *sivamet*. This will not harm you. I will hold the necessary temperature in your mind for you. Trust me. You do not want that blood in or on your body."

"I don't want any of this," she replied, trying not to cry. She was not about to be a crybaby in front of him, not when he was angry with her. Still, his voice had gentled and she didn't want that either because then she really might cry, so no matter what, she was in trouble. "I just want to go home."

"I am your home, as you are mine. Hold still. Close your eyes."

She swallowed hard and did as he instructed. She heard the crack of lightning and behind her eyes was a terrible, blinding flash. Her back felt hot. Really, really hot. Not burning. The sensation was strange. She didn't like it at all. Then it was gone and with it the pain boiling through her flesh down to her bones. It still hurt, but not in the same way. The moment it was done, she donned a shirt to cover the damage to her body.

Andre put her from him. Again his touch was gentle. She opened her eyes. His chest was a mess. He had a hole in it and his face had a few deep scratches, but there were far worse lacerations on his shoulder and arms, not to mention the two bullet wounds that seemed the least of his worries. He was bleeding profusely from the chest wound and some of the deeper lacerations.

Teagan looked down at her midriff. Andre bunched her shirt in his fist and lifted it so he could see the laceration that went all the way across her front, from rib to rib. Blood dripped steadily and ran down her belly.

Csitri.

There it was. Silk and velvet. Rough. Tender. Turning her stomach upside down. Even her heart did a little strange tremor.

"You are killing me, Teagan. I cannot have my woman in battle." He sighed softly, caught her hips with both hands and bent his head to the slash.

Teagan closed her eyes as his tongue slid so very gently along the wound.

I cannot. I am not the kind of man that can have his lifemate in danger.

Her heart stuttered again. It felt ... delicious. Amazing. More, his soft confession, a mixture of tenderness, regret and steely determination, took her breath. Went all the way through her to her soul. She heard him. She knew his anger was all about the laceration on her body, the vampire's blood dripping onto her, the undead touching her. In his mind was the specter of his human family, their bodies lying broken all around him, the vampire's hands on his adopted little sister and mother. She heard him. She got him. She knew what that moment had cost him when he saw her in danger.

Teagan pushed at his wild hair with gentle fingers. A

caress. "I'm sorry, Andre. I can't stand seeing you in danger. I was so afraid for you. I didn't think you saw Keith creeping up behind you."

He continued to lap at the long, angry line on her midriff. His fingers tightened on her hips. *I see everything in battle, Teagan. I have been fighting vampires for centuries. These were easy. The humans I could have stopped even easier. You cannot put yourself in danger. Promise me.*

She closed her eyes, her fingers moving in his hair. She couldn't promise him. She couldn't. She wanted to give him that reassurance, but she knew if she saw him in danger again, she would rush to help. That was part of who she was and it wasn't going to change.

"I want to give you everything, Andre. I hate that I brought that memory so close to the surface again, but I can't be anyone but who I am."

With one last swipe of his tongue he straightened and looked down at her with his blue eyes. His palms went to the wound. Both of them. Pressing into her skin, spanning her midriff, taking in every inch. She felt the warmth. The healing. He was good. No, he was better than good, and deep inside, the healer in her watched and remembered his every move.

He turned her around, lifting her shirt so he could examine her back. She felt the slide of his hair. All that silk against her skin. The velvet rasp of his tongue followed. She closed her eyes. The action was sensual. Primitive, but still very sensuous. Her body grew hot and wet.

When he lifted his head and turned her back around to face him, his expression was gentle, not at all angry. "I do not know what I am going to do with you when I must go into battle. Chain you inside a cave perhaps. To the bed. So you will be waiting for me when I get back."

351

"Um. No. Just no to that one. I wouldn't be waiting with open arms. You try that one and you'll find out how much damage a modern woman can do when she's really annoyed with her man."

Her gaze fastened on his chest. The hole in his flesh. The lacerations. She couldn't tear her eyes from the damage. Everything in her, every cell in her body pushed her to heal those terrible wounds. How he was standing, she didn't know. More, he had taken the time to heal her.

Her hand smoothed over the worst wound. Her body swayed toward him. "I'm fully Carpathian, right?"

His gaze burned over her. She felt it, even though she didn't lift her eyes to his. Hot. He was so hot. Her fingers caressed the edges of the hole there. She instantly felt the reaction in her own body, her cells rushing to the surface to build flesh and take away pain. As if she could share her own skin.

She leaned into him and used her tongue as he had, closing her eyes so she wouldn't see what she was doing, so much as feel. He tasted like she remembered in her dreams. Hot. Masculine. Addictive. More, she knew she had that same healing agent in her saliva and she could do what he had done. She could heal his terrible wounds. She loved being a healer. It was her purpose. It had always been the one thing that made her feel she was worth something.

She'd chosen to study geology because she wanted to study rocks, gems and crystals, know their origins and feel how each could be used. This method was just as instinctive, a tuning of her body to his, just as she had done all her life, but closer. More intimate. She loved this.

Andre's hands came up to her hair. She felt the bite as he fisted bunches of silk in his large hands, but nothing could stop her. She lapped at the wound, taking every care to make certain the healing agent spread and did its work. Her fingers smoothed over the edges, as if she could push her own cells into his skin to build a bridge of tissue. She took her time, even when she heard him groan.

You have to stop. I am as hard as a rock.

I can't stop. Not until I have every single scratch on you healed.

He lifted her into his arms. She didn't stop, not even when she felt the wind in her hair, flowing across her body, and heard it whistling in her ears. She knew he was taking them back to their cave.

Teagan slipped her arms around his neck, using her tongue along his now bare chest, following the worst of the lacerations. Then they were in the dark of the cave and her body was as bare as his. His fingers were between her legs doing all sorts of distracting and delicious things to her body.

She decided she might like being Carpathian after all.

19

Teagan knew she was caught in the middle of a nightmare. The terrible dream couldn't be anything else, because Andre's human family surrounded her. They lay broken and dying all around her. The ground beneath her feet was saturated with blood. A vampire gripped her with bony claws, digging his talons into the side of her neck all the while turning his head to one side, looking away from her, laughing hideously.

She followed his gaze and saw Andre. The look on his face broke her heart. He was on the wall, his body bloody from the four stakes holding him pinned there. No matter how hard he struggled, there was no way for him to gain his freedom. He looked so young, so broken. She couldn't stand that look on his face, the mixture of sorrow, agony, guilt and hatred for the undead. She had to do something.

Teagan reached up with both hands and ripped at the vampire's face. He screamed and screamed. She heard the echo of it resounding through her mind. She realized it was Andre's scream, not the vampire, because Ciprian, Andre's uncle, had twisted his head and sunk his teeth deep into her neck.

She gasped and for one horrible moment realized she had no air. She was buried alive. Panic rushed over her and she dug at the heavy soil, trying not to suffocate, her heart pounding so hard she was afraid it would explode. She kept her eyes closed, terrified of seeing the dirt surrounding her, knowing she had only moments to figure out what to do to save herself.

She was aware of her every frantic heartbeat. Of Andre's body lying still and lifeless, wrapped around her own. Of the feeling of the soil on her skin and the tiny hairs of roots brushing over her. She thought about the open air. How it felt. How she could breathe it in. She wanted the soil gone and both of them out of the earth and onto the bed, totally clean. She built the picture in her mind, putting every ounce of fear, determination, will and strength she had into it.

Just like that, the weight was gone from her and she felt the blessed fresh air on her face and body. Gasping with relief, she dragged air into her lungs, still keeping her eyes closed tightly. She actually felt the refreshing wash on her skin, much like the sensation of a shower, yet without the water. Even her mouth felt clean.

She became aware of the mattress on her back and Andre's body curled tightly around hers. Her lashes lifted and she stared at the ceiling of the cave, triumph rushing through her. She'd done it. She'd managed to open the earth and get not only herself out, but Andre as well.

Instantly she became aware of hunger beating at her. Dark hunger clawing at her insides until every cell in her body was desperate. At the same time, the burning between her legs started. Not gentle. Not a little. Desperate. Needy. That same dark hunger but in an entirely different way.

Teagan turned her head and looked at the man lying curled around her. In his sleep, he didn't look any younger. If anything, he showed the many battles in the lines of his face. That didn't make him any less attractive. In fact, she thought he was all the more handsome. Her gaze drifted possessively over his long, thick lashes, the hair spilling around him, his straight nose and strong jaw to his wide shoulders.

Andre was a big man physically. Everything about him was big. He seemed to take up an entire room when he walked into it. His chest was thick and heavily muscled. She smoothed her hand over the places where he had been injured. She didn't see so much as a line there. Still, she sent healing warmth along the spots where each wound had been.

She came up on her knees so she could really look at him, this man who was her other half. This man who was beautiful to her. A handful for a modern woman, but still, her man. Her lifemate. Looking down at him, there wasn't a doubt in her mind that she loved him. She wasn't going to have any regrets.

The one thing she'd worried about most was that she'd lose her family again and again over the centuries. Of course she could look at it that way, but she would choose to look at it as a great privilege. She would see future generations of her sisters' children's children. She would learn to accept the circle of life just as Andre had done. Learning that acceptance would take a while, but she would have him to see her through. Andre. Her gorgeous, beautiful man.

She pressed a kiss to his chest and continued to study his body, committing it to her memory. He had a narrow waist, narrow hips, and he was gifted in the male department, which, truthfully, she found a little intimidating. Still, he was beautiful and he was hers.

She bent over him, licking along his flat belly, following

the lines of his muscles there. *Wake up, Andre. Come to me. I need you. I want you to wake up and let me taste you. Let me feel you inside of me. I have this burning need and only you can do something about it.*

She hadn't been the one dreaming, that had been Andre and she somehow had shared his terrible nightmare. If she could do that, she might eventually find a way into the dream to at least comfort him.

She wished she was sexy and knew everything there was to know about sex. She wanted to wake him and push the nightmare far from his consciousness, to replace that memory with something incredible. She made a silent vow to find a way to ease his nightmare, even if she could never fully get rid of it for him.

She ran her hands over his body, feeling him warm. She pressed her lips to the spot directly over his heart and caught his first breath, his first beat. Strong. So strong. His hands came up, fingers settling in her hair. She watched his lashes lift and she caught the amazing glacier blue before his eyes warmed and set her own heart pounding.

"I have needs, honey," she murmured, and bent to lap at the spot just over his heart. The blood ebbed and flowed there. The taste of him was already in her mouth. Perfect. Andre. All male and all hers.

His hands tightened until she felt that familiar, arousing bite on her scalp. "The best way to wake up, my woman's hands and mouth on me."

"Glad you like it, because you can expect it a lot," she said, her attention on his hard, warm body.

Teagan lapped at the spot several times and felt his cock stir against her thighs. She nipped him with her teeth and his cock jerked. Hard. She smiled. "You like this."

One hand smoothed down her back, over her buttocks to

the junction between her legs. He found a warm welcome. Hot liquid met his fingers. She squirmed over those, clever, pressing fingers, wanting them deeper. He moved his thumb in lazy circles, never really penetrating. Not enough.

"I like this very much. Apparently so do you."

"Touch me."

"I am touching you."

"Inside me." It was an order.

"Take my blood." That was a soft command.

Her heart jumped. She knew she was going to do it, all on her own, just as she'd healed him on her own. She craved the taste of him, but healing him was different than feeding. She had been totally concentrating on curative measures. This was . . .

"Sensual," he supplied.

"Erotic," she breathed, and felt her teeth slide into place, sharp incisors, not the canines like the vampire had, but still, sharp. She nipped him again and felt his body shudder. His thumb slipped inside, just the tip.

Teagan bit down, sinking her teeth deep and the exotic, masculine flavor of him burst through her senses like champagne bubbles. He sank his thumb into her and her body clasped greedily at him. It felt . . . wonderful.

"Ride my hand, *sivamet*. I want you to give it to me, your orgasm. Come for me while you feed."

That was hot, too. His taste. His hand. Those magic fingers. Her body tightening and his hard, hard cock like a steel spike pressed tightly against her inner thigh. She couldn't do anything but ride his hand. She was helpless with need. With urgency. She fed at his chest, drawing that unbelievable taste that was only his into every cell while her body rode his fingers, coiling tighter and tighter.

"So beautiful," he breathed. "So absolutely exquisite.

Harder, *csitri*. Give it to me. Let me have that beautiful gift right now."

At his command, she felt her body tense. Tighten. Unleash. A storm of quakes, hard and hot and unexpected. She pulled her mouth away from him, followed the little ruby beads down his muscles with her tongue and then lapped at the twin pinpricks until they closed.

She waited a moment, breathing deep as her body subsided. His fingers moved, which was delicious, but she was fixated on the pearly drops she felt on her thigh. "I'm not finished," she whispered, and kissed her way down his belly.

"Are you sure?" he asked softly.

She hadn't been sure. She'd been intimidated, but then she heard the husky note in his voice. That near groan. That made her more than certain. That made her determined.

"You might have to give me a little instruction, but I'm very sure. I want to know every single inch of you, Andre." Her tongue lapped at his belly and then she kissed her way through rough hair.

His gasp was very satisfactory. He didn't say anything. He didn't tell her what to do, so she slipped into his mind and found ... anticipation. Pleasure. It didn't seem to matter to him how good she was at this, only that she wanted to give him pleasure, and that alone, the want in her, was all he needed to be hard and ready for her.

"I do wish I knew more," she murmured as she wrapped her hand around the base of his heavy erection. And it was heavy. She lifted the steely spike from his stomach. Velvet soft yet definitely steel.

"I am grateful that I am the one to be your teacher, Teagan," he admitted. "You belong only to me and that is a gift. A rare and precious gift. As far as I am concerned, you cannot do anything wrong as long as you are enjoying what you do for me. Do what you wish and if you want more guidance, look into my mind. You will feel what I am feeling."

She liked that. She liked that he gave her the time and opportunity to explore on her own. She bent her head again and lapped at the crown of his cock, swirling her tongue over the sensitive head, licking up those pearly drops. He tasted the same as when she fed at his chest, only more exotic. More erotic. There was no resisting him.

"I like that you're all for me," she murmured, breathing warm air over him.

She shaped him with her fist. "You really are gorgeous, Andre. Gorgeous, hot and sweet . . . " Her eyes met his for one moment, filled with amusement. "Most of the time."

"I am very thankful you feel that way."

She dipped her head and licked him like an ice-cream cone and then swirled her tongue under the crown. That got another shudder, his hips jerking and a swift indrawn breath. She liked that because he liked it. She did that a few more times and then used her tongue on the thick shaft, curling around and over it, lapping at the thick, long flesh.

His fingers curled around hers, tightening so that her hand curled into a fist. He used an up and down motion, keeping her fist wrapped around him. The hand in her hair urged her head down over him. She took the hint instantly, opening her mouth and drawing him in even as she touched his mind to feel what he was feeling.

She shivered and the blood rushed through her, hot and wild. Her sex spasmed. The sensations she was creating in Andre were *glorious*. Perfect. She loved it. Her confidence grew. As long as she could feel what he was feeling, she knew she was giving him pleasure. So much pleasure, and she was excited that she could. She wanted this for him. Her mouth tightened and she suckled strongly, her tongue dancing while her fist moved under the instruction of his hand. She liked that, too. She liked that he was so willing to teach her, that he had patience and even enjoyed the fact that she'd been with no one else.

"Not enjoy, *sivamet. Love.* I didn't have parents, not even when I was born. Neither of them. I had the Borois for a brief time and they were taken. I counted them mine, but really they were not mine, in spite of the fact that I loved them. I had the family that raised me, loosely had them. I ran wild, and the triplets followed me so I was not always welcome. You are mine alone. Really mine. You belong to me."

She was glad she was busy loving on him, using her energy in a very good way that sent so much pleasure streaking through his body he could barely get the words out, barely think straight.

I love belonging to you, but, Andre, you had them. The Borois, they were yours.

She used her tongue again under the crown and he groaned and tugged at her hair. "You need to come up here now, Teagan. I want you on your hands and knees."

That sounded intriguing. She gave his cock one last lick and did what he said, going to her hands and knees there on the mattress. Instantly he knelt up behind her, one hand going to the nape of her neck to push her head down. A streak of fire rushed through her body. She didn't know why the position and the way his hand on her nape and the arm sliding around her waist to drag her back to him felt so erotic to her, but it did.

"Stay like that," he instructed softly, and his hand moved down over her back to her buttocks and then he grasped both hips.

She closed her eyes as she felt that burning crest lodge at her entrance. Then he slammed inside. Hard. Jolting her body with every stroke. She thought she knew fire until that moment. He began a fierce, brutal rhythm, surging into her over and over. Heaven. She didn't know anyone could feel that good.

At the bite of his fingers on her hips, she moved back into him, just as hard. "More," she breathed. "I love this, Andre. I want more." Her tone was breathy. Pleading even. Eager. She didn't care. She knew he shared her mind, he could feel what he was doing to her, and what he was doing was more than good.

"My woman," he said softly between his teeth.

She loved the way he said it. Possessively, just like the hands on her hips. He gripped her harder and lifted her off the mattress so only her head and forearms were down with her legs curled tight under her. His strokes increased in strength. She had no choice but to reach out and hold on to the headboard to keep from being thrown off the bed. Each thrust sent storms of fire bursting through her body to radiate outward to every cell.

She was coiled tight. Too tight. She didn't want to let go, not without him.

"Give it to me," he instructed, his voice harsh.

"With you." Her breath hissed out of her lungs. She was desperate to hang on. She was so close, her body wanting to spin out of control.

He was relentless, driving her higher. "Give it to me," he bit out between his teeth. *"Now."*

There was no stopping her body from obeying. She came apart, a brutal, hard orgasm that tore through her entire body so that she screamed her release. He powered right through it. Never stopping. A machine moving in her, prolonging the orgasm, stretching her out on a rack of pure pleasure, her muscles grasping at that spiked steel invader.

Abruptly he withdrew and turned her, rolling her under him, yanking her legs apart and pushing them over his shoulders. His tongue took one long swipe that sent hard aftershocks rippling through her. Then he was over top of her, his body blanketing hers, and he thrust into her brutally again, nearly triggering another orgasm.

Andre slowed the pace, although each thrust was hard and deep, sending waves of pleasure through her. He leaned over her, his dark hair brushing her skin sensuously. It felt so amazing, especially when the strands trailed over her sensitive breasts. His mouth found hers and he kissed her. His mouth on hers added to the fire in her sex and streaking through her body.

His mouth trailed kisses down her chin, her throat and over the swell of her breast. Her heart nearly stopped. His hips kept moving, jolting her body when he surged deep, but she could barely breathe when she felt his tongue on her breast. For one moment he lapped at her nipple and tugged with his teeth and she nearly lost all control, but his mouth moved back to the swell of her breast, tongue swirling and teeth nipping. This time she felt the sharp edge of his incisors.

Her feminine sheath clamped down hard around him. His teeth sank deep and she cried out, her head tossing, both hands anchoring in his hair as he drank from her. He was in her mind, filling her with him. Every part of her mind, every lonely place she thought no one would ever see or know. He was deep in her body, stretching, burning, bringing that fire to her and her blood mingled with his. Soaked into his cells. They shared the same skin. It was . . . beautiful. Perfect. Erotic.

There was no stopping her body from milking his. She didn't try. She lifted her hips to meet his, wanting him deep—so deep anyone would have to pry them apart. She pushed against his mouth, urging him on, while her fingers stroked caresses in his hair. He was hers. All hers. Every inch of him. Every single gorgeous Carpathian inch of him.

Baby, I can't hold back, she whispered into his mind. *It's too lovely. Too perfect.*

Give yourself to me and take me with you. He filled her mind with his consent, with his command, his voice a silken velvet rasp that always undid her.

Teagan let the fire consume her. Her body clamped down hard around his, grasping, making demands of its own, refusing to burn alone. She felt his cock swell, a seemingly impossible feat, but it did, she knew it did. Then there were the hot splashes that added to the beauty of the moment.

He swept his tongue over the swell of her breast and threw back his head, groaning her name before dropping his head against her neck. Her body didn't want to stop. She had no idea an orgasm could last as long as this one did. All the while he stayed hard, feeling her body strangling his, feeling the pleasure sweeping through both of them.

"I love you, Andre," she whispered softly. "I want to give you everything you want, but I don't know how. I don't know how to be anyone but who I am."

He knew what she was talking about instantly. She felt him moving through her mind. Felt his soft caresses. That was beautiful, too. She couldn't stand by and watch her man fighting a vampire and not help if he was in trouble. She just couldn't. She wanted to give him what he needed, and she knew that reassurance was a need of his. He wasn't being arrogant or bossy, he needed to know she was safe from vampires.

He rolled, taking her with him, so that she was sprawled over top of them. They were still locked together. She felt full. Stretched. Part of him. She let him push her head down to his chest, his fingers massaging the nape of her neck.

"I have given this some thought and I think I have worked out a solution to our problem. One that allows you to be you and still gives me peace of mind."

"Really?" She *loved* that he'd thought about their problem. Loved that he wasn't trying to dictate to her, but genuinely wanted to find something that would work for both of them, not just him. Since her head was on his chest, she pressed little kisses over the heavy muscles. "Thank you, Andre."

His hand slid back into her hair. "*Csitri*, do not thank me until you've heard what I have to say. You may not agree."

"I'm thanking you because you cared enough to give the problem some thought instead of dictating to me." She lifted her head to look at him, her gaze drifting over his face. She loved his face. Every expression. Every line. The strong line of his jaw and the darker shadow that she found so attractive.

"I want a partner, not a slave, Teagan. I was never hoping for a 'yes' woman."

She laughed softly. "That's a good thing, honey, because there isn't anything remotely 'yes' about me."

She leaned down and brushed kisses over his lips. Back and forth. Light. Gently. Tasting him. Her stomach fluttered. "Tell me about your solution."

"I thought a lot about what you said, how you would need to come to my aid if you thought I was in trouble."

She nodded and nibbled on his chin just because it looked so delicious. "I want to contribute in some meaningful way. What you do is important and you've been doing it for so long, I doubt you'll just stop."

"I would not know how to stop. I have too much experience, Teagan. I promised you I would move to the States and that we would live near your grandmother and we will. Tomas, Matais and Lojos are already there. I told them I would follow when I could and now I have even more reason to join them in the States."

"There are many Carpathians like you in the United States?"

"We have many reasons to change locations, but vampires have spread out and that means hunters have to follow. They try to find places where there are no hunters and they are free to kill. For your grandmother to have joined the human society of vampire hunters there had to be some major event that precipitated her believing in vampires."

Teagan froze. Her gaze searched his. "Do you mean she might have come across an actual vampire?"

"Why else would she suddenly decide vampires are real? Could someone convince her?"

She shook her head. "My grandmother is very intelligent. She's very grounded in reality, that's why none of this made sense to us. We tried to talk to her about it, but she just wouldn't tell us a thing."

"She would want to protect you."

"Even knowing we all thought she was going round the bend? Bonkers? Completely crazy?"

"You tell me, Teagan. Would she protect you from the knowledge that the world had real monsters living side by side with humans?"

She took a breath. It would be something Grandma Trixie would do, especially for her because she was afraid of so many things.

"My grandmother is the best, Andre." Her voice softened. "She's always loved us and taken such care of my sisters and me."

He rubbed her bottom. It felt good. More than good. She could feel the burn starting all over again. Not as desperate or as hungry, but building slow and easy. Still, she felt something in his mind.

366

"Tell me," she whispered. "Even if you think I can't take it."

"If she tried to harm you, *sivamet*, I would protect you. I would not hesitate to protect you. My protection is, as a rule, very permanent."

She knew what he was saying. "I appreciate you might think you would have to protect me from her, after all the things I've said, but she would never, under any circumstances hurt me. She would protect me even if she thought I was the undead. Family is everything to her. Absolutely everything. If she accepts you as family, you'll see what that truly means. She's fierce, outspoken, funny and I love her more than anything . . . except maybe you and I don't know how that's possible."

He nodded, but she noticed he didn't reply. He wouldn't. He wasn't going to argue with her, or belabor his point. He'd warned her straight up what would happen if her grand-mother tried to harm her, but she knew, without a shadow of doubt, that Grandma Trixie would die before she harmed her so she wasn't worried.

"Tell me your solution," she said again. "We keep getting off the subject and I think it's important."

"You are unique in a lot of ways, at least I think your gifts are. I have not heard of other lifemates, when they were human, being able to take down safeguards in the way that you could. You can also tune your body to a vampire's. That gives us an advantage when hunting. You can find them and bring down their safeguards."

She drew in her breath. Andre was actually talking about using her as a partner. She loved that he thought she would be such a help.

"I would not want you to participate at all in the battle, no matter how bad things look," he warned. "That would be forbidden. You would have to give me your word you will follow instructions."

367

She bit her lip hard. She wanted desperately to be his partner, but she knew, if he were in trouble, she would go back on her word.

"I can open my mind to you the entire battle. I cannot be distracted in any way, but you can see clearly what I am aware of and what I plan to do. That way, you will know if I am really going to be surprised or not. If you cannot see awareness in my mind, you will be able to warn me."

She liked that. She liked that *a lot*. "That sounds reasonable." She wouldn't be paralyzed in the body of an owl feeling helpless.

"And then, there is the fact that you are a superior healer."

"I am?" She liked that a lot, too. More than anything, she wanted to be good healer. She wanted to be able to help others.

"For most wounds such as those I encountered—other than the gunshot, which was no more than a couple of flesh wounds—I would have had to stay in the ground more than one rising. I could actually feel the tissue regenerating when you were healing me. You definitely are good. That will be a huge bonus to me as well, knowing you are close by and can see to any wound."

She didn't like the fact that he so readily accepted that he would be wounded in his battles with the undead, but he'd been hunting and destroying them for centuries, so he knew what he was doing.

"I like your idea very much, Andre," she whispered. She brushed her lips back and forth against his and began a slow undulation of her hips, moving lazily.

His hands slipped to her waist and he urged her into a sitting position. The moment she sat up, she could feel him pressing deep inside her. So deep. So thick. Filling and stretching her. She loved that *more* than a lot. His hands moved up her body, lingering a moment where the vampire had slashed her midriff and then higher still until he was cupping her breasts.

"Do you see why your breasts are so perfect for me?" he whispered. "So beautiful." His palms covered her breasts completely. She fit perfectly into his hand. He had a large hand and the warmth engulfed her. He massaged and kneaded the small curves gently. "So soft. So sensitive."

Her nipples went hard, pushing into the center of his palms. Two stiff peaks begging for attention. She threw back her head, her hair cascading around her shoulders and down her back to slide over his belly and hips. She began to move faster, riding him the way she had his fingers.

"See, *sivamet*. Look how beautiful you are." He watched his palms drift down over her slight curves to once again cup them in his hands.

Teagan looked down at herself. With each movement of her body, her small breasts swayed against his hands. She loved the way they looked together—him so big, her so small. She'd never loved her body before that moment. She was flushed and aching.

"Keep watching, *csitri*." His voice was a rough, velvet rasp. Sexy. His eyes were hooded and dark with growing hunger. Pure sensuality.

There was something very decadent and forbidden about watching his fingers grasp her nipples, watching them roll and tug, while streaks of fire shot from her breasts straight to her sex. Her muscles clamped down tight around him and her body bathed his shaft in liquid heat. She moaned and licked at her lips, forcing herself to keep her gaze on the erotic sight of his fingers at her nipples. Her hips, of their own volition, began a more urgent pace.

Andre half curled his body so he could pull one breast

into his mouth, suckling hard. She cried out, the fire raging hotter. Her blood went thick and molten. Her eyes closed because she could barely stand the pleasure. The fire had begun slow and lazy, but now the temperature was hotter than ever, the burn storming through her like a fireball out of control.

"Watch," he commanded.

His hand slid down her belly. She watched the path it took. Those fingers, long and strong, thick and clever, sliding in a caress over her skin. She swallowed hard as she watched Andre's body coming together with hers, as she lifted up and then rode down over his steely spike. The beauty of it nearly brought her to tears. The pleasure of it made her entire body glow with heat, with excitement.

She gasped as his finger homed in immediately to her most sensitive spot. It was shockingly sexy. His other hand moved up her body until his finger was sliding back and forth over her lips.

"Open for me."

She did immediately, sucking his finger deep into her mouth while she rode him harder and harder, faster and faster, gasping for breath while his other finger stroked her bud right straight into paradise. Her orgasm snuck up on her much faster than she anticipated, roaring through her, leaving her breathless and a little shocked at the intensity when she'd been moving into it so slowly.

She didn't have time to catch her breath because he rolled her under him and took over, his hips not in the least slow and leisurely, building the tension in her all over again. Suddenly everything was even more amazing. She looked up at his face. His beautiful face. His blue eyes blazed down at her, so intense, so filled with ... love.

She really couldn't catch her breath. There it was, all of it, everything she could ever want, right there in the intensity of his blue eyes. Love. For her. Stark. Raw. Fierce.

Teagan reached up and stroked a caress through his hair. "You're so gorgeous, Andre, and I love you so much." Sometimes, like that very moment, the way she felt for him crept over her, then grew and grew until she couldn't contain it. She could barely stand looking into his eyes, his emotions were so close to the surface, so strong they nearly overwhelmed her. How could anyone feel like that about her?

"Keep looking at me, *sivamet*," he whispered in his silken tone. "I need to look at you when you give yourself to me."

She realized he had done that before, rolling her at the last moment to stare down into her eyes. She trailed her fingers down his face and then, as the tension coiled tighter, dropped her hand and let pure feeling take her. Her head tossed on the pillow, but she didn't look away from him. Her body writhed under his, hips bucking, her fingers digging into his back while her legs wrapped him as tight as she could.

Every inch of her that she could possibly press to him, she did, all the while staring into his eyes. The breath left her lungs, leaving them raw and burning. Still the tension grew, coiling tight deep inside. She needed it now, that wonderful, soaring release, but he didn't give it to her.

"Andre," she whispered. "Andre, I can't take any more."

Her body clamped down on his, the friction a terrible, perfect thing, but still, she couldn't quite reach her goal, and those blue eyes didn't help. Sensual. Hooded. Watching her intently. Pushing her higher than she'd ever been.

"You can," he said softly, and proceeded to show her he was right.

She wrapped him up tighter. Her legs hooked around his hips and she tipped her body at another angle, to draw him deeper, to get what she wanted. His hands adjusted her more, tilting her hips and then holding her there so the long, thick length of him ground down over that delicious bundle of nerves, that perfect sweet spot, over and over.

She cried out as she felt her body slip out of control. She felt that moment when her muscles gripped him in a velvet vise and strangled, determined to get what it needed from him. She couldn't look away from the blue of his eyes.

Possession. Satisfaction. Love. Lust. And then his own release overtook him, and her eyes widened at the sheer beauty of it. She'd given that to him. Just what he gave her, she gave to him.

Teagan closed her eyes to savor the expression in his eyes, to burn it into her memory. "I don't know how I got so lucky," she murmured against his shoulder as he collapsed over her, burying his face in her neck. "My miracle."

He let her take his crushing weight just for a few moments, his face against her neck, her arms around him, his cock deep inside of her. It didn't matter that she could barely breathe, he gave her that moment and it was important to her.

"Teagan."

A shiver went down her spine and she blinked back tears.

"You are my miracle, Teagan. I am more than pleased that I am yours."

She held him tighter, reluctant to allow him to take his weight from her, even though it was becoming impossible to catch her breath.

He smiled against her neck, kissed her there, his mouth and teeth moving sensuously, and then he rolled them again so that she sprawled on top of him.

"Did you just bite my neck?" she accused at the feel of a little sting there.

"Yes," he admitted, with a laugh in his voice. "I intend to

leave my mark on you everywhere. I like taking little bites out of you."

Playing. He was playing with her. Teasing. She loved that she had been the one to give him that. She buried her face in his neck and held him all the tighter. She couldn't look at him when she said it, but it had to be said. "Thank you, Andre. For bringing me into your world. I might be afraid, but I'm so happy I'm with you and I want this. I want us to be together in every way and I couldn't be unless I was Carpathian."

His hand stroked caresses in her hair. "You were frightened when you woke and found yourself deep in the ground. You fight my commands, Teagan, and even in your subconscious you unravel them. I did not protect you as I should have from your awakening. I should have been up before you."

"You were wounded and the soil was healing you." She made the statement softly, suddenly remembering that moment when she was caught in his dream. Other things had registered, but she hadn't noticed them because the nightmare was too vivid and so had been the terror at being buried alive.

"Yes," he said softly, allowing her to figure it out for herself.

He gave her that. Acknowledged that she had a brain. All the fear she had living in her skin didn't matter because she refused to let it rule her life. She was a geologist for heaven's sake. She loved rocks. She loved soil.

She had automatically registered the various layers of soil so rich with minerals. If she hadn't been so shocked at being under the ground, buried under those layers, she would have been caught up in her need to identify and count them. She would have known how they were healing Andre and rejuvenating both of them.

"I won't be so afraid next time, Andre. You do not have to shield me from what I am. I think I can handle it."

"I never doubted your ability to handle it," he murmured softly.

She could tell he was pleased with her by the tone of his voice, all velvet and rasp. His hand continued to move over her body, tracing the line of her spine down to the curve of her buttocks.

"We have a vampire to catch, *csitri*. This one is unlike the others. He will be difficult to bring down. He is cunning and ruthless and has plenty of tricks. There are few surprises to a hunter who has been bringing the undead to justice for so many years, but sometimes it can happen."

"Do you recognize most of them?" she asked tentatively. It stood to reason that he would run across childhood friends.

"The older ones. I have been gone many years. This one, I knew. His name is Costin Popescu. He is alone now, his pawns defeated. He will try to sneak away, not face me, but I cannot allow that. He is extremely dangerous, and he cannot, under any circumstances, find you. He will go after you in order to destroy me."

Her eyebrows shot up and shock slid through her. *He will go after you in order to destroy me.* Andre wasn't just meaning he would be grief-stricken if something happened to her. He had alluded to more several times, but she wasn't getting it.

"How would that destroy you, Andre?" she asked quietly, holding her breath, knowing his revelation would be huge. And it would be the truth.

"You are my lifemate. I cannot exist without you, now that I have found you. If he manages to destroy you, he is destroying all light in my soul, leaving nothing but the darkness. I lived with that for centuries, but it came on gradually, over time. To have that happen, the connection severed, it would throw me into madness, into the thrall. I would have to follow you immediately, or become the very thing I have hunted throughout these long centuries. I would be the undead."

Teagan bit her lip. "You wouldn't."

"I would. That is the curse and the blessing of our species. We cannot continue without our lifemate. We are too dark inside."

She chewed on her lip for a moment. "So basically, you're saying I'm saving you *again*."

His smile was slow in coming but she was rewarded. His smile was beautiful and this one lit his eyes. "Yes, Teagan, you have saved me."

She kissed him. He took over her kiss, just like he did most intimate contact between them, but only after she was able to kiss him for a long time.

"Do you see why it is important that you stay away from vampires?" he asked gently.

"It was important to you before you explained this to me, so yes," Teagan said. "Tell me the plan and I'll follow it to the letter."

His eyes searched hers for a long time and then he nodded, the glacier blue melting into a deep, sea blue, warming her with his love.

20

Two owls flew through the evening sky. The male flew slightly above the smaller female, his wing just over her, just enough to protect her from any attack coming from above them. They executed lazy circles in the air, in perfect synchronization, as if they were two dancers performing a stunning ballet against a backdrop of clouds.

Teagan scanned the ground below them carefully. Not because she thought she would spot the master vampire they hunted, but because the scenery was breathtaking. Breaks in the forest presented boulders covered in green moss, lining a series of small, tumbling waterfalls, cascading through the boulders and falling into a clear, shallow pool. Small rocks made up the pool floor. The pool spilled into a larger stream that seemed to meander through the tall trees. Ferns sprang up along the banks, crowding other plant life, vying for coveted space.

Her body picked up the rhythm of the stream and

waterfalls. She heard the music and her own body sang that song with nature. Trees added the drumbeat of branches in the wind as well as the softer, flowing music of the sap running in the veins through the variety of trees.

She felt free. Complete. Part of nature. Part of the wild, wonderful mountains and the dense forest below. Above her rose the higher, enshrouded peaks where she knew the monastery was located. Inside that sacred place were the ancients who had not yet left the world, but had no hope of finding lifemates. They could no longer afford to hunt and destroy the undead. Each kill brought them closer to becoming vampire. They weren't safe around humans or any other temptation, and yet they could not walk into the sun and destroy themselves because it felt so wrong to them.

She felt them as well, although they were in the distance, felt the emotions they couldn't feel. Despair. Loss of all hope. Sorrow. Pain not physical, but mental. The air groaned with those heavier emotions, but the ancient Carpathians couldn't feel any of it themselves. She knew she had to find a way to ease those burdens, and her heart hurt for them. She had felt them before, but she hadn't recognized when she'd first found the cave that she'd been feeling the emotions of the lost ancients in the monastery.

Teagan.

Andre's voice wrapped her up in velvet. The raspy tone licked over her skin and the silk pushed deep inside. She would always love the way he said her name.

You cannot take on the burdens of the ancients. It is too much.

Actually, I think I can help. In the cave. She'd been sitting right on it. She had followed her tuning fork through the various chambers of the cave, looking for a stone to cure her grandmother of insanity, but her grandmother clearly wasn't insane and didn't need a stone. All along she'd felt that heavy

377

burden, the weight of the ancient Carpathians, yet she hadn't acknowledged it. Hadn't known what it was.

When she'd sunk to the floor of the cave to meditate and open her mind, she had inadvertently connected with the stone she needed. It wasn't her grandmother's stone, but it was the one that would help ease the suffering of the ancients in the monastery. Elated, she nearly fell from the sky.

Do you really think you can ease the burden of an ancient? There was hope in Andre's voice. *My adopted brothers, Tomas, Matias and Lojos are skating very close to the edge of the insanity. If you could ease them, give them more time . . . Even if it is a few more years . . .*

She had no idea what her stone would actually do, but she knew it would help—and she had to help those ancients in the monastery. That need had now become a compulsion. The stone was somewhere beneath the spot where she had chosen to meditate. She would have to dig carefully to find it, making certain not to destroy it in the hunt for it. Now, when she heard the cautious hope in Andre's voice, she wanted to be able to help the ancients even more.

I think I can . . . She trailed off.

Her stomach lurched, a discordant note jarring the beautiful symphony of the mountains and forest. She took a careful look around, using the owl's superior vision.

Andre. He is somewhere close by. Beneath us.

The moment she sent Andre the information, he acknowledged her. *I do not feel him at all, Teagan. He is a master and is able to hide himself well. Your gift is incredible and will be an enormous aid to us.*

She couldn't help but feel a little glow at his words. This was far better than sitting on a tree branch, paralyzed and feeling useless. Andre made her feel important to him—always—in every capacity.

What does it feel like?

He was already slipping deeper into her mind, but she liked that he asked. It was a form of asking permission, even though she knew he needed to feel the discordant note for himself.

We're moving away from him, she reported, as the jarring note became fainter.

Circle back around. I need to hear it. You tune yourself to that note and when it is strongest, we can follow the trail, Andre said.

The two owls rose higher, turning in a slow circle, moving up into the higher elevations. She could see the mountain rising up above the dense forest of trees. The canopy swayed, drawing her attention back to the leaves, silver against the backdrop of the evening sky. The night was staining the sky a darker blue. A few brave stars sparkled above their heads, and the moon managed to make itself seen against the darker sky.

Shrouding the mountain peaks was a heavy mist that seemed impenetrable. Once again she felt the heavy burden of the monks pressing into her. They had their own music, but it was infinitely sad. Filled with despair and sorrow. Worse, although they radiated it, sending those notes of intense pain into the universe, they clearly weren't aware of it.

Can you tune them out? Andre asked gently. *You are taking on their sorrow, sivamet. They would not want that for you, for any woman. They honor women and have their entire lives. They are ancients without the other half of their souls and it is far too dangerous for them to continue looking. They are lost and they know it.*

I can help them, Andre. Perhaps give them a few more months or years.

Perhaps, Teagan. You are a miracle so I have no doubt if anyone can do such a thing, it would be you, but not like this. Not taking on their burden.

She didn't know how to tune them out. All that sadness slipping into nature's joyous symphony. The notes weren't at all unharmonious. In fact, they added to the richness of the music she heard. And then ... there it was. Her stomach lurched and she felt a jarring, as if something vibrated wrong through her insides.

Did you feel that, Andre? He's there. I need to hear more to find his trail and follow it. That one note out of place.

Teagan Joanes was a true miracle. Andre felt the note through her. He would never have discovered a master vampire's lair. Never. They didn't leave blank spots, giving away to the hunter that their presence was close. Not if they were a true master. They were far better at vanishing than that or they never would have survived so many centuries to become a master.

The discordant note grew stronger as the two owls began to narrow in on the jangle of sound, so out of place among the beauty of the song Teagan could hear and had shared with him.

Teagan had been so beautiful, so unexpected, so sexy, waking him up, replacing nightmares with her sweet, sensual body. Giving herself to him. He didn't know what other males had, what went on between lifemates, but he was thankful she belonged to him and that she understood he belonged to her. She had taken him into her keeping in the same way he had her.

He stayed very alert in her mind. She wasn't flying headlong into danger. She felt her way, sharing with him without holding back. She was afraid. Her fear beat at him, but that didn't stop her. It didn't slow her down or make her hesitant. His woman had a backbone of pure steel.

To the right. We need to drop down closer to that area in the mist there, Andre, but I think if we do, he'll know we're here.

Popescu's pawns had used a web inside the fog to find victims. Andre had seen that particular trick used in the past, but it wasn't a well-known one. Not many vampires had managed to acquire the necessary knowledge to do such a thing. It was complicated, and most didn't have the cunning or patience. But Costin Popescu did, and that said a lot about his battle knowledge.

Let me move ahead of you, Andre said. *Stay circling right here until I can get a feel for what he has wrought there in the fog. If I can find a way for us to move through it undetected, we will get closer and try to pinpoint his exact location.*

Why didn't he leave?

He was either wounded much more severely than I first thought, which I doubt and will not count on, or he is not moving so he does not leave a trail for me to follow. A master will forgo his meals to throw a hunter off the trail. This one is very dangerous, Teagan. He poured a warning into his tone, hoping she understood the knowledge he imparted to her.

I have no wish to encounter him up close and personal, Andre, she assured.

He found himself wanting to smile at the snippy little tone she used. He liked her snippy. He liked the way, when she was nervous, she blurted out anything that was in her mind. He found the trait both funny and endearing.

Neither do I, he admitted. *Keep your mind in mine, just in case I find us a way in.*

He was using his bossy tone, which he knew she disliked as a rule, but she didn't seem to mind so much when they were hunting vampires.

She made a little sound in the back of her throat. *I don't know what I'm doing hunting vampires. That's your territory so be as bossy as you want. Anything else, you might want to consider I've been known to bash people over the heads with frying pans.*

You hit a serial killer over the head, he reminded. *That was entirely justified. Hitting me would just be mean.*

Um. No. What exactly is the definition of a serial killer? Doesn't that label go with multiple bodies stacking up?

He choked on his own laughter. She had a point, but she didn't need to make him laugh when he was entering the web of a master vampire. He had to go delicately, and without a body of any kind that could trip the shimmering wires trailing back to the undead.

Andre shifted, leaving the form of the owl to become nothing but molecules moving through the air. He entered the mist cautiously, feeling for each of the fine filaments that would lead back to the master.

Now you have called me an old dog and *a serial killer.*

I'm just saying.

The smile was gone from her voice, even though she went along with his teasing. He didn't like that she was afraid for him, and he knew she was. She was in his mind, just as he was in hers, and she knew what he was doing was very dangerous. The vampire's traps surrounded him.

Sivamet. He tried to wrap the endearment in his love. *I have done this for centuries. Believe in me.*

I do.

She said it fast. Sincerely. Meaning it. But she was terrified *for* him, just as he had been terrified for her when she'd been so close to the vampire. He had never considered that his lifemate would feel the same intensity of fear for her man as he did his woman when she was in the path of danger, and he didn't like it. He more than didn't like it. His woman shouldn't have to ever feel that kind of fear.

You do, she shot back, revealing she was becoming even more adept at reading his thoughts than she had been at rising. She learned at an outrageous pace. He was going to have to work hard to stay in front of her.

It is not the same thing. Deliberately he made his reply decisive.

She would never convince him, although he knew she would try, that she had every right to worry over his safety as he did hers. For him there would always be a difference. She was his woman. Precious. A treasure to cherish. No matter that she had a spine of steel, she was fragile in his world. She might not think so, but she was. She always would be. It was his duty and his privilege to protect her.

You make me crazy when you think like that, Andre. Of course I am going to worry about you facing monsters. I love you. You're my . . . family.

That was everything. Family, to Teagan, was her everything. Sacred. For her to say that, she was revealing her vulnerability to him. She was giving him another gift and he knew it was huge. He wasn't going to spoil it by arguing with her. He was who he was and he couldn't change his nature. He could find ways to compromise because above all, he wanted her to be happy, but he didn't want her worried or in danger.

I love you, sivamet. You are my heart and soul. She had just given him hers, he needed her to know she wasn't alone in that.

Andre spotted the first filament and elation swept through him. On his own, he couldn't hear the discordant notes jarring nature's symphony, but through Teagan, he knew the vampire was below him and to his right, smack in the middle of what appeared to be solid rock.

I am going to drift as close as I can to that boulder just to my right. Do you see it, Teagan? I think he may be somewhere in that vicinity. I cannot pinpoint his location.

The female owl made another slow circle, dropping lower.

Do not touch the mist, he cautioned.

I think I can make a pass just beneath the fog, come down as if I was hunting and missed my prey. I might be able to feel his exact location.

He was grateful she waited for his permission. If she allowed her owl to actually scan the ground looking for mice or any other food source, and then allowed the bird to take over, giving it very little guidance, she would be safe enough. The vampire wouldn't expect a female owl to be any threat to it.

Still, Andre was uneasy. If Popescu hadn't fed in days, he might be just starved enough that he would go after an animal—a bird flying that little bit too close.

Csitri, if he catches you, he would tear you apart with his teeth before I could get to you.

I don't have to get that close. I just need to get below the mist, drop as if I'm hunting and feel the strength of those notes. I can pinpoint his exact location.

Popescu wasn't under the ground, not if those filaments were anything to go by. The master vampire had set his lure and he was waiting—hoping—a victim would come by so he wouldn't have to move. Moving meant leaving a trail. He was staying very still and waiting for the hunter to leave the area, just as he'd done for centuries.

I can do it, Teagan said.

Her fear beat at him, and Andre was grateful he had had the presence of mind to mask her presence just in case they had come across the master vampire. At the same time she felt fear, her determination poured off of her. She wanted this. It made her feel a part of him. Maybe she even needed it.

She wasn't asking to go into battle, just to be of aid, to feel as if she gave him some advantage. It was the most difficult thing he'd ever done, and it went against his nature, but he was in her head and he could see, this was everything to her. By giving his consent—and it said a lot about her that she waited for it even when she wanted to give him this—he knew he would be giving her self-respect. More, he knew she could live with the division of their partnership, if he could concede.

I want you to remember, to always hold in your heart, in your head, what will happen should anything happen to you. I need you, Teagan, far more than you will ever need me. I love you. I have never really had anyone in my life until you. I cannot go back to emptiness. Do you understand what I am saying to you?

He still was uncertain he could give her his consent. He drifted even closer to the boulder where the filaments seemed to lead. He wanted to be close just in case the vampire made a grab for the bird.

I understand that and I also understand what you're giving to me. Her voice was soft. A caress. Filled with love.

Do it then. Feed me the information and then get far away. Into the trees where the owl can hide. I will need you when I am done. No matter how bad the wounds are, take me to ground and I will heal. Do you understand? Get me into the ground.

Absolutely. I won't let you down, Andre. Just stay connected to me, even when you're afraid I'll feel pain. Don't shut me out, because if you do, I'll panic. As long as I know you're alive, and you have a plan, I can stay where you tell me.

Teagan didn't hesitate, but then he knew she wouldn't. She dropped out of the sky, sliding beneath the bank of fog, talons extended toward a mouse rustling in the vegetation.

An actual mouse. Luring the owl in. The mouse wasn't close to the boulder Andre suspected held the vampire. The mouse was near a thin sapling shooting out between two smaller rocks.

Get out of there. Andre called the warning just as the owl veered away from the ground, away from the straggly tree nearly bent double from the winds that often raged over the mountain.

385

He heard the crash of notes, the cacophony of sound that jarred every cell in Teagan's body. She heard it as she had come in, following his instructions, allowing the owl to be close to the surface. At the last possible moment, when she heard the discordant notes, she had reacted, taking control back.

Andre hadn't expected that, not so soon, but he was grateful as the vampire lunged out from between the rocks, throwing the decoy of a sapling off of him as he reached for the bird.

Andre used his speed, shifting as he rushed through the distance separating them, inserting his body between Popescu and Teagan, slamming into the vampire with the force of a freight train, driving him backward, his fist slamming home, deep into the chest of the undead. The fierce momentum sent both of them tumbling together over the cliff. Andre locked onto the vampire with his free arm, even as he dug through tissue, muscle and bone to try to find the withered, blackened organ that ensured Popescu would rise again and again.

Teagan rose behind them as the two men went over the cliff and landed in the canopy of the taller trees, breaking branches as they fell through to the lower, heavier limbs. She could see Andre clearly, his free arm deflecting teeth and talons, while his fist continued to burrow through the agonizing acid blood. She felt it burning through his skin, right down to his bones, but he didn't stop. Didn't flinch. He kept after his prize, no matter that the vampire leaned forward and tore open his neck.

Her heart plummeted as she saw the vampire gulping at the bright red blood. It took everything she had to do as her lifemate had commanded. She had promised. She felt his agony and fear lived and breathed in her, every bit as terrible a monster as the master vampire, but she held on.

Andre had told her to look inside his mind. See his plan. Know that he had one and he would use it to make the world a safer place. She hid herself in the thickest branches possible, all the while staying in his mind. She kept silent even when she wanted to whisper to him that she was there, she was with him. He wasn't alone in this fight and she would do anything at all to help him.

He had said by staying safe that would help the most and she had to trust that he was right. He had blocked all pain so he didn't feel the damage the vampire inflicted on his body. He didn't seem to notice the terrible rake marks down his chest as Popescu dug his talons into flesh and ripped at it, even gulping some of that in his eagerness to feed on rich Carpathian blood.

The sight sickened her. She had never seen anyone so torn and bleeding. Still, he didn't stop. The resolve in his mind was absolute. He would destroy this vampire to keep it from ever again preying on humans or Carpathians. He wasn't afraid. He had buried his emotions somewhere deep where even she couldn't find them. He didn't feel the raw agony, but *she* did.

Her stomach churned and for a moment she thought she might actually black out. She knew better. She didn't dare. Andre would be distracted and he was in a fight for his life. More, he was relying on her. He would have tried to move away from Popescu's attack had she not been there to take his back.

The pressure was enormous, but at the same time, she was elated, no—more—she was honored that he would trust her to save his life no matter how badly he was wounded. She swallowed down bile and forced herself not only to watch, but to assess the damage to his body, which lacerations were superficial, which were life threatening.

Coming up with a plan of action that continually changed as the battle raged on kept her mind occupied, and she could compartmentalize the pain. At first she wasn't even aware that she was doing it. She was far too busy mapping out Andre's body and following every single rip and tear. Monitoring his blood supply and helping him to slow the blood loss. She found she could even, because she was entrenched so deeply in his mind, repair some of the damage to his veins and arteries even from the distance.

She wanted to do as he had done and become pure healing energy, but she didn't dare leave her body behind and unprotected, not until she knew the vampire was dead. The two combatants disappeared from her view. The broken branches from the tree they'd hit were blackened, the leaves withered and dried as if all the energy had been sucked out of it—or if it had been poisoned.

She caught a glimpse of the master vampire and Andre under two healthy trees, but one bent toward Andre, branches reaching like two hands toward the back of his head. Vines sprang from the limbs and wrapped around his neck. Her heart in her throat, she nearly jumped from the tree and spread her wings to get to him, but she forced herself to look into his mind. To stay still. To keep her promise. It was so difficult. She knew she was weeping inside the body of the owl. Her heart pounded and every cell in her body wanted—*needed*—to get to Andre, but she held herself in check.

His mind was utterly consumed with the battle. He had known Popescu had directed the battle path toward the two trees. He had even known what would happen and he hadn't tried to escape. He still didn't try. Instead, he withdrew his arm from the vampire's chest.

She could see Andre's fist was closed. His arm was

mangled, bloody and the flesh was gone all the way to the bone where the vampire's blood had eaten through skin and tissue. The vines whipped around him fast, covering him from his head down his shoulders and arms, pinning his arms to his side.

Teagan heard rolling thunder and lightning forked across the sky.

Sivamet. You know what to do.

Andre dropped the blackened organ at his feet, lowered his head, vines and all, and drove his shoulder into the vampire, driving him backward and off his feet, away from the heart.

Teagan didn't have time to think. She saw the instructions in Andre's mind and she took control of the lightning, dragging a whip from the sky and slamming it to earth. The first pass hit inches from the target, but she steadied her aim, ignoring the vampire tearing strips of flesh from her man, ignoring the nasty teeth ripping into his bones. The whip of lightning hit the small target dead center, incinerating the heart.

Popescu's shock showed on his face. He was certain Andre was helpless to control the white-hot energy pouring from the sky. He turned his head slowly to look toward the trees where Teagan hid. She shivered at the mask of evil, the terrible hatred she saw there. The red, burning eyes went vacant and his body toppled to the ground. As it did, the vines around Andre loosened and then dropped away, no longer under the vampire's control.

She waited until Andre stepped away from the body, until he went down on one knee and dropped his head, sagging. She slammed the whip over Popescu's body and watched it incinerate. She held the energy there for Andre. He didn't move toward it and, heart in her throat, she moved it closer to him. It took him too long to bathe his arms and chest in the heat to burn every drop of vampire blood from his body. As soon as he was done, he let himself sag to the ground.

Teagan allowed the energy whip to go back to nature and she flew as fast as possible, shifting as she touched the ground. Again, she forgot her clothes, but as she rushed toward Andre, she managed to add jeans and a T-shirt. Not that it mattered. Nothing mattered but Andre and healing his wounds.

Up close, the task of healing him appeared impossible. No one could live through those terrible lacerations. He was practically gutted. His belly was open, his chest, his neck. She'd started the repairs to his veins and arteries, but the vampire had done even more damage in those moments while Andre extracted the undead's heart. For one, horrible, time-stopping moment, she feared she couldn't heal him. It was too much.

She took a breath. He had stopped his heart from beating to keep from losing all of his blood. He lay lifeless, his large frame there on the ground, so completely ravaged she almost didn't know where to start. She even looked around her, as if she could find another healer, one far better than she was, but there was no one else.

She had asked for this task. She had wanted it. And Andre believed in her. He had put his life in her hands because he believed in her. She closed her eyes and let go of doubts. Of ego. Of fear. Fear was the most difficult, but she couldn't help him as long as that damaging emotion clung to her. So no fear. She could do this. She *would* do this. There was no other choice.

For one bizarre second she hung there, teetering between physical and spirit because the fear, entrenched for a lifetime in her very skin, held tight, but she had no other option. This was Andre. Her other half, and he wasn't afraid. He had gone into battle with a plan. That plan included her saving his life. He had known what the vampire would do to him and he had quietly accepted the pain and damage because he believed in her.

Teagan let go of the last of her fear and allowed her spirit to enter Andre's body. She had a plan and, although she had to slightly alter it, she stuck with it, applying the healing energy from the inside out. She was meticulous and took her time, knowing if she missed something vital, she wouldn't have the energy to go back and fix it.

She had no idea how long she worked on Andre, but his belly, chest and neck wounds were horrendous. She had to stop when she felt her spirit faltering. She found herself in her own body, swaying with weariness, terrified at the loss of strength, mostly because the moment she came to her unprotected body, she knew she wasn't alone.

Teagan spun around, facing what could only be an enemy. She had been in Andre's mind during the entire fight with the master vampire, and she knew what it took to kill one, but she had no strength left. Even standing there, keeping her body between Andre's and the stranger, she was swaying, her legs like rubber, knees weak.

"We heard the battle," the stranger said softly.

He kept his distance from her. His hair was very long and flowed down his back, as black as a raven's wing. He was tall, not as tall as Andre, but almost. He also looked extremely dangerous. His eyes were midnight black, no hint of any other color and his mouth suggested he had no knowledge of what a smile was.

She swallowed hard. Notes of music wept into the harmony of nature's song, giving her his identity. "Are you from the monastery?"

He nodded slowly. "Andre is your lifemate?"

Teagan stepped closer to her man. She should have picked

up a weapon. A rock at least. Andre had told her it was far too dangerous for these men to be in battle—or around anyone at all. There was blood all over the ground. All over Andre.

"Yes." What was she supposed to do?

"He needs blood."

"I was going to give him that next. I have a plan," she blurted out, and then bit her lip, annoyed with herself. Andre found her strange idiosyncrasy funny and cute, this man didn't so much as get a light in his eyes. He was all predator.

"You are too weak to give him what he needs. I will provide for him."

"No, you won't. I don't know you. I don't know anything about you. I can take care of my man." She lifted her chin, giving him her sternest, scariest look.

He, like Andre, didn't seem impressed.

She knew the worst of Andre's wounds had begun the healing process. It would take time, blood and soil, but she was certain the gaping holes in his neck, chest and belly would eventually heal. She had a long way to go though.

"You are too weak to give him what he needs."

They stared at each another. She refused to back down or look away.

He sighed. "I am called Fane. You called, and we decided to answer."

She frowned. "I didn't. I wouldn't know how to call you."

"But you know I am from the monastery. You must know I mean you no harm. We all felt your reach, that you could feel what we could not. That has never happened before, not ever, in all the centuries we have lived."

Teagan felt a stirring in her mind. It took great effort not to shift her gaze to Andre. She knew he was awake. That gave her confidence.

"I'm sorry if I disturbed you." She knew she was stalling

for time. Still swaying from weariness, she was uncertain if she could protect Andre.

"I do not understand the connection between us, but there is one. I will give blood to Andre and then to you."

She bit down hard on her lip. *Tell me what to do. I don't want him to give me blood.* The idea of taking or receiving blood from anyone but Andre was repulsive. She had just begun to accept her new life. She wasn't ready for that.

Let him come to me. Step to my other side. There are words he must say to me. If he does not say them, I will know he is our enemy. If he says them, he will keep his word.

Reluctantly Teagan moved back, her gaze on Fane's face. She worked around to Andre's other side, giving Fane access to her man. "Won't it make you weak, giving both of us blood?"

"The others are nearby to see to me and to protect all of us while you heal your lifemate. I wish to examine him. You are clearly a strong healer, but ..." He trailed off, and crouched low, beside Andre.

Teagan couldn't help but think his movements were elegant and graceful. He moved in harmony with nature, not against it. She heard him murmuring ancient words.

"Kuñasz, nélkül sivdobbanás, nélkül fesztelen löyly."

Andre interpreted the words as the ancient continued to chant more obviously ritual words of healing. *You lie as if asleep, without beat of heart, without airy breath. I offer freely, my life for your life. My spirit of life forgets my body and enters your body. My spirit of light sends all the dark spirits within fleeing without. I press the earth of our homeland and the spit of my tongue into your chest, your belly and your neck. At last, I give you my blood for your blood.*

Teagan thought there was beauty in the ancient chant. Certainly there was power. She felt it. Fane leaned close to

Andre, and her heart jumped. She tried to stay relaxed, but it was difficult when the fierce beauty of the man, all predator, scared her.

"Andre, take what is offered freely. My life for your life." Fane slashed his wrist and pressed it to Andre's mouth.

Andre's hand moved. He took Fane's offering respectfully. Teagan nearly sagged with relief. Almost at once, she felt the ancient's presence in Andre's body. She bit down harder on her lip, knowing he was examining her work. She had a long way to go. There were so many lacerations. Too many. She'd gotten tired just trying to repair the worst of the damage. She wanted the help for Andre, but still, it was her job and she'd blown it.

Fane returned to his body, still giving generously of his blood to Andre. "You did an amazing job. Too good. You are out in the open unprotected. Just the two of you. He shut down his heart so he would not lose more blood. Save the heavy repairs for when you are safe. Do the minimum, give him blood and get him to safety. Remember to set your safeguards and then heal as best you can before putting him in the ground."

That is my failing. I should have told you, Andre said.

Teagan nodded at Fane, eager for more advice. "I don't understand what you mean by *too* good. How can healing be too good? He had terrible wounds and he would have died from them."

"You are too weak to continue. You need blood and you cannot give what you do not have to your lifemate. How you could repair such wounds without soil or saliva, just you, I do not know. You have a tremendous gift. Just do enough to get him to safety. Once there, you can be more meticulous and precise."

She understood, although his advice went against her

394

nature. She could understand what he meant. She was weak—too weak to get Andre back to the cave and in the soil like he needed.

"I think I can help you and the others," she offered timidly. She'd never been timid, but something about the set of his shoulders, his aloofness, his very loneliness, made her aware she was intruding. "I feel it. I've felt it since I arrived here in the mountains. Just ease you a little. Give you more time."

Those eyes, beautiful eyes but so dangerous moved over her face. "I thank you for thinking of us, but we are beyond all help."

"Andre had thought to enter the monastery. He is one of you, isn't he? That's why you're here helping him. He's one of you and he found me. If he found me, there's hope for the rest of you."

"We cannot feel hope. We are extremely dangerous."

"I understand. Still. I know I can help. I'm just letting you know that the offer is there."

He inclined his head. "I will take your offer to the others."

Andre swept his tongue across the ancient's wrist and for the first time opened his eyes. "Thank you, Fane."

"I gave blood. She healed your wounds. The ones that matter. The rest can be healed in the ground. Can you make it back to your place of rest?"

Andre nodded. "Yes."

Fane slashed at his other wrist and held out his hand to Teagan. "I offer freely. My life for your life."

Teagan closed her eyes for a moment, trying not to see the ruby beads or feel the hunger clawing at her stomach. She knew it would be a terrible insult if she couldn't do this. The ancients didn't leave the monastery, not for anyone, yet they had come to aid Andre and her.

Can you help me, Andre? He would never know what it cost her to ask. She valued her independence, but she was not going to insult this man, not when she felt his every sorrow, the terrible agony of his lonely existence—both emotions the ancient Carpathian couldn't feel for himself.

At once Andre was in her mind, directing her movements so that she took the ancient's wrist and respectfully accepted his offering. She was aware of what she was doing, yet far removed from it all. The night was nearly gone. That was how long she'd worked on healing Andre. That was how long they had been unprotected. Fane was right, she should have done what she could to keep Andre alive and then gotten him to safety.

The moment she knew she had enough of the rich ancient blood to be at full strength, she closed the wound and bowed her head to him. "Thank you, Fane. For everything. For your advice, which I will always follow. For your blood that we both desperately needed, but also for your protection. Please thank the others for us as well."

Fane had gone very pale. He didn't try to rise, not even when Andre did. Blood seeped from the lacerations Teagan hadn't gotten to, but her lifemate was alive. He needed to go to ground, but she had closed the worst of those wounds. For that she was grateful.

"The others are close. They will come for me. Go now before the sun begins to rise," Fane instructed.

Andre reached down to grip Fane's forearms in the way of his people. *"Kaδa wäkeva óv o köd."*

What does that mean? Teagan asked, curious. It was a beautiful moment between two warriors who clearly understood each other.

Stand fast against the dark, Andre interpreted.

Teagan felt tears burn. "Please do, Fane. Please hold on

and let me help." That was all she could do for him. It was his choice.

Andre slipped his arm around her and took to the air. Below them, she caught a glimpse of four other men, moving in to aid Fane.

21

Teagan woke to a multitude of sensations. Pleasure, no, much, much more than pleasure bursting through her. She found herself flat on her back, in the bed Andre had fashioned for her. She was stark naked, her hair everywhere, when she distinctly remembered braiding it before the earth closed over them. The most delicious sensation was Andre's mouth working between her legs.

She lifted her head to look at him, at his beautiful, glacier blue eyes, so dark now with intensity. With stark hunger. With possession. His tongue, his teeth, his fingers all worked at her, sending familiar fire streaking through her body, building tension so fast, so hard she fragmented before she even caught her breath. Perfect. Beautiful. The greatest start to the night she could imagine.

Andre wasn't done. He never was. He wanted more. He kept his eyes on her face, a demand there. He didn't stop, not even when her hips bucked and her head tossed. Not when she gasped his name and pleaded with him that it was too much, that the sensations rocketing through her refused to stop. She couldn't catch her breath. Couldn't think. He drove her higher. Demanded more.

Not enough for me, sivamet. I need it all. Give yourself to me.

She knew what he meant. She had to trust that he would know when she had enough. But truly, the firestorm raged through her body. The orgasm spread like a wildfire out of control, consuming her. Still his mouth was relentless.

Again. I need it again.

She wasn't certain the first had ever stopped. Her body rippled and quaked, the first running into the second, and now he was demanding a third. His tongue was clever and his teeth just perfect, but the way he suckled as if he was dying of thirst and needed every single drop of liquid he could possibly get was her undoing.

Every cell in her body coiled tighter and tighter until she feared she might go insane with pleasure. Was that even possible? If it was, Andre was driving her there. There was no way to think. No way to be anything but what he wanted. He took her higher than she'd ever been and she reached for him, needing him. Needing to feel something solid beneath her fingertips as she flew apart, fragmenting into tiny little pieces, all of them soaring.

She heard herself scream. Call his name. Plead with him. She wanted him to fill her. She needed that. And then he was there, holding her thighs apart and slamming into her tight sheath. She heard him groan as her muscles gave way and he drove deep. His thick shaft invading her felt like a burning brand of steel.

"Hard, Andre. I need hard this time."

One large hand swept back her hair so he could look down into her eyes. She could see by the look on his face he intended hard. Rough. Brutal even. Perfect. She needed him like that. She needed primitive. A claiming. She could barely breathe with needing him exactly as his possessive look told her the way he planned on taking her.

He gathered her hips in one arm, lifting her to the angle he wanted and he began to thrust hard and deep, setting a fierce rhythm, a vicious pace, pistoning into her over and over with enough force to rock her body with every stroke. She ran her hands up and down his back, stretching to reach his hips, taking in as much skin as possible, reveling in the way he was as hungry for her as she was for him.

She was already so sensitive, and her fourth orgasm burst over her before she even knew she was close. She transferred her hold to his hair, clutching tightly, afraid she was going to come apart. He didn't even slow the pace. His eyes never left hers—not for a moment and he didn't even blink. He watched her, drinking in every orgasm. Wanting more. Demanding more from her.

Andre. She whispered his name in his mind. Filled him with her. Gave herself to him.

You are mine. All of you, Teagan. Every scorching inch of you. Your heart. Your soul. Your body. Your mind. You belong to me.

His body surged harder into hers, sending what felt like white-hot forks of lightning streaking through her. She was going up again, even higher. Scary. Wonderful. Impossible.

Did you doubt that for even a moment? You are mine, Andre. My man. My lifemate. I would follow you anywhere. Do anything for you. And she would. Modern woman be damned. This man was her everything and she was going to love him just as fiercely as he loved her, wherever that led her. And right now, at this moment, it was leading her to paradise. Unless she could die from too much pleasure.

She watched his eyes, those beautiful eyes. So gorgeous.

So in love. So soft and tender when he looked at her. So fiercely possessive. *How did I get so lucky?* She meant it, and she didn't care if she was giving away the fact that he really was everything to her. Andre gave that to her all the time. Now, she knew he really meant it. He deserved to hear it back. To know it.

He suddenly leaned forward and took her mouth. He took it the same way he was taking her body. Rough. Savage even. Demanding. Hard. Hot. Wet. So incredibly perfect. She gave herself up to his hands. His mouth. His cock. She gave herself to him because she knew if she did, the reward would be awesome ... and it was.

She felt him swell, then the stretching and burning that was part of the perfection of that amazing friction as he slammed home, filling her, raking over her bud so that her body tipped right over the edge and she began a free fall, this time with him. His groan in her mouth, pouring down her throat, a delicious, amazing *perfect* moment when they shared everything, skin, bodies, minds, hearts and soul.

Andre buried his face once again in her neck, holding her to him, his body buried deep, the weight of him crushing her while he surrounded her completely. It didn't matter that she could barely breathe, she knew *exactly* why she loved this moment, this aftermath. Andre surrendered completely to her—to his love of her. He was completely vulnerable to her in that moment. Every time.

He gave her that gift every *single* perfect time. Her big, bad, Carpathian warrior, who could take down a master vampire and had hunted them for centuries, gave her that gift. She held him tight, lifting her legs to circle his hips, to hold him as close to her as possible. She loved that her heart found the rhythm of his. She loved that, although she could barely breathe, he made certain she had air.

"I love you, Teagan. More than life." Andre lifted his head and brushed a kiss across her mouth before rolling off of her.

There was always that moment of loss—of bereavement when his body left hers. She wanted him back, but then when a woman had a lover like Andre, she supposed it wasn't wrong to get a little greedy.

"It worked. Our partnership. You found the vampire and you healed me."

"We've been in the earth a week. I wasn't the only one to heal you. There was Fane's blood, which was huge, and the soil helped as well." She felt compelled to point that out. "I actually took a look at the minerals in the soil to see what would help and that's why I moved our resting place."

He stood, uncaring of his nudity. "I love looking at you," she blurted out, reaching out with lazy fingers to stroke his shaft. "You're really gifted in the looks department, Andre. I think you're the most gorgeous man I have ever seen. All over." Her fingers caressed and then wrapped around him.

"How many men's bodies have you seen?"

"Um. Just yours, but look at you. Really. If someone was going to sculpt a nude male, you should be their model. Not that I want other women looking at you. I'm just saying I love looking at you."

"I'm very glad you do."

He reached for her, forcing her to reluctantly give up her prize. "You need the hot springs. I was not gentle."

"I loved every second." But he knew that, he'd been in her mind. "I'm not certain I'll ever get used to being naked in front of you, but since I really loved looking at your body I suppose it's a small price to pay."

"I love looking at your body," he said as he carried her to the hot springs. "I am very particular about that point." He set her on her feet and Teagan sank down into the water.

Her cell phone sang to her from across the room. "How can I get service here? That's crazy. We're up the mountain, inside a cave. *Deep* in the cave."

"I know keeping in touch with your family is important to you," Andre said. "So I made certain you had enough reception to text." He waved his hand and floated the cell phone through the air to her.

Her heart turned over. "Seriously, Andre, you make me want to cry when you're so thoughtful and sweet." She plucked the phone out of the air and checked her message. "Uh-oh, Andre. Brace for this. You're going to need to. Grandma Trixie is on her way so that she can make certain I don't hook up with some crazy foreigner who is out for my virtue and will most likely lock me up in his harem or take me to some deep, dark cave and make me his sex slave."

He burst out laughing. A real laugh. Genuine. It was a beautiful, musical sound and Teagan loved it.

"Did she really say that?"

"Yep."

"Too late. She's far, far too late," Andre said.

Teagan had to agree.

APPENDIX 1

Carpathian Healing Chants

To rightly understand Carpathian healing chants, background is required in several areas:

1. The Carpathian view on healing
2. The Lesser Healing Chant of the Carpathians
3. The Great Healing Chant of the Carpathians
4. Carpathian musical aesthetics
5. Lullaby
6. Song to Heal the Earth
7. Carpathian chanting technique

1. THE CARPATHIAN VIEW ON HEALING

The Carpathians are a nomadic people whose geographic origins can be traced back to at least as far as the Southern Ural Mountains (near the steppes of modern-day Kazakhstan), on the border between Europe and Asia. (For this reason, modern-day linguists call their language "proto-Uralic," without knowing that this is the language of the Carpathians.) Unlike most nomadic peoples, the wandering of the Carpathians was not due to the need to find new grazing lands as the seasons and climate shifted, or the search for better trade. Instead, the Carpathians' movements were driven by a great purpose: to find a land that would have the right earth, a soil with the kind of richness that would greatly enhance their rejuvenative powers.

Over the centuries, they migrated westward (some six thousand years ago), until they at last found their perfect homeland—their *susu*—in the Carpathian Mountains, whose long arc cradled the lush plains of the kingdom of Hungary. (The kingdom of Hungary flourished for over a millennium—making Hungarian the dominant language of the Carpathian Basin—until the kingdom's lands were split among several countries after World War I: Austria, Czechoslovakia, Romania, Yugoslavia and modern Hungary.)

Other peoples from the Southern Urals (who shared the Carpathian language, but were not Carpathians) migrated in different directions. Some ended up in Finland, which accounts for why the modern Hungarian and Finnish languages are among the contemporary descendants of the ancient Carpathian language. Even though they are tied forever to their chosen Carpathian homeland, the wandering of the Carpathians continues as they search the world for the answers that will enable them to bear and raise their offspring without difficulty.

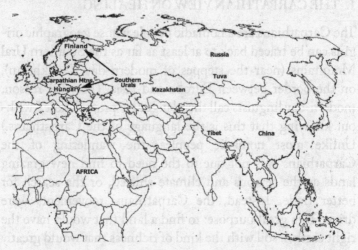

Because of their geographic origins, the Carpathian views on healing share much with the larger Eurasian shamanistic tradition. Probably the closest modern representative of that tradition is based in Tuva (and is referred to as "Tuvinian Shamanism")—see the map on the previous page.

The Eurasian shamanistic tradition—from the Carpathians to the Siberian shamans—held that illness originated in the human soul, and only later manifested as various physical conditions. Therefore, shamanistic healing, while not neglecting the body, focused on the soul and its healing. The most profound illnesses were understood to be caused by "soul departure," where all or some part of the sick person's soul has wandered away from the body (into the nether realms), or has been captured or possessed by an evil spirit, or both.

The Carpathians belong to this greater Eurasian shamanistic tradition and share its viewpoints. While the Carpathians themselves did not succumb to illness, Carpathian healers understood that the most profound wounds were also accompanied by a similar "soul departure."

Upon reaching the diagnosis of "soul departure," the healer-shaman is then required to make a spiritual journey into the netherworlds to recover the soul. The shaman may have to overcome tremendous challenges along the way, particularly fighting the demon or vampire who has possessed his friend's soul.

"Soul departure" doesn't require a person to be unconscious (although that certainly can be the case as well). It was understood that a person could still appear to be conscious, even talk and interact with others, and yet be missing a part of their soul. The experienced healer or shaman would instantly see the problem nonetheless, in subtle signs that others might miss: the person's attention wandering every now and then, a lessening in their enthusiasm about life, chronic depression, a diminishment in the brightness of their "aura," and the like.

2. THE LESSER HEALING CHANT OF THE CARPATHIANS

Kepä Sarna Pus (The Lesser Healing Chant) is used for wounds that are merely physical in nature. The Carpathian healer leaves his body and enters the wounded Carpathian's body to heal great mortal wounds from the inside out using pure energy. He proclaims, "I offer freely my life for your life," as he gives his blood to the injured Carpathian. Because the Carpathians are of the earth and bound to the soil, they are healed by the soil of their homeland. Their saliva is also often used for its rejuvenative powers.

It is also very common for the Carpathian chants (both the Lesser and the Great) to be accompanied by the use of healing herbs, aromas from Carpathian candles and crystals. The crystals (when combined with the Carpathians' empathic, psychic connection to the entire universe) are used to gather positive energy from their surroundings, which then is used to accelerate the healing. Caves are sometimes used as the setting for the healing.

The Lesser Healing Chant was used by Vikirnoff Von Shrieder and Colby Jansen to heal Rafael De La Cruz, whose heart had been ripped out by a vampire as described in *Dark Secret*.

Kepä Sarna Pus (The Lesser Healing Chant)
The same chant is used for all physical wounds. "Sívadaba" ["into your heart"] would be changed to refer to whatever part of the body is wounded.

Ku'nasz, nélkül sívdobbanás, nélkül fesztelen löyly.
You lie as if asleep, without beat of heart, without airy breath.

Ot élidamet andam szabadon élidadért.
I offer freely my life for your life.

O jelä sielam jörem ot ainamet és soŋe ot élidadet.
My spirit of light forgets my body and enters your body.

O jelä sielam pukta kinn minden szelemeket belső.
My spirit of light sends all the dark spirits within fleeing without.

Paj´nak o susu hanyet és o nyelv nyálamet sívadaba.
I press the earth of our homeland and the spit of my tongue into your heart.

Vii, o verim soŋe o verid andam.
At last, I give you my blood for your blood.
To hear this chant, visit: http://www.christinefeehan.com/members/.

3. THE GREAT HEALING CHANT OF THE CARPATHIANS

The most well-known—and most dramatic—of the Carpathian healing chants was *En Sarna Pus* (**The Great Healing Chant**). This chant was reserved for recovering the wounded or unconscious Carpathian's soul.

Typically a group of men would form a circle around the sick Carpathian (to "encircle him with our care and compassion") and begin the chant. The shaman or healer or leader is the prime actor in this healing ceremony. It is he who will actually make the spiritual journey into the netherworld, aided by his clanspeople. Their purpose is to ecstatically dance, sing, drum and chant, all the while visualizing

411

(through the words of the chant) the journey itself—every step of it, over and over again—to the point where the shaman, in trance, leaves his body, and makes that very journey. (Indeed, the word "ecstasy" is from the Latin *ex statis*, which literally means "out of the body.")

One advantage that the Carpathian healer has over many other shamans is his telepathic link to his lost brother. Most shamans must wander in the dark of the nether realms in search of their lost brother. But the Carpathian healer directly "hears" in his mind the voice of his lost brother calling to him, and can thus "zero in" on his soul like a homing beacon. For this reason, Carpathian healing tends to have a higher success rate than most other traditions of this sort.

Something of the geography of the "other world" is useful for us to examine, in order to fully understand the words of the Great Carpathian Healing Chant. A reference is made to the "Great Tree" (in Carpathian: En Puwe). Many ancient traditions, including the Carpathian tradition, understood the worlds—the heaven worlds, our world and the nether realms—to be "hung" upon a great pole, or axis, or tree. Here on earth, we are positioned halfway up this tree, on one of its branches. Hence many ancient texts often referred to the material world as "middle earth": midway between heaven and hell. Climbing the tree would lead one to the heaven worlds. Descending the tree to its roots would lead to the nether realms. The shaman was necessarily a master of movement up and down the Great Tree, sometimes moving unaided, and sometimes assisted by (or even mounted upon the back of) an animal spirit guide. In various traditions, this Great Tree was known variously as the axis mundi (the "axis of the worlds"), Ygddrasil (in Norse mythology), Mount Meru (the sacred world mountain of Tibetan tradition), etc. The Christian cosmos, with its heaven, purgatory/earth and hell, is also worth comparing. It is even given a similar topography in Dante's *Divine Comedy*: Dante is led on a journey first to hell, at the center of the earth; then upward to Mount Purgatory, which sits on the earth's surface directly opposite Jerusalem; then farther upward first to Eden, the earthly paradise, at the summit of Mount Purgatory; and then upward at last to heaven.

In the shamanistic tradition, it was understood that the small always reflects the large; the personal always reflects the cosmic. A movement in the greater dimensions of the cosmos also coincides with an internal movement. For example, the axis mundi of the cosmos also corresponds to the spinal column of the individual. Journeys up and down the axis mundi often coincided with the movement of natural and spiritual energies (sometimes called kundalini or shakti) in the spinal column of the shaman or mystic.

En Sarna Pus (The Great Healing Chant)
In this chant, ekä ("brother") would be replaced by "sister," "father," "mother," depending on the person to be healed.

Ot ekäm ainajanak hany, jama.
My brother's body is a lump of earth, close to death.

Me, ot ekäm kuntajanak, pirädak ekäm, gond és irgalom türe.
We, the clan of my brother, encircle him with our care and compassion.

O pus wäkenkek, ot oma ´sarnank, és ot pus fünk, álnak ekäm ainajanak, pitänak ekäm ainajanak elävä.
Our healing energies, ancient words of magic and healing herbs bless my brother's body, keep it alive.

Ot ekäm sielanak pälä. Ot omboʹce päläja juta alatt o jüti, kinta, és szelemek lamtijaknak.
But my brother's soul is only half. His other half wanders in the netherworld.

Ot en mekem ŋamaŋ: kulkedak otti ot ekäm omboʹce päläjanak.
My great deed is this: I travel to find my brother's other half.

Rekatüre, saradak, tappadak, odam, kaŋa o numa waram, és avaa owe o lewl mahoz.
We dance, we chant, we dream ecstatically, to call my spirit bird, and to open the door to the other world.

Ntak o numa waram, és mozdulak, jomadak.
I mount my spirit bird and we begin to move, we are under way.

Piwtädak ot En Puwe tyvinak, eʹcidak alatt o jüti, kinta, és szelemek lamtijaknak.
Following the trunk of the Great Tree, we fall into the netherworld.

Fázak, fázak nó o ʹsaro.
It is cold, very cold.

Juttadak ot ekäm o akarataban, o sívaban és o sielaban.
My brother and I are linked in mind, heart and soul.

Ot ekäm sielanak kaŋa engem.
My brother's soul calls to me.

Kuledak és piwtädak ot ekäm.
I hear and follow his track.

Sayedak és tuledak ot ekäm kulyanak.
Encounter I the demon who is devouring my brother's soul.

Nenäm ´coro, o kuly torodak.
In anger, I fight the demon.

O kuly pél engem.
He is afraid of me.

Lejkkadak o kaŋka salamaval.
I strike his throat with a lightning bolt.

Molodak ot ainaja komakamal.
I break his body with my bare hands.

Toja és molanâ.
He is bent over, and falls apart.

Hän ´caδa.
He runs away.

Manedak ot ekäm sielanak.
I rescue my brother's soul.

Alǝdak ot ekam sielanak o komamban.
I lift my brother's soul in the hollow of my hand.

Alǝdam ot ekam numa waramra.
I lift him onto my spirit bird.

Piwtädak ot En Puwe tyvijanak és sayedak jälleen ot elävä ainak majaknak.
Following up the Great Tree, we return to the land of the living.

Ot ekäm elä jälleen.
My brother lives again.

Ot ekäm we'n'ca jälleen.
He is complete again.
To hear this chant, visit: http://www.christinefeehan.com/
members/.

4. CARPATHIAN MUSICAL AESTHETICS

In the sung Carpathian pieces (such as the "Lullaby" and
the "Song to Heal the Earth"), you'll hear elements that
are shared by many of the musical traditions in the Uralic
geographical region, some of which still exist—from Eastern
European (Bulgarian, Romanian, Hungarian, Croatian, etc.)
to Romany ("gypsy"). Some of these elements include:

- the rapid alternation between major and minor
  modalities, including a sudden switch (called a
  "Picardy third") from minor to major to end a piece
  or section (as at the end of the "Lullaby")
- the use of close (tight) harmonies
- the use of *ritardi* (slowing down the piece) and *cre-
  scendi* (swelling in volume) for brief periods
- the use of *glissandi* (slides) in the singing tradition
- the use of trills in the singing tradition (as in the final
  invocation of the "Song to Heal the Earth")—similar to
  Celtic, a singing tradition more familiar to many of us
- the use of parallel fifths (as in the final invocation of
  the "Song to Heal the Earth")
- controlled use of dissonance
- "call and response" chanting (typical of many of the
  world's chanting traditions)

416

- extending the length of a musical line (by adding a couple of bars) to heighten dramatic effect
- and many more

"Lullaby" and "Song to Heal the Earth" illustrate two rather different forms of Carpathian music (a quiet, intimate piece and an energetic ensemble piece)—but whatever the form, Carpathian music is full of feeling.

5. LULLABY

This song is sung by women while the child is still in the womb or when the threat of a miscarriage is apparent. The baby can hear the song while inside the mother, and the mother can connect with the child telepathically as well. The lullaby is meant to reassure the child, to encourage the baby to hold on, to stay—to reassure the child that he or she will be protected by love even from inside until birth. The last line literally means that the mother's love will protect her child until the child is born ("rise").

Musically, the Carpathian "Lullaby" is in three-quarter time ("waltz time"), as are a significant portion of the world's various traditional lullabies (perhaps the most famous of which is "Brahms' Lullaby"). The arrangement for solo voice is the original context: a mother singing to her child, unaccompanied. The arrangement for chorus and violin ensemble illustrates how musical even the simplest Carpathian pieces often are, and how easily they lend themselves to contemporary instrumental or orchestral arrangements. (A wide range of contemporary composers, including Dvor̆ák and Smetana, have taken advantage of a similar discovery, working other traditional Eastern European music into their symphonic poems.)

Odam-Sarna Kondak (Lullaby)

Tumtesz o wäke ku pitasz belső.
Feel the strength you hold inside.

Hiszasz sívadet. Én olenam gæidnod.
Trust your heart. I'll be your guide.

Sas csecsemőm, kuńasz.
Hush my baby, close your eyes.

Rauho joņe ted.
Peace will come to you.

Tumtesz o sívdobbanás ku olen lamt3ad belső.
Feel the rhythm deep inside.

Gond-kumpadek ku kim te.
Waves of love that cover you.

Pesänak te, asti o jüti, kidüsz.
Protect, until the night you rise.

To hear this chant, visit:
http://www.christinefeehan.com/members/.

6. SONG TO HEAL THE EARTH

This is the earth-healing song that is used by the Carpathian women to heal soil filled with various toxins. The women take a position on four sides and call to the universe to draw on the healing energy with love and respect. The soil of the earth is their resting place, the place where they rejuvenate, and they must make it safe not only for themselves but for their unborn children as well as their men and living children. This is a beautiful ritual performed by the women together, raising their voices in harmony and calling on the earth's minerals and healing properties to come forth and help them save their children. They literally dance and sing to heal the earth in a ceremony as old as their species. The dance and notes of the song are adjusted according to the toxins felt through the healer's bare feet. The feet are placed in a certain pattern and the hands gracefully weave a healing spell while the dance is performed. They must be especially careful when the soil is prepared for babies. This is a ceremony of love and healing.

Musically, the ritual is divided into several sections:

- **First verse:** A "call and response" section, where the chant leader sings the "call" solo, and then some or all of the women sing the "response" in the close harmony style typical of the Carpathian musical tradition. The repeated response—*Ai Emä Maye*—is an invocation of the source of power for the healing ritual: "Oh, Mother Nature."
- **First chorus:** This section is filled with clapping, dancing, ancient horns and other means used to invoke and heighten the energies upon which the ritual is drawing.
- **Second verse**
- **Second chorus**
- **Closing invocation:** In this closing part, two song leaders, in close harmony, take all the energy gathered by the earlier portions of the song/ritual and focus it entirely on the healing purpose.

What you will be listening to are brief tastes of what would typically be a significantly longer ritual, in which the verse

and chorus parts are developed and repeated many times, to
be closed by a single rendition of the final invocation.

Sarna Pusm O Mayet (Song to Heal the Earth)

First verse

Ai Emä Maye,
Oh, Mother Nature,

Me sívadbin lañaak.
We are your beloved daughters.

Me tappadak, me pusmak o mayet.
We dance to heal the earth.

Me sarnadak, me pusmak o hanyet.
We sing to heal the earth.

Sielanket jutta tedet it,
We join with you now,

Sívank és akaratank és sielank juttanak.
Our hearts and minds and spirits become one.

Second verse

Ai Emä maye,
Oh, Mother Nature,

Me sívadbin lañaak.
We are your beloved daughters.

Me andak arwadet emänked és me kaɲank o
We pay homage to our mother and call upon the

Põhi és Lõuna, Ida és Lääs.
North and South, East and West.

Pide és aldyn és myös belső.
Above and below and within as well.

Gondank o mayenak pusm hän ku olen jama.
Our love of the land heals that which is in need.

Juttanak teval it,
We join with you now,

Maye mayeval.
Earth to earth.

O pirä elidak weńća.
The circle of life is complete.

To hear this chant, visit:
http://www.christinefeehan.com/members/.

7. CARPATHIAN CHANTING TECHNIQUE

As with their healing techniques, the actual "chanting technique" of the Carpathians has much in common with the other shamanistic traditions of the Central Asian steppes. The primary mode of chanting was throat chanting using overtones. Modern examples of this manner of singing can still be found in the Mongolian, Tuvan and Tibetan traditions. You can find an audio example of the Gyuto Tibetan

Buddhist monks engaged in throat chanting at: http://www.christinefeehan.com/carpathian_chanting/.

As with Tuva, note on the map the geographical proximity of Tibet to Kazakhstan and the Southern Urals.

The beginning part of the Tibetan chant emphasizes synchronizing all the voices around a single tone, aimed at healing a particular "chakra" of the body. This is fairly typical of the Gyuto throat-chanting tradition, but it is not a significant part of the Carpathian tradition. Nonetheless, it serves as an interesting contrast.

The part of the Gyuto chanting example that is most similar to the Carpathian style of chanting is the midsection, where the men are chanting the words together with great force. The purpose here is not to generate a "healing tone" that will affect a particular "chakra," but rather to generate as much power as possible for initiating the "out of body" travel, and for fighting the demonic forces that the healer/traveler must face and overcome.

The songs of the Carpathian women (illustrated by their "Lullaby" and their "Song to Heal the Earth") are part of the same ancient musical and healing tradition as the Lesser and Great Healing Chants of the warrior males. You can hear some of the same instruments in both the male warriors' healing chants and the women's "Song to Heal the Earth." Also, they share the common purpose of generating and directing power. However, the women's songs are distinctively feminine in character. One immediately noticeable difference is that, while the men speak their words in the manner of a chant, the women sing songs with melodies and harmonies, softening the overall performance. A feminine, nurturing quality is especially evident in the "Lullaby."

APPENDIX 2

The Carpathian Language

Like all human languages, the language of the Carpathians contains the richness and nuance that can only come from a long history of use. At best we can only touch on some of the main features of the language in this brief appendix:

1. The history of the Carpathian language
2. Carpathian grammar and other characteristics of the language
3. Examples of the Carpathian language (including The Ritual Words and The Warrior's Chant)
4. A much-abridged Carpathian dictionary

1. THE HISTORY OF THE CARPATHIAN LANGUAGE

The Carpathian language of today is essentially identical to the Carpathian language of thousands of years ago. A "dead" language like the Latin of two thousand years ago has evolved into a significantly different modern language (Italian) because of countless generations of speakers and great historical fluctuations. In contrast, many of the speakers of Carpathian from thousands of years ago are still alive. Their presence—coupled with the deliberate isolation of the Carpathians from the other major forces of change in the world—has acted (and continues to act) as a stabilizing force that has preserved the integrity of the language over the centuries. Carpathian culture has also acted as a stabilizing force. For instance, the Ritual Words, the various healing chants (see Appendix 1), and other cultural artifacts have been passed down through the centuries with great fidelity.

One small exception should be noted: the splintering of the Carpathians into separate geographic regions has led to some minor dialectization. However the telepathic link among all Carpathians (as well as each Carpathian's regular return to his or her homeland) has ensured that the differences among dialects are relatively superficial (e.g., small numbers of new words, minor differences in pronunciation, etc.), since the deeper, internal language of mind-forms has remained the same because of continuous use across space and time.

The Carpathian language was (and still is) the proto-language for the Uralic (or Finno-Ugrian) family of languages. Today, the Uralic languages are spoken in northern, eastern and central Europe and in Siberia. More than twenty-three million people in the world speak languages that can trace their ancestry to Carpathian. Magyar or Hungarian (about fourteen million speakers), Finnish (about five million speakers) and Estonian (about one million speakers) are the three major contemporary descendants of this proto-language. The only factor that unites the more than twenty languages in the Uralic family is that their ancestry can be traced back to a common proto-language—Carpathian—that split (starting some six thousand years ago) into the various languages in the Uralic family. In the same way, European languages such as English and French belong to the better-known Indo-European family and also evolved from a common proto-language ancestor (a different one from Carpathian).

The following table provides a sense for some of the similarities in the language family.

Note: The Finnic/Carpathian "k" shows up often as Hungarian "h." Similarly, the Finnic/Carpathian "p" often corresponds to the Hungarian "f."

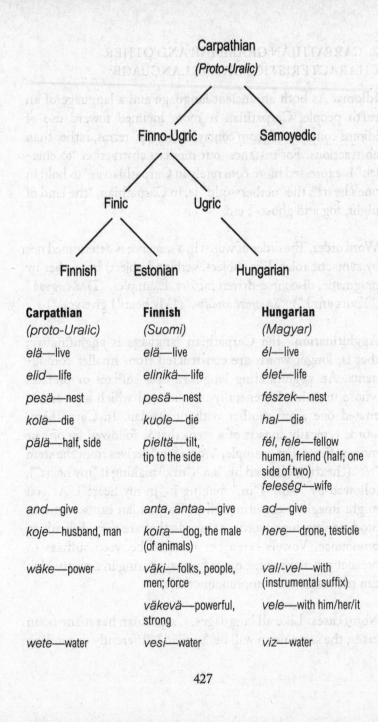

Carpathian
(Proto-Uralic)

Finno-Ugric   Samoyedic

Finic   Ugric

Finnish   Estonian   Hungarian

Carpathian (proto-Uralic)	Finnish (Suomi)	Hungarian (Magyar)
elä—live	elä—live	él—live
elid—life	elinikä—life	élet—life
pesä—nest	pesä—nest	fészek—nest
kola—die	kuole—die	hal—die
pälä—half, side	pieltä—tilt, tip to the side	fél, fele—fellow human, friend (half; one side of two) feleség—wife
and—give	anta, antaa—give	ad—give
koje—husband, man	koira—dog, the male (of animals)	here—drone, testicle
wäke—power	väki—folks, people, men; force	vall-vel—with (instrumental suffix)
	väkevä—powerful, strong	vele—with him/her/it
wete—water	vesi—water	viz—water

427

2. CARPATHIAN GRAMMAR AND OTHER CHARACTERISTICS OF THE LANGUAGE

Idioms. As both an ancient language and a language of an earth people, Carpathian is more inclined toward use of idioms constructed from concrete, "earthy" terms, rather than abstractions. For instance, our modern abstraction "to cherish" is expressed more concretely in Carpathian as "to hold in one's heart"; the "netherworld" is, in Carpathian, "the land of night, fog and ghosts"; etc.

Word order. The order of words in a sentence is determined not by syntactic roles (like subject, verb and object) but rather by pragmatic, discourse-driven factors. Examples: *"Tied vagyok."* ("Yours am I."); *"Sívamet andam."* ("My heart I give you.")

Agglutination. The Carpathian language is agglutinative; that is, longer words are constructed from smaller components. An agglutinating language uses suffixes or prefixes whose meaning is generally unique, and which are concatenated one after another without overlap. In Carpathian, words typically consist of a stem that is followed by one or more suffixes. For example, *"sívambam"* derives from the stem *"sív"* ("heart") followed by *"am"* ("my," making it "my heart"), followed by "bam" ("in," making it "in my heart"). As you might imagine, agglutination in Carpathian can sometimes produce very long words, or words that are very difficult to pronounce. Vowels often get inserted between suffixes to prevent too many consonants from appearing in a row (which can make the word unpronounceable).

Noun cases. Like all languages, Carpathian has many noun cases; the same noun will be "spelled" differently depending on its role in the sentence. Some of the noun cases include: nominative (when the noun is the subject of the sentence), accusative (when the noun is a direct object of the verb), dative (indirect object), genitive (or possessive), instrumental, final, supressive, inessive, elative, terminative and delative.

We will use the possessive (or genitive) case as an example, to illustrate how all noun cases in Carpathian involve adding standard suffixes to the noun stems. Thus expressing possession in Carpathian—"my lifemate," "your lifemate," "his lifemate," "her lifemate," etc.—involves adding a particular suffix (such as "*-am*") to the noun stem (*"päläfertiil"*), to produce the possessive (*"päläfertiilam"*—"my lifemate"). Which suffix to use depends upon which person ("my," "your," "his," etc.) and whether the noun ends in a consonant or a vowel. The table below shows the suffixes for singular nouns only (not plural), and also shows the similarity to the suffixes used in contemporary Hungarian. (Hungarian is actually a little more complex, in that it also requires "vowel rhyming": which suffix to use also depends on the last vowel in the noun; hence the multiple choices in the cells below, where Carpathian only has a single choice.)

	Carpathian (proto-Uralic)		Contemporary Hungarian	
person	**noun ends in vowel**	**noun ends in consonant**	**noun ends in vowel**	**noun ends in consonant**
1st singular (my)	-m	-am	-m	-om, -em, -öm
2nd singular (your)	-d	-ad	-d	-od, -ed, -öd

429

Person				
3rd singular (his, her, its)	-ja	-a	-ja/-je	-a, -e
1st plural (our)	-nk	-ank	-nk	-unk, -ünk
2nd plural (your)	-tak	-atak	-tok, -tek, -tök	-otok, -etek, -ötök
3rd plural (their)	-jak	-ak	-juk, -jük	-uk, -ük

Note: As mentioned earlier, vowels often get inserted between the word and its suffix so as to prevent too many consonants from appearing in a row (which would produce unpronounceable words). For example, in the table on the previous page, all nouns that end in a consonant are followed by suffixes beginning with "a."

Verb conjugation. Like its modern descendents (such as Finnish and Hungarian), Carpathian has many verb tenses, far too many to describe here. We will just focus on the conjugation of the present tense. Again, we will place contemporary Hungarian side by side with the Carpathian, because of the marked similarity of the two.

As with the possessive case for nouns, the conjugation of verbs is done by adding a suffix onto the verb stem:

Person	Carpathian (proto-Uralic)	Contemporary Hungarian
1st (I give)	-am (andam), -ak	-ok, -ek, -ök
2nd singular (you give)	-sz (andsz)	-sz

3rd singular (he/she/it gives)	— (and)	—
1st plural (we give)	-ak (andak)	-unk, -ünk
2nd plural (you give)	-tak (andtak)	-tok, -tek, -tök
3rd plural (they give)	-nak (andnak)	-nak, -nek

As with all languages, there are many "irregular verbs" in Carpathian that don't exactly fit this pattern. But the above table is still a useful guideline for most verbs.

3. EXAMPLES OF THE CARPATHIAN LANGUAGE

Here are some brief examples of conversational Carpathian, used in the Dark books. We include the literal translation in square brackets. It is interestingly different from the most appropriate English translation.

Susu.
I am home.
["home/birthplace." "I am" is understood, as is often the case in Carpathian.]

Möért?
What for?

csitri
little one
["little slip of a thing," "little slip of a girl"]

ainaak enyém
forever mine

431

ainaak sívamet jutta
forever mine (another form)
["forever to-my-heart connected/fixed"]

sívamet
my love
["of-my-heart," "to-my-heart"]

Tet vigyázam.
I love you.
["you-love-I"]

Sarna Rituaali (The Ritual Words) is a longer example, and
an example of chanted rather than conversational Carpathian.
Note the recurring use of *"andam"* ("I give"), to give the chant
musicality and force through repetition.

Sarna Rituaali (The Ritual Words)

Te avio päläfertiilam.
You are my lifemate.

Éntölam kuulua, avio päläfertiilam.
I claim you as my lifemate.

Ted kuuluak, kacad, kojed.
I belong to you.

Élidamet andam.
I offer my life for you.

Pesämet andam.
I give you my protection.

Uskolfertiilamet andam.
I give you my allegiance.

Sívamet andam.
I give you my heart.

Sielamet andam.
I give you my soul.

Ainamet andam.
I give you my body.

Sívamet kuuluak kaik että a ted.
I take into my keeping the same that is yours.

Ainaak olenszal sívambin.
Your life will be cherished by me for all my time.

Te élidet ainaak pide minan.
Your life will be placed above my own for all time.

Te avio päläfertiilam.
You are my lifemate.

Ainaak sívamet jutta oleny.
You are bound to me for all eternity.

Ainaak terád vigyázak.
You are always in my care.

To hear these words pronounced (and for more about Carpathian pronunciation altogether), please visit: http://www.christinefeehan.com/members/.

433

Sarna Kontakawk (The Warriors' Chant) is another longer example of the Carpathian language. The warriors' council takes place deep beneath the earth in a chamber of crystals with magma far below that, so the steam is natural and the wisdom of their ancestors is clear and focused. This is a sacred place where they bloodswear to their prince and people and affirm their code of honor as warriors and brothers. It is also where battle strategies are born and all dissension is discussed as well as any concerns the warriors have that they wish to bring to the Council and open for discussion.

Sarna Kontakawk (The Warriors' Chant)

Veri isäakank—veri ekäakank.
Blood of our fathers—blood of our brothers.

Veri olen elid.
Blood is life.

Andak veri-elidet Karpatiiakank, és wäke-sarna ku meke arwa-arvo, irgalom, hän ku agba, és wäke kutni, ku manaak verival.
We offer that life to our people with a bloodsworn vow of honor, mercy, integrity and endurance.

Verink sokta; verink kaŋa teräd.
Our blood mingles and calls to you.

Akasz énak ku kaŋa és juttasz kuntatak it.
Heed our summons and join with us now.

To hear these words pronounced (and for more about Carpathian pronunciation altogether), please visit: http://www.christinefeehan.com/members/.

See **Appendix 1** for Carpathian healing chants, including the *Kepä Sarna Pus* (The Lesser Healing Chant), the *En Sarna Pus* (The Great Healing Chant), the *Odam-Sarna Kondak* (Lullaby) and the *Sarna Pusm O May et* (Song to Heal the Earth).

4. A MUCH-ABRIDGED CARPATHIAN DICTIONARY

This very much abridged Carpathian dictionary contains most of the Carpathian words used in these Dark books. Of course, a full Carpathian dictionary would be as large as the usual dictionary for an entire language (typically more than a hundred thousand words).

Note: The Carpathian nouns and verbs below are word stems. They generally do not appear in their isolated, "stem" form, as below. Instead, they usually appear with suffixes (e.g., "*andam*"—"*I give*," rather than just the root, "*and*").

a—verb negation (*prefix*); not (*adverb*).
agba—to be seemly or proper.
ai—oh.
aina—body.
ainaak—forever.
O ainaak jelä peje emnimet ŋamaŋ—Sun scorch that woman forever (*Carpathian swear words*).
ainaakfél—old friend.
ak—suffix added after a noun ending in a consonant to make it plural.
aka—to give heed; to hearken; to listen.
akarat—mind; will.
ál—to bless; to attach to.
alatt—through.
aldyn—under; underneath.

alə—to lift; to raise.

alte—to bless; to curse.

and—to give.

and sielet, arwa-arvomet, és jelämet, kuulua huvémet ku feaj és ködet ainaak—to trade soul, honor and salvation, for momentary pleasure and endless damnation.

andasz éntölem irgalomet!—have mercy!

arvo—value; price (*noun*).

arwa—praise (*noun*).

arwa-arvo—honor (*noun*).

arwa-arvo olen gæidnod, ekäm—honor guide you, my brother (*greeting*).

arwa-arvo olen isäntä, ekäm—honor keep you, my brother (*greeting*).

arwa-arvo pile sívadet—may honor light your heart (*greeting*).

arwa-arvod mäne me ködak—may your honor hold back the dark (*greeting*).

ašša—no (*before a noun*); not (*with a verb that is not in the imperative*); not (*with an adjective*).

aššatotello—disobedient.

asti—until.

avaa—to open.

avio—wedded.

avio päläfertiil—lifemate.

avoi—uncover; show; reveal.

belső—within; inside.

bur—good; well.

bur tule ekämet kuntamak—well met brother-kin (*greeting*).

ćaða—to flee; to run; to escape.

ćoro—to flow; to run like rain.

csecsemõ—baby (*noun*).

csitri—little one (*female*).

diutal—triumph; victory.

436

eći—to fall.

ek—suffix added after a noun ending in a consonant to make it
    plural.

ekä—brother.

ekäm—my brother.

elä—to live.

eläsz arwa-arvoval—may you live with honor (*greeting*).

eläsz jeläbam ainaak—long may you live in the light (*greeting*).

elävä—alive.

elävä ainak majaknak—land of the living.

elid—life.

emä—mother (*noun*).

Emä Maүe—Mother Nature.

emäen—grandmother.

embε—if, when.

embε karmasz—please.

emni—wife; woman.

emnim—my wife; my woman.

emni hän ku köd alte—cursed woman.

emni kuŋenak ku aššatotello—disobedient lunatic.

én—I.

en—great, many, big.

én jutta félet és ekämet—I greet a friend and brother (*greeting*).

én maүenak—I am of the earth.

én oma maүeka—I am as old as time (*literally: as old as the earth*).

En Puwe—The Great Tree. Related to the legends of Ygddrasil,
    the axis mundi, Mount Meru, heaven and hell, etc.

engem—of me.

és—and.

ete—before; in front.

että—that.

fáz—to feel cold or chilly.

fél—fellow, friend.

fél ku kuuluaak sívam belső—beloved.

fél ku vigyázak—dear one.

feldolgaz—prepare.

fertiil—fertile one.

fesztelen—airy.

fü—herbs; grass.

gæidno—road, way.

gond—care; worry; love (*noun*).

hän—he; she; it.

hän agba—it is so.

hän ku—prefix: one who; that which.

hän ku agba—truth.

hän ku kaśwa o numamet—sky-owner.

hän ku kuulua sívamet—keeper of my heart.

hän ku lejkka wäke-sarnat—traitor.

hän ku meke pirämet—defender.

hän ku pesä—protector.

hän ku piwtä—predator; hunter; tracker.

hän ku vie elidet—vampire (*literally: thief of life*).

hän ku vigyáz sielamet—keeper of my soul.

hän ku vigyáz sívamet és sielamet—keeper of my heart and soul.

hän ku saa kuć3aket—star-reacher.

hän ku tappa—killer; violent person (*noun*). deadly; violent (*adj.*).

hän ku tuulmahl elidet—vampire (*literally: life-stealer*).

Hän sívamak—Beloved.

hany—clod; lump of earth.

hisz—to believe; to trust.

ho—how.

ida—east.

igazág—justice.

irgalom—compassion; pity; mercy.

isä—father (*noun*).

isäntä—master of the house.

438

it—now.

jälleen—again.

jama—to be sick, infected, wounded, or dying; to be near death.

jelä—sunlight; day, sun; light.

jelä keje terád—light sear you (*Carpathian swear words*).

o jelä peje terád—sun scorch you (*Carpathian swear words*).

o jelä peje emnimet—sun scorch the woman (*Carpathian swear words*).

o jelä peje terád, emni—sun scorch you, woman (*Carpathian swear words*).

o jelä peje kaik hänkanak—sun scorch them all (*Carpathian swear words*).

o jelä sielamak—light of my soul.

joma—to be underway; to go.

joŋe—to come; to return.

joŋesz arwa-arvoval—return with honor (*greeting*).

jörem—to forget; to lose one's way; to make a mistake.

juo—to drink.

juosz és eläsz—drink and live (*greeting*).

juosz és olen ainaak sielamet jutta—drink and become one with me (*greeting*).

juta—to go; to wander.

jüti—night; evening.

jutta—connected; fixed (*adj.*). to connect; to fix; to bind (*verb*).

k—suffix added after a noun ending in a vowel to make it plural.

kaca—male lover.

kadi—judge.

kaik—all.

kaŋa—to call; to invite; to request; to beg.

kaŋk—windpipe; Adam's apple; throat.

kać3—gift.

kaδa—to abandon; to leave; to remain.

kaδa wäkeva óv o köd—stand fast against the dark (*greeting*).

kalma—corpse; death; grave.

karma—want.

Karpatii—Carpathian.

Karpatii ku köd—liar.

käsi—hand (*noun*).

kaśwa—to own.

keje—to cook; to burn; to sear.

kepä—lesser, small, easy, few.

kessa—cat.

kessa ku toro—wildcat.

kessake—little cat.

kidü—to wake up; to arise (*intransitive verb*).

kim—to cover an entire object with some sort of covering.

kinn—out; outdoors; outside; without.

kinta—fog, mist, smoke.

kislány—little girl.

kislány kuŋenak—little lunatic.

kislány kuŋenak minan—my little lunatic.

köd—fog; mist; darkness; evil (*noun*); foggy, dark; evil (*adj.*).

köd elävä és köd nime kutni nimet—evil lives and has a name.

köd alte hän—darkness curse it (*Carpathian swear words*).

o köd belső—darkness take it (*Carpathian swear words*).

köd jutasz belső—shadow take you (*Carpathian swear words*).

koje—man; husband; drone.

kola—to die.

kolasz arwa-arvoval—may you die with honor (*greeting*).

koma—empty hand; bare hand; palm of the hand; hollow of the
    hand.

kond—all of a family's or clan's children.

kont—warrior.

kont o sívanak—strong heart (*literally: heart of the warrior*).

ku—who; which; that.

kuć3—star.

440

kuć3ak!—stars! (*exclamation*).

kuja—day, sun.

kuŋe—moon; month.

kule—to hear.

kulke—to go or to travel (on land or water).

kulkesz arwa-arvoval, ekäm—walk with honor, my brother
     (*greeting*).

kulkesz arwaval—joŋesz arwa arvoval—go with glory—return
     with honor (*greeting*).

kuly—intestinal worm; tapeworm; demon who possesses and
     devours souls.

kumpa—wave (*noun*).

kuńa—to lie as if asleep; to close or cover the eyes in a game of
     hide-and-seek; to die.

kunta—band, clan, tribe, family.

kutenken—however.

kuras—sword; large knife.

kure—bind; tie.

kutni—to be able to bear, carry, endure, stand, or take.

kutnisz ainaak—long may you endure (*greeting*).

kuulua—to belong; to hold.

lääs—west.

lamti (*or* lamt3)—lowland; meadow; deep; depth.

lamti ból jüti, kinta, ja szelem—the netherworld
     (*literally: the meadow of night, mists, and ghosts*).

laña—daughter.

lejkka—crack, fissure, split (*noun*). To cut; to hit; to strike
     forcefully (*verb*).

lewl—spirit (*noun*).

lewl ma—the other world (*literally: spirit land*). *Lewl ma* includes
     lamti ból jüti, kinta, ja szelem: the netherworld, but also
     includes the worlds higher up *En Puwe*, the Great Tree.

liha—flesh.

lõuna—south.

löyly—breath; steam (*related to lewl: spirit*).

ma—land; forest.

magköszun—thank.

mana—to abuse; to curse; to ruin.

mäne—to rescue; to save.

maɣe—land; earth; territory; place; nature.

me—we.

meke—deed; work (*noun*). To do; to make; to work (*verb*).

mića—beautiful.

mića emni kuŋenak minan—my beautiful lunatic.

minan—mine; my own (*endearment*).

minden—every, all (*adj.*).

möért?—what for? (*exclamation*).

molanâ—to crumble; to fall apart.

molo—to crush; to break into bits.

mozdul—to begin to move, to enter into movement.

muonì—appoint; order; prescribe; command.

muonìak te avoisz te—I command you to reveal yourself.

musta—memory.

myös—also.

nä—for.

nâbbŏ—so, then.

ŋamaŋ—this; this one here; that; that one there.

nautish—to enjoy.

nélkül—without.

nenä—anger.

ńiŋ3—worm; maggot.

nó—like; in the same way as; as.

numa—god; sky; top; upper part; highest (*related to the English word: numinous*).

numatorkuld—thunder (*literally: sky struggle*).

nyál—saliva; spit (*related to nyelv: tongue*).

nyelv—tongue.

odam—to dream; to sleep.

odam-sarna kondak—lullaby (*literally: sleep-song of children*).

olen—to be.

oma—old; ancient; last; previous.

omas—stand.

omboće—other; second (*adj.*).

o—the (*used before a noun beginning with a consonant*).

ot—the (*used before a noun beginning with a vowel*).

otti—to look; to see; to find.

óv—to protect against.

owe—door.

päämoro—aim; target.

pajna—to press.

pälä—half; side.

päläfertiil—mate or wife.

palj3—more.

peje—to burn.

peje terád—get burned (*Carpathian swear words*).

pél—to be afraid; to be scared of.

pesä (n.)—nest (*literal*); protection (*figurative*).

pesä (v.)—nest (*literal*); protect (*figurative*).

pesäd te engemal—you are safe with me.

pesäsz jeläbam ainaak—long may you stay in the light
   (*greeting*).

pide—above.

pile—to ignite; to light up.

pirä—circle; ring (*noun*). to surround; to enclose (*verb*).

piros—red.

pitä—to keep; to hold; to have; to possess.

pitäam mustaakad sielpesäambam—I hold your memories safe in
   my soul.

pitäsz baszú, piwtäsz igazáget—no vengeance, only justice.

443

piwtä—to follow; to follow the track of game; to hunt; to prey upon.

poår—bit; piece.

põhi—north.

pukta—to drive away; to persecute; to put to flight.

pus—healthy; healing.

pusm—to be restored to health.

puwe—tree; wood.

rambsolg—slave.

rauho—peace.

reka—ecstasy; trance.

rituaali—ritual.

sa—sinew; tendon; cord.

sa4—to call; to name.

saa—arrive, come; become; get, receive.

saasz hän ku andam szabadon—take what I freely offer.

salama—lightning; lightning bolt.

sarna—words; speech; magic incantation (*noun*). To chant; to sing; to celebrate (*verb*).

sarna kontakawk—warriors' chant.

śaro—frozen snow.

sas—shoosh (*to a child or baby*).

saɣe—to arrive; to come; to reach.

siel—soul.

sieljelä isäntä—purity of soul triumphs.

sisar—sister.

sív—heart.

sív pide köd—love transcends evil.

sívad olen wäkeva, hän ku piwtä—may your heart stay strong, hunter (*greeting*).

sívamet—my heart.

sívam és sielam—my heart and soul.

sívdobbanás—heartbeat (*literal*); rhythm (*figurative*).

sokta—to mix; to stir around.

soŋe—to enter; to penetrate; to compensate; to replace.

susu—home; birthplace (*noun*). At home (*adv.*).

szabadon—freely.

szelem—ghost.

taka—behind; beyond.

tappa—to dance; to stamp with the feet; to kill.

te—you.

Te kalma, te jama ńiŋ3kval, te apitäsz arwa-arvo—You are nothing but a walking maggot-infected corpse, without honor.

Te magköszunam nä ŋamaŋ kać3 taka arvo—Thank you for this gift beyond price.

ted—yours.

terád keje—get scorched (*Carpathian swear words*).

tõd—to know.

Tõdak pitäsz wäke bekimet mekesz kaiket—I know you have the courage to face anything.

tõdhän—knowledge.

tõdhän lõ kuraset agbapäämoroam—knowledge flies the sword true to its aim.

toja—to bend; to bow; to break.

toro—to fight; to quarrel.

torosz wäkeval—fight fiercely (*greeting*).

totello—obey.

tsak—only.

tuhanos—thousand.

tuhanos löylyak türelamak saɣe diutalet—a thousand patient breaths bring victory.

tule—to meet; to come.

tumte—to feel; to touch; to touch upon.

türe—full, satiated, accomplished.

türelam—patience.

türelam agba kontsalamaval—patience is the warrior's true weapon.

tyvi—stem; base; trunk.

uskol—faithful.

uskolfertiil—allegiance; loyalty.

varolind—dangerous.

veri—blood.

veri-elidet—blood-life.

veri ekäakank—blood of our brothers.

veri isäakank—blood of our fathers.

veri olen piros, ekäm—literally: blood be red, my brother; figuratively: find your lifemate (*greeting*).

veriak ot en Karpatiiak—by the blood of the Prince (*literally: by the blood of the great Carpathian; Carpathian swear words*).

veridet peje—may your blood burn (*Carpathian swear words*).

vigyáz—to love; to care for; to take care of.

vii—last; at last; finally.

wäke—power; strength.

wäke beki—strength; courage.

wäke kaδa—steadfastness.

wäke kutni—endurance.

wäke-sarna—vow; curse; blessing (*literally: power words*).

wäkeva—powerful.

wara—bird; crow.

weńca—complete; whole.

wete—water (*noun*).